The

Phantom's Apprentice

The

PHANTOM'S APPRENTICE

a novel

Heather Webb

SONNET PRESS

ISBN-13: 978-0-9996285-0-8
ISBN-10: 0-9996285-0-X

PRINTED IN THE UNITED STATES OF AMERICA

Original Cover Art by James T. Egan, copyright 2017
www.BookflyDesign.com

Praise for the novels of Heather Webb

Becoming Josephine

"Webb holds up a light into the inner recesses of a fascinating and contradictory woman . . . Becoming Josephine is an accomplished debut." *—New York Journal of Books*

"A brilliant debut novel. Exquisite detail . . . with the completion of this book Ms. Webb has made her name as a novelist and historian." *—Portland Book Review*

"Perfectly balancing history and story, character and setting, detail and pathos, Becoming Josephine marks a debut as bewitching as its protagonist." *—Erika Robuck, National Bestselling author of Hemingway's Girl*

Rodin's Lover

"Masterfully crafted . . . . Webb captures the era and characters to perfection." *—RT Book Reviews, starred review*

"You'll be drawn into this story of obsession and passion." *—Cosmopolitan*

"Webb's novel gives a fascinating insight into the power of art and love set against the colorful backdrop of the Parisian art world." *—France Magazine*

"This well-researched book takes you on an emotionally gripping and passionate ride that hardly lets up for a minute." *—Dish Magazine*

"An entertaining guide that will take readers in and out of the salons and studios of 19th-century Paris and introduces them to one of history's most tragic and unsung rebels." *—Kirkus Reviews*

Last Christmas in Paris

"A moving and heartfelt story of love and bravery"—*Library Journal, Starred Review*

"Beautifully told . . . the authors fully capture the characters' voices as each person is dramatically shaped by the war to end all wars."—*Booklist*

"[A] searingly romantic crisis of the Great War . . . hold your breath"—*Sunday Independent*

"The storytelling will touch readers with its human portraits of lost youth."—*RT Book Reviews*

The Phantom's Apprentice

"Webb combines music and magic seamlessly in The Phantom's Apprentice, weaving glittering new threads into the fabric of a classic story. Romantic, suspenseful and inventive, this novel sweeps you along to its breathless conclusion." —*Greer Macallister, USA Today bestselling author of The Magician's Lie*

"A performance worthy of the Paris Opera...Christine's evolution from 'damsel in distress' to self-reliant woman is masterfully done, hooking the reader from the first page. Webb's work is immersive, well-crafted, and beautifully paced. A must-read!" —*Aimie K. Runyan, author of Daughters of the Night Sky*

"Webb's beautiful writing made this story unputdownable . . . and unforgettable."—*Booktrib*

"In her captivating novel, Heather Webb casts an intriguing new light on a much-loved tale . . . . Full of magic and atmosphere, lush historical detail and page-turning suspense, The Phantom's Apprentice is sure to enthrall, enchant and delight . . . . Brava!" —*Hazel Gaynor, NYT bestselling author of The Cottingley Secret*

For my beloved sister Jennifer, believer in magic

"All of Paris is a masked ball."
—Gaston Leroux

"The stage should make as complete as possible the illusion of reality."
—Victor Hugo

Dear Reader,

The first time I listened to the musical of *The Phantom of the Opera*, I was sixteen. My parents had attended the show and enjoyed it so much, they purchased the CDs. Little did they know how I would lap up this captivating music, so different from anything else our family had ever listened to, and it filled the house until I knew every word and every note. There was something special about this Gothic tale. I fell in love with the enchanting backdrop of the Opéra de Paris, the lush and dark tone, the romance. And yes, the tortured souls.

Years later, I read the novel by Gaston Leroux that had inspired Andrew Lloyd Webber, and noted the way the composer had taken pieces of the story that spoke to him, and left behind those that didn't. As I mulled this, I noticed something glaring to my feminist mind. Why were the female characters of that era portrayed in a certain light? Why were they either haughty and demanding, or sweet and simpering? I began to question who was this Christine Daaé truly—her heart, her dreams, her strengths—beyond the men who dictated her comings and goings. One day, the Muse answered, and I began to hear Christine's voice. It was soft as a whisper at first, but slowly, Christine began to trust me. The secrets she held surprised me, and I quickly got to work!

This book is the result of my questioning who Christine Daaé might have been in all her beauty, talent, love, and darkness. In *The Phantom's Apprentice*, I weaved together both the original novel and the popular musical, and added new dimensions to characters and story alike, creating a secret world all my own.

So without further ado, I give you my passion project: a dramatic tale of loss, love, and magic and, of course, the incomparable world of the Paris opera.

Sincerely,

Act One

"Angel, I hear you speak, I listen."

—Andrew Lloyd Webber's
The Phantom of the Opera

Overture

New York City, 1891

I was not the innocent girl they thought me to be. Though many never witnessed it, my honeyed warmth disguised a spine of steel. It took time to find my strength, but it had been there all along. Didn't everyone hide behind a mask at one time or another? In my experience, yes, very often, yes. Yet I longed to be free of my own.

I walked backstage and collapsed into a chair before the vanity mirror. My wine-colored gown blended with the shadows, leaving only the whites of my eyes and pale skin visible in the gloom. Shivering, I turned the knob of the lamp and a flame flickered to life. My knees still trembled from the mysterious vision I'd seen in the west balcony.

"You're imagining things," I whispered.

With a shaking hand, I grasped a pot of cream to remove the many layers of rouge and powders. The familiar clamor of stagehands and props, and the din of a dissipating crowd floated through the hall, but did little to calm my nerves. I must have been seeing things. I had to be. Yet terror licked up my spine.

My eyes shifted focus to a reflection in the mirror behind me. The glass tub slipped from my fingers and clattered to the floor.

There, on the table beside the sofa, lay a single red rose tied with a black ribbon.

~1~

Paris, 1877

I inhaled a breath and released a final high note. My voice shattered the stillness of the audience, and applause ruffled through the room. I beamed as I glanced at Papa, who lowered his violin and bowed. Smiling, I followed his lead and bowed beside him, proud to be his musical partner. He had trained me with singular vision since Mother died; I needed a skill to survive should anything happen to him, and my talents in music grew by the day. I wanted it, too, more than air—at least, I told myself this practice after practice, year after year.

"Remember: Head high, shoulders back, and project," Papa instructed. He turned to our small audience: Madame Valerius, Claudette the maid, Albert the footman, two cooks, and a coachman—our benefactor and her staff. "Christine is guided by the Angel of Music, is she not?"

"Hear, hear!" Madame Valerius cried.

Papa insisted an ethereal being had watched over me since Mother died. Though he assumed the image soothed me, it made Mother's absence feel more pronounced, more final. Countless nights I had cried for her, my child's heart raw with loss, until her scent and the warmth in her eyes faded from memory. The Angel of Music stayed beside me, yet my own Mother did not. I didn't understand this disparity; and now, after all of these years, I didn't believe in spirits at all. I forced a smile and rubbed the rose brooch at my neck; the only thing left of Mother.

A thick cough rattled in Papa's chest. When it passed, he wiped his lips and scarlet drops seeped into his handkerchief.

"I'm going to call on the doctor," I said firmly.

The bleeding had become more frequent.

He held up his hand. "There is nothing a doctor can do for me." His eyes softened when he saw my expression. "There's no sense in wasting money. We won't have many more opportunities to work together, *min kära*, and I intend to save every centime for you for when I am gone."

Again, talk of his death. A familiar rush of fear squeezed my chest. My companion and protector, Papa dictated my every move and I followed him without question. When I dared to disobey, I paid the price in chores and endless singing drills. Though Papa was unbearably strict at times, I couldn't imagine my life when he was gone. He was my partner, my only family. My dream of being onstage would dissolve without him; no one would host a lowly sixteen- year-old without family or connections.

I cast my gaze to the floor to hide the sudden flood of tears. I hated to admit it, but Papa's final months were in sight. His frame withered more each day, his vivacious spirit waned, and even the passion in his music dimmed. I choked back a clot of emotion.

Desperate not to cry, I drank deeply from my water glass while he launched into a rendition of his favorite piece of music: "Lazarus." I'd heard it so many times I hummed the melody without thinking.

Papa cradled his instrument's burnished amber face in his hands as if it were his child. The violin, a masterpiece crafted by Jacob Stainer, had cost more than two years of performance earnings, but he insisted on the finest quality for his music. I didn't blame him for our sacrifice, despite a lifetime of moving through the outskirts of Paris from one abandoned barn or hovel to the next. We hadn't lived in a proper home since leaving Sweden so many years before. Not until now.

When he finished his song, he twirled his finger in the air and said, "Do your exercises once more."

He relinquished his violin to its case and sat down to nibble a wedge of apple.

Relieved to see him eating, I smiled. "Can I bring you some tea?"

"You mean, can you ring for tea." Madame Valerius folded her hands in her lap. "You're not going to wait on anyone, Christine," she reminded me. "I like to think of you as family. What once was mine is now yours, too."

We had met the elderly woman one perfect summer in Normandy four years before, and she had never forgotten Papa's music. When he called on Madame Valerius for help—to request that she adopt me when he passed—she opened her home to us on the rue Notre-Dames-des-Victoire. Relieved, we moved into her modest apartment overlooking a park, complete with a gurgling fountain and burgeoning flowerpots. Madame lived exclusively on the first floor for ease of use with her wheelchair, and generously gave me the largest room on the top floor. All was tidy and warm. For the first time, I didn't choke on the odor of rotting hay and animal droppings but instead relished the faint scent of roses perfuming the air.

"Of course, Madame," I said, softly. "Thank you."

Though not luxurious, Madame's home seemed abundant with her maid, footman, and carriage, not to mention ample firewood. I couldn't get used to the new privilege of a full belly, much less someone else pouring my tea. To hide my discomfort, I fished a deck of cards from my oaken box, a gift from a long-lost childhood friend, Raoul de Chagny. Papa taught him to play the violin the summer we'd spent in Normandy, the very same summer we met Madame. When not practicing, I enticed Raoul to play card games and indulge my interest in small illusions. He looked on as I tinkered endlessly with an assortment of brass knobs and twisted springs, and built simple machines that produced some special effect. Somehow, Raoul understood that my hobbies made me feel closer to Mother. She had enjoyed trifling with such diversions, too, even though they did not suit our sex.

I hadn't seen Raoul since that summer, yet I thought of him still. With the constant moving, I had no other friends.

I shuffled my cards, their worn edges yielding to my hands.

"Your affinity for card tricks is rather astounding, I must say,

Christine." Madame touched her gray chignon, a nervous habit I often noticed. "Such a clever girl. I thought . . . Well, I thought you might enjoy seeing a real conjurer. Your father needed a bit of prompting, but I think I won him over."

"I don't understand." I stacked the cards into two piles.

"I have taken the liberty of purchasing tickets for you."

"You mean it?" I squealed, first embracing Papa and then Madame. "Oh, thank you! I have always longed to go."

"Well, *min kära*, isn't that wonderful," Papa said, in Swedish, his lips pinched.

His tone quelled my enthusiasm. He seemed upset, resentful even.

"Madame Valerius"—he nodded at our hostess, changing to French once more—"has been very kind." He smiled and his wan face softened, reminding me of his once-jovial nature. "The show is this evening."

I squealed again, in spite of Papa's poorly veiled chagrin. I didn't understand his disdain for my favorite hobby, but I could hardly wait! How I wished Mother were here. She would share my delight, without doubt.

I kissed Madame on the cheek and she smiled widely, pleased she had made me so happy.

Plopping into my chair, I chose a card from the stack in front of me. A magic show! I could hardly believe it. With my thumb, I covered the plump heart floating beside the Queen of Hearts. The image blurred as I lost myself in memories of a summer evening years before—the only occasion I'd seen a conjurer. Papa and I had performed at a nobleman's salon. As luck would have it, a conjurer presented directly after us. I recalled how the gentleman wore a regal dress coat with winged collar and navy foulard, and a curious smile throughout his show. Rapt, I stared in awe while he commanded everyone's attention with the smooth authority of his voice. When he transformed silk handkerchiefs into a pair of doves and coaxed carnations from an empty pot, applause thundered through the room.

For me, the world had tilted then, taken on a new hue as if before, all had been coated in a gray residue. Now everything appeared awash in color and light. My fingers tingled and an awakening blossomed inside of me. I understood why Mother had found illusions so enchanting.

After his act, the conjurer approached us. "You enjoyed my show, as I enjoyed your daughter's."

Papa nodded stiffly. "Thank you."

"You sang like an angel." The conjurer smiled at me. "You look like one, too, with your golden hair and white dress."

I looked down at the scuffed toes of my boots, suddenly timid. "*Merci*, Monsieur. I hope to be a real singer one day, on a stage."

His lips twitched with amusement. "Continue to practice and you will."

Emboldened by his faith in me, I risked an impolite question. "Will you show me one of your secrets?"

His eyebrows shot up in surprise.

"Christine, mind your manners," Papa said.

I ducked my head in shame. "I'm sorry. I—"

The conjurer reached behind my ear and produced an orange. "For you."

I smiled and accepted the gift, stroking the fruit's leathery skin in anticipation. I had never tasted an orange. "How did you do that?"

"I can't share all of my secrets." Delight danced in his eyes. "I will, however, show you this." He gathered a deck of cards from a box on the stage and directed me to a side table away from the crowd. "You hold the cards like this." He palmed the entire deck and wrapped his fingers around the sides of the stack with the exception of his index finger, which crooked over the top edge of the cards. "Watch closely."

From that day forward, I practiced what the conjurer had shown me and attempted illusions of my own. Noticing my enthusiasm, Papa scolded me if I spent too much time "learning tricks." It seemed to anger him, though I tried to make him understand. To be able to step inside a world of make-believe—to escape our poverty and simple existence, and the anguish I'd suffered losing Mother—imprinted on my heart that day.

"Magic," I whispered. It *did* exist.

The clock in the salon chimed and I refocused my gaze on Papa's slight frame. He flipped open his pocket watch and looked pointedly at the deck in my hand. "We need to move along, or we'll be late."

"I can't wait, Papa!" We were going to see a conjurer!

After a light supper, Albert the footman helped us into the carriage, and we set out for the Theatre Margot. Papa coughed the entire trip, inflaming my guilt for dragging him from bed. I knew he didn't want to go, but humored me just the same.

I rubbed his back to comfort him. "Are you all right?"

"Fine, fine," he said, though he couldn't hide the worry in his eyes.

When the carriage deposited us outside the theatre, Papa's anxiety deepened. I frowned, both bemused by his attitude and annoyed he would hamper my amusement at my first real magic show. I couldn't let it ruin my night.

"We're here!" I clapped in delight, and exited the carriage.

A sign spanned the front of the building with curled red lettering that read: THE MASTER CONJURER. Beyond the sign, the building lacked frills of any kind; it had no ornate gilding, no imposing entryway. It was a nondescript structure; the only oddity was its proximity to not one, but three sewer holes in the street. As we approached the door, steam rose through the grates, carrying the odor of waste drowning in a watery underground. I wrinkled my nose in disgust. I would never have chosen such a location for a theatre.

As we filed in behind the crowd, I studied the patrons who, despite their numbers, remained mostly silent.

"Why is everyone so solemn?" I asked.

Papa leaned into me. "They have come to see the conjurer contact the dead. The papers claim he caused a riot in London when he toured there last. The spiritualists clashed with those who don't believe it's possible to summon ghosts." He pressed his lips together. "You know how I feel about spirits."

I knew well. He spoke about Mother at times as if she were there, or at least could hear him speak. Yet spirits seemed unlikely to me, silly even.

"If there is the slightest concern, we will leave immediately." His expression mirrored the drawn faces of the audience. "I will not put you in danger."

"I understand." I kissed him lightly on the cheek.

Once settled in our seats, I studied the audience. Weren't they excited, at least a little, to see the show? One woman's eyes shifted, and she turned to look over her shoulder as if she expected a ghost to sneak up behind her. I snickered at her expression. It was an illusion— all of it. Every act had a logical explanation, though the crowd seemed to believe differently.

Perhaps it was I who was missing something. Maybe spirits lived among us after all, and I was foolish to doubt.

Papa squeezed my hand and brought it to his lips.

I rewarded his gesture with a smile. After, I gazed at the pair of rich black curtains draping the stage. Two balconies nestled against the wall on either side of them, and along the ceiling, a frieze of instruments popped from the upper casing. Lanterns lined the proscenium, flickering brightly in the otherwise dark auditorium.

Just then, the curtain twitched and shivered and a gentleman emerged from between the center of its folds. His silver beard consumed most of his face, and his round middle straddled his legs.

My heart leapt into my throat. This was it!

"Good evening, ladies and gentleman." He folded his hands and placed them on his belly.

The last of the murmurings died away.

"I am Monsieur Pichon, owner of the Theatre Margot. Tonight, I am pleased to present the greatest illusionist Paris has ever seen." The audience gazed at him, captivated by his words. "He will enthrall you with bodiless musicians, amaze you as a woman disappears before your eyes." The man lowered his voice, and slowed his words for effect. "He will astound you when he raises the dead."

Deep silence enveloped the theatre.

"Never before has anyone seen such feats on one stage," Pichon

9

continued. "Please welcome the Master Conjurer!"

A trio of latecomers climbed over the audience and seated themselves directly in front of us, the largest man blocked my view of the stage. Frustrated, I leaned to my left. The brim of my hat brushed the gentleman next to me and he glared. I couldn't miss the show! I leaned to my right, toward Papa. He smiled and allowed me to crowd him. Still, with the other person in front of him, much of the stage was obstructed from view.

As the curtains opened, a smattering of applause rippled through the room. The stage was empty, save for one small table and chair in the middle of the platform. Two torches sparked to life on the recessed wall, revealing a figure standing on the left side of the stage. Still, shadow obscured most of his body. As the illusionist stepped forward, the crowd murmured. I couldn't make out the gentleman's features; between his hat, the lighting, and my position, it was impossible. Furious, I crossed my arms over my chest like a petulant child. I could hardly see! Then I remembered Papa. Quickly, I dropped my arms and folded my hands in my lap, hoping he didn't notice my frustration. He didn't feel well or want to be here at all, but he had come for me. I sneaked a glance at his face. He looked as if he might faint. His brow scrunched into a frown, his pale lips quivered, and perspiration dampened his forehead.

"Should we go?" I whispered, covering his hand with mine. "We can leave if you're not feeling well. Return another time."

The crowd gasped.

My head jerked toward the stage. What had I missed? A blond woman in bejeweled clothing and mask, and a top hat with mesh, bowed and backed away until she disappeared behind the curtain. His assistant, I assumed.

"Do we need to go?" I slipped my hand under Papa's elbow.

"No, *min kära.* Enjoy the show. I can endure."

For the following hour, I shifted between worrying over Papa as his body curled into a half-moon, and studying the conjurer's performance. To my dismay, I could only guess two of the illusionist's secrets.

I glanced at Papa again. His skin had taken on an ashen hue.

"I insist we go," I whispered in as firm a tone as I could muster.

"I insist we stay." He placed his hand upon my knee. "I don't want to disappoint our hostess, or you, my dear."

I longed to watch the show, but not at the expense of his comfort. Madame would understand, and I could return another time . . . someday.

Papa raised his eyebrows in a question, waiting for my consent. At last, I nodded and trained my eyes back on the stage.

Each illusion grew more complicated than the last: sleight of hand, birds escaping their cages, and a disappearing act. I shifted to see better, but with Monsieur Blockhead in front of me I despaired at how much of the show I lost.

"This cabinet is empty," the illusionist's voice boomed. "Mademoiselle Cartelle will now step inside."

The assistant reappeared in a showy ensemble of sequins and gold beading. She flourished her hand to present the empty cabinet.

I shifted to my left and peeked between the two seated in front of me.

The assistant climbed inside the cabinet.

I gazed intently, examining every detail. The structure sat on four legs, about a meter off the ground. No one could disappear from its bottom, and no curtain or fixtures were attached to the top of the box.

The Master Conjurer closed the cabinet and, within seconds, flung open its doors. The assistant had vanished, and the crowd roared with delight. With a swift motion, the illusionist closed the doors again and quickly reopened them.

Mademoiselle Cartelle smiled and waved at the crowd. Her gesture fed the excitement of the already-cheering audience.

I grinned, impressed by the conjurer's clever trick. How had he done it? The woman had reappeared so quickly. Perhaps there was a revolving door inside the cabinet. I envisioned the hinge, fixed with a special spring. But we would be able to see the door from our seats.

"Do you know how he did it?" I leaned over to whisper in Papa's ear. He smiled, in spite of himself. "Magic."

A stagehand emerged from the wings to remove the cabinet.

"Now, ladies and gentlemen, the act you have come far and wide to see." The Master Conjurer's voice dropped lower than his natural tenor.

All noise ceased. Gone were the odd coughs and whispers, the creaking chairs. Despite my understanding of illusions, doubt mingled with fascination. I wanted to believe, even if it wasn't real. What did mankind truly know about the soul? We could only guess at the realities of life beyond the grave.

The air grew saturated with fear.

"There comes a time when we must all face death." The conjurer paused as the fear thickened.

Suddenly, I found it hard to breathe. I couldn't help but think of Papa, and the way illness eroded his fiery nature. One day, his light would go out.

I squeezed his hand again.

"We cross the threshold to the beyond," the conjurer continued. "Are we still in pain, or do we pass on, blissful in the release of our fleshy selves? Some believe our darkest moments leave their marks on the soul." His voice dropped once more. "And for those, we are punished."

The lamps on the walls went out.

A few women shrieked, cleaving the tension in the air.

The illusionist had been difficult to see before, but now I could hardly make out his form on the stage.

"Tonight, I shall call on the spirit world, and summon those who have a message to share with us."

"He's a devil!" shouted a man in the audience.

Others shushed him.

The illusionist's voice turned coaxing, liquid. "Let the border between worlds dissipate. We beseech you, spirits, to come forth with your troubles. Let us guide you from this earth to a resting place, once and for all." He held out his right hand, palm up. "Come! Come to us. We can assist you."

The silence in the hall grew heavy, crushing us against our seats.

I stared in amazement as a prick of light gleamed in the space over the conjurer's hand, and grew into a pulsing orb.

A collective gasp arose from the audience.

The orb grew bigger and elongated, stretching to take on a human form. An ethereal light encapsulated its limbs and finally, a blurred face emerged.

I gaped, in spite of myself.

"Who is it?" a voice called out.

"Silence, please!" the illusionist commanded.

The spirit held out his hand and pointed at the audience.

I gripped the edges of my seat.

"What does it want?" someone shouted.

"Who do you seek, spirit?" the illusionist asked.

The spirit floated across the stage and pointed again, toward the back of the theatre.

"Someone in this audience will pass from this world soon," the Master Conjurer said. "The spirit has come to warn us."

Fear pooled in my stomach. I clutched Papa's arm. This was an illusion, I reminded myself. No one was going to die, not yet. Still, my agitation increased. I glanced over my shoulder. Something wasn't right. The energy in the room had shifted.

The crowd murmured. A few couples jumped to their feet and left the theatre in a disenchanted huff.

The illusionist ignored the disturbance and spoke to the spirit again. "Can you tell us how this death will take place? Or perhaps, how to avoid it?"

The ghost slowly raised his hands to his neck.

A man stood and waved a fist in the air. "This is a hoax!"

Others strode to the exit.

More spectators jumped to their feet, shouting. Papa struggled to stand.

"What are you doing?" I asked, tugging at his coat sleeve.

With all the breath he could muster, Papa shouted, "Mademoiselle Cartelle!"

I stood, confused. Had his illness affected his brain? "Papa, please. Why are you shouting at the assistant? Sit down."

The assistant stared out at the crowd, eyes finding us at last. Her mouth fell open. In a second, she was at the conjurer's side, directing his gaze toward us. Embarrassed by Papa's uncharacteristic behavior, I focused my attention on helping him back into his chair, hoping the assistant and those who rushed toward the exit would obscure us from the illusionist's view.

The assistant returned her attention to the illusionist.

"Remain calm, everyone," the conjurer shouted over the crowd. "We must not spook it."

Some laughed at the illusionist's pun.

"You're a demon!" A man hurtled insults at him. "How else could you call on the dead?"

The audience shouted back and forth at one another until the din grew to a roar.

The spirit faded—just as a trapdoor on the stage flew open and smoke billowed into the theatre.

In the same instant, I smelled it—the unmistakable odor of charred wood.

"Fire!" someone screamed.

Panic surged through me like a rushing river. I'd heard of theatres catching fire, trapping the patrons within. Few survived.

Papa attempted to stand again, but a cough clogged his throat and he fell back into his chair. I struggled to help him up. His lungs seized and his body convulsed. I watched in alarm while he fought against the disease. When he finally regained his breath, I dragged him to his feet.

The audience pushed and shoved, devolving into a terrified mob.

I clutched Papa against me, horrified at the scene unfolding. Quickly, I evaluated the chaos. We were opposite the door, across the room. God help us.

"We have to go. Now." I pulled Papa's arm.

He fell into another fit of coughing and couldn't stop. "I-I need a minute," he rasped through labored breath.

Rubbing his back, I glanced at the stage.

Two men lunged at the proscenium. My mouth fell open as I watched one of them smash a lantern open with a club, lighting both club and curtains on fire. Flames devoured the fabric within seconds, spread across the ceiling, and engulfed a crossbeam. The fire swelled as if the entire theatre had been doused in something flammable.

I hauled Papa forward with all my strength. Halfway there. Eyes glued on the exit, I focused on the only thing that mattered: making our escape.

Just then, a horde of men pushed past us. I lost my grip and Papa staggered and fell. A blur of black coats and colorful gowns flew by as others rushed ahead. Someone shoved me out of the way.

I fell to my knees beside Papa, people streaming around us.

"You have to get up," I shouted. "We'll be trampled!"

He curled into a ball, clutching his handkerchief. The entire square of fabric bloomed red with blood. Half pushing, half pulling, I dragged him toward a wall away from the stampede, a prayer on my lips. There was no escaping until the crowd thinned. I looked back at the stage, my eyes stinging with smoke. The proscenium—the entire outer frame—was ablaze, yet two men and the assistant still lingered there. The illusionist and the man with the club wrestled on the stage floor.

I frowned in confusion. What was happening? The assistant screamed and launched herself at another of the attackers. A scene in a nightmare. All around me people heaved against each other to escape, smoke choking the air. No one could help the conjurer, least of all me. Tears spilled down my cheeks, washing the sting from my eyes, if only for a moment.

The crackle of splintering wood rent the air.

For an instant, a deafening crash drowned out the screams. I cried in terror, clutching Papa's hand. A beam had broken loose from the ceiling, crushing rows of seating and the bodies of the unlucky.

We were going to die. *I* was going to die—at sixteen. I would never sing again, never again watch the sunset in a blaze of gold, never fall in love. Suddenly I despised myself, my childish desires. My love of magic, a foolish pastime, would be the death of me—and of my beloved Papa.

Papa collapsed against me.

Tears bathed my cheeks as I watched him choke on ash-filled air. With a trembling hand, he touched my cheek, then lay on the floor beside me.

I glanced at the exit. The crowd had thinned! We might still make it, if we could skirt the pile of wreckage and avoid the caved-in ceiling. It was then I noticed them—the people dragging themselves toward the exit on broken limbs, and the others who lay lifeless with impaled torsos.

I covered my mouth with my hand. We must go *now.* I reached for Papa's arm, prepared to drape him across my back, if need be—and stopped.

A trickle of blood snaked down his chin. He gasped a final time and then his body relaxed. His head tilted away from me.

"Papa?" I screamed, gathering his head in my lap.

The light faded from his eyes.

"Papa! Don't leave me," I sobbed, my lungs burning. "How will I do this without you?"

His glazed, unseeing eyes stared up at me. I buried my face in his neck. My body shook with sorrow until my head grew faint. I couldn't breathe.

The fire consumed all, sucking the remaining air from the room.

I leaned my head against the wall, too weak to move. There was no time. The fire would consume me, too. I surrendered to the smoke, the heat on my skin, the grief searing my insides.

A black graininess invaded the edges of my vision, and I closed my eyes.

~ 2 ~

I didn't know how long I lay against the wall, laboring for breath, images of my paltry existence swimming behind my eyes. The tug of darkness grew stronger by the second; it seemed calm there in the abyss, alluring in its oblivion. I reached for it, grasping at curled black ribbons that undulated at the edges of my mind. In the darkness there would be no pain.

The spirit on stage had been correct. Someone would die tonight. *Many already had.*

Something tugged my arm.

With immense effort, my eyelids peeled open a fraction, but I didn't have the strength to lift my head.

A bloodied hand reached for me.

In the next instant, I was yanked to my feet. My legs collapsed beneath me and I pitched forward into someone's arms. A hand slid under my legs, and I felt myself hovering above the ground.

"Papa," I moaned with what little strength remained. My head lolled backward.

My rescuer tightened his grip, and we escaped to the safety of the street.

I awoke with a start and found myself in bed, surrounded by lace-covered pillows and frothy blankets. The haze of sleep dissipated, and I squinted at the onslaught of daylight. As reality washed over me, the hollow in my chest split open and pain gushed forth once more.

Three years had passed, and still I dreamed of fire, terrified screams, and Papa's unseeing eyes. I felt the burn of smoke in my lungs.

My hand rested on my throat. I had sung every day since Papa's death in a feverish plea for his forgiveness, wherever he might be. Somehow, he had to know how sorry I was; I had to show him. It was my fault he had died such a horrible death. Had I enjoyed a hobby fit for ladies, we wouldn't have been at the show at all. My girlish desires had taken my only family from me.

Now, at the grand age of nineteen, I was certain of only two things: I would become a celebrated singer at any cost, and I would never again dabble in illusions. Perhaps then, someday, I would no longer despise myself.

My beautiful oaken box lay safely locked in the bottom drawer of my armoire, my cards and trinkets along with it. I'd nearly sacrificed it to Madame's fireplace, but I couldn't bring myself to destroy it. I had already lost too much to fire—I would give it nothing more.

I slipped from bed and went through the motions of my daily toilette, though I didn't know why. I had nowhere to go. Still, if I didn't, I would melt into sleep and while away my days in bed. Lose myself in a torrent of loss and loneliness. I toyed with a dove-shaped brooch that was on my vanity tabletop. The jewelry had adorned my dress the day of Papa's funeral. Madame had ordered a small burial service in one of his favorite places—the Bay of Perros, in a small church plot overlooking the sea—even though we had no body to bury. It rained so hard that day, the water drove sideways from the sky, soaking my mourning gown through until it sagged on my frame. The argent waters of the Atlantic had churned and thrashed against the shore, unsettled under a bleak sky. As unsettled and bleak as I felt that day— as I did still.

Thankfully, Papa had chosen well in Madame Valerius, to whom he had entrusted my future.

After his burial, she took my hands in hers and said, "Christine, you are not without friends. Please, let us remain living together as before."

I embraced her, grateful for this lovely woman who owed me nothing and offered me all. I couldn't imagine how I had earned such kindness.

Drawing myself away from memories, I started for the large brass cage in the salon near the window. As I removed the cloth covering it, my trio of canaries blinked, blinded by the sudden light. Within seconds, they rustled and flapped their wings, and greeted the morning with a song. Outside of an occasional game or a walk with the maid, Claudette, the birds were my only source of happiness.

"*Mes amours,*" I cooed. "Sing for me."

I popped the spring on the miniature door and reached inside. Bizet, the friendliest of the three, hopped onto my finger. I stroked his yellow breast and planted a kiss on the strip of black that wrapped his head like a bandit's. He chirped his delight and I smiled. Mozart and Berlioz grew jealous, their songs changing from happy chirps to squawks.

"Now, now. I love you all." I caressed Berlioz's gold-marbled breast, and then Mozart's.

"Mornin' to you." Claudette whisked into the room and drew open the last of the drapes, a sunny smile on her face. "I'm going to market today. Care to join?"

I regarded the maid, so pretty even with her red curls smoothed under a cap. Her Irish family had moved to Paris a few years before to seek work after losing their farm. When they discovered few pronounced their daughter's name correctly, *Clodagh* became Claudette. Both outsiders, and of similar age, we formed an attachment instantly.

"Madame wouldn't like it if I helped you." Madame Valerius had taught me what people expected of a lady, since I had only the most rudimentary lessons. Even so, I didn't see myself as a society woman, and doubted I ever could. I would be a poor musician always, a girl without parents or property; a girl with few options.

"Oh, come, now. She'd rejoice to see you out and about." Claudette gave me a pointed look. "Been weeks since your last outing. Besides, she gave me a little extra today. Told me you should buy yourself something."

The last outing had been a soirée with Madame. I had felt as stiff and wooden as a marionette, parroting the polite words I knew I should say. The entire evening, I wanted to be at home, tucked in bed in solitude. I didn't know who I was, who I should be—not anymore. And parading around someone's high society salon emphasized my awkwardness.

I sighed. "I suppose a change of scenery might do me good." I coaxed my pets from my shoulder and returned them to their cage.

"Why don't we try the market cross town instead of our local? See a bit of the city. You can choose the strawberries for the tarts."

I managed a wan smile. "My favorite."

We set out for a market in the Latin Quarter, an ancient neighborhood still thriving, and a favorite spot to purchase produce, spices, and dishes prepared by *étrangères*. When we arrived, I slung my basket onto my arm and joined the swarm of shoppers. My nose detected the fishmongers before we saw them, along with a cheese stand ripe with aromas of Roquefort, chèvres, and so many others. We skirted around a pair of elderly women in bonnets perched on an overturned crate, speaking in heated tones and waving their arms with such passion, they seemed to be arguing, until one began to cackle.

Just beyond a table littered with leather handbags and journals, I stopped at the oddest stall I'd seen at a street market. The vendor was selling an array of square and rectangular boxes, even some cylindrical, and each contained a lock of some sort. The vendor cursed as he tried to open a peculiar metal box with a screwdriver.

Curious, I picked up a metal sphere and rolled it between my hands.

"You enjoy lock puzzles, Ma'moiselle?" His weathered skin sagged under the weight of his wrinkles.

"These are puzzles?" My mood brightened a little.

"Some have hidden compartments with little gifts. But really, the reward is to best the designer. Crack the lock."

I picked up another box and ran my fingers over the grooved panels and miniature levers. They were similar to the secret puzzle box Papa

20

had given me for my sixteenth birthday, made of pine and containing a surprise inside. It had taken me three days to learn how to open it. Inside, I had found a sack of marbles and a rabbit made of glass. I drew my hand away from the table. We couldn't afford such a frivolity. We'd already sold the carriage, let the cooks go, and shifted our meals from five courses to three.

"Go on," Claudette said. "Madame said you could pick something out for yourself."

"I shouldn't," I said, guilt creeping in. Madame must have forfeited one of her own small pleasures, just for me. I lifted an intimidating lock puzzle made of steel and shaped like a square with a loop handle.

"Ah, yes. The German trick lock," the old man said.

"If you don't choose, I will," Claudette insisted with a wink. "I'm carrying the money, after all."

I played with the German lock a few moments, and at last capitulated. "I like this one."

The vendor watched me, curiosity dancing in his eyes. "Are you sure about this one? It will keep you busy for a while. Maybe forever."

"That's precisely what I need."

He chuckled. "All right. Remember you brought this on yourself."

Claudette gave me the change purse, and I paid him the correct number of francs. I slipped two extra coins in my handbag. I wasn't the only one receiving a gift today.

The vendor wrapped the lock in paper. A grin split his face as he gave it to me. "Good luck, Ma'moiselle. Those Germans are never easy."

I placed the heavy item in my shopping basket, and followed Claudette to another stall. When she turned her back, I snagged a measure of green and pink silk ribbons, paid the vendor quickly, and slipped them into my handbag. My friend deserved something pretty, and I knew Madame would agree. I glanced over my shoulder at Claudette and smiled. She held my hand when loneliness got the better of me, and soothed me with stories about her siblings or the latest gossip. I consoled her as well when she longed for the green pastures of Ireland, or her family who had recently moved away again.

Claudette sorted through cartons of onions, baskets of lettuce and endives, and a dozen other vegetables lining the table in a cheerful array of summer reds, yellows, and greens. I joined her, squeezing a plump tomato for good measure.

"You try?" the vendor behind the table asked, with a thick accent I couldn't place. He produced a knife from his apron pocket and sliced a wedge of tomato. Its juice ran over his thumb as he held it out to me.

I popped the morsel in my mouth. I had to admit, I was happy Claudette had insisted I join her.

"A kilo, please," Claudette said.

I moved to the next cluster of merchants selling flowers.

Claudette dipped her face into a bouquet of pink roses and inhaled. When she looked up, her eyes grew round. "Did you see that man?"

I glanced over my shoulder. "Which? I didn't see anyone."

"He's disappeared now. Wears a mask o'er half his face. Eerie fellow. I wonder what happened to him."

"It must be uncomfortable to be stared at all the time," I said absently, cradling a bouquet of lilies in my arms. Madame's favorite. I placed them in the basket. "You've seen the beggars who hang around the markets. Many are disfigured. He's probably one of them."

Claudette continued to stare in the same direction. "I suppose, but it was eerie the way he looked at you."

Unease turned my stomach as we rounded the corner to the next set of stalls. Perhaps the man recognized me from one of my performances years ago, I reasoned. Nothing to worry about.

"He's there!" Claudette said. I glanced up as a frown marred her face. "He's disappeared again."

I laughed. "Stop pointing, Claudette." We ambled to a row of booths packed with a display of soaps. "Can we buy our fruit now? I haven't forgotten the tart." A genuine smile touched my lips for the first time in weeks.

"I think he's following us," she hissed.

"He has no reason to follow of us," I said, yet a shiver traveled over my skin.

Claudette slipped her arm through mine. "Well then, let's buy some berries and leave right away, just to be certain."

We wound through the crowd until we reached a fruit stand featuring all sorts of berries and golden Mirabelle plums. As I reached toward one, I stopped.

Goose bumps rose on my skin.

From the corner of my eye, I felt a figure staring at me. Had Claudette's masked man really followed us?

I spun around.

No one was there. Instead, I faced a posting board papered with advertisements. Dozens of eyes stared back at me from the papers. Among them, Mephistopheles—the devil in *Faust*—beckoned with his dark gaze.

I laughed softly at my vivid imagination and took a strawberry from the sample tray.

As I tasted the fruit, I thought of the Opéra de Paris. The fall performance season would begin soon. I could audition for a role in *Faust*, if I truly wanted to pursue a career on the stage. But the directors wouldn't open their doors to just anyone, and certainly not to a woman without connections and lacking experience. I needed a word from a friend or a well-connected figure. I stared blankly at the strawberries in my basket. In all honesty, I lacked the talent required for the grand opera anyway. I would only make a fool of myself on such an illustrious stage.

The uneasy sensation came again, this time from the other direction. I looked up quickly. Again, no one was there.

Later that night, I sat at the table in my bedroom poring over the trick lock. It would open with a key eventually, if the person used the correct series of left and right turns to release the inner latches. On a sheet of paper, I recorded each combination of turns, including my twists of the handle on the bottom of the box. After each attempt, the contraption clicked but didn't yield. After an hour I paused for a break, touching the four screws on the lock's front panel. Once I deciphered the system, I would open the cover with a screwdriver, assuming it wasn't soldered on, and niggle with the levers, perhaps draw a map of its innards. Learn from my new toy.

I sat in silence, staring at my tools. The thrill of puzzling through a challenge dissipated, and the weight of melancholy tugged at my temporary contentment. I couldn't go on this way, grief-stricken, filled with longing and remorse. I floated through the days without direction or purpose, without hope. But I didn't know yet what I should change. Sighing, I reapplied myself to my task, focusing on something that could be solved.

"Christine?" Claudette knocked at the door and poked her head inside. The aroma of sugared strawberries and butter wafted in behind her.

"Come in." I tossed the key on the desk. I'd tried more than twenty combinations on the lock already, without luck.

On the desk she set a tray laden with coffee and a slice of fresh-from-the-oven tart. "Hope they're as good as the last batch."

Noticing the silk ribbons threaded through a long plait in her hair, I grinned. My gift accented her beauty, as I knew it would. "I'll take this in the salon with Madame." I rose from my chair and stretched my hands overhead.

"She can't make it to the salon. Not unless we carry her."

"What?" My arms fell to my sides. "Why not?"

"Her wheelchair is broken," Claudette whispered, afraid Madame would overhear. "We can't afford a new one."

I glanced at the lock, guilt swishing in my stomach. Supporting me cost Madame too much of her already-limited stipend. I had to do something before Claudette and Albert found themselves without employment, and I was on the street again.

For now, I would start by repairing her chair myself.

The tinkle of Madame's silver bell rang through the house.

"I'd best see what she needs," Claudette turned to go.

"I'll go with you, and take a look at her chair."

We joined Madame in the study, where she sat on a chaise longue positioned beneath the only portraits on the wall in the whole room: one of Papa, one of Monsieur Valerius, and another of a handsome but intense-looking gentleman I'd never met.

Forcing an upbeat tone, I said, "I'll work on your chair tonight and have you up and about by morning."

"Thank you, child, but please sit down." She touched her hair. "I have something to discuss with you."

I paused at her tone. "What is it?"

"Well, dear, you've grown into a young woman," she began. "Beautiful and kind."

"Thank you," I said calmly, though my pulse thudded an erratic beat. She wanted to marry me off and rid herself of my expenses. Though a reasonable suggestion, the thought made my stomach twist into knots. I didn't know any gentlemen, certainly none willing to take on a woman of my limited circumstances.

Madame nodded at the tray Claudette placed on a side table, and said, "You would make a lovely bride for the right gentleman, Christine. Someone with a steady income and comfortable home."

I sucked in a deep breath. "I fear my lowly station will be off-putting."

"With your voice and beauty, you will enchant a hundred men. You'll have your choice, child. They won't care a whit about where you come from, I assure you."

I sat in silence, mulling over her words. If I met someone I could love, it would be a fine solution, though the notion stirred panic inside me. The vibrant memory of Raoul de Chagny sprang to mind—the only man for whom I had ever had feelings. I wondered where he was now. I looked down at my hands, once again without gloves. Too busy with trifles, as usual, and lacking in *gentillesse*. What man would embrace my eccentricities? More unattractive still, I longed to perform on stage. I couldn't imagine a husband who would condone such a life.

"As you know," Madame continued, "we're struggling to keep up with our expenses."

Another pang of guilt hit, and I dropped my eyes to the worn carpet covering the floor. "Yes."

"Very well, then, we agree." Her lips relaxed into a smile. "I've decided to throw a salon next week, and invite everyone I know. Though you're a bit on the older side to be debuting in society, I'm calling it a *debut* so the guests will bring their sons and nephews or cousins."

"But the expense," I protested.

She held up her hand. "I have been saving for this since you moved in with me three years ago. We'll make it a fine show with lovely food and champagne, and divertissements."

My mouth opened, but no sound escaped. I glanced at Claudette, who shot me a rueful look. She didn't want me married off any more than I did, but I couldn't argue with Madame. I must do what was expected and, in fact, should be utterly grateful for the opportunity.

I forced a smile. "We will make a fete of it."

Claudette threaded the last of the faux pearls into my hair. Their iridescence complimented my porcelain skin, flaxen curls, and the delicate shimmer of my pink satin gown. I couldn't help but admire the way my cheeks bloomed, despite the somberness lurking in my eyes. I didn't look forward to the evening ahead.

"You're beautiful tonight," Claudette said.

"Thanks to you." I squeezed her hand. I had contrived every possible excuse to take to my bed, but couldn't insult dear Madame.

My reticence deepened as a gloomy fog rolled in, uncharacteristic for August.

"Should we close the windows?" I asked, rubbing my arms. "It's damp."

"You'll be needing the air soon enough, with all of those bodies cramping the apartment." Claudette slid the vanity drawers closed.

"Maybe we can sneak away, play cards tonight," I said.

"I doubt you'll be left alone in that dress." She winked. "And I'm sure to be kept running."

Madame had filled me in on each of the gentlemen attending, including their backgrounds, properties, and professions. I groaned and rested my head on my arm. At least I didn't have to sing. It was the one thing I had refused to do. I hadn't performed in public yet without Papa and tonight, with so much at stake, I didn't want to make a spectacle of myself. Performing was bound to make me emotional. Fortunately, Madame agreed, if reluctantly.

"Up with you." Claudette pulled my chair out. "They'll be here in minutes."

I grimaced and stood. "What happens if I don't like anyone?"

"You'll think of something." She squeezed my shoulder and swept from the room.

I looked over the list of attendees and the notes I'd written about each one. Monsieur Delacroix, a particularly important guest and a dear friend of Madame's, was a famed professor at the Académie des sciences in Paris. As part of the entertainment he would bring in a medium to lead a séance with *une table tournante*–a special table used to contact spirits. Butterfly wings beat inside my stomach. If we reached out to Papa, would it be his true, benevolent spirit that answered, or some other incarnation?

I reminded myself that none of it was real.

Since Papa's death, I had envisioned his soul hovering around me but had yet to feel it–just as it had been with Mother's passing. In truth, I hoped I was simply blind to their presence. If nothing waited for us beyond the grave, and all we had was the here and now . . . I stared at the worn rug covering the floor, the mostly blank walls, and the old lace curtains. Meager things filling our meager lives. It was too depressing to consider.

I slipped the list into the desk drawer and headed to the salon.

As the guests arrived I did my duty, playing the grateful ward. I pasted a smile on my face, laughing when appropriate and smiling to encourage conversation. After a glass of champagne, my shoulders relaxed and the roomful of guests seemed less intimidating.

When Claudette circulated with another tray, I snatched a second glass.

"Go easy," Claudette said, leaning toward my ear. "You aren't much of a drinker. You don't want to give the wrong impression." She winked. "Or perhaps you do."

"Don't worry. I still have my wits about me." I leaned in closer. "Unfortunately, there's a strange man who keeps following me around the room." I nodded at the petite man with carefully styled blond hair and a suit in the latest fashion. Of all the men here, he appeared the wealthiest, or at the least the one who cared the most about appearances.

He caught my gaze and winked.

Claudette grinned and spun off around the room with her tray, like a merry little top.

I groaned inwardly, but forced myself to smile at the gentleman—and then moved across the salon away from him. I didn't want to marry a man who considered himself prettier than me.

Within the hour, Madame introduced me to a clerk, a journalist, an attorney, and three professors. A slew of fine would-be husbands, should any find me suitable.

I reminded myself of this while smothering a yawn.

"And I immediately gave him the key," Monsieur LaRousse said, and laughed at his own joke.

I feigned amusement, secretly wishing someone—*anyone*—would rescue me. The clerk had rambled about his cumbersome duties in the governor's office without so much as a single inquiry about me, or anyone else in our circle for that matter. He seemed interested only in himself. Just as well. I stood two heads taller than him, and his teeth jutted from his mouth like a goat's.

Abruptly he leaned too close and said, "You're the most beautiful woman I've ever seen, Mademoiselle Daaé. If you would have me—"

"It has been so lovely to meet you, Monsieur," I interrupted, in hopes of preventing him from asking the dreaded question. "I apologize for my abrupt departure, but I must tend to Madame Valerius."

He blushed. "Of course."

Without hesitating, I checked in with Madame, and then meandered across the room.

Several of the guests looked at me with wolfish expressions, well aware of the real purpose for our salon, but none seemed interested in courting me—or even engaging me in real conversation—aside from the awkward clerk.

I positioned myself by the refreshment table and nibbled on a biscuit. Just beyond, the study doors stood open to the balcony overlooking the courtyard. Several gentlemen congregated outside, smoking and conversing in the cool night air.

"Nice party," one man said.

"If you like a lot of talking, and too few women."

The others laughed.

"Jeanne's ward is a real beauty," a third man said. "If you're a red-blooded male, you can't deny it."

My cheeks grew hot.

"If you like that sort, sure," the attorney said. "Docile on the surface, yet a singer, I've been told. You know what that means." He made a motion with his fist.

The others laughed again.

"Not a bad thing, is it? No one wants a lady in the bedroom."

Heat spread across my chest, followed by shame.

"She's beautiful, but my family would never accept her. Anyway, she doesn't have a franc to her name. Not much incentive there."

One of the professors chuckled. "I'd enjoy her for an evening or two, though I suppose I wouldn't be the first."

I wanted to tell them to jump off the roof. Instead, I gulped down my outrage and the threat of tears along with the remainder of my champagne. The cruelty of their mockery speared me through. Deep down I wondered where I belonged, what came next for me in this life, and these wretched men had managed to rub an already-tender spot raw.

I stood tall, turning from the balcony—and met the unfaltering gaze of Monsieur Delacroix, the professor of whom Madame had spoken all afternoon. A shock of dark hair hung over the edges of his collar. Though aging, he was handsome with his sculpted features and the silver flourishing at his temples. Still, his direct gaze made me uncomfortable.

The man commanded attention; that was clear.

Monsieur Delacroix's voice boomed from across the room. Three women laughed in response. He looked past them and smiled at me. With effort, I hid my anger and hurt, and nodded. I didn't want to be rude to Madame's dear friend.

After a supper of sole *meunière* in capered lemon sauce, herb-roasted potatoes, fruit tart, and cheeses, we retreated to the salon for spirits and the infamous table *tournante*. Nervous, I accepted another flute of champagne. As I sipped from my glass, I felt a hand at my elbow.

"Mademoiselle, I am pleased to find the rumors true." Monsieur Delacroix smiled, baring perfect white teeth. His eyes shone icy blue with irises ringed in cobalt, giving his gaze an intensity that startled me. "You are indeed more lovely than I would have thought possible."

"I— Good evening, Monsieur."

"Do not let those ingrates get to you." He tilted his head in the direction of the men I'd overheard on the patio. "They're fools. If I knew them better, I would give them a tongue-lashing for their offensive behavior."

A rash of embarrassment stained my cheeks. He had noticed my angry expression? Or perhaps he'd heard the men talk about me earlier.

"Thank you." I smiled, warmed by both his flattery and his kindness. "You are the mysterious gentleman in the third portrait." I motioned to the painting next to those of Papa and Monsieur Valerius.

He nodded. "Professor Gustave Delacroix. Family friend and

colleague of the late Monsieur Valerius, at your service."

"Madame spoke of your accomplishments," I said, not missing the arrogant tilt of his chin. "You work in the sciences, I hear."

"I test theories regarding supernatural occurrences. Prove they aren't real through science." He drank from his glass, his eyes never leaving my face.

"A fascinating pursuit," I said, shifting from one foot to the other. In spite of his amicable nature, the man oozed a sense of power and self-assurance. And there was that unmistakable intensity.

"I hear you have quite the affinity for cards," he said. "Sleight of hand, and so forth. I'll save you a place at the table this evening. Perhaps you will show me a trick?"

My head snapped up. Madame had mentioned my magic? My sullen behavior had not gone unnoticed, I knew, but I hadn't touched the magic box in more than three years. They had been a diversion at one time, a comfort. Not now. What once consoled me now flushed me with pain and guilt.

"I no longer indulge in such games," I said softly. "But I'll join the festivities at least, since Madame wishes it. Mediums and spirits do not interest me much, I'm afraid."

The professor didn't need to know that contacting the dead unnerved me.

"She would be disappointed if her cherished ward didn't participate." He smiled to soften his insistence.

Taken aback by his blunt nature, I remained silent. He was right, of course, and clearly cared for Madame's happiness.

"Forgive me for my directness," he said, noting my expression. "I really should learn to hold my tongue."

I smiled. He meant well, I could see. "You're right, of course. Madame would want me to join the others and see the medium."

"Perhaps she will also ask you to sing? I hear you are quite talented."

"Thank you." I smiled again. "It has been some time since I performed in public." Madame hadn't wanted me to perform on my own, and I obeyed her wishes, just as Papa had taught me.

"I see you've met Monsieur Delacroix," Madame said, rolling toward us. She squeezed my hand. "I hope you find him as wonderful as I do."

She smiled up at the professor, her skin radiant.

"You are too kind." He took Madame's hand and brushed it with his lips. "Are we ready to begin? Mademoiselle Daaé, why don't you invite Madame Claire to the table."

"Please do, dear." Madame twisted her wedding ring on her finger.

"Of course." I nodded and skirted the room.

The medium already sat at the *table tournante*, awaiting the signal to begin. She looked nothing like I expected. I had anticipated a woman with head scarves and colorful skirts, too much rouge, and stacks of beads around her neck, perhaps a turban. Instead, Madame Claire resembled an ordinary, middle-aged washerwoman with limp hair, mousy features, and thick fingers crowned by dirty fingernails. I wondered how she had come to be a medium.

"Good evening," I said. "Thank you for joining us. We're ready to begin the ... event."

Despite my skepticism, my insides churned. What if I was wrong, and spirits not only existed but refused to leave once summoned?

The medium smiled, revealing a set of decaying teeth. "As you wish."

I flinched at both her accent and her lack of hygiene. I'd spent enough time on the streets and in ramshackle homes to recognize an indigent from the streets of Paris. Some soothsayer.

"Ladies and gentlemen"—Delacroix's voice silenced the room—"our gracious host has given us permission to begin the séance. Those who would like to participate, please be seated around the table."

I looked down at the round table, remembering the way it felt as I stroked the lattice woodwork inlay at the start of the evening. Within the design, a series of numbers fanned out around the table's edges. Each number stood for a letter of the alphabet, I was told by an overeager guest. The medium would ask a question and, allegedly, the spirit would turn the tabletop, pausing in the proper places to spell its reply. Time to see it in action.

A flurry of moving chairs and nervous laughter filled the air as the guests relocated around the table. Some excused themselves and took refuge in the courtyard garden, drinks in hand, to avoid the "tool of the devil." The Catholic Church would not forgive meddling in the affairs of the dead.

In a few quick strides, I distanced myself from the table and sat on the sofa. Madame would want me present, even if I didn't participate, and I would oblige her from across the room. Nervous, I suppressed thoughts of Papa. I didn't want to unwittingly invite him—were that even possible. I picked at the cotton fringe on the arm of the sofa. My foot bounced beneath my gown in a steady rhythm.

Alfred dimmed the lanterns while Claudette rushed about lighting candles. Within moments, candlelight flickered on the walls and ceiling, casting an orange glow throughout the salon.

A hush blanketed the room.

"First, we must clear our minds," the medium said. "Dispel your worries, the daily lists, the gossip we enjoyed during this evening's fine meal."

Soft laughter followed.

"Allow the sacred to enter your hearts, the space around you."

I froze in my chair. How similar her words were to those of the illusionist, all those years ago on the night of the fire.

Let the border between worlds dissipate, the conjurer had said.

After several moments pause, the medium continued, her voice soft. "Come forth. Let us guide you."

Let us guide you from this earth to a resting place, once and for all.

My hands began to tremble.

"We can help you resolve what you have left unfinished," she said.

We can help you.

My breath came in uneven spasms. I gulped down the remainder of my champagne, willing the fizz to burn away the acrid memories of ash that settled on my tongue. I squeezed my eyes closed, praying the images would dissipate.

"Now close your eyes and breathe," the medium said. "Another deep breath. That's right."

I could go, join those drinking aperitifs in the courtyard. Madame would understand. Yet I remained glued to the chair, sucking in one steadying breath after another. I wasn't at the theatre. I wasn't in the midst of a ravaging fire, I reminded myself, but in the safety of Madame's home.

"Another breath," the medium said.

I studied the guests' faces as the medium's words pressed down upon them; the twitch of a brow, the fading of crease lines, jaw muscles relaxing. The inadvertent smile tugging at an unbeliever's lips.

"We will contact Benoît Valerius this evening," the medium said.

A gasp arose from those at table, though Madame Valerius remained perfectly still.

I gaped at her. She had agreed to this! I couldn't believe she would lay her heart so open before a crowd. Her husband had died in a boating accident on the Normandy coast many years ago—the very same accident that had left her disabled. It happened the summer Papa and I had visited the region for a series of performances; it was our first acquaintance with them. Monsieur Valerius's accident had only validated my fear of water.

Madame never spoke of the incident, and I dared not ask. To cause her pain hurt me as well. My loyalty to the dear lady flared.

I shot up from the sofa. "I don't think—"

"It is all right, *ma chérie*," Madame Valerius said quietly. "If I can communicate with my beloved . . . with Benoît . . . It is all right."

I sat slowly and clasped my hands together. This would not end well.

"Silence, please, everyone." The medium's voice took on a commanding quality. After a moment's pause, she continued, "Press your fingertips lightly on the surface of the table."

All did as she instructed.

"Spirit world," she went on, "open our hearts and minds to your presence."

Dread settled on my shoulders.

"Benoît Valerius, we beseech you to join us. Your wife awaits a sign."

After a moment's pause, the table top turned slowly on its casters.

Click, click, click.

The spinning increased in speed. A woman in a lavender muslin gown gasped, and whispered in her friend's ear. The friend bobbed her head forward, her lips forming an "o" of surprise.

"Is it you, Monsieur Valerius?" the medium said.

Click, click, click.

A series of turns spelled: *N-o.*

Madame's face fell. The hopeful light that bubbled around her all evening disintegrated. I breathed a sigh of relief. Regardless of Madame's hopes, I didn't want to see her weep at a party in front of everyone. Or at all.

"Spirit, will you speak to us?" the medium asked.

The table moved again.

Y-e-s.

I clutched the edges of my chair, leaning closer in spite of myself.

"With whom have you come to communicate?"

The table stilled for a long moment. The only sound arose from the faint sizzle of burning candlewicks. I watched Monsieur Delacroix, shadow and light playing across his features, and the sheen of his dark hair. He wasn't a believer, I knew. I wondered what could be going through his mind.

He caught my eye and winked.

Embarrassed, I refocused my gaze on the immobile table.

Just as the guests grew restless, the casters squeaked and the round turned, more slowly than before.

I held my breath as it spelled: *M-a-d-e-m-o-i-s-e-l-l-e.*

My heart pumped against my rib cage. There was only one other mademoiselle in the room, aside from me: a woman advanced in years.

It couldn't be Papa. It couldn't be. Or . . . Mother? My breath grew shallow.

More turns came.

D-a-a-é.

My stomach bottomed out. I hadn't asked for this—I didn't want it. I tried to tear my gaze away but couldn't.

"Who are you?" Delacroix interrupted the session.

Click, click, click.

A-n-g-e-l.

"Well, you've invoked an angel, Mademoiselle. Far better than a devil," Delacroix said, his voice low.

Soft chuckles filled the room.

I couldn't stand this. I pushed to my feet. "I do not wish to—"

The table spun again.

M-u-s-i-c.

"The Angel of Music," I whispered. Blood drained from my face and limbs, leaving me cold. It wasn't Papa, but the Angel? It couldn't be true. Spirits, angels, ghosts . . . these were beings of our dreams; beings for little girl whimsies and the elderly poised on the threshold of death. A means of comfort as the dying looked back over the regrets of their lives, and toward the infinite night ahead. This must be a hoax.

The table began to turn once more.

G-o. S-i-n-g.

Monsieur Delacroix smiled.

I clutched my middle as if I'd been struck.

The medium looked at me, her eyes brimming with a curious emotion I couldn't pinpoint. "The Angel of Music calls, Mademoiselle Daaé."

~ 3 ~

Shaken to the core, I spent the remainder of the week skittering around the house, startling at the smallest noises. The séance had confounded my perception of life and death, of what it meant to exist. I couldn't make sense of it. While in bed, I left a candle burning as I clutched the covers to my chin and stared at the long shadow of the armoire bleeding across the floor. Flickering candlelight teased the darkness, tempting it to snuff out its golden rays. I turned my ear to the whispering of drapes over floorboards, the moan of wind against windowpanes, until the last flame sputtered out. When the light surrendered to the dark, I squeezed my eyes closed. Yet the air pulsed as if alive. Were spirits here, watching me, even now? Maybe we always walked in the company of the dead without knowing, without seeing.

The dreams I had stuffed down years ago resurfaced with a vengeance: the image of the Master Conjurer and his assistant floating across the stage, their shrieks as fire licked the curtains and an attacker rushed them with a club. I wondered if their spirits haunted the ruins of the Theatre Margot, or hovered protectively around their loved ones.

Despite the disturbing images, songs flooded my dreams. The Angel commanded my music.

One afternoon in the garden, I sat beside Madame beneath the shade of a beech tree, wondering how I might broach the subject weighing on my mind. I'd had several nights of fitful sleep and battled a nervous energy until I couldn't stand it another minute. No one wanted me, not in the way Madame had hoped, and we needed a way to pay for her increasing doctor bills. I had to *do* something.

Drawing on my courage, I stuffed my sewing into my cloth sack. "Madame, I think it's time I started performing again."

She looked up from the novel she cradled in her hands, and studied me silently for several long moments. At last she said, "I hoped your time with me would lead to a happy marriage. As you know, your security has been on my mind these last few years. I'm not convinced singing will bring you happiness, Christine." She closed her book. "Also, it could make pairing you with a gentleman more difficult. Remember the salon."

I remembered it all too well.

"But it will bring added income, and build my experience. I see this as a means to aid my security." I lowered my eyes. "And yours."

"It's just . . . your reputation, dear."

Avoiding her gaze, I rubbed a spot on the arm of her wheelchair with my thumb. "The damage was done long ago. I've been a singer all my life. We need this, Madame. Marriage may lie in the distant future, or not at all. In truth, I could never see myself marrying for money alone."

"I wouldn't expect that, dear. I married Benoît for love." Her eyes took on the far-away look of memory. "But you're right, and your father would want you to devote yourself to music."

She closed her book. "I know just the person to get you started. In fact, he sent a letter this morning and I forgot to pass it along. Goodness, where is my mind going?" She rang a bell on the table beside her and Alfred arrived promptly.

"How may I assist you?" He bowed, sending a lock of hair over his overly large forehead and into his eyes. What the man lacked in looks, he made up for in manners and hard work.

"I'd like the post from my desk," she said.

In seconds, I held a letter imprinted with Monsieur Delacroix's elegant script.

Madame closed her book and laid it on her lap. "It's addressed to me, but the message is intended for you."

I skimmed a lengthy personal note about Benoît Valerius, and

Monsieur Delacroix's regrets for the failure to contact his spirit. I was surprised he apologized to Madame, given his skepticism, but he was a good friend, I supposed.

At the mention of my name, I slowed to read carefully.

Mademoiselle Daaé seems like a pleasant young woman, but so glum. I believe she could benefit from some entertainment. To that end, I would be delighted to escort her to the Cirque du Fantasme this evening—along with a maid, of course, if you think an additional escort necessary. I assure you, my intentions are purely of friendship and to aid you in any way I can, as always. Send word through Alfred should you decline. Otherwise I will arrive at eight o'clock.

Avec tout affection,

Gustave

I grimaced. If a perfect stranger could detect my unhappiness so easily, melancholy must blanket me like a shroud.

"He is truly a gentleman," I said slowly, remembering his compliments from the night of the salon. Though his letter insisted otherwise, I hoped he wasn't courting me. At last, I said, "The circus would be great fun."

Madame Valerius nodded. "And while you are with him, perhaps you can ask for his assistance."

I frowned. "In what way can he help me?"

"Gustave has many friends in the theatre circles. Perhaps if you accept his invitation, you can ask him who you should approach, or if he can connect you with someone." Madame Valerius eyed my hands. "Darling, your nails. You need to have them buffed, if not by Claudette then perhaps someone in town."

I fidgeted in my chair. "I don't like to ask Claudette for more than her usual share of work. And the money . . . I'm not comfortable—"

"My dear, I have never had a daughter. Please"—her eyes grew moist—"permit me to care for you as my own."

I knelt beside her mahogany wheelchair. "I'm truly grateful."

39

And I was. Not only did I feel gratitude, but I had grown to care for this generous woman. Her kindness and affection, along with Claudette's, had saved me from utter despair, from disappearing completely.

A smile carved a path into Madame's sagging cheeks. She adjusted her lower body with her hands, grunting as she lifted one leg and shifted in her velvet-covered seat.

"Would you like some help?" I asked.

"Oh goodness, no." She averted her eyes and touched her hair, embarrassed someone had seen her move her damaged body. "Why don't you do a card trick for me?" she said, changing the subject. "It has been so long since I've seen you practice."

I picked at a ragged nail. "I can't." I looked up and met her blue eyes. "I don't practice illusions anymore."

She held my chin between her thumb and forefinger. "I have noticed, *ma chérie*, but one day, you will find what you love again. You will pursue it, and not just because your papa did, but because it is who you are."

I saw my torn expression reflected in her eyes. I would never pursue the pastime that killed Papa, though abandoning my magic made me feel adrift—so far from Mother and all that I was before the fire. My eyes misted.

"Now, what do you say to the circus? Have you been?"

"No."

"Oh, it's marvelous!" She clapped her hands in joy. "You need to wear something elegant. You'll not want to look out of place from the other society ladies."

I glanced down at my unadorned day dress. Madame—and Monsieur Delacroix—were right. I needed time out of the house. And perhaps the professor could help me with an audition or two, if he was as well-connected as Madame said.

"I suppose I can't refuse." I smiled. "By the way, how do you know Monsieur Delacroix?"

"My Benoît worked with him. Gustave was new to the Académie

40

and very young at the time we met. When my husband died, Gustave helped me keep the household together. He gathered Benoît's dossiers, recommended an attorney, and so forth. He was very kind to me." She looked down at her wrinkled hands. "I don't know where I would be without him."

"He's a good man," I said, relieved Madame truly counted the professor among her dearest friends. It would make it easier to request his help.

She smiled. "Yes."

Mind reeling, I kissed her cheek and returned indoors.

Some hours later, Claudette helped me into a blue satin gown with a full bustle and black bows at the elbows and bosom. I smiled as I envisioned clowns and contortionists, a lion tamer and his whip, a crew of bleating goats, trick dogs, and perhaps an elephant decked in feathered plumes and beads with a woman on his back. I hoped I could enjoy the show, despite my nerves. I had never asked someone for help, and didn't feel comfortable now, particularly with nothing to offer the professor in return for his possible favor. But I must ask. We needed the income too desperately.

An hour later Monsieur Delacroix called at the door.

"I've been looking forward to our rendezvous all afternoon." He entered, wearing an elegant suit and cravat.

I smiled. "It was very kind of you to invite me."

"Thank you, Gustave," Madame Valerius said. "As always, you are a gentleman and friend."

He bowed over Madame's hand and kissed it. "I'm happy to assist you and yours as always, Jeanne."

She smiled warmly.

"Will Mademoiselle Daaé be accompanied by her maid this evening?"

"I don't think that's necessary," Madame replied.

My eyebrows arched in surprise. Madame was usually one for propriety. She must trust Delacroix implicitly to allow such a thing.

Claudette curtsied and left the room, but I saw disappointment in the slump of her shoulders. She wanted to see the circus more than I did.

I kissed Madame on the cheek. "I won't be late."

"To the Cirque du Fantasme!" Delacroix motioned to the door.

I climbed into the carriage and settled on a plush seat saturated with the heady scents of tobacco and bergamot. The night landscape streaked by as we rode across town: purpled skies, buildings in silhouette, and the sparkle of city lights on the watery face of the Seine. Monsieur did not attempt conversation and I tried not to twitch. I longed to discuss the burning question on my mind, but knew better than to bring up his connections and auditions so abruptly.

If the professor granted me his help, would he expect a price in return? I suppressed a sigh. I had nothing to give him in return, but I must ask him either way.

"Monsieur Delacroix," I said quickly, afraid to lose my nerve.

He turned from the window, a smile curving his lips.

"I wondered if . . ." I fumbled for the right words. "How often have you been to the circus?"

"Oh, a few times, I suppose. You're looking forward to it, I hope?"

I nodded, while silently berating myself for my lack of confidence. Before the end of the night, I *must* ask him.

"You know, Christine, after the séance I hoped you would share that voice of yours. Perhaps at the next soirée?"

I brightened at the serendipity of his statement. This was my chance. "I'd be delighted to, Monsieur. I—"

The coach came to a stop.

"We're here." He reached for the door handle.

I swallowed my words. I would have to try again later.

We alighted from the carriage and paused in front of a grand panel posted on the outer fence that read Cirque du Fantasme in silver lettering. Patrons flowed through the entrance in an adagio rhythm, the slow yet steady melody of marching boots complementing the *tap-tap* of silk-covered heels over the planks.

"Allow me." Monsieur Delacroix held out his arm.

I blushed. I had never been so near a man, other than Papa.

The professor paid the entrance fees and we strolled through the grounds. One tent boasted an aquarium, complete with reptiles and rare amphibians. Another housed a colony of sea lions, and a third, a family of elephants. I gaped at the strange creatures from distant lands. Most of the animals I had seen only in Madame's books. We continued along the dirt path between tents, grime soon covering my only pair of silk mules, as animated patrons pushed by us. The scent of straw and the earthy musk of animal feces permeated the air. Cheering arose at random moments, a horn blared somewhere, and music played in the distance.

Gratitude and awe bloomed in my chest and filled my heart to bursting—for the wonder, for the escape from the shriveled life that had engulfed my spirit. Here, life throbbed around me, rich and raw and stinking in its glory. A smile spread across my face. It felt as if my life lurched forward again—like a rusted wheel finally coated in fresh oil, and I was ready for it to turn.

My gaze flickered to Delacroix's face and darted away. At the periphery of my vision, I saw him smile. He seemed as happy as I was.

Now was as good a time as any.

"I know so little about your work, Monsieur." I initiated the conversation, hoping to steer it in the right direction. "What's it like being a professor?"

"Conducting studies and comparing their results, mostly," he said. "Recording my findings, giving demonstrations. In my field, it's difficult to measure results. It's no easy task to expose a ghost for a fraud." A dark chuckle rumbled in his chest. "But there must be a rational explanation for the supernatural. Never mind the mediums. They're a bunch of charlatans. Conjurers are the worst of them."

My steps faltered. I knew something of conjurers and the way they affected the audience.

"An interesting subject." I ducked beneath a banner of flags. "What drew you to it?"

His ebullience waned and he pressed his lips together. "It's a rather long story. Best for another day. For now, all I will say is: Tragedy has a way of shaping a person."

A notion I knew well. Though his reply sparked my curiosity, I didn't want to dampen his mood, especially when I needed something from him. "I beg your pardon. I didn't mean to pry."

"Not at all." He smiled.

As we turned down another pathway between tents, the rich aroma of caramel wafted around us.

"I can't imagine there are many in your field of expertise?" I pressed, anxious to keep him talking. "Do you work alone or with a team?"

"Mostly alone, though I work with assistants on occasion. There are more in the field than you might think. Professor Émile Lebard, for instance." A shadow hovered about his features.

"Monsieur Lebard?"

"A man intent on finding the connection between science and spiritualism. He believes in the nonsense, and seems to enjoy making me look like a fool."

So the professor was competitive. I wondered if all academics were the same. To me, it seemed as if they should work in tandem; one person's studies helping another. I didn't know how to respond, so I remained silent.

"And you?" He interrupted my thoughts. "Do you believe the soul can exist separately from the body?"

I never had before, but after the séance and the vivid dreams I wasn't certain of anything. I paused amid a stream of jugglers. "I never considered it possible until Papa died, and the other night..."

As I said the words, the familiar ache of loss resurfaced, pushing at the lightness of spirit I had felt only moments before.

Sensing my sadness, he took my hand between his and pressed it gently. "Please accept my condolences." His voice was soft. "The fire was a tragedy and you were so young. You didn't deserve to suffer such a cruelty."

"I was sixteen," I said, relieved he appeared sensitive to my loss.

"And now you are a woman, still stricken by grief." He squeezed my hand again. "Shall we enjoy ourselves? What would you say to having our fortunes read?"

He motioned to a small booth just ahead.

Within it, a soothsayer named Madame Huet bared a toothless smile with glistening pink gums.

I wrinkled my nose. "Perhaps the lions instead?"

He grinned. "The lions it is."

We moved around the soothsayer, and I nearly toppled a dwarf in a curious blue disguise. His pointed hat and floppy shoes elicited a giggle from the young ladies waiting in the queue outside the grandest tent of all—the equestrian ring and main event, where the lions would make their appearance.

"Pardon me," I said to the little man.

The dwarf glowered and continued on his way.

When we entered the tent, I tilted my face skyward to take in the hundreds of cables and poles propping up the canvas overhead. Acrobat ropes and wires crisscrossed near the ceiling or dipped just above a net poised to catch those who fell. I stared in awe at the cables' distance from the ground. How could an acrobat ever get used to swinging so high?

"This way." Delacroix led me to an empty seat on the topmost bench.

As I settled in next to a couple already seated, their conversation drifted in my direction.

"I heard Sergio is the best around," the gentleman in the brown morning coat said. "He sleeps with the lions."

"*Ce n'est pas vrai,*" the woman said.

"If it's true, he's completely mad." The man caught me eavesdropping and winked. He projected his voice to include me this time on purpose. "Can you imagine sleeping in the same room as a

45

predator? He watches you while you sleep, while you dress. He watches your every move."

I shivered at the thought.

"Ladies and Gentleman"—a man in redingote, bow tie, and top hat bellowed into a copper speaking trumpet—"what you are about to witness will surprise you, thrill you, and terrify you." He paused. "Tonight, we welcome Sergio, Master of the Beast, with his pride of lions. Not only will he impress you with tricks, he will defy death!"

Drums boomed a warning from the orchestra near the rear of the tent. Several men pushed an enormous cage to the center of the ring, while others pulled in a train of animal carriers on wheels. One by one, four lions sauntered from their cages. When Sergio appeared, applause arose from the audience. The tamer climbed onto his stool and unfurled the coiled whip at his side, his coat as scarlet as a hunk of flesh. I cringed at the proximity of the cats, and the menace of their large paws.

"*Dieu*, they could scratch out his eyes!" said the woman to my right.

"They say the lions have their claws removed," her companion replied. "Cut out by surgery, though I don't know if it's true. But they could still easily crush him, maul his face or shred his throat with their teeth."

"Marceau, please!" she exclaimed. "You're frightening me."

I grimaced as Sergio began his routine. What if the lions didn't follow his cues? Surely he wouldn't put himself in danger. The animals must be well-trained.

A lioness growled and sat up on her hind legs as instructed. Sergio tossed a chunk of raw meat into her mouth. He gave the male lion a command. The animal didn't budge. Sergio flicked his wrist and his whip snapped the air. The lion roared, but remained in position. I watched the tamer's bravery with awe. He stood nonchalantly in front of a large audience, surrounded by a cast of beasts watching him through amber eyes. An incredible feat.

After another moment, he cracked the whip again, mere centimeters from the lion's hide. The animal roared and batted the air with his paw, narrowly missing the man's head.

The audience gasped.

Leave the lion alone, I thought. He doesn't want to play today, and *I* didn't want to witness a gruesome death.

Man should not wrangle with beasts.

The day's lingering heat made the tent an oven, and perspiration trickled down my back. I yearned to escape the stench of body odor and fear, but I couldn't tear myself away.

"He's supposed to put his head in the big one's mouth," the man to my right said. "Looks like he could have it bitten off tonight."

Sergio shouted. Still, the lion disobeyed. The beast's roar reverberated through the tent, alerting the lionesses. Without pause, the females joined the male, hissing and growling.

I covered my eyes. The pride would attack and the tamer would be torn to pieces in front of everyone.

Someone shouted from the crowd, cleaving the tension in the air. People murmured with their neighbors.

"Are you all right?" Monsieur Delacroix whispered. A muscle in his jaw twitched. Apparently the act was getting to him as well.

I nodded. Gripped by macabre fascination, I removed my hand from my eyes.

Sergio shouted something. The next instant, the lion closed his mouth around the man's forearm.

The crowd's murmurings grew louder.

Two armed men entered the cage.

"It is all part of the show!" Sergio called to the audience. "Remain calm!"

A third man divvied out meat to the lionesses. The large cats devoured it. Within seconds, the men ushered them out of the ring. Sergio seemed to be cajoling the lion, though we couldn't hear his words. A man carrying a gun circled behind the beast. The woman beside me buried her face in her escort's shoulder, unable to watch.

I clutched Monsieur Delacroix's arm, hardly daring to breathe.

He covered my hand with his. "Do you want to leave?"

I didn't answer, just stared at the ring.

Sergio coaxed the lion to release him. At last, the beast relaxed his jaw, shook his mane, and sauntered across the cage to claim the last piece of raw meat. The tamer stood on his miniature platform and bowed.

The stunned audience didn't clap. A few men cheered.

"He certainly defied death," Marceau said, laughing. "Barely."

I exhaled and my shoulders relaxed.

"Care for a walk?" Delacroix asked. Perspiration wetted his forehead. "Some fresh air?"

"Yes, please," I said, ready to be far from the lion tent.

As we stepped into the cool night air, the ringleader rode past us on a white stallion, trumpet poised at his lips. We walked past a troop of exotic women in orange-and-white costumes holding ribbons at their sides, or stretching their limbs. Behind them, an irate clown shouted at another, who ignored the first clown's rage and lit a cigarette.

"That gave you quite a fright," Delacroix said. "I must admit, it had me nervous as well."

"The lion could have ripped the man's arm off!"

His tone turned cold. "Idiot. Performers do the most absurd things for an audience."

I glanced at Delacroix, surprised by his change in demeanor. His forehead bunched into a frown, his eyes pensive.

Suddenly I remembered my agenda. I had to speak to him, soon. Before we knew it, the evening would end and I would lose my chance.

"I have something I'd like to ask you." The words burst from my lips without time to finesse them. My careful planning dissolved.

"Certainly, but first, come with me. This is important."

I gulped down my disappointment at yet another lost opportunity. "Where are we going?"

"I have something to show you. This way." He picked up speed as he led me farther from the largest tents, past the crowds, and to the outermost edges of the fence.

When he stopped abruptly, I almost plowed into him.

"What is so impor—" The words died on my lips.

Just beyond the final tent, a theatre abutted the property. The theatre that had taken Papa.

The barrier holding my emotions in check—stretched thin and taut inside me—punctured at the sight. I blinked rapidly to hold the deluge of tears at bay and inhaled deeply. I hadn't been near the site since that horrible day. In fact, I hadn't remembered the address or even the surroundings. But I recognized it now. The trembling in my knees confirmed it.

Voice low, Monsieur Delacroix said, "It's time for you to move on, Christine. And I would like to help you. I have a few friends at the opera house, and I know they're holding auditions for the autumn and winter seasons very soon. Why don't you sing for them, and see how things go. I'll put in a good word for you. Your father would be so proud to see you try."

Surprised, my mouth fell open but emitted no sound. It was uncanny how he had read my mind. I gazed at the crates of new wood stacked beside the charred ruins. Apparently, the theatre would be restored and filled with patrons again. The thought made me strangely hopeful.

I looked at Delacroix. For a second I wondered why the professor wanted to help and seemed so eager to do so, but I dismissed the thought. My wish would be granted. That's all that mattered. I could help Madame, and move forward, at last.

"You're right." I nodded. "I can think of nothing that would please my father more."

~4~

I tried to sleep but lay tangled in the sheets, staring at the flowered frieze in the plaster ceiling. With my eyes, I followed the lines along the crown molding and down the wall to the casing around the windowpanes. Seeing the theatre again brought flashes of heat on my skin and the memory of Papa's sad, accepting gaze as blood oozed down his face. I pulled a pillow over my head to banish the image. Papa's proud face rose behind my eyes again, but this time, I saw him the day I received a standing ovation. My nerves had been wrecked until I'd stepped into the pool of warm light on the stage, and looked out at the entranced faces of the audience. I had come alive that day. I wanted to make him proud again, to somehow make up for what I'd done.

I threw the covers aside and tiptoed across the cool tile. Beyond the heavy drapes at the window, moonlight crept over paving stones in the courtyard, leaving a silvery luminescence in its wake. The urge to be outdoors overwhelmed me. I pulled on a pelisse and boots, lit a candle, and tiptoed down the stairs to the salon. For a few moments, I looked around the room, deciding whether or not it was truly safe to go outdoors at this hour.

A board creaked behind me.

I swiveled around, heart beating wildly. The noise hadn't come from my own footfall. Did the Angel of Music hover over me, even now?

It had to be the natural groans of the house, oaken floors disturbed at such an ungodly hour.

"Coward," I whispered. Yet I pulled my pelisse more tightly about my shoulders. I stole through the salon to the cupboard where I knew the decanter of brandy would be tucked away among the glasses. Some alcohol should help me relax. I poured a serving and walked outside around the side of the building to the courtyard. Despite the late hour, the air was still warm. I sat on the bench, swigged deeply from the glass–and coughed from the burn. I never drank brandy. A sip of wine here and there was all I could muster, but as the alcohol soaked into my blood and my muscles relaxed, I was grateful for its potency. Perhaps it would help me sleep.

Beneath the moon, my senses sharpened. The night's music filled the air as leaves rustled in the breeze and insects chirped from an unseen cranny on the patio. I closed my eyes and let the orchestra of sounds wash over me, feeling them twine around my fear and pluck it like guitar strings. The softest note fell from my lips, and then another, stretching into a melody.

After the first song, hope flooded the cavity beneath my ribs, pushing against the despair lodged there for so long. Another melody sprang from memory; a lullaby Mother had sung to me. As the familiar lyrics flowed over my lips, a sense of serenity slipped through my veins. I should sing–I *would* sing. It was time to do my duty. More than that, it was time to find my place.

A cool breeze lifted the hair from my neck. Goose bumps rose on my arms. Where had the breeze come from? The evening was so warm. I threw a furtive glance over my shoulder. Pots bursting with thirsty geraniums fanned out behind me. Their peaked branches hadn't rustled in the wind as my hair had. Oddly, the breeze hadn't seemed to reach them.

Cool air brushed my skin again, leaving a charged tinge in the air. I shivered and looked to the bushes again. Something moved among them.

I stood, heart thumping. "Who's there?" My imagination reeled with thoughts I didn't want to entertain. Perhaps I shouldn't be out in the dark, alone, at this hour, after all.

The breeze brushed my cheek this time, and still, the bushes did not stir.

I screeched and bolted from the courtyard.

As I locked the front door, I laughed softly and leaned against the wall. It had likely been a cat rustling the branches—no ghosts or angels. And what predator would be hanging around a garden in hopes someone might show? Such ridiculous notions.

Still, I darted to my room as fast as I could and locked the door behind me.

Each morning for the next two weeks, I awoke with notes on my tongue. From soft pianissimo to fortissimo, from melodies to arias, I sang, relishing the feel of my lungs burning for air, the vibrations in my head and throat, the power of emotion rising from within and weeping from the lyrics, or bursting into the room. Madame Valerius broke into applause, then tears, when my voice floated through the house.

Finally, the day of my audition arrived. Clutching the edges of my vanity table, I leaned closer to the mirror, stomach as riotous as a stormy sea. I told myself I could do this. I could stand before the most discerning musical ears in the world and perform, after years of hiding from society. The worst that could happen would be that I made a fool of myself—failing completely and destroying Papa's dreams as well as my own.

A hysterical laugh escaped my lips. Anxiety flamed through me in waves and my face flashed hot. I needed to get hold of myself.

A light tap came at the door.

"It's time," Claudette said, her voice muffled.

Madame Valerius had relinquished Claudette from her daily chores so she could go with me to the audition.

"Christine?" Claudette knocked a second time.

I opened the door and stared at her, lips stretched tight over gritted teeth.

She laughed and took my hands in hers. "You look terrified. Don't worry. You'll be wonderful."

I squeezed her hands. "You really think so?"

"I'd sooner scrub a floor than sing in front of a crowd myself. But then, I sing like a frog." She fluffed her skirts. "Do you like it?"

The pink dress embroidered with roses accented her lovely freckled complexion and red hair. I was relieved she would be with me for support. I needed a friend.

"You're stunning." I kissed her cheek.

Her smile widened. "Never thought I'd see the day I look like a real lady."

My gown had been carefully chosen as well: summer green to set off my complexion and highlight my blue eyes. I touched the matching felt hat pinned in my hair. I hoped I would stand out.

We hailed a coach, careful not to crush our pressed bustles. Once on our way, the city sailed by as we traveled to the Boulevard des Capucines, home of the Opéra de Paris. I didn't know how much time I would have to warm up my voice, and immediately put myself into proper position. Perched on the edge of the seat, I sat tall, pushed my shoulders back, and relaxed the muscles in my jaw with the heels of my hands. After several deep breaths, I sang a set of scales. Next, I placed my tongue on the roof of my mouth just behind my teeth and blew until it vibrated, all the while varying my pitch. Finally, I hummed for several minutes. Though Claudette had seen me practice many times, she smothered a giggle. The exercises had made me laugh when I was a little girl, and likely would put a smile on any non-singer's face.

When the carriage stopped at the Opéra de Paris, I gaped at the grand façade. Sets of columns framed the front of the building in twos, capped by statuettes. Golden figures poised atop the far spires. A large copper dome popped from the roof, and a sculpture of Apollo watched over the city from its peak.

My stomach quivered like jellied fruit as I took in its grandeur.

The coachman jumped down and opened the door. "Mademoiselle?"

"I-I don't know. I . . . Please, just drive on. I'm not ready. I can't do this." My voice came out as a hoarse whisper. How could I audition if I couldn't speak?

"No." Claudette's lips were set in a determined line. "I won't let you miss this. Why don't I slip into the back of the theatre? Won't do you any good if I'm loitering about in the cast room. You can focus on me. That would help, wouldn't it?"

I threw my arms around her. "Would you?"

"I've never been inside a theatre." She slipped her arm through mine. "Let's get to it, then, shall we?"

I gathered my nerve, and we headed to the entrance on the west side of the opera house. The building seemed to draw in a breath when I swung open the door. As I stepped inside, a strange sensation rushed over my skin. I tried to ignore it and continued on, wandering through a corridor to the foyer on the first floor.

As we rounded the corner, I gasped. A grand staircase made of marble swept upward to a landing, split in two directions, and continued to the second floor. Above us, tiered balconies gilded in gold wrapped the interior walls. On the topmost floors, the gold became iron vines that coiled in rows between banister and floor.

Claudette whistled. "Amazing."

I stood in stunned awe. The building demanded reverence.

"Look at her!" Claudette pointed to a statue of a woman holding a candelabrum above her head, her haunted face and bronzed body lustrous in the light.

The statue was one of a pair guarding the steps. I looked past her outstretched arms, at the ceiling. Panels of cherubs, beautiful maidens, and nymphs brought the domed ceiling to life in pastels and gold leaf. Yet, in spite of all the beauty, the opera house emanated an ominous ambiance. Something dark and unseen, something almost tangible.

I shook my head. The thought didn't help my tumbling stomach. I needed to find the cast room and practice more, focus on the task at hand. I looked around me, prepared to ask someone for directions. A workman in dusty clothing and boots carried a toolbox; a pair of men in expensive suits crossed the room while deep in conversation. Others appeared as lost as me, or intent on their own thoughts.

A second workman started in the same direction as the first.

"Pardon me, Monsieur, but where is the cast room?"

He stared at me, eyes greedy, before saying, "Walk along the west side of the foyer. There is a set of steps there. Take them and follow the hallway to the second door on your right."

"Thank you," I said, avoiding his eyes.

Claudette snickered as he walked away. "He looked at you like he'd never seen a woman before."

I shuddered. "I tried not to notice."

When we reached the cast room, a woman stopped us. "You're both here to audition?" Her voice was flat, as if she had asked the question a hundred times.

"I won't be singing," Claudette chimed in.

The woman twisted her mouth in disapproval. "Then you'll not be allowed inside the changing rooms or the cast room."

"Can I wait in the theatre?" Claudette asked. "I won't be in anyone's way."

She huffed with impatience. "The directors won't allow it. Wait in the main foyer or outside."

Claudette shot me a conciliatory look.

"It looks like I need to do this on my own."

"Bonne chance," she said, her Irish brogue as thick as ever. She leaned to my ear and whispered, "I'll find a way in. Don't you worry your pretty head about that."

The woman put her hand on her bony hip. "Are you coming in or not?"

I nodded and was ushered through a dressing room divided by stalls, and on through another hallway. As we neared a final door backstage, the woman bent over her paper and added my name and address to the list. "You're number twelve. When your number is called, go through this door to the stage. The chorus director and his assistant will signal you when it's time."

She pushed the door open.

A dozen others peered at their newest competition.

My stomach churned as I glanced at the singers. Some hummed or trilled to warm their voices; others sang at full tilt but covered one ear to block the discordant racket of sopranos, tenors, and baritones. How could they hear themselves? I'd never had to compete just to practice.

A man poked his head through the doorway. "Number eight, you're next."

The woman seated against the wall stood, held her head high, and left the room. She seemed so at ease. I envied her confidence. With a deep breath, I sang a set of scales and did another of my exercises. The door opened every few minutes and another singer joined us in the queue. The competition grew by the minute.

A half an hour later, the assistant appeared again. "Number twelve!"

My stomach plummeted to my feet. I was on. I followed him through the door and onto the stage, just behind the curtain. Number eleven was still singing a piece from *Le Mariage de* Figaro. The woman's nasal register rang thick and her vowels were not as elongated as they should be. Her notes sounded forced, as if she strained her vocal chords to produce the sounds.

I hoped I sounded better than that.

"Thank you," the chorus director said, not allowing her to finish the song. "That will be all. Next!"

The assistant said, "State your name for the directors clearly, as well as the piece. When finished, exit the stage down the left stairs and leave through the door on the west wall."

I must have looked terrified because he chuckled softly and said, "It's over quickly. Good luck."

I emerged from behind the curtain, breathing deeply to calm my nerves. As I walked across the stage, I was struck by the magnificent theatre. Hundreds of ruby-red seats sat in neat rows like soldiers at attention. Box seats in the same scarlet paneling, framed by golden balconies, lined the walls. A large chandelier hung from the ceiling. I stared out at the parterre. A hundred years ago the floor-level seats wouldn't have existed at all, and laborers would have stood in the space, conversing and laughing, creating their own spectacles. The stage would have been rimmed in candles, making the air hazy with smoke. The audience may or may not have given their attention to the players and singers, caring more to be seen than to be entertained. Until now. It had changed in recent times, Papa had said, and it was a better time to be a performer. In this moment, I couldn't help but wish for the days when no one listened.

I scanned the faces of the few people in the audience. Three gentlemen and a single woman sat several rows from the stage. Claudette hadn't made it inside. Disappointment fed my nerves and my eyes fluttered shut. I needed to be calm, to relax my vocal chords. I took in another steadying breath and imagined Madame Valerius's salon. There I stood, in front of the fireplace.

"We don't have all afternoon, Mademoiselle," someone said. "State your name and get on with it, please."

My eyes flew open and I cleared my throat, stepping into the well of light pooled in the center of the stage. "My name is Christine Daaé. I will be singing "Habanera" from *Carmen*."

The man with blond hair wrote furiously in his notebook. When he finished, he looked up. "You may begin."

Good posture and projection, I reminded myself as I pulled my shoulders back a fraction. I lifted my chin and stared at the back wall. Would I hear the accompaniment over my thundering pulse?

The pianist on the far end of the stage started, and the familiar tune I had practiced so often in the previous weeks filled the theatre. At the right moment, I began. As the first lyrics left my lips, the directors' faces faded and the red-and-gold paneling blurred. I could be somewhere else, be *someone* else, transform into the character of my role.

Note after note, the song built toward the crescendo. Energy flowed through me and I felt powerful. The emotion swelled until a familiar release swept me into a world containing only music. Until the end. Just as I neared the last few stanzas of the song, my pitch wavered. I recovered quickly and finished strong.

The music stopped and my mask fell away once more.

One of the gentleman said, "Thank you, Mademoiselle Daaé."

When he said nothing else, my hope wavered. I had botched the song at an important moment. Too many vied for a position in the chorus—they didn't need someone who couldn't sustain even a full song.

All four in the audience leaned in to confer.

Blood pounded in my ears. What could they be saying? The seconds felt like hours. At least I tried, I consoled myself. And at least the directors had not stopped me in the middle of the song, like they had the previous woman.

Finally, the blond gentleman spoke. "We'll post the list next Monday in the cast room. Next!"

"Thank you." I scurried from the stage, relieved to be on my way.

Once I escaped through the designated door, I heaved out a breath. A full week to wait. I didn't know how I'd stand it. I wound through the maze of corridors to the foyer. The stack of unpaid bills on Madame's desk flitted through my mind and my anxiety flared again. If they didn't choose me, I would have to think of something else, some other way.

I found Claudette waiting in the foyer along with a handsome gentleman in a pin-striped coat and a perfectly trimmed mustache. He appeared taken with Claudette. I didn't blame him. She was a vision today.

She smiled as I approached. "Are you finished then?"

"Yes." I gave her a relieved smile.

"I'll be on my way," the man said. "Good day to you, Mademoiselle O'Malley." He tipped his hat at us both and hurried up the staircase.

"Who was he?" I asked.

"A handsome devil," she said. "He asked if he could call on me, but I put him off. He would drop me the minute he discovered I'm a housemaid." Her lips formed a pout. "I wish I were you sometimes."

"You forget I'm a musician's daughter from the streets. I won't marry well, either, and when Madame . . . Well, we'll both be out on the streets again."

Her eyes grew contrite. "I know. I just want something more to my life than sweeping floors. Maybe one day."

"It will happen." I kissed her cheek. "Remember, we're in this together."

She smiled weakly and said, "How'd you fare?"

"All right. I tripped over a syllable that threw off my pitch near the end." I sighed. "But it's finished and I'm glad about that."

"I'm sure it went better than you think."

As we climbed aboard the coach, I cast a glance over my shoulder at the building's imposing face. "I hope you're right."

After the audition, I picked apart every note of my performance. I reassured myself I sang as well as I could, and then minutes later decided my voice was atrocious. With such an inferior performance, I didn't deserve a spot in the famed opera chorus. Exhausted by the constant wavering, I focused on my plans to move forward. If the opera wouldn't have me, I would find another venue in which to sing. Yet I had no accompaniment and it would be improper, even laughable, to assume I could tour from salon to salon on my own. I knew no one.

The only bright spot came from my trick lock, which swung open on the fifty-sixth combination. Inside, I found a string of tiny silver bells. Delighted, I fastened the string around my wrist and began sketching an image of the lock's many complex levers. Who knew when I might use the puzzle's tricks again.

When casting day arrived, I rose from the breakfast table, unable to eat. In less than an hour, I would return to the opera, see if I had survived the audition. I slipped out into the courtyard and paced across the patio.

"Monsieur Delacroix is here." Claudette interrupted my thoughts. "He's brought you roses this time."

I had seen a lot of the professor the last few days. Each visit he brought gifts, and assured me of my place at the opera house. Though I accepted them, I confessed my unease to Madame Valerius. If he was courting me, he wouldn't get very far. I was too young for him, and though he endeared himself to me, I didn't see him in a romantic light. I didn't care how silly and modern the notion was, I couldn't marry someone I didn't love.

Madame had confronted him at my insistence.

After the meeting, she soothed my fears. "He's only seeking your friendship, Christine. Don't forget, he's a dear friend of mine. Why wouldn't he take my ward under his wing? He said you need a male figure guiding you, and wants to look after you like a father. I quite agree."

I breathed a sigh of relief. "Thank you for asking. It must have been a delicate question to pose."

She looked down and clasped her hands in her lap. "We have endured a far more delicate time."

I wondered what she meant, but assumed she referred to her husband's death and didn't want to pry.

"Besides, he has a mistress." Madame's eyes took on a faraway look and she touched her hair.

Her anxious habit emerged again, but why? I watched her closely. Did she have feelings for the professor? But she was well beyond his age, as he was beyond mine.

Lightly, I had said, "Is his mistress anyone I have met?"

"No." She had gripped the wheels of her chair. "I'll just be off to my room for a rest."

I had stared after her, surprised by her abrupt departure.

"What are you thinking about?" Claudette grinned as her words brought me back to the moment. "You're scowling."

I ignored her and headed to the salon.

Delacroix stood in the middle of the room, holding a cone of pretty paper stuffed with yellow roses.

"You spoil me." I took the flowers and unrolled them from the paper to trim their ends.

"I came to celebrate your good news." He flashed his chalk-white smile.

I bit back a self-deprecating remark. Instead, I said, "It's kind of you to be so supportive, but if you had seen the queue of singers, you wouldn't be so sure."

"Now, that's no way to behave. You must think like a star." He watched me slice off the end of each stem and place the flowers in a vase. "Come, let me go with you."

"That won't be necessary—"

"I insist." He took me by the arm with a firm hand.

I regarded Delacroix's vivid eyes, his unmistakable air of authority. He was the reason I had an audition in the first place. His belief in me had buoyed me the past week, and if he wanted to accompany me . . . I smiled. "Very well."

"I'll take you for coffee after. My carriage is in the drive."

When we entered the foyer of the opera house, the sensation I noticed on my first visit returned. A heavy foreboding settled on my shoulders and attached to my spirit. I shivered and continued onward to the cast room. Somehow, the building felt alive, and looked on its visitors with begrudging acceptance. I remembered the opera house's history from the newspaper clippings Papa had strewn across the farm table in our barn. Executions had taken place in the underground cellar during the Commune. I could still see the parody of those deaths captured on a waterlogged newspaper as clearly as if I had read it that morning. I wondered if those souls were trapped within the walls. An unsettling thought. Perhaps it was only the building's dark history, but I couldn't shake the feeling: Something lurked in this magnificent theatre.

"This place is a labyrinth," Delacroix said behind me, his voice low.

I wanted to say—And haunted!—but instead said, "We're almost there. It's the next corridor on the left." In this building of many doors and winding corridors and multiple floors below ground, I was grateful for my innate sense of direction.

At last, we reached the casting room. Inside, a crowd had gathered around two lists pinned to the wall: one paper listing the dancers, the other the singers.

I held my breath. This was it. Now or never.

"Yes!" a young man shouted, his features alight with happiness. He stepped to the side to let the others push forward.

One by one, each singer either whooped in glee or shrugged and sauntered away. I chewed my bottom lip as I waited for the crowd to thin. I could wait. I would prefer to mull over the verdict in relative privacy.

A young woman hung back next to me. Her slight frame suggested she was a ballerina.

"I'm Meg Giry," she said when she caught my eye. "Maman works as a concierge here. I've done a few productions, but the spots are always competitive. Are you a dancer?"

I warmed to her open face. "I'm Christine Daaé. A singer, but I've never performed at the opera, or any place so grand." I laughed nervously.

"You have nothing to fear." Monsieur Delacroix patted my shoulder.

He seemed so certain, almost vehement.

Meg held her hands beside her in a classic ballerina pose, wrists slightly bent, pinkies and forefingers extended. She looked as if she might leap away any moment. "If we both make the list, you'll have a friend already."

I smiled. "Thank you."

When the last woman's head drooped in disappointment and she walked away, I approached the list. Heart clamoring against my ribs, I ran my finger over the names. As I neared the end of the list, my hope shriveled more and more like a deflated balloon. Until—there it was!—second to last in bold lettering: Christine Daaé.

I suppressed a screech of joy and turned to tell the professor, but before I could say a word, he gripped my arms and kissed each cheek.

"Congratulations," he said with a grand smile. "You see?"

I had done it! Somehow, the directors overlooked my error and wanted me to take part in their chorus. At the Nouvel Opéra! I could scarcely believe it.

"I made it!" Meg squeaked. "You must have, too? Congratulations."

I laughed at her enthusiasm. "The same to you."

"Lovely to meet you, Christine Daaé! I'll see you on Monday." Meg scampered away on feet that didn't seem to touch the ground.

"Shall we celebrate?" Delacroix held out his arm.

"Oh, let's!" I took his arm eagerly, joy brimming inside me.

Practice began the following Monday, and so did my new life.

~5~

Upon my return to the opera—as a *real* member of the cast—I ambled through the corridors, taking in the magnificence of the building, the endless stream of new faces, and the magnitude of my luck. I couldn't believe I was here! When I reached the cast room, I shrugged out of my pelisse and slung it over my arm.

"Christine, is that you?"

I turned to find the ballerina I'd met at the audition. Relieved to see a familiar face, I smiled. "It's nice to see you again, Meg. I'm a little nervous."

She patted my shoulder. "You'll become one of us quickly. Meet Jocelyn." She presented the woman at her side. "She's in the chorus as well."

Though not pretty, the chorus girl's smile was warm and welcoming. She kissed my cheeks and said, "Welcome."

Surprised by the informal way the players and singers greeted each other, I hesitated before saying, "I'm Christine Daaé. Lovely to make your acquaintance."

Jocelyn giggled. "Goodness, we'll have to cure you of all that formality. We're a tightly knit group here."

Cheered by her friendly nature, I felt my shoulders relax. "The cast is immense. I had no idea it would be so intimidating. How many people work here?"

"Oh, seven hundred to . . . about a thousand, would you say, Meg?" Jocelyn grinned. "Impressive, isn't it. But the show won't run itself."

I nodded. Like cogs in a machine. How would I make a name for myself among such a cast? I fidgeted with the sleeve of my pelisse.

"Have you got a copy of the libretto yet?" Meg asked. "I have an extra." She rummaged inside her bag and produced a rumpled copy of the script.

"Not yet. Thank you." I skimmed through all five acts, noting the number of arias verses *cavatinas*—the shorter, melodious songs— making a mental note of when the chorus sang. Some operas had three acts, others five. Some were Bel Cantos featuring the beauty of the song, like the operas of Bellini and Rossini; others focused on grand theatrics, like Meyerbeer's, while others were comical or tragic. Every variety one could think of, really, and I knew only a few. The popular *Faust* was the perfect place for me to begin.

"Let's see . . . other things you need to know to survive around here." Jocelyn counted them off on her fingers. "The machinists ogle the dancers. The costume designer is an absolute genius—stop by his workshop on the second mezzanine. Be on time for practice with Gabriel, the chorus director, or he yells a lot. Goes purple, in fact." She paused, biting her lip. Suddenly her eyes lit up. "Many of us meet for drinks or dancing after most shows, if you'd like to join us. Oh, and whatever you do, don't make the prima donna angry."

"Who is the prima donna?"

"Carlotta," Meg and Jocelyn said in unison.

"She can be charming and helpful, even, but once you're on her bad side, she'll have it in for you until you're kicked out of the show," Jocelyn said, brown eyes earnest. "Trust me. Be careful around her. I've seen it happen twice."

Duly noted. I didn't need to make trouble for myself. "I'll do my best. Thank you."

Meg laced her arm through mine. "Let's take a tour of the ballet rooms. You can see where we practice, and where we meet with our patrons after the show."

I smiled, genuinely grateful for my new friends. "I'd like that."

Every day I passed new faces in the halls and backstage at the opera house. Machinists constructed sets, fly boys shifted the flats and drops painted with faux scenery, musicians practiced with the orchestra. Ballerinas danced until their feet bled. When I felt more comfortable with my surroundings, I followed Jocelyn's advice and met the costume designer. Fabien welcomed me into his workshop, boasting happily about his multitude of fabrics and accoutrements, and presenting his sketch boards with pride. His latest designs included an array of seventeenth-century court gowns. They would premiere in a new *opéra comique* called *La Mascotte,* about a virginal good-luck charm. Delighted, I let the designer show me more.

I found myself observing the crew whenever time permitted. I wanted to learn it all. One afternoon during practice, the lighting manager perched on a seat in the audience, studying our rehearsal with a hawk's eye. He took copious notes and paced around the outer fringes of the stage. At one point, he strode to the back of the parterre, and eventually wound up on a balcony, observing the show from above.

I listened with fascination while he spoke with the stage director.

"I want footlights along the proscenium and lanterns on the gantry." The manager motioned to the bridge-like structure overhead.

"For the garden scene?" the stage director asked.

The man nodded and put his hands on his hips, staring hard upstage. "We'll also need lighting behind the drops for the scene when Mephistopheles enters."

"You shouldn't illuminate the wings during the ballet," the stage director replied.

"Yes, I know. Let me do my job, Sean." He motioned to his crew to begin the adjustments.

I'd never considered the importance of stage lighting, yet it seemed it could determine the ambiance and tone of the entire show. Though I hadn't yet grown used to my place, I was proud to be a member of such a talented crew.

The most celebrated cast member of them all—Carlotta Arbole, the Italian diva—stood out among the singers. On Thursday evening, I watched her from my position near the back of the stage. A row of braids was pinned to the crown of her head, and the rest of her glossy dark hair waved down her back. A full-busted woman, she wore an expensive silk gown with a low neckline, and refused to practice in costume. That way, she claimed, the costumes would have more impact on opening night. Carlotta was a handsome woman with a bold voice and unmatched stage presence. I looked on in awe as she swished from one corner to the next, never losing her sense of rhythm or showing any breathlessness. She went beyond just singing on cue; she embodied the characters she played, though I considered her a touch melodramatic for my taste. Even so, I envied her self-possession.

"I'm finished for the day," Carlotta said with a toss of her dark mane. "I'm tired."

"Mademoiselle, please." Consternation tugged the corners of Gabriel's mouth into a frown. "Two more songs and we'll be finished."

"I am finished now," she insisted. "Let the others practice. They need it far more than I do." She whirled around and headed toward the east wing of the stage.

"Carlotta, come back this instant!" Gabriel shouted.

She tossed her head again and continued on her way, singing out, "I'll come and go as I please."

Exasperated, Gabriel clamped his mouth closed for an instant before raising his voice again. "All right, everyone. Let's begin with the soldier's chorus. To your places."

I covered a grin. The woman knew how to get her way.

We went through two songs. Each time, my voice wouldn't stay in tune with the others. I shifted anxiously from one foot to the other. This had happened for days and I couldn't think why. Why wasn't my voice cooperating? I redoubled my determination.

We began again, from one verse to the next and—

"Stop!" Gabriel wiped his perfectly dry brow with a handkerchief. Everyone paused while he folded the square of linen and stuffed it ceremoniously in his pocket. "Mademoiselle Daaé, you are projecting your voice."

Several in the row below me turned to glare.

"I'm sorry. I'm trying—"

"Do not try. Do," he said, exasperated.

Or I might find myself without a position. The director's unspoken words hung in the air. I looked down to avoid his glare. Why couldn't I harness my voice? I must not be focusing well.

"We're going to start over, from the beginning," Gabriel said.

Jocelyn leaned toward me and whispered, "You have a lovely voice. Don't let him scare you."

I smiled in thanks.

"Encore!" Gabriel said, raising his hands in the air.

I pulled myself up to my full height, shoulders back, and locked on to the director's hands. When the time came for sopranos to join the song, I followed his directives—until we hit a middle C note.

The note surged from my lips and my voice sailed above the others.

"Stop, stop, stop!"

"Will you stop showing off?" a man to my right asked. His beady eyes almost disappeared in his rotund face. "We have to keep starting over because of you. *Every time*," he said, emphasizing his disdain. "I don't understand why they don't send you on your way."

A lump lodged in my throat. The man was horrible, and yet, I feared he was right. But I could do this, I told myself. I *had* to do this.

The director stepped down from his platform, tugged at the edges of his suit jacket, and headed straight for me, the clack of his shoes beating in tune with my thumping pulse. "Mademoiselle Daaé, a word please. Everyone else, take a break."

I flushed and followed the director to his office.

Gabriel closed the door behind us. In the enclosed space, the strength of his spicy cologne clogged the air.

"I apologize for my performance today. And all week," I added hurriedly. "I'll work harder, if you just give me another chance. I—"

He held up his hand. "I didn't bring you in here to reprimand you. It's true you are having trouble blending your voice with the others, and they assume you aren't a skilled singer. Had I not known your difficulties for what they truly are, I would have the same opinion."

I frowned. "I don't understand."

"You, Mademoiselle, have the voice of a lead."

My eyes widened in disbelief. "You mean—"

"You're struggling to integrate your voice with the others because you aren't one of them. You possess far more talent." He cracked a smile. "A *diva*," he repeated and emphasized for effect, "does not integrate well, as her voice rises above the others naturally. Your voice is rich, yet you are able to project a clear coloratura soprano. I haven't heard a voice so fine since we appointed Carlotta as our leading lady. You need practice, but in time, your voice might match hers. At the very least, you make a fine stand-in."

A surge of joy warmed my veins. I remembered the rude man in the chorus and grinned.

"I would like you to learn Carlotta's lines. She hasn't had an understudy in ages, but we need one. She comes and goes whenever she wants, and it causes . . . issues." He leaned closer, as if imparting a secret. "She can be a difficult woman, if you hadn't noticed. She may resist, but I have the final say."

This was it! The opportunity I was hoping for. Elated, I grasped his hand without thinking and shook it vehemently. "Thank you for this opportunity, Monsieur. I'll make you glad you've chosen me."

"I sincerely hope so." A hint of amusement shone in his eyes. "Report to my assistant immediately and gather the scripts. You'll continue to learn the chorus songs as well."

I smiled. "You can't know what this means to me."

He gave me a crisp nod and retreated through the door.

I imagined walking past the chorus, ignoring their sour expressions, and practicing the lead! I ran in place in my exuberance. Papa would have been so proud. He would have said . . .

What would he have said? I grasped for the sound of his voice, his wise counsel, but couldn't recall it. A sudden pang rippled through me. I had forgotten the sound of his voice. The familiar despair began to well, but I held on to my emotions tightly, the way a seal on a bottle grips the glass. No, I wouldn't let it pull me under again.

Directing my gaze to the ceiling, I whispered, "Papa, I hope you're watching. This is for you."

Each day after practice I returned home and pored over Carlotta's lines. I had been in the diva's presence plenty, and yet, she hadn't even glanced in my direction. She seemed to ignore me intentionally. I didn't know what to think of her behavior—I posed no threat to her position. The music-loving crowd worshipped her, and the papers raved about her as excitement built for the upcoming season.

"Stop!" Carlotta shouted at the orchestra, her voice shrill. "You're off-key again." She stalked across the stage and drank from a water glass.

"*They* were not off-key," Gabriel said.

"Are you insinuating I was?" She glared at him. "I will have you fired, you ingrate! And you, little dancer"—she pointed at Meg—"are out of step."

Meg's face drained of color. I shot her a look of sympathy. Meg danced beautifully as always, but *La Italiana* seemed to enjoy being spiteful.

Chagrin stamped the choral director's face. "Why don't you take a break, Carlotta. We'll practice the recitative when you return. Christine, you're on."

Carlotta brushed past me, calling over her shoulder, "Lift your chin while you finish your aria this time, Daaé. And be sure to work on your breathing. Gasping like a fish is unacceptable. It would be a shame to have you replaced when you've only just begun."

The first sparks of anger flickered in my belly. Through a false smile I said, "I will do my best. It's an honor to be called your understudy."

She stopped abruptly and turned, her skirt swaying around her flower-painted boots. She looked me over, taking in the muslin patterned with bluebells, my tightly pinned hair. "*Tua bellezza* isn't

71

enough to secure your place here." She waved her hand toward the rows of empty seats in the theater. "You are a novice and it shows. No amount of pretty-girl pucker or fluttering eyelashes will persuade the audience to love you. Nor the directors to keep you."

Heat bloomed in my chest and seeped into my cheeks. I needn't see the rash to know it was there; it always betrayed me when I most needed to stand up for myself but couldn't. The words—a perfectly formed retort—stuck in my throat like day-old bread. I wanted to tell her I was grateful for this chance to prove myself, that I would make them happy they chose me. Most of all, I longed to tell her she was a bully. Yet, in spite of the unfamiliar anger growing inside me, my eyes darted to the worn boards of the stage. Papa's warning about speaking out of turn, and the regret that would inevitably follow, echoed in my ears.

Carlotta grasped my chin between her thumb and forefinger. "I tell you these things not to hurt you, *bella*, but to warn you. Female singers and actors are treated like cattle that can be bought and sold. You must prove your worth or lose everything."

Tongue-tied still, I nodded.

She scoffed at my silence and swept off the stage.

"Christine!" Gabriel called to me. "We don't have all day."

The sheen on his impeccable blond waves caught the light and his features appeared unmoved by the exchange. He had witnessed Carlotta's less-than-friendly behavior but said nothing. He'd been bullied by her many times, I knew. Carlotta held all the power. They had no other true *vedette*, no other star, and her celebrated status filled every seat in the theater. I walked to my place and stuck out my chin. If I must earn my respect here, I would.

After a grueling practice with the chorus one afternoon, I lost myself in *Notre-Dame de Paris* in Madame's salon. I needed an escape to the luxurious stained glass of the cathedral, the kind yet beastly

Quasimodo, and his respite among the bells. I sighed happily, as I nestled into the cushions of the sofa.

Monsieur Delacroix's baritone floated in from the hall, interrupting my diversion.

"What brings you across town?" I stood and we exchanged kisses on each cheek.

"I thought I would pay you and Jeanne a visit," he said.

"She's resting." I rang a bell to summon Alfred. "She hasn't been feeling well lately. The pain in her back seems to be getting worse."

Alfred entered and bowed. "What can I bring for you, Mademoiselle? Monsieur? Coffee or tea?"

"I'd like a brandy." Delacroix hung his bowler on the hat rack. "I've had a long day already."

I noted the agitation in his voice, the wrinkle between his eyes. "I hope all is well?"

Alfred brought a snifter glass and decanter, set it before Delacroix, and served him.

After a drink of the potent liquor, the professor studied me silently. He seemed to wrestle with a decision. At last he said, "A most troubling rumor has surfaced from the opera house."

"Oh?" I clasped my hands together in my lap, suddenly nervous. I hoped it had nothing to do with me. I had worked hard these last weeks to fit in, and to please the choral director—to stay out of Carlotta's way.

"You may think me foolish when I explain." He paused.

I motioned to Alfred to put on the kettle for tea.

"There's talk of a ghost at the opera."

"A ghost at the opera house?" I echoed. First the séance, now this?

"Someone claims to have seen a floating head. Several of the ballerinas and choir girls reported hearing voices. The incidents appear to be growing more fantastic by the day."

The intensity of his gaze chilled me.

I rubbed my arms to banish the unwelcome rash of goose bumps. How had all of this happened around me without my knowing?

Suddenly it seemed as if ghosts were everywhere.

He clasped his hands. "As you know, this is my line of work. Or a part of it, anyway."

"Indeed, yes, but you're certain it's at the Opéra de Paris? This is the first I've heard of it and I'm there almost every day. I—"

"I have a very good source." He perched on the edge of his chair.

I frowned at his tone. "If you believe they're true, then so shall I."

A grim smile crossed his face and he visibly forced himself to relax. "The rumors intrigue me. In fact, the directors have contacted me to assess what is happening. They'd like for me to locate the problem. I will help when I can, but as you know, I have my own work to do at the Académie. I certainly can't be there every day." He traced the rim of his empty glass with his thumb. "But you can."

I stared at him in surprise. "You want me to chase a ghost?"

"Chase it, no. But if you could document any disturbances or odd happenings, listen to the gossip among the cast and report it to me, it would be helpful. I'll make it a point to tour the building thoroughly as well."

"It could all be a series of pranks." I didn't want to disappoint Delacroix—he had been so kind to me the last months—but, should I draw attention to myself, I could be dismissed. Or become the ghost's next target. In spite of the ridiculous notion, my goose bumps returned. The building had a life of its own, and apparently it held secrets, too.

"Christine, it could help me with my research either way," he said, his exasperation plain, "but it will also help the directors. I owe them a favor."

Alfred placed the tea tray on the table. He had taken the liberty of bringing a variety of biscuits as well.

"I must admit, your request makes me uncomfortable," I said. "Should I be caught sneaking about, I might get into trouble."

"I assure you, you needn't do anything dangerous or too intrusive. Leave that to me." His words came out in a rush, like he was on the verge of victory. He scooped up my hand in his and squeezed it harder

74

than necessary. I winced at the pressure. "Perhaps for your efforts, I may treat you to a new gown? You'll need something beautiful for all of the parties you'll attend once the season starts."

"Thank you, but that won't be necessary." I pulled free of his grasp and massaged my palm. His eagerness bordered on forceful. I wondered, once again, how he had come to his profession. It seemed odd for a man of academic achievements to devote so much time to rumors and supernatural phenomena.

Given his request, I deserved some answers. I cradled my full teacup in my hands. Its warmth seeped into my fingers and began to burn my skin. "Tell me, Monsieur, how did you come to work in your profession? I recall you saying it was a story for another day. I think that day has arrived."

His absorbing gaze penetrated my very skin.

I shifted on the sofa and focused on his square-toed ankle boots, polished to a shine. "I fear jeopardizing my position at the opera, but if you help me understand . . . If this is something so dear to you . . ."

"You can't imagine how dear." He seemed to relax with my concession and poured himself another brandy. Once he'd had a sip, he said, "My mother died when I was a boy of eight. Consumption. My father was grief-stricken beyond consolation. In fact, he never recovered. He saw apparitions of her everywhere, claimed he heard her whispering to him at night. He solicited medium after medium to perform séances to contact her spirit. Time stopped for us, just as it had for her. Father became obsessed with her ghost, with the dead. Enough to forget his son who still lived."

He swilled the last of his drink. "When I confronted him, we argued. I would hide in the library for hours."

My unease ebbed and sympathy replaced it. I regarded the sorrow lines around his eyes, the determined set of his jaw. He was all alone after his mother's death, even with a living parent at his side. Though I had been orphaned, I never doubted my father's love.

Delacroix sought to disprove his father's theories to spite him. He'd had no one to comfort him, or watch him grow into a man. This was why the professor didn't believe in the spirit world.

I touched his arm gently. "I'm so sorry."

"It's all long past. He was a fool. I've had two dead parents most of my life, and friends who have perished, and yet I've never seen a spirit, nor heard one." He looked up. "Except on a conjurer's stage at a show my father and I attended one night. After the show, Father took his own bullet—all because the conjurer made him believe my mother was at the theatre, and that he should join her in death."

I squirmed inwardly. Conjuring was dangerous—something I knew all too well. Communing with the dead triggered grief, outrage, fear. Yet it was all an act. I felt a prick of guilt for enjoying the illusions anyway.

A fierceness returned to Delacroix's tone. "I will find that conjurer one day. Expose him for the fraud he is. I've narrowed the list considerably over the years. So you see, my work is quite personal, as well as professional."

I studied him in silence. A vein pulsed in his neck and anger clouded his eyes.

"As for the opera house," he continued, "if the directors need my help to rid them of a nuisance, I'm more than happy to oblige. I will expose this ghost as nothing but a fraud, a man disturbing the cast for his own amusement. It can only help my career as well. After, I'll add the findings to a book I've been writing for some time. I plan to approach a publisher with it next year."

I placed my hand atop his. "If tracking this . . . this ghost becomes too uncomfortable, or if it causes any trouble I will—"

"Cease all enquiries at once," he finished my sentence.

I nodded. "I'll do it." The moment I said the words, anxiety stirred in my stomach.

"You're an angel." He kissed my gloved hand and stood abruptly. "I must go. I have some urgent matters to look into, but I'll be in touch very soon."

I rose from my chair, taken aback by his abruptness.

"Enjoy your evening." He collected his hat from the rack and ducked through the door without hesitation. I didn't even have the chance to say goodbye.

I slumped on the sofa and mulled over the strange conversation. Of late, I'd been questioning my beliefs. The dreams, the noises at night. Now this? I shook my head. I'm certain I wouldn't find anything at the opera. Someone must be up to a rash of silly pranks, I tried to convince myself.

Ghosts didn't exist.

~6~

I felt more than a little foolish the following two weeks, skulking about the cast and the dressing rooms to eavesdrop, but I hadn't caught word of anything about a ghost. I wondered where Delacroix received his information. Perhaps someone had fabricated the rumors to mislead the directors. None of it made sense.

When opening day arrived, I could hold my tongue no longer.

"Meg, can I ask you something?" She plaited her hair in her dressing stall among the others. "Have you heard anything about a ghost haunting the opera? There are some rumors, apparently."

She dropped her arms to her sides and narrowed her eyes. "Who wants to know?"

"Let me help you." I scooped up her fine dark hair and finished plaiting the last section. "Oh, just me. I was curious. It seems ridiculous, doesn't it?"

"Who mentioned the ghost to you?" She lowered her voice.

"I overheard a couple of the ballerinas talking about it on their way to practice," I lied.

She turned in her chair to face me. "If I tell you, you can't say a word about it. Promise me."

I hesitated to reply. I would have to lie to her again, and I didn't like the idea. But I promised Monsieur Delacroix I would help.

"Don't worry. I'm not one to spread rumors."

She motioned for me to lean closer. There's a *fantôme*. He lives here, in the building. Some claimed to have seen him. There have been threats. All I can tell you is: Don't stay after the show ends, and try to avoid being alone. And we can't tell *anyone*."

"Who is 'we'?" I asked.

She pulled back to study my face. "I can't tell you."

79

My eyes widened. She knew more! "I won't tell anyone. I don't have any other friends here."

"Another time," she said, turning to face the mirror. "I need to finish getting ready. Sorelli will make me do barre exercises all day tomorrow if I'm late."

Hiding my disappointment, I squeezed her shoulder. "Good luck tonight."

I made my way to the rooms backstage where the cast congregated. Excitement stirred the air. The rumble of conversation grew louder as patrons poured into the theatre. Frantic machinists levied cables into place and prepared the set flats that would shift during the production. Chorus members queued in the order they would file on stage, while others milled about in various costumes.

Mephistopheles bent over a red curled shoe, his black horns catching on the gossamer angel wing that Sorelli wore.

A devil ensnared by an angel.

Sorelli yanked her wing free, leaving a small hole in the delicate fabric. She swore at the devil.

I smothered a laugh and skirted around her to the other side of the cast room. Though I was Carlotta's understudy, I didn't need to dress for the show. In fact, Gabriel told me I didn't need to be in the building at all unless I wanted to be. I had sagged instantly at the thought of being excluded. Everyone knew Carlotta wouldn't miss a show—especially opening night—and that being the diva's understudy, while somewhat prestigious, meant lots of practice with little-to-no stage time. I shrugged off my disappointment. It was opening night at the opera and I had never seen a show. Tonight, I would enjoy my first production from backstage—not something most people could say.

"*Vite, vite!*" An assistant dashed through the room, clapping her hands. "The curtain goes up in five minutes."

Cries erupted in the room. Everyone finished tinkering with their costumes and dashed to their positions.

When the opera began, I settled in the west stage wing for the best view.

"What are you doing here?" asked Pierre—the same man who had shown his irritation with me in the chorus. Waves of disapproval rolled off his shoulders and assaulted me in their silent, yet potent way.

"Watching the show," I said firmly, my eyes fixing on the bean-shaped mole just above his thin lips. How did he emit beautiful sounds out of such a mouth?

His face twisted into a scowl and I felt the urge to say something rude. Between the anger I'd felt a few days ago toward Carlotta, the brazen way I'd demanded Delacroix tell me his history, and now this, I was beginning to not recognize myself—in a good way. My lips stretched into a smile of their own accord.

Pierre's eyes narrowed. "What's so amusing?"

Meg leaned over my shoulder. "Leave her be, Pierre. It's her first show and she just wants to watch. Come on." She tugged my hand, pulling me in front of her so I could see the stage.

When the show began, I watched Carlotta carefully.

Meg ran her hands over her white tulle skirt and leaned to my ear. "Carlotta is *magnifique* as Marguerite, isn't she? It's true, as much as I hate to admit it."

I nodded. The diva's voice and stage presence captivated the crowd; her charisma charged the air. Now I understood how she had reached stardom. Yet in spite of her talent, I felt no envy toward Carlotta, no expectation, but something else entirely. *Need* throbbed in my veins—a need to make my own place.

When the act finished and the curtain closed over the stage, the fly boys and machinists set to work, changing the set pieces and shifting the drops. I marveled at their speed and precision.

"Off I go," Meg said.

I stepped back as a herd of ballerinas pranced to their positions, the wooden tips of their slippers thumping softly against the floor. They remained as still as statuettes dressed in white sequins, waists encircled with fluffy tulle. Sorelli stood in the middle of them, wings pointed toward heaven. When the curtain lifted and the music began, their bodies came to life like toys sprinkled with magic dust. I watched them in awe, though I had passed their practice room day after day. Their elegant ensemble left me breathless. Yet the crowd chattered through the entire performance. The mid-show intermission meant very little to them, save the true dance connoisseurs.

After the dance and the final act of the opera, the crowd dispersed. The cast made their way to the dressing rooms, and headed home. Though I wanted to leave as well, I remembered my promise to Delacroix. I loitered, ears perked, hoping to catch something useful. But the players dwindled until I was one of the final singers in the dressing room, and still, I hadn't heard or seen a thing. Pierre and his large mole were the last to go, and he left without an offer to escort me.

What a gentleman, I thought, as I gathered my handbag and umbrella.

I glanced around the empty cast room and paused. This was the perfect opportunity to sneak around a little, poke into things. If I did, I could tell the professor with honesty I had looked and found nothing, assure him no ghost existed. I rifled through the drawers and vanity tops, pawed through an errant handbag left by accident, and found nothing. Finally, I slipped into the dimly lit corridor.

A pair of male voices echoed in the distance. A door thudded closed.

Avoiding the direction of the sound, I walked quickly down a passageway I had yet to explore. Somewhere on the same floor, the clunk of costly sets shifted, and a few male voices laughed or shouted orders at each other. A janitor passed me carrying a broom. He tipped his hat as he went, leaving the hall empty once more. One by one, the lights began going out.

My pulse pattered against my throat. Though finding a ghost in the dark might be more likely, I walked quickly to a lit corridor, the only sound coming from my ragged breath and the clicking of my heels.

I didn't believe in ghosts.

I didn't believe in ghosts!

I peeked inside a room. Nothing.

I continued on, and after two more turns, peaked inside a dark room. I fumbled on the wall for some sort of lamp or switch. Parts of the building had been fitted with electricity, but much of it still used gas lighting. Unable to find a switch plate, I decided to try the opposing wall. I squinted and made out the faint outline of a set flat or large piece of furniture. My ears perked like a spooked mare as I waded through the darkness.

Then I heard it. A faint scratching—or was it breathing?

I held my breath and glanced over my shoulder. I was being a coward. I had lived in far more frightening places, and had walked by dozens of scoundrels with Papa as we picked our way through the rubble that once was our home. I could be tough when I wanted, I reminded myself.

When I reached another doorway on the opposite wall, I stepped through to find a staircase leading to a lower level. A light glowed faintly at the bottom of the steps. I had heard about the seven stories below the stage; most were used to store sets, costumes, and tools, but there was also a cistern in case of fire. And a prison cell.

I shivered. Why did I have to think of that now?

The scratching came again.

"Who's there?" I turned, my skirt whisking around my feet.

A deep silence greeted me.

The urge to flee twitched in my legs. After a moment's pause, I exhaled a breath, annoyed with myself. There was nothing here, and in just a few more minutes, I could leave, be on my way. I gathered my courage and descended the stairs.

A vast storage room sprawled out before me. Stage props cluttered the space: a large bed with flowered *couverture*, lamps and tables, false trees, the frame of a house, and more. I touched the cool glass of a hand mirror and a flute tossed carelessly on a table. I continued on to an adjoining room packed wall to wall with scenery flats.

"Can I help you, Mademoiselle?"

I jumped at the voice and turned, hand over my pounding heart. "I—

I don't know. No, thank you."

"Having a look around, were you?" the man said.

My eyes locked on his frying-pan face, his hulking shoulders. I clutched my umbrella tighter.

"Yes, I wanted to see ... I've heard ..."

He took a step closer. "You heard something?"

A lump lodged in my throat. He was just a machinist or a stagehand, no ghost. Nothing to fear.

"There's talk of a ghost haunting the opera." The machinist took two steps closer. "Have you heard such a thing? Ridiculous, isn't it?"

My eyes darted to the staircase where I had entered.

He raised a brow as a lascivious smile split his face. "I would be glad to see you out, Mademoiselle. If you need help finding an exit, that is."

He stepped closer still.

My heart slammed against my ribs. In two strides he would have me cornered, my back against the wall.

I cleared my throat and used my sternest tone. "Thank you, but that won't be necessary. I'll just be on my way. You must have a hundred things to do."

"Not at the moment, and I've grown rather tired of this charade. I'm no more a machinist than you are a diva." He rocked forward on his feet as if ready to pounce.

I swallowed hard. "I'm not sure what you mean."

"I'm here to find him, like you. The ghost," he hissed.

Blood pounded like a drum in my ears. "I'm not here to find a ghost. I am a singer." I inched away from him toward the door. "Do you think the ghost is real?"

"Oh, he's real, all right." In a swift movement, he closed the space between us and pinned me against the wall. "Real as I am."

I cried out. "What are you doing? You're frightening me!"

"You're easy to look at, aren't you?" He ran a calloused thumb down my cheek, sending a wave of disgust down my throat.

"Please," I said. "Let me be and I won't tell anyone you're here."

He laughed. "I am not worried about what you might say." His arm slid around my waist and wrenched me toward him.

I cried out again. *Get away,* my head screamed. *Kick him, bite him. Run!* Yet I felt helpless in the crush of his arms. "Please, don't hurt me."

He laughed. "This won't hurt if you're quiet. You might even enjoy it." He fumbled with the buttons of his pants.

Terrified, I kicked his leg with the sharp point of my boot and thrashed in his hold.

"Putain!" he shouted. "Hold still."

I aimed for his other leg and screamed. "Someone help me!"

The lights went out.

Something rattled in the dark.

"Get off of me!" I shouted, struggling in the man's grip.

He pressed himself harder against me, smashed his face in my neck. "You smell sweet, too."

I screamed again.

"Shut your mouth or I'll have to hold you down."

Terror locked every muscle in my body. There was nothing I could do. He had me pinned. I said a silent prayer this would end quickly.

The next instant, a thud sounded near my head.

The man grunted and his arms released me.

"Go!" a sinuous voice said in the dark. "Leave now or you will regret it."

I bolted in the direction I thought was the staircase at once. I slammed into a flat. Its edge cut into my wrist before it crashed to the floor. I screamed, and continued running blindly in the dark.

At last a faint glow appeared, lighting the staircase from above. Someone had lit one of the lanterns. I flew up the stairs, through a maze of corridors and rooms. Once at the exit, I launched myself at the outer door. It flew open on impact and smashed against the outside wall. I dashed into the street, gasping for breath.

Streetlamps buzzed and a stray dog trotted over the cobblestones, his coat mangy and matted with dirt. And there, across the road, sat Monsieur Delacroix's coach. I frowned, puzzled by his sudden appearance for a moment, then dashed toward him. I didn't care why he was here, I was just relieved.

The door swung open, and the professor stepped into the night. "Good heavens, are you all right?" He ushered me inside the carriage. With one look at my stricken expression, his surprise shifted to concern. "I was just waiting for the directors. They're joining me for cards at the gentlemen's club. It's a good thing I'm here. Tell me, dear, what happened?"

"A man—he . . . he grabbed me and—"

He clenched his fists. "Who was this man?"

"I don't know." I gulped in a breath to steady my nerves, my racing heart. "He said he was done pretending to be a machinist. He's tall and broad with a large face."

He grimaced. "Did he hurt you?" He fished a handkerchief out of his breast pocket and gently dabbed my face.

"He tried. He pushed me up against the wall." The tears began in earnest.

"What were you doing there so late? Hasn't the cast already gone home?"

"I was looking for the ghost. Trying to help you."

"Dear girl." He squeezed my hands and rubbed my back until the tears dried.

"I'm so glad you're here."

"I am, too. There, there." His soft voice steadied my nerves.

Several minutes later, he lowered his gaze. "Christine?"

"Yes?" I exhaled a calming breath.

"Did you find anything?"

I sniffed. "No one knew anything about a ghost except one of the ballerinas. She said there were rumors, but no proof. Said I shouldn't talk about it."

"I see." He dabbed at the tears that began again. "More importantly, did this man take advantage of you?"

I shook my head.

"Thank goodness." He breathed a sigh of relief.

"Just as he pinned me against the wall, the room went dark. The machinist must have been hit because there was a thump and he released me." I wiped my face. "I heard a voice. He told me to run. Said I would regret it if I didn't."

His dark eyebrows shot skyward. "A voice, you say?"

"Yes, a voice." I shivered at the memory.

A light filled his eyes and he smiled. "That, my dear, was our opera ghost."

I couldn't stop thinking about the incident, dreaming about it, worrying about it. When it was time to return to the opera for practice, I was exhausted. Though I didn't want to, I had to tell the directors about my attacker. Delacroix had warned me they might consider me a liability, or that the truth might cause trouble for me among the other cast members. Just the same, I planned to talk to them that day. I didn't see how they would consider me at fault, and I didn't feel safe in the same building as my would-be molester.

As I approached the office, I paused before knocking. Angry voices drifted into the hall.

"He has some nerve demanding we keep box five reserved for his personal use." Monsieur Moncharmin's voice rumbled behind the door.

"I don't give a damn about box five," Monsieur Richard replied. "It's the money. I say to hell with him!"

"Are you certain this is the ghost? Have you seen his handwriting before?"

"Who else would have made such a demand!" Monsieur Richard's boots shuffled across the floorboards.

I froze. The ghost had left them a note! Straining to hear better, I rested my cheek against the door.

"We will carry on as usual tonight. This has to be a prank from a disgruntled employee."

Monsieur Richard chimed in, "I concur. But what do you think the tyrant will do if we rent box five?"

"Nothing. This is positively ludicrous."

"What about Carlotta's request for increased pay? She's the main event, whether we like it or not."

"She hasn't shown us her loyalty," Montcharmin interjected.

"She's difficult and temperamental. She threatened to quit again only yesterday when you were at the bank."

My nerves twitched in anticipation. If Carlotta left, would I take the stage?

"She threatens to leave at least once a week. Let her go. We'll hire someone else."

"You know very well there isn't anyone to replace her."

"Of course there is. We have the understudy."

"The chorus girl?" Montcharmin asked, his voice thick with disbelief.

"Gabriel says she has a decent voice."

I winced at the offhand remark. *Decent* was not how I wanted to be described.

"We'll have to do better than decent. The show won't go on without a suitable replacement. We'll keep Carlotta happy for now, but if she becomes too big of a problem, we'll hold another audition. Daaé can cast her lot against the others. I have a friend at the opera in Vienna. He might be able to send someone."

I dropped away from the door and rushed off in the other direction, legs numb and heart heavy. When I reached a vacant alcove, I leaned against the wall and stared at the ceiling. Its embellishments looked too beautiful for a simple woman like me—just like the rest of the opera house and its cast. Despair swept over me and I blinked several times to clear the tears. Though I longed to be on stage, I had no business being a part of this production.

Malaise stirred in the pit of my stomach—the same sensation I felt each time I entered the building. Rubbing my arms, I looked down the empty hallway. I should force myself to turn back, tell the directors about what happened. Even if they didn't care that I worked here at all.

Something stirred in the wall behind me.

I jumped and turned abruptly.

There was nothing there. Of course not. Had I gone mad? It was probably a rat in the walls. I chewed on my nail, unsure if I could really face the directors now. I could always approach them later.

"Do not be sad, beautiful one," a melodious voice said.

My heart seized in my chest. It was the voice from last night!

"Who's there?" I whispered, looking down the drafty corridor.

"I'm here to help you."

"Who are you?" I looked at the ceiling, fear rippling through me. I turned to the wall and ran my shaking hands over the paneling. In a building with many floors, secret recesses, and a dozen covert staircases, I knew there must be more undetected doors.

"You won't find me there." Instantly, the voice emanated from a different place across the hall. "But I was with you last night, in your hour of need."

This must be him—the opera ghost—just as Delacroix had said. A rustling sounded behind me and I flinched again.

"Joseph Buquet will leave you alone, now, anyway." The timbre of his voice turned sinister.

"The machinist?" Had this mysterious voice hurt the man? I didn't know whether to be frightened or relieved.

"Or so he called himself, yes. He is a criminal."

"You speak in riddles. Are you . . ." I swallowed hard. "Are you going to hurt me, too?"

A haughty laugh reverberated off the walls and ceiling. "I fear it is I, who will be hurt by you."

I looked overhead as I moved to the other wall. "I don't understand."

The slightest swishing came from my left. My face jerked in that direction.

No one was there.

"You don't need to understand." Amusement crept into his voice. "All you need to do is to follow my instructions. Meet me each evening during the performance, unless you are on stage, in which case you

89

will meet me afterward. When there's no show, you will still come to practice daily in your dressing room. You have talent, but have had poor training."

In spite of my fear, his words stung. Papa would certainly disagree. "And if I don't?"

"You will never be ready to compete for Carlotta's place. As it stands, she's a far better singer than you, but together, we can develop your voice into what you long for it to be."

The voice hummed a melody, notes flowing into one another until I recognized a beloved song: a piece from *Carmen* in which Don Jose sang of his tortured love for the beautiful, wild Carmen, though she wanted only the handsome Escamillo. How had this ghost known I loved *Carmen* most? The poetic lyrics and stunning finish with Carmen's death had entranced me from the first time I had heard it.

As the song faded, silence enveloped me once more.

Voice hoarse, I said, "Please, if I am to do as you say, at least tell me who you are."

A sliding noise came from inside the walls.

The voice whispered in my ear, "I'm not only the *fantôme de l'opéra*, I am your Angel of Music."

Act Two

"Painted Faces on Parade"

—Andrew Lloyd Webber's
The Phantom of the Opera

~7~

The following evening, I practiced with the chorus, but my head buzzed with the Angel's words. Just as Papa had always said, the Angel was here for me. It felt like a dream—a terrifying one, but a dream nonetheless. Surely my mind played tricks on me. I sang on the greatest stage in the world and now a spirit would help me become a star—if I did as he asked.

When the show ended, I left the stage and walked quickly to the dressing rooms. As I neared Carlotta's, I picked up my pace. I didn't want to run into the prima donna.

"Christine, how convenient," she called as I passed the door.

Luck was not on my side.

"Please, come in," she called.

Reluctantly, I walked to the doorway of her dressing room and stopped. Carlotta wore a magnificent costume made of muslin, dyed chestnut brown and trimmed with animal fur. A pointed helmet sat atop her head, a band of studded leather encircled her naked wrists and neck, and one long plait ran over her shoulder. The costume designer stood at her elbow, fussing with some pins along her hem.

I had to admit, she made a stunning Odella. I wondered when they expected to run Verdi's *Atilla*. I'd heard nothing about it. I frowned, confused. Why hadn't I been asked to learn her parts as the understudy? In fact, I hadn't heard much about the happenings at the opera at all. I needed to pay more attention when Meg prattled on after practices.

Carlotta motioned to me, pulling her elbow from the designer's grip. "Ouch! Be careful." She glared at him.

"I've asked you not to move a half dozen times," he said, not bothering to hide the annoyance in his voice.

She ignored him. "Christine, I wanted to invite you *a casa mia.* You've heard that I'm hosting a soirée next week at my apartment, I'm sure. Half of the city will be there, so it should be quite a fete."

Startled by her sudden warmth—and suspicious of her intentions—my voice faltered. "I . . . No, I hadn't. It's very kind of you to invite me."

No one had spoken of the party around me, or included me in their conversations. My chest tightened a little at the thought. I hadn't integrated well with the cast, it seemed, and didn't understand why. Jealousy, perhaps?

I looked past Carlotta into her dressing room. Several bouquets of exotic blooms filled the tables, and an armoire gaped, displaying gowns and costumes of all kinds. A vanity stood against the far wall, showcasing a magnificent mirror framed in gold leaf. On its tabletop, a clock struck half past eleven.

"I'm honored you would think of me."

"Think of you?" Her penciled-on eyebrows shot up in surprise. "Oh, *cara mia,* you are one of us now. I like to take the understudies into my fold. I have struggled to make a name for myself, to stand on solid ground. Now my ground is rather glorious, no? But you must put in the effort. *Sii forte!* Be strong!" She thrust her fist forward to prove her point.

"Besides"—her eyes raked over my frame—"you could benefit from my expertise. If I ever need you to stand in for me, I can't have you driving away the crowd I've worked hard to attain."

An offer of help, wrapped in thorns. This was the woman I expected. "Carlotta—"

She dismissed me with a wave. "Be on your way."

"You were wonderful tonight."

"Of course, darling. *Buonanotte.*"

Though Carlotta's assured response hit a nerve, I smiled before hurrying to the dressing rooms. Perhaps I would make friends at her soirée, or at the very least, enjoy myself. Meg was kind, but often too busy helping her mother, Madame Giry, with her duties as box keeper and concierge, or practicing dance routines. Claudette was dear, but lacked the freedom I had to come and go. I was tired of being alone.

I turned down the hallway leading to the dressing rooms. My stomach clenched at the thought of being with the Angel at this hour of night, but I had to see if this was real. If *he* was real.

A laugh of disbelief bubbled in my throat. My emotions swung from terror to doubt to excitement within seconds. This was a ghost who truly understood music; the one Papa had promised looked after me all those years. Perhaps the Angel's aid would be exactly what I needed. Perhaps he was my only hope. I was meeting an angel-ghost to practice? Good God, I was losing my mind.

"You do plan to keep your word?" The Angel whispered near my ear.

"Oh!" I stumbled in surprise and backed against a marble column, its cool surface seeping into my skin. "I'm—I'm tired."

"Do you wish to improve or not?" A hint of impatience tinged his words.

"Yes," I said, shrinking against the pillar. "Am I to meet you in the dressing rooms?"

"Of course not." His impatience flared again. "Meet me in yours. We will have more privacy there."

"I don't have my own."

"It's the last door at the end of the hallway. You will find it as luxurious as that of *La Italiana*."

My own room? I wondered what Carlotta's reaction would be when she learned of it. She would see it as competition. Hearth thumping, I walked swiftly past a cluster of weeping candles and a series of empty rooms. Everyone had gone home or joined the revelry at a dance hall. Everyone but me. When I reached the last room, I stopped. A plaque had already been affixed to the door. I traced the curve of the letter "C" and smiled. The letter "i" was dotted with a star and shimmered gold. In spite of my hesitation, my heart swelled at the sight.

Inside, a resplendent room sprawled before me, lavishly furnished with velvet-covered chairs and walls lined with crimson silk. A burnished cherry armoire skulked on the far wall. Carved into the topmost ledge of the furniture, a face jutted from the frame, its undulating hair serpentine and a smile on its lips that could only mean mischief. I moved to the vanity in the middle of the far wall. Light spilled from lamps on either side of its large mirror, and on the tabletop was a single scarlet rose. Mind whirling, I stroked the petals, still dewy and fresh as if the blossom had just been plucked. I smelled the flower and rested it against my cheek, relishing the velvet on my skin. It didn't make sense that the choral director hadn't mentioned my dressing room, unless... unless he didn't know about it.

"Beautiful, isn't it?" The Angel of Music's voice sounded low, but insistent.

I spun around. "Where are you?"

"Here," he said, from the opposite corner of the room.

"And now here," he sang, his tenor reverberating from the ceiling.

Bumps rose on my arms. He must be a ghost. No human could move so quickly. Forcing out a steadying breath, I said, "May we begin? My benefactor is ill, and I don't like to leave her alone too long."

"You're eager. I quite like that." His tone turned jaunty, his amusement plain. "First, you must listen. To become a fine musician is to understand what you hear, to emulate it, and then to embody it."

The voice began to sing and his rapturous tenor filled the room. Without thought, I swayed to the playful yet addictive song and admired the purity of his beautiful voice, understanding the difficulty of flowing from one phrase to the next at such speed.

The Angel of Music, indeed—he was a brilliant singer.

When he finished, I was breathless. "I don't recognize the song."

"You don't know *'La Donna è Mobile'*?" He sounded incredulous. "It's from *Rigoletto*, based on Victor Hugo's play *Le roi s'amuse*. 'Woman is unstable, like the feather in the wind; she changes tone, and thought.'" His laugh echoed through the dressing room. Abruptly the laugh stopped, and his tone took on an exasperated edge. "There's so much you do not know. We need to get to work at once. We'll begin by warming up your vocal chords. Start with a lip and tongue trill. Follow with humming a set of scales."

"I've already practiced today."

"You have worked with those beneath you, who don't understand music," he insisted. "Now, begin."

I stood in ready position with my chest out and arms loosely at my sides. I completed one drill after another, quick to follow the Angel's lead. I didn't want to disappoint him.

When I finished, he said, "This time, sing an arpeggio with the word 'nah.' Mind your mouth position."

I formed my lips into an oval and followed his instructions. Slowly, my tightened muscles relaxed, my unease ebbed.

"Excellent. You are at ease, I see, and it shows."

A warm sensation coursed through my limbs. I smiled, genuinely happy. Though the Angel's presence made me nervous, his praise encouraged me in a way Papa's never had.

"Now," he continued, "I'd like you to sing 'Habanera.' "

From *Carmen* again. It seemed no coincidence that he'd chosen a favorite of mine. If spirits walked among us, wouldn't they know our secrets? I closed my eyes as the notes awakened in my throat and danced to the tip of my tongue. The melody cantered around me, caressed the air, and filled the room.

"Arrête!" the Angel thundered.

My eyes flew open and the song died on my lips.

"You are singing from your throat, not your diaphragm, and there's no resonation through the head." The Angel sounded exasperated. "This is why your voice is deeper than it should be. You are a coloratura soprano, not a mezzo, and your tone is off. Carlotta outshines you in this regard."

Stunned by his change of mood, I stared at myself in the large mirror spanning the back wall. I was encapsulated in a beam of light, making my hair look like spun gold, my features as delicate as a porcelain doll. But my vocals were those of an amateur, apparently, and I'd never realized I had quite so much work to do. Not even Papa had been so critical.

At last, I managed to say, "I have never had a proper tutor."

"You have one now."

"Why are you helping me?"

After a long moment of silence he said, "I promised to look after you."

"Promised whom?" I assumed it must be my father. But, if so, why had the Angel come to me only now? Perhaps, it was because I had locked my music away when Papa had died. I'd closed the door to everything and everyone.

"That doesn't matter," he said. "What matters now is your voice. I will make you into a star, if you do as you are told. We will oust Carlotta together."

A pang of guilt hit me. Carlotta, though prickly at times, had invited me to join her at her home and offered her assistance—not an easy concession on her part. Though I wanted to be on stage, I didn't want to do something untoward to force her out, or to embroil myself in a scheme. Yet . . . if I did succeed her, I'd achieve a dream beyond my imaginings. And my wages would help support Madame—and me.

"Very well." I turned to the voice, now coming from a corner swathed in darkness. "Tell me what I must do."

For the following week I practiced with the Angel of Music daily. I tingled when I felt his dark presence pervade my dressing room, his passion saturate the air. Enthralled by his talents and flattered to be worthy of his attention, I obeyed his every request. I didn't know what I had done to deserve his instruction, but I relished learning from him. He didn't mind my lowly station, my lack of connections, or my weaknesses. He believed I could be shaped into a star. In spite of his generosity, his mercurial moods kept me on my toes. I absorbed so much from his lessons, even when he roared for me to stop and picked at every syllable or flat note. It wasn't long before I learned to detect the moment his patience wore thin. I knew how to do as I was told, regardless of my own desires. I'd been obedient my whole life.

I smothered a yawn with the back of my hand. Last night our lesson was fraught with more stops and starts than usual. He had been unsatisfied with everything. When I managed to get home and climb into bed, it was only a few hours before dawn.

When Monsieur Delacroix arrived at the door first thing in the morning, Claudette pulled me from heavy slumber.

"What brings you here, Monsieur?" I tugged at the dress I'd thrown on in haste.

"I would like to speak with you. Walk with me?" He offered his arm. "We can take a turn through the Luxembourg gardens."

"Can we stop for coffee and croissants first?" I asked, stomach grumbling.

The professor led me to his favorite café across town. When finished with our repast, we continued on to the gardens. As I stepped down from the carriage, I turned my face to a despondent sky. A little dreary weather didn't deter me after years in the streets. With a snap, I popped open my umbrella and peered out from beneath the fringe, eyes still bleary with fatigue. The clouds wept upon its bowed arch, my shoes, and my hem, and rainwater pooled in the path around the central fountain of the garden.

"It's quite a day for a walk." I twirled the umbrella handle between my hands in a nervous gesture. Perhaps the professor had learned my secret: The ghost he sought had become my teacher, and my friend. I had no idea how I could put him off the notion. I was a terrible liar.

Monsieur Delacroix motioned to a thicket of elm trees. "Autumn is early this year. The leaves have already begun to brown."

"Yet the flowers are as beautiful as ever." Blooms embellished the many flowerpots scattered throughout the garden. I would humor him with polite conversation, hoping my instincts were wrong. But the weighty topic—the opera ghost—hung in the air between us.

He rolled a dried leaf between his fingers until all that remained were the threads of its veins. "As you know, I have spent some time at the opera house."

Unwittingly, my feet picked up their pace. "Yes, I assumed so." Though I had yet to see him there myself, and frowned at this oddity.

"It has come to my attention that the ghost has made some threats, one of which was made to secure a dressing room for you." He turned his cobalt eyes upon me.

A hot flow of anger rushed to my cheeks. "Pardon my frankness, Monsieur, but I had nothing to do with it, if that is your implication."

He plucked more leaves from a branch and crushed them in his palm. "You've heard the ghost speak once before. Has he spoken to you again? If so, you must tell me at once. It isn't just for my studies, Christine. The directors demand to know."

Friend or not, the professor had no right to push me this way.

For the first time, the Angel of Music had made me feel as if someone understood me. I needed the Angel to get to the stage. I cared for Delacroix, and respected the directors, but I had to look out for myself as well.

A gust of wind blew rain from the umbrella's fringe and sprayed my cheeks. I stopped in the path as I realized a sudden, liberating truth: I didn't *have* to tell Delacroix anything. I didn't have to continue on as if I were a child, my father's daughter, bound by strict rules and expectations. I was a woman. I didn't need a man to dictate my every move.

Helping Delacroix didn't benefit me, and it threatened the Angel's trust. If my teacher abandoned me . . . the thought inspired an unexpected ache in my gut. I would be on my own in the opera house, left to defend myself, without a tutor or a protector.

"I haven't heard the ghost's voice since that night." I ran my fingers along the fringe of my umbrella. "And thank goodness. It scared me half to death."

"That's unfortunate." He pressed his lips together. "If you do hear something, please let me know. It's imperative to keep abreast of the ghost's actions. I can't protect you otherwise."

"I'm not sure what you mean."

"I have your best interests at heart." He took my free hand in his, kissed it, and squeezed it—a little too hard. "You needn't keep anything from me. I hope you know that."

His tone, for the first time, frightened me. "Of course." I swallowed a sudden lump in my throat.

He proffered another gleaming smile. "Let's escape this drizzle, shall we? It's not as nice a day as I thought."

~ 8 ~

When the evening of Carlotta's party arrived, my stomach churned. Carlotta had said half the town would be there. I toyed with my comb, making music as my fingers strummed its teeth. I pictured myself in a corner near a punch bowl, feigning nonchalance while cringing inside. I would recognize some castmates, more than likely, but Meg wouldn't be there and I had yet to make more friends. My time had been consumed by the Angel. He would be angry with me for missing our lesson tonight, but I needed a reprieve. I hoped the note I'd left on my dressing room table would excuse my absence.

Surely he would understand—he wasn't a monster.

I smoothed the skirts of a royal blue gown with lace overlay across the bodice. Meg insisted I borrow it, and I was glad I'd taken her advice. At least I looked the part of one of Carlotta's wealthy friends.

Carlotta's luxurious apartment was in the fourth arrondissement, a charming and affluent quarter of Paris. The moment I entered, I felt transported to Italy. Silk the blue of a robin's egg, imprinted with shiny leaves, stretched over the walls. Gold drapes with long tassels adorned the windows, and chandeliers made entirely of glass hung in each room in varying shades of turquoise, sea green, and vivid cornflower blues. The chaises wore flowered silk like elegant women, and a wall of mirrors reflected the room to make the space appear twice as large. Upon each gilded table rested a statuette of a nude woman in a tasteful yet sensual display. All was spectacular and dramatic, just like the owner.

I accepted an aperitif from a butler and sauntered through the salon. Over the fireplace, a portrait of Carlotta in full costume dominated the mantel. I hid my smile and skirted around the edge of

103

the crowd in search of a familiar face—without luck. Dismayed, I stationed myself by a window just as a silvery tinkle of laughter drifted across the room. It belonged to a pretty woman dressed in white satin, who pushed out her chest enough to bump the man's forearm standing opposite her. Though attractive, her overt flirtation made her seem desperate. After another moment of forced giggling, the woman whispered in the ear of the younger woman on her right.

The gentleman bowed his head, as if to excuse himself, and turned to go.

My stomach plummeted to my feet. It couldn't be . . .

I stared at the gentleman. His eyes were the color of the sea and his tousled sandy hair accented the regal cut of his jaw—a grown Raoul de Chagny, the boy who had starred in my dreams for years, stood only a few paces away, here, in Carlotta's salon. Time had made him even more handsome than I remembered.

My heart fluttered like a starling's wings in a morning sky. Memories flooded, catapulting me to another time: a time when Papa was alive and well and walked with me along a Normandy beach.

My current surroundings faded, replaced by the pungent odor of seaweed, the feel of my hair blowing freely around my face, and the sensation of frothy surf soaking my hem.

"I saved it," Raoul had said, his trousers sopping from the knees down. He had rescued my scarf when a salty gale caught hold of its fringe and pitched it into the waves. Afterward, he had plopped down beside me on the sand.

I had accepted the sodden fabric, secretly pleased he showed me such deference. He knew I feared deep water or swimming of any kind, and respected me rather than ridiculed me as his brother's friends had. I had thought of little else beyond his bright smile, his constant teasing, and the soft sea green of his eyes since we had met a few weeks before.

"I hope you didn't ruin your trousers." I picked a strip of seaweed from the heap we'd collected and weaved it into a wreath.

Earlier, we had caught a pail of crabs and tried to make them race each other. To our amusement, they ignored our track of driftwood and seashells. We had forgotten they scurried sideways. How we had laughed at the sight.

Raoul reached for his own piece of kelp, his hand brushing mine. He smiled as he met my eyes.

I wrapped the wreath around his neck. "Your very own scarf, *Monsieur le Vicomte*." I couldn't resist emphasizing his title to tease him. He didn't care for his noble status, disliking the way it separated him from his friends, an attitude for which I admired him all the more.

Raoul laughed and slung wet kelp in my lap.

I rolled the strip in the sand and slung it back at him—too late. His hand caught mine midair. Our laughter ebbed as he cradled my hand in his. My whole body warmed to his touch—a sensation I would never forget. I wondered if he had felt the tingling as I had. I wondered about the softness of his lips.

"This thing stinks!" He pulled the wreath over his head, breaking the spell.

I had laughed again, brushed the sand from my skirts, and headed toward Papa, who lounged on a blanket some meters away, picnicking with Raoul's father and brother. The Comte de Chagny had met Papa years before at a fete. He never forgot my father's skill and hired us for a performance at a gala in his vacation home nearby. Violin lessons for Raoul soon followed.

My memories of sand and sea fell away as I stared at Raoul—now elegant and assured in his suit, among the educated and elite where he belonged. I stared at him as if under a spell, possessed by the aura of memory, and this dream of a man. My cheeks flushed. Would he remember me? I glanced at the women fanned around him, attempting to win his affections. My insides twisted. I couldn't blame them. With his handsome face and a fortune to match, he would make an excellent husband.

My heart skipped in my chest at the thought.

Married to Raoul.

I gulped down my wine and, with it, my heart. A poor musician's daughter was of no consequence in a nobleman's world. That fact had been reestablished firmly in my mind after Madame's salon, and those men hadn't even been nobility. Raoul would marry a woman of his own class to preserve the family name. Love would play no part in his decision.

I tore my gaze away and glanced around the room, eyes settling on Carlotta. She winked and a feline smile curved her lips. I felt exposed, as if she'd peered inside my heart. Embarrassed, I looked down into the bottom of my glass. When I glanced at her again, Monsieur Delacroix was handing her a fresh drink. He brushed her forehead with his lips.

My eyes grew wide. When had he arrived? Was *she* the mistress he mentioned in passing? Carlotta exchanged a look with him and then set her sights on me. She said something to Delacroix and they made their way across the room.

"Mademoiselle Daaé," she said in a singsong voice. Ever the performer.

Monsieur Delacroix leaned in to kiss my cheek. "*Ma belle!* I didn't expect to see you here."

"Likewise, Monsieur." I glanced from him to Carlotta and back.

"Could you excuse us for a moment, Professor?" Carlotta gave me a conspiratorial wink. "Christine and I need to have a little woman-to-woman chat."

"Of course." He swigged from his glass and gave me a pointed look. "I would like to speak with you later as well."

I suppressed the instant uneasiness his tone inspired. Had he learned I'd been speaking with the phantom after all? Suddenly I felt like a child caught being naughty.

"If we have time, of course." I shifted from one foot to another.

"You are busy with new friends?" He raised his brow. "Well, enjoy yourself at the party. I can always pay you a visit another time *chez toi.*"

I clutched my glass tighter. At some point, I would have to tell him the truth.

Before Carlotta could pull me away, three gentlemen joined our circle, two of whom engaged Delacroix immediately. The third leaned toward me with the hungry look on his face I had come to recognize. Though handsome, his expression made me uneasy.

"You are Carlotta's new protégé, I hear," he said with a wink. "And my, aren't you a beauty."

"Thank you. Yes, I am new to the Opéra de Paris, though not new to singing."

"I bet." He laughed heartily, then swallowed a mouthful of spirits. "I look forward to seeing you *perform*, shall we say?"

My mouth fell open. The man was vile.

"I'd like to refresh my drink," I choked out the words. "If you'll excuse me."

As I darted to the refreshment table, I stole another quick glance at Raoul. He conversed heatedly with a gentleman. I couldn't help but feel relief the women had dispersed, at least for now.

"Men can be such beasts," Carlotta said from behind me.

"So I'm learning." I turned, not missing her amused smile.

"You know, dear, we would make a fine pair, you and I. Two beautiful women, both singers destined for fame. We could rake in the attentions of the *abonnés*, if we chose. On our own terms, of course. It would bring in a tidy fortune for us, and the theatre."

I stiffened at her mention of the *abonnés*; the male season ticket holders. They doled out jewels to ballerinas vying for advancement on the stage. Not only did the *abonnés* shower the chosen ones with fine gifts, but they donated large sums to the opera house to keep the coffers full and to ensure they received certain . . . privileges. After the show, their money bought them a *petit rat*, as the impoverished and desperate ballerinas were called. Often, the arrangement included sexual acts in exchange for their generosity. I'd been an impoverished girl, but thankfully I had never been forced to such a level of desperation. Perhaps, without Madame Valerius, I would have. I felt a keen sense of pain on the ballerinas' behalf.

"I don't understand," I said at last. "I'm not a dancer, and neither are my circumstances desperate."

"They court singers as well if there is an attraction, or a willingness." She batted her heavily painted eyelashes as if I were a man she could win over.

The seed of anger I'd been harboring grew stone-sized in my gut. "Are you suggesting I forfeit my decency? I have no intention of allowing a man to despoil me. At the very least, not unless he intended to be my husband."

"Don't act as if you are better than me," she said, eyes flashing. "I worked my way up from nothing, just as you are now. My mother died in a brothel at the hand of some brute, and I learned to accept favors when they came my way. You may be high on your luck now, Daaé, but it changes in an instant." She leaned closer, a cloud of her jasmine perfume clogging my throat. "Besides, I know you have lost your innocence already."

My mouth fell open for the second time that evening. How did she know the machinist attacked me? And she had her information all wrong. "How—"

She waved her hand, the diamonds on her bracelet flashing like a warning. "It's my opera house. Why shouldn't I know what goes on there. Without me, the show doesn't go on. Without me"—she paused and leaned closer—"you have no allies. You have *nothing*."

I opened my mouth to reply but quickly closed it. My retort shriveled on my tongue, as it always did. Another thought came, unbidden, and chilled me to the core. Did Carlotta talk to the Angel of Music?

"I assure you, nothing happened with the machinist." I willed my voice to remain calm. "I was accosted, but I managed to get away. Had it not been for—" I stopped myself, almost too late.

Carlotta grinned her feline smile once more. "Had it not been for what?"

In need of escape—from Raoul, from the overwhelming feeling I didn't belong here, from Carlotta and this horrid conversation—I set down my wineglass. "If you will excuse me, I'm going to call it an evening. I'm afraid I'm not feeling well."

She stuck out her bottom lip. "You poor dear. I do hate when my guests leave early. But, Christine? Just one more thing."

I braced myself for insult.

"Steer clear of the Vicomte de Chagny. He's courting a friend of mine. It would do you no good to get foolish notions in your head. He's a beautiful man, but taken already."

I couldn't hide the shock I felt. "I haven't even spoken to him."

"You have such an expressive face, dear," she said sweetly.

I blushed in humiliation. "Thank you for the invitation, Carlotta. I bid you good night."

Her brow wrinkled in false concern. "Do feel better."

I gathered the shreds of my dignity and strode to the door, pausing for a final glance over my shoulder.

Raoul de Chagny stared after me, eyes wide.

Sleep did not come easily. Memories of Raoul swirled around me like flurries in a snowstorm, glistening and magical, yet leaving me cold. I could still see the sheepish expression on his face from so many years ago when he gave me the magic box. My exclamation of delight had put a wide grin on his face. We had spent so many afternoons laughing.

I pushed up on my elbows and peered over the tented blanket across my feet. My magic box lay inside the armoire just beyond the bed, untouched since the fire. The series of visions I'd come to expect whenever I remembered that night flashed through my mind once more: the Masked Conjurer, his "spirit" floating above the stage, the beautiful assistant in her glittering costume and mask. And then the flames, the falling beams.

I huffed out a sigh and flopped back onto the mattress, wondering what Raoul thought when he saw me across the room. He seemed as surprised as I had been when I discovered him at Carlotta's. I tossed in my sheets, finally ending up on my back and throwing my arm across my eyes. Carlotta's warning rang in my ears. Raoul was spoken for, and I must watch my step if I wanted to remain in her good graces—as well as those of the directors.

Not a problem, I reminded myself. I wouldn't see Raoul again anyway.

After another two hours of fitful sleep, I crawled from bed and completed my toilette, preparing to go to the opera house early. At home, I would do nothing but fixate on Raoul and the unknown woman to whom he was essentially engaged.

I walked through the opera house corridors later that morning, holding my breath, knees wobbly as noodles. Day after day, I waited for a voice to whisper in my ear, or for someone else to corner me as Joseph Buquet had. I wondered when the fear would finally dissipate. Perhaps the only way was to learn the building's secrets, to make it less mysterious and eliminate the unknown.

I would give it a try, now. Today.

I found a staircase, descended to the floor below, and continued through the room beneath the stage. Machinists buzzed about, while others constructed scene flats for a new set. I watched in awe as the stage floor lowered from eye level to the deep cellar to make way for another platform. Envisioning the gears and mechanisms responsible for such a feat, I continued to the recesses of the stage. Three men teetered on a bridge overhead, painting a forest on a muslin drop secured to a wooden frame. It would span the entire wall when finished. A fourth man on ground level puttered with a horizontal pocket along the drop's hemline, designed to disguise a pipe or chain to pull the cloth taut on stage.

"Would you like to help us, Ma'moiselle?" One of the men in paint-spattered pants and apron called down to me.

I smiled. "You're doing a great job already." I would sooner enjoy working on the mechanics of the sets, see how the pieces fit together to create a certain effect. Still, I admired the lush foliage expertly painted on the drop, the sweep of branches shading a grotto in the foreground. The set looked almost real.

"It's beautiful," I said.

"Thank you." The painter winked.

I continued to the next section of the stage where a machinist struggled with a long rod fitted with a series of wheels.

"Is it not working?" I asked, peering over his shoulder.

"It's jammed." He pointed to a cord tangled along the track. "Can't move the bedroom furniture on the stage tomorrow night without it."

"If you fit the screwdriver under the edge here"—I pointed to the metal end—"and force the cord upward, it will release the bearing." I glanced at the machinist's face to see if he understood.

He smiled, showing a large hole where his front bottom teeth should be. "You interested in machines, Mademoiselle?"

"I like to understand how things work. Machines are like puzzles."

"Haven't seen many ladies fussing with them, I must admit." He scratched his unshaven chin. "I could tinker with them for hours."

I nodded. "I just solved a lock puzzle, at home. A German trick lock. I managed to open it after a few weeks, but I can close it again and you can have a go, if you like."

He whistled in amazement. "You opened one of those by yourself? I'm impressed."

His praise inspired a happy warmth in my veins. I smiled again. "Thank you."

"I'd like to take a crack at it, if you don't mind sharing."

"Not at all. I'll bring it in tomorrow."

"Say, you care to see the rigging loft? I can show you the flies."

"Oh, yes!" I followed him to the wings of the stage and climbed a spindly ladder after him, careful to keep my dress from tangling in my legs.

"You go out on these platforms." He demonstrated, walking along a narrow wooden plank that floated over the stage. Dozens of people milled about beneath us. "When it's time, you crank the right lever at the same time the fly boys pull the ropes below." He gestured to a series of ropes and wires. "And voilà! You've got yourself a set change. The drops are painted cloths with the background scenery. And these pieces here"—he motioned to thin sheets of wood—"are called borders. They're used to change the skyline."

Though it made sense, I couldn't imagine keeping it all straight during a production. There had to be dozens of wires and ropes, and if someone chose the wrong one during a show one night, they'd likely be dismissed.

We descended the ladder and continued on our tour, the machinist explaining the function of each backstage area. I felt myself relax as we continued. It took far more people than I had realized to run an opera.

When he finished, I touched his shoulder lightly. "That was very kind of you. Thank you, Monsieur—?"

"Call me Georges. Anytime you'd like, I'll show you more."

I smiled. "Georges, then. I'll be sure to bring the lock tomorrow. Good day to you."

He nodded and scurried back to his station.

Curious to have a look at the other sets, I wound through a maze of abandoned flats in a more secluded alcove, pausing to admire a bedroom. Another resembled an amphitheatre. As I examined a tavern on a cobbled street, a male voice drifted toward me from the other side of the flat.

"You've got to see this," the voice said. "I think I found the passageway."

A prickle of fear ran up the back of my neck. I recognized that voice—it belonged to Joseph Buquet, the machinist who tried to molest me. Disgust and hatred swarmed my stomach, yet I willed myself not to flee. I had to see what he was up to. Perhaps then I could tell the directors how he attacked me and relay his scheming. That must be enough to warrant his dismissal.

"I followed a series of trapdoors and found a staircase hidden in the walls," he went on, tone brusque.

I peeked around the edge of the flat.

Buquet ushered another man—smaller in stature, and with a thin mustache—to a recess in the wall. I tiptoed several feet and ducked behind another flat. Shielded from view, I leaned closer, straining to hear their conversation.

"There are at least another three floors down, maybe more, but it was so dark I couldn't see. I didn't have enough oil in my lantern to continue and still find my way back."

"We'll bring two lanterns," the mustachioed man said. "Run one until it goes out, and use the second for backup."

"There must be lighting, but I didn't find a damn thing. I was afraid of getting lost."

Why were they trying to go further underground?

"I didn't see any signs of—"

The zip and swish of a saw grinding through wood drowned out their voices. I blew out an impatient breath and leaned against the partition. After a few moments, the sawing ceased.

"We'll get the ghost." Joseph's voice drifted toward me again. "Bring him to the boss for questioning."

The blood drained from my face. They were hunting the opera ghost, my Angel—now, while everyone was here. I paused, surprised by my assertion. *My* Angel? Somewhere along the way I had laid claim to this soul who helped me to become a better singer, to become a stronger version of myself. Though he frightened me with his mercurial moods, I felt almost wedded to him . . . at least professionally.

At the very least, I owed him a warning.

"I'll show you the entryway." Joseph looked over his shoulder and scurried across the room.

Blood pumped in my ears as I followed them into the hall, hanging back just far enough to hide. What in the world had gotten into me? I wasn't brave or daring. I wasn't strong, and certainly couldn't fend the men off, should they discover me. I shuddered at the thought—but I had to know. I could warn the ghost and then tell Delacroix all I had seen, which would secure both of their faith in me.

"This way." Joseph lowered his voice.

The men turned down another corridor and through a series of storage rooms. Racks of old costumes, battered flats, and forgotten props lay turned over and stacked in heaps. As I skirted around an empty glass case, my shoe caught the edge of the frame and I stumbled. I gasped, catching myself on a set of movable stairs. Its wheels squeaked, and the stairs rolled.

"Did you hear something?" Joseph's hand flew out to his side, signaling them to stop.

I slipped between racks of costumes and held my breath, pulse thumping in erratic beats. An emperor's robe crusted with sequins hung like the skin of a sickly old man, once beautiful but now sagging and laden with dust. I eyed it warily—dust made me sneeze.

"Want me to make sure no one is around?" the other man asked.

"I've got it," Joseph growled, striding back through the room toward me.

I retreated deeper into the costumes, willing myself to shrink between the folds of fabric. My rustling shook the dust loose. An invisible cloud of particles invaded my nose.

Joseph's footsteps grew louder, closer.

I twitched my nose like a rabbit, praying I wouldn't sneeze.

At the edge of the rack, Joseph paused.

My eyes watered and my throat shivered as I held the spasm at bay.

"There's no one here," he said, turning back toward his companion.

"Chasing a ghost has a way of making you hear things that aren't there." The second man goaded.

"There's no ghost here, either, Serge," Joseph rumbled. "Come on, the doorway is over there."

I covered my nose and mouth with my sleeve, and sneezed, stifling the noise as much as I could. My head and nose vibrated with the force. Thankfully, the men were just far enough away and too engrossed in their exploration to notice the whisper of sound. I crept slowly from the cover of the costumes and peered around a nearby cabinet.

Joseph stopped in front of a mirror with chipped beveled edges; the glass showed the smokiness of age. He pumped an invisible lever near the floorboard with his foot, and the wall panel slid inward, revealing a passageway shrouded in darkness.

Excitement raced through my veins. A secret passage!

"That's easy enough," Serge said. "I'll finish the job I'm working on and we'll go. No one will notice us missing. Meet back here in two hours?"

Joseph nodded.

I scrambled back to my hiding place, not daring to move until their footsteps receded. After dusting grime from my clothing, I walked quickly to the mirror. I stopped in front of it. I didn't have a lantern or the slightest idea where to go or how to get back. I could get lost, as Joseph said, and who knew how long it would be before someone discovered me—or who would make the discovery.

I stepped backward, shaking my head. It wasn't smart. I needed to speak to the Angel from my dressing room. But I had been absent last night, at Carlotta's. If the Angel was angry I'd missed our lesson, he might not return for a while.

I set off for my dressing room. I had to try, at least. If Joseph and his friend discovered him somehow, or a secret he needed to hide, who knew what might happen? I had to protect the Angel. I owed him that much.

Inside my dressing room, I locked the door and laid my cheek against the wall paneling.

"Angel?" I called softly. "Are you there? I need you."

My stomach swam with nerves.

"Angel?" I raised my voice. "Please, I'm sorry I missed our lesson. Don't be angry with me. This is important." I waited for several minutes, then called, "Someone is after you!"

I heard no movement, no hint of the luxurious tenor I had come to know so well.

"I'm trying to help you," I pleaded.

Still no answer.

I glanced at the clock on my vanity. I still had time to try the secret passage myself before Buquet and his thug showed, but I would have to hurry. Threading through the corridors in a rush, I reached the storage room quickly and crouched in front of the mirror. With a probing hand, I felt along its base. A thin metal lever jutted above the warped floorboard. The latch! I pressed it with my hand.

It didn't budge.

Grumbling under my breath, I straightened and stomped on the lever with my foot. The door whooshed as it receded into the dark passage.

Success!

I peered inside the opening, and found nothing but a dark hallway. I paused, doubt clouding me like a fog. What was I doing here? Should Joseph find me, who knew what he would do.

I knew. I clenched my fists at my sides. Now was not the time to be a coward. I could do this. I *needed* to do this—I controlled my own life, my own fate. Despite my loyalty to the Angel, I needed to prove I was my own person, not a shrinking coward in constant need of protection. With a deep breath, I entered the passageway.

A faint light shone in the distance like a lantern veiled in cloth. I recalled Joseph's comments about the darkness and frowned. There was enough light. Joseph could have found his way without a lantern. Besides, he wasn't the sort to be tentative. He was an ox, smashing through a tearoom.

I sucked in a breath to calm the blood racing through my veins. Reaching gingerly for the wall, I tried to banish the image of cobwebs sagging under the weight of fat spiders with frightening eyes and rows of hairy legs. A smooth surface met my fingertips. I sighed in relief and inched forward, leaving behind the welcome light of the storage room.

A breeze thick with dust blew against my cheek. There must be an opening somewhere. Frowning, I took another step.

My foot met no pavement.

I screeched as I plummeted downward, the sensation of falling lasting only a moment before my hip connected with the edge of a step, then another, and several more. I rolled, limbs flailing, until I landed in a heap at the bottom of the staircase. Groaning, I pushed

116

myself into an upright position and felt along the floor until my fingers brushed the edge of the landing. I peered over the edge. An additional set of stairs led farther, deeper into an abyss of darkness.

Footsteps clattered in the passageway behind me.

Heart pounding against my ribs, I scrambled to my feet and descended the second staircase, pushing aside my fear of what lay below. A dangerous man followed somewhere behind—I had to find a place to hide. *Now.* Using the wall as my guide, I plunged deeper into the heart of the building. At last, my hands closed around a doorknob. I turned it, and threw open the door.

I squinted in a flood of light. As I attempted to get my bearings, the whinny of horses floated through the air. There was a stable down here? Stunned, I gaped at the strange spectacle. I sorted through my memories, seeking the details of the opera house's history. The building had been built at Emperor Bonaparte III's request. The stable must have been for his private use, but that was a decade ago. Perhaps they used horses in the shows? I faintly recalled Gabriel mentioning horses, though I didn't remember how, or in what context.

The rumble of male voices came from the hall behind me. I raced for the cover of the stable. In my rush, I closed the door behind me with a bang.

"Who's there?" Joseph called.

My breath hitched as I slipped into a stall occupied by a white stallion. The horse peered at me warily, but calmed as I caressed his nose. He whinnied and nibbled my shoulder.

"That's it. Be a good boy," I whispered, thankful for the many times Papa and I had slept in stables and cared for horses in exchange for shelter.

The stallion pawed the ground with his hoof, stirring up the pungent odor of manure and straw. In spite of my caresses, he didn't like sharing his space.

As I crouched, the stable door crashed open against the wall. The horses neighed at another unexpected intrusion.

"I know you're in here," Joseph shouted.

My breath froze in my lungs.

"Show yourself!" he shouted.

I flattened against the wall, wishing I could become invisible.

"We're going to have some fun when we find him," Serge said.

Momentarily relieved, I rocked back on my heels. They thought I was "a him."

"Grab the broom," Joseph said. In seconds, the broom handle thwacked against the wood, over and over again. "Come out, opera ghost! Show yourself like a man."

Each time he hit a stall door the horses pranced about and snorted their dismay. The white stallion seemed more rattled than the others. He stamped nervously behind me.

Please don't crush me, I prayed.

"There's no one in the stalls, Joe," Serge said.

"We heard the door close. He's here. Come out, ghost!" Joseph shouted.

My heart thumped in my ears. I prayed the Angel would show up, scare them with his ominous voice, or do something. Anything.

The men continued through the stalls, slamming doors, nudging the horses with the broom. Any moment they would find me, and have their way with me. Panic seized me. The thought of Joseph Buquet, his rotten breath, his rough hands pawing beneath my clothes. I gasped in a breath and the odor of perspiration and horse manure filled my lungs. I tugged at my high-necked collar, trying to breathe. He might even kill me when he finished. Stupid, stupid girl, I berated myself.

I squeezed my eyes closed. *Please, Angel. You promised to protect me.*

The shuffle of their boots grew closer, the slamming louder. As they approached the last row of stalls, my stallion snorted and shook his head.

Serge cracked the broom against the stallion's door. The horse blew out an angry breath, and danced around his stall in agitation.

Serge poked the horse with the broom handle.

The stallion backed away from the broom. A screech tore from my lips as the horse narrowly missed my legs.

"Well, what have we here?" Serge poked his head into the stall. "Aren't you one of the chorus girls? Did you go looking for the ghost yourself?"

I remained silent, too terrified to speak. I wished violently that I had stayed in the safety of my dressing room—that I hadn't felt the need to prove myself, and to what end, exactly?

Joseph stopped beside him. When he recognized me, his eyes narrowed to slits and a malicious grin spread across his face. "Well, well. It's not just any chorus girl, it's you. The beautiful understudy. The one who had me beaten that night. Lost a few teeth because of you." He opened his mouth to show me a large space where two of his top teeth should be.

Though my insides quaked, the injustice of his statement fueled my hate. "You deserved it! You should have been dismissed as well."

His laugh had jagged edges. " 'Dismissed'? I'm well liked among the machinists and cast. Everyone knows what a jolly fellow I am. They wouldn't believe you, no matter what you told them." With that, he opened the stall door.

Serge took the horse's halter to calm him, while Joseph advanced toward me. In seconds, he stood over me, gripped my arm, and hauled me out of the stall.

"I'll go straight to the directors. Tell them what you've done."

He shoved me to the floor.

I threw out my hands to catch myself, scraping my palms against the floorboards.

"They'll thank me for finding the ghost. I'm sure they'll be so happy to have him eliminated, they won't care about you a bit."

Despite my fear, I considered the absurdity of Buquet's statement. If the Angel was truly a ghost, could he even be located, much less eliminated? This man was mad.

"She sure is pretty, isn't she?" Serge's expression shifted from anger to hunger.

"A real beauty. And delicious. I've tasted her once before."

Bile surged up my throat. I wrapped my arms about me like a shield.

"Stay away from me. I swear, I'll tell them! I'll go to the police."

Serge ignored me and stepped closer. "That's hardly fair. You've had a go and I haven't."

Panic surged through my limbs. I couldn't believe I was in this place —again. My eyes darted around the stable, searching for a weapon or a way out. A pitchfork sat near the door. I could reach it, but I would have to keep them talking to distract them.

"Why are you hunting the ghost?" I asked, my voice tremulous. Slowly, I stood.

"We need to have a word with him," Joseph growled.

I turned on my heel and raced for the pitchfork.

"Get her!" Joseph shouted.

"Angel, help me!" I screamed. Three more strides and I would have the weapon. "Angel, help!"

Just as I grasped the rusted handle, Joseph caught me and spun me around. It felt as if a brick smashed into my face.

I reeled backward and everything went dark.

~9~

I awakened to a cold sensation burning my skin. My eyes fluttered open to find Meg standing over me, concern shining in her doe eyes.

"You're awake." She dropped the compress she held against my face and sighed in relief.

I sat up, wincing at the pain throbbing through my cheek and the back of my head. "What happened?"

The secret passageway . . . at once, the events came flooding back. I felt my dress, felt my limbs, my abdomen. I hadn't been defiled and nothing seemed broken, thank God. I exhaled in relief. In fact, my clothes showed no signs of struggle. Had the men just left me? That seemed unlikely, given the way they had acted. Someone must have come to my rescue. Someone or *something*.

My Angel had saved me again.

Meg sat on the edge of a chair in her leotard and skirt. She tucked her slippered feet beneath her. "Maman told me to tend to you in your dressing room. The ghost told her you were hurt."

"The ghost?" I asked, feigning surprise. "He helped me?"

Meg shrugged. "I assume so, since he told Maman. Can a ghost carry a human?" She shuddered. "The whole thing is strange. And horrible."

I probed my swollen cheek tentatively. I wanted to go home, but first I had to thank the Angel, and find out what had happened.

"You're shaking." Meg rubbed my arms. "It's all right. You're safe."

I wasn't safe until I told the directors about the evil men and had them arrested. Pain throbbed behind my eyes and along my jaw. Groaning, I held the compress to my swollen face. What had I been thinking? I was lucky I hadn't been killed.

"May I ask you something?" Meg leaned forward in her chair. "Why haven't you been practicing with Gabriel and the others?"

"I've been practicing on my own." When I needed them, lies sprang to my lips before I had a chance to think. My Angel had inspired more than one change in me, and not all for the better.

Meg's face changed, and a cloud perched on her fair brow. "There are rumors going around about you, Christine. They say the opera ghost is your teacher. And now he's rescued you. We all assume. . . I won't tell anyone, because it'll make it worse. He's not exactly the most popular . . . being around here. You should be careful."

A nervous laugh stuck in my throat. "I don't believe in rumors, or ghosts."

She leaned forward again. "I know the ghost is real, Christine. He rescued you, and Maman delivers messages for him. She's told me everything."

"Has she seen him?" I dropped my voice to a whisper, though I knew if the Angel wanted to hear us, he could. Somehow, he was everywhere—and nowhere—all at once. Each time I decided he was a man, he convinced me otherwise. Either way, I couldn't deny his presence made my heart race, or that I was grateful for him.

"Maman says the only person who seems to know the ghost, other than herself, is a Persian man in a multi-colored turban who visits from time to time. I've seen the Persian in the opera house as well, though he never speaks to anyone. He's odd." She frowned for an instant and lowered her voice. "She also says the ghost demands payment from the directors. And now he wishes to dethrone Queen Carlotta." She giggled and clapped a hand over her mouth. "You mustn't tell anyone I said that. Maman would be furious."

"I will keep your secret," I said, my mind racing.

I was sickened at the prospect that my Angel was capable of blackmail and assault. Like it or not, I cared for him. He watched over me, inspired me. I couldn't deny his constant aid, or his fierce loyalty. He had saved my life and taught me so much. But I knew he harbored a darkness I had yet to see. His sinister laugh echoed in my mind, his snappy tone edged with menace when I didn't do precisely as he asked.

Meg frowned. "Are you all right? You just blanched white as a sheet."

"What do you mean by the ghost 'wishes to dethrone Queen Carlotta'?"

"He keeps demanding they put you on the stage instead of her. But, as you know, they have yet to follow his orders. Bad decision." She rubbed her filmy skirt between her fingers in a nervous gesture. "Maman says we will all pay for ignoring the ghost's requests. She talks about the ghost so often I . . ." She trailed off. "I'm afraid of her association with him. And her feelings."

"Her feelings"? Meg seemed to imply there was something more between them. An uncomfortable emotion prickled inside of me. "Try not to worry." I squeezed her hand. "If he communicates with her, he must trust her discretion."

"I need to know something, Christine." Curiosity shone in her eyes. "Is the ghost your tutor?"

I studied her earnest expression. If her mother already worked for the ghost, she must be good at keeping secrets. And she was one of my few friends. I hoped I could trust her.

"Yes." I averted my eyes. "He comes to my dressing room at night, though I can't see him, sometimes during performances, sometimes after them." I clutched her hand. "But please, tell no one. I don't want to anger him. He might leave."

"I knew it!" She pounded her knee with her fist. "Just think. If he helps you take a lead role, you'll be a star. Your voice is so lovely."

"Thank you." I smiled weakly, and winced as the movement stretched my bruised cheek.

I wondered what the Angel was planning—his promise to dethrone Carlotta both rattled and excited me. If he succeeded, I would gain true recognition, and secure Madame's household. I could do whatever I liked from there. The thought dislodged something inside me; hope—not guilt—filled the hollow of my chest. *I could do whatever I liked.*

Ideas I hadn't entertained since Papa's death flooded into my mind.

Meg rose to her feet. "You should go home and rest. Perhaps when you're better you'll join us at the dance hall?"

I tried to smile without luck—my cheek was too sore. "I would like that."

Meg opened the door to go, and a figure in the hallway.

"Christine!" Monsieur Delacroix rushed inside. "You've been hurt." Though concern brimmed in his voice, he studied the large mirror covering the wall over my head. "I've been following the hidden staircases through the first few floors. Combing them for clues and information. I thought I heard a voice, but couldn't trace it, and I haven't heard it again." He glanced at my face, as if remembering I was there—and injured. "*Mon Dieu*, how did this happen?"

Something about the wildness in his eyes, the way he had to remind himself to be concerned, kept the truth locked firmly inside me. "I fell and hit my face."

"Goodness." He touched my hand. "Do you need assistance?"

"Thank you, but no. I'll just rest a bit longer and then be on my way."

"Very well." He stood abruptly and returned to the door. "I will visit you at home soon."

As he left, I heaved a sigh and closed my eyes. Meg's words rushed back. People knew the Angel worked with me, yet I couldn't imagine how they knew—no one had heard us talking, at least to my knowledge.

My head throbbed. Light flashed around the edges of my vision. I needed to go home, get proper rest. I pulled on my cloak and gloves, and locked my dressing room door behind me.

Claudette administered laudanum to ease the pain in my jaw and throbbing temples over the next few days. The blow across my cheek turned from angry welt to a bruise that spread in a frightening patchwork of blue-black and purple. Madame Valerius gasped when she saw me, and then her eyes had filled with tears.

"I fell on the stairs." Another lie slipped out before I could stop it. "I slammed my face against the marble casing at the base of a statue."

"Darling, you must be careful. You will wreck your pretty face." She motioned to Albert to fetch a cold compress.

I stewed over the horrible chain of events for the next three days. Why had I lied to cover for the monster who attacked me? Keeping the incident to myself meant Buquet would go free—again. Then it dawned on me. I hadn't lied to protect Joseph, or to cover my own foolishness.

I lied to protect *him*—the ghost, my Angel.

If I explained what Joseph and Serge were looking for, or admitted why they attacked me, it would alert the directors. They would send for the magistrate and hunt the Angel. I had to protect my teacher, my savior. My pulse quickened at the thought of his beautiful tenor in my ear.

But Madame Valerius knew me too well. She didn't buy my lies.

Claudette poked her head into my room. "Madame wants to speak with you."

I closed my book and joined her in her bedroom, sitting carefully on the edge of her bed. "How are you feeling?"

"Fine, fine," she said, dismissing my concern. "I think the better question is how are you feeling, my dear?" She eyed the bruise on my face.

"Better," I said, shifting my gaze away from hers.

I'd spent the better part of a week recovering. Albert had delivered a note to Gabriel to inform him of my illness, and that I would return in a few more days. The opera went on. They didn't miss their understudy, or even need me, really. Carlotta would sooner croak than allow me to step into her shoes.

She waved me closer. "Come here, child."

I moved within reach of her soft, wrinkled hands, and she cupped my chin in them. "I want you to protect yourself, should you ever need to."

Taken aback, I flinched. "I don't know what you mean."

"I don't know what's really going on, Christine, but you need to assume there are less-than-good people in the world."

She rang her bedside bell and Alfred entered the room, carrying an item between his thumb and forefinger. He held it away from him as if it were a poisonous snake.

A gun.

"This is my pistol," Madame said. "I'd like you to keep it with you."

Too shocked to speak, I stared back at her. She didn't seem the type to own a weapon.

She chuckled at my expression. "Don't look so surprised. I bought it during the invasion ten years ago, when Emperor Bonaparte was captured. You probably don't remember. You were just a girl."

"I remember the Prussians. Everyone was starving, not just Papa and me."

"Yes, and they looted and destroyed many homes. I wanted to protect myself. Now it is time you did the same. For a while, at least. When things are safe again, you can return it to me."

Somehow, she knew more than I had told her. Claudette must have revealed at least part of the truth. I couldn't argue with Madame, though the thought of carrying a pistol made me queasy. Suddenly I wondered if my own mother would have given me a weapon or met with the police on my behalf. Would she stroke my hand the way Madame did, teach me to sew, and read books with me, encourage me to learn her magic?

Madame touched my chin, pulling me from my thoughts. "Be careful, my dear."

I stared at the weapon in my hands. "I'll just put this away for now." I closed her bedroom door behind me.

Perhaps I would return it to her desk without her knowing. The unwelcome thought of seeing Joseph again made my hands tremble, and propelled me swiftly down the hallway. Maybe the pistol wasn't such a bad idea after all. I unlocked the drawer of my armoire and placed it next to my magic box for safekeeping.

My magic box.

Unable to resist, I wiped clean the layer of dust on the lid. With my finger, I traced my carved initials for the hundredth time. A vision of Raoul flitted through my mind: his flawless cravat, and the satisfied expression on his handsome face, radiating from beneath a bow of golden maple leaves. I wondered how he might react if he knew I still had his gift. I ached to open the box, sift through its contents, and test my memories of the well-loved illusions, but doing so might engender more longing for a pastime I had sworn off for good.

A longing I should ignore.

I shoved the box back into the drawer. With a sigh, my eyes shifted to the pistol's carved handle, inlaid with pearl and decorated with curling vines designed for a woman's taste. What in the world would I do with a gun? I couldn't imagine shooting someone, and hadn't the slightest idea how to use one. I closed the drawer and turned the key as the knocker on the front door clacked.

I descended the stairs and found Monsieur Delacroix waiting for me in the hall.

"You are looking quite well, considering, Christine." He removed his hat and handed me a package of sugared fruits before seating himself.

Claudette slipped into the room quietly, bearing a tray with coffee, a dish of sugar cubes, and a baguette with butter and confiture.

"It's healing." My fingertips grazed the spot on my cheek.

The doctor had stopped by that morning, leaving another hefty bill in his wake for examining me as well as Madame, who grew weaker each autumn day with the cool air and the rains. He recommended she spend the winter somewhere southern and warm, but we couldn't afford to maintain an apartment elsewhere and also a residence for me in Paris. The stress of our financial situation made my fingers itch to seek the comfort and distraction of my tools and gadgets. My cards. Instead, I dropped a sugar cube in my coffee and watched it disappear as it melted. My magic, again—I had to stop thinking about it. I sighed as I stirred.

"Carlotta said everyone is worried about you." Delacroix sipped the rich brew.

I held my composure, though I wanted to protest. Her behavior confused me. One minute she was polite, even nice; the next, I had to brace myself for a strike. Perhaps she meant well after all, but was simply a difficult woman.

"In fact," he went on, "that's why I'm here. To make sure you're recovering. Have you seen a doctor? I would hate for you to lose your coveted position. You should return to the opera as soon as possible."

Coveted position? An understudy's position came with a certain amount of prestige, but I rarely had the chance to perform. I was no closer to becoming a star and only marginally adding to our income. I stirred my coffee again, agitating the liquid until it sloshed over the porcelain rim.

"Are you all right?" Delacroix arched a thick eyebrow.

Surprised my unrest was so apparent, I forced a smile and sat taller. "I'm ready to return to work, is all. I have been restless."

"Anxious to meet with your tutor, perhaps?" Delcroix asked smoothly.

I gripped my cup. He had heard more rumors about the ghost, and was baiting me. Had Meg revealed my secret? That seemed the only way the rumors could have spread. A twinge of betrayal twisted my gut. I had trusted her. I liked the ballerina, but perhaps I should have kept my mouth closed. Unless someone else had overheard—or Delacroix had uncovered the news while at the opera, somehow. He was hanging outside my dressing room door while Meg and I talked about it.

"I don't have a tutor, Monsieur. You know that."

"I see." His eyebrows knitted into a frown. "Well, the cast is saying the opera ghost speaks to you. Do you deny it?"

For the first time, I didn't retreat into my skin, wishing I could find the right words. I met his gaze evenly. "All I've seen and heard, I have told you."

"And your face? I'm not certain a little fall could make it look like this." He gestured to the fading bruises. "How did this happen exactly?"

"Your line of questioning feels as if I am before a jury, Monsieur."

He chuckled and sank back into the sofa. "I apologize. I've been working with incompetent fools the last week and it has set me on edge. I only ask because I care for your well-being. Nothing more. I've been worried you will find yourself embroiled in the scandal. Opera ghosts, threatening letters, and now your injury."

"It's kind of you to ask, but I am well." I blushed on cue, not from embarrassment, but from anger that I should be forced to lie again. "As I said before, I smashed my face on the marble base of a statue. I was clumsy and lost my footing. I feel foolish about the whole thing."

"There is no need to chastise yourself, my dear." He peered at me over the rim of his coffee cup. "I thought you should know, I've gone over the maps of the opera house quite thoroughly, as well as examined each of the staircases and halls. I've only found one hidden staircase, and it led to the stables. Not quite the secret I had hoped to find. The directors are ready for me to wrap my investigation. They will call the gendarme if any other damning business occurs with this ghost."

Something told me there were many other secret passages the professor hadn't yet discovered. He couldn't be as thorough as he thought—and for some reason, this pleased me to bits. To hide my satisfied grin, I gulped the remainder of my coffee, the liquid scalding my throat as it went down. Apparently, there was a lot he didn't know, including the evil men searching for the ghost. Delacroix would go into a tirade if he knew others might achieve his goal before him. Yet, despite his veiled warning, he couldn't make me share what I knew. My loyalty to the Angel was too strong. The Angel trusted me, and I needed him.

Delacroix leaned forward to squeeze my hand. "You know you can come to me if you hear something, or if anything is amiss. I would never let anyone hurt you."

"Goodness, why would anyone hurt me?" I spoke an octave too high and my fingers rested on my throat in forced surprise. I hoped I didn't appear as false as I felt.

He assessed me with his vivid gaze.

129

For a moment, I thought he would call my bluff, but at last he said, "I don't want to alarm you, but a beautiful woman—particularly one in an exalted position—is always a target. Carlotta has had many admirers take things too far. I hope you are taking proper precautions."

"Thank you for your concern, but all is well, I assure you."

"Very good then."

His tone indicated satisfaction, but I noted his clenched jaw and the way his left hand balled into a fist. He knew I withheld something, but he wouldn't try to pry more from me, at least for now.

I pressed my lips together and reached for a hunk of buttered bread.

The happy chirp of canaries wrenched me from my thoughts. I had neglected them of late, abandoning our daily song. With a snap, I popped open the lid to their cage and reached inside for Bizet. He puffed out his proud golden belly to be stroked, then cooed and rubbed his head against my thumb.

"I'm sorry, *mes amours.* I've been so busy."

Bizet cocked his head and peered at me with an inquisitive eye. I reached into the cage again and Mozart hopped on my finger. I brought him to my mouth so he might perform his favorite trick—a gentle peck to my lips.

"A kiss from my sweetest bird."

Mozart tweeted a reply, pleased with the work he had done. He hopped from my finger to my forearm as I fetched Berlioz from the cage next. Berlioz nipped the wrinkled flesh on my knuckle, angry I had left him for last.

I yelped. "That is no way to treat a lady."

Berlioz squawked in defiance. He didn't appreciate being abandoned. Simple mealtimes were not enough attention for my beloved pets. I hummed *"Se vuol ballare"* from *Le Mariage de Figaro*, a song Papa used to sing to me. Bizet and Mozart joined in with their own songs, chirping merrily. I scrubbed Berlioz's head softly with my finger until he decided he was no longer angry and joined the others in singing.

"You're a stubborn fellow, aren't you?" I asked.

Berlioz chirped and rubbed his head against my finger.

"Tomorrow we'll play some more, I promise."

All three canaries hopped into their cage. I flicked the string of bells dangling from a wire ring. Bizet clasped the rope in his beak and jingled them in reply. After cinching the cage door closed, I swept up the pile of seed hulls and feather wisps from the floor beneath the cage.

Tomorrow I returned to the opera. I had decided to tell the directors everything about the violent machinist, once and for all. Though afraid of the repercussions, I had to speak up—for my own safety and the safety of anyone else Buquet might target, including the Angel.

Which posed another problem. I would have to explain why I was wandering through the stables the night he attacked me.

Someone knocked at the front door.

I frowned, setting down the broom. Monsieur Delacroix had come just yesterday so it couldn't be him. Someone for Madame Valerius, perhaps.

"I've got it," Claudette called from the kitchen.

I glanced out the window, wondering who might visit in the rain, but discovered it had stopped. Soggy sunlight streamed over the hedges and condensation glistened on the windowpane. I had hoped to go for a walk and get some fresh air before I braved my return to the opera. Now I could. I would slip from sight, once Madame Valerius joined her guest, and take a carriage to a park across town with Claudette.

"There's someone here to see you." Claudette looked in on me in the study.

I shot her a puzzled look. "Monsieur Delacroix again?"

Claudette lowered her voice. "A gentleman. A *very* handsome gentleman." She grinned at my startled expression. "The Vicomte de Chagny requests your presence, Mademoiselle," she said with mock formality.

A fluttering began beneath my rib cage. Raoul? I rushed to the mirror on the wall. My hair appeared in order, but my violet day dress was rather plain. With no time to change, it would have to do. I pinched my cheeks and took a deep breath, though it didn't slow my suddenly racing pulse. He had found me somehow, must have asked someone for my address.

When I turned, Claudette whispered, "You're gorgeous as always. Must not keep him waiting."

At times Claudette seemed like the sister I never had. I tugged on one of her loose curls before following her from the room.

In the foyer, the vicomte held his hat in his hands. When I joined him, a smile crossed his face that could devastate a room.

"*Bonjour*, Mademoiselle Daaé. Allow me to introduce myself. You probably don't remember me, but we met as children. I am Raoul de Chagny." He smiled. "The boy who rescued your scarf in the surf? We spent the whole summer on the beach in Normandy, terrorized crabs, and spied on my brother." He chuckled.

Still surprised he stood in my apartment, I remained speechless, forcing myself to continue breathing in and out.

"I hope I've not interrupted something important." He frowned. "Forgive my impertinence. I should have written to introduce myself."

"No! Not at all." I reddened as I realized the vehemence of my reply. "Of course I remember you, Monsieur le Vicomte. It's a pleasure to see you again. May I offer you some tea or coffee?"

He bunched his hat in his hands. "Would you allow me to escort you on a walk instead? After two days indoors from the rain, I'm feeling rather cagey. Your maid could accompany us, of course."

"Only if you will consider dining with us after, Monsieur," Claudette said, before I could reply.

My eyes widened at her bravado. Claudette rarely held her

tongue—something I adored about her, usually—but her forward behavior wasn't appropriate with nobility, least of all a vicomte about whom I admittedly couldn't stop thinking.

Raoul released another of his powerful smiles and said, "I would like to join you very much."

I couldn't prevent the grin that leapt to my lips.

"Very good, Monsieur." Claudette curtsied. "I'll let the kitchen know right away."

I hid my amusement. We didn't have a kitchen staff, and her curtsy looked more like a stumble.

"A walk, Mademoiselle?" Raoul persisted.

"I would be delighted, though I won't have an escort, I'm afraid. Forgive my impropriety. We are . . . short of staff just now and I have no siblings."

"Think nothing of it," he said, smiling. "I will be a perfect gentleman."

As I slid on my pelisse and pinned on a bustle hat with black ribbon and plume, I was grateful he couldn't hear the galloping horses in my stomach.

A gust of fall air greeted us at the door, sweeping through Raoul's naturally tousled locks.

"You must wonder how I found you, after all this time?" he asked, breaking the silence. "I saw you at Carlotta's party. You were leaving, and I knew I had to find you." He stopped, as if realizing he had said too much.

He *had* to find me? The horses in my stomach began to race again. "Oh? It's a shame I missed you that evening. I knew very few there and felt a bit out of place."

"It was an odd gathering, I'll admit."

"Is Monsieur le Comte well?" The words felt stiff on my tongue. I had never called Raoul or his brother, Philippe, by their proper titles.

"Please, you must call me Raoul. That hasn't changed."

Relieved, I smiled again. "As you wish."

His smile reached his lovely eyes, and the world felt more joyous, my heart lighter. Embarrassed by the rush of emotion, I focused on the cobblestones leading to a row of manicured hedges that ringed a fountain. Still wet from the rain, the stones glistened in the fall sunshine as if coated in silver.

"Philippe and I have been arguing these days. I am a sailor, but Philippe insists I quit the navy and return to our estate. He would like us to manage it together." A muscle in his jaw clenched. "It *is* a large job, but I've never felt at home there. I haven't been able to bring myself to stay. Besides, I know my brother well. I would be underfoot and he would resent my interference. It's best I carry on, create my own path."

"And your father?"

"He passed away some time ago."

"I'm so sorry. Forgive my intrusion."

"He has been gone a long time. The summer after Normandy he passed."

I wanted to squeeze his arm, to tell him I understood the pain of his loss. Instead, I continued on in silence, gravel crunching underfoot as we wandered along the garden paths.

On a patch of grass, two children played with their cup-and-ball toys. With a flick of the wrist, the wooden ball sailed into the air as far as the attached string allowed, and then the children attempted to catch it in the cup. The little boy hadn't mastered the delicate nature of the toss. Over and over the ball bounced from the edge of his cup and dangled beside the handle. I smiled at his puckered brow, his tongue poking between pink lips as he concentrated on his task.

"It isn't fair!" the boy said, crossing his arms over his chest. "You always win."

"You're flinging it too hard." His sister demonstrated her maneuver several times.

We sauntered around the edge of the park, beneath a row of maples shifting to a fiery hue with the autumn change.

Raoul held his hands behind his back in an easy manner. "You are Carlotta's understudy, I hear. Congratulations. You were always a fine

134

singer."

I felt myself redden from the tips of my ears to my toes. "Thank you, yes. It's an honor." *And a frustrating one*, I wanted to add. The woman was threatened by me and I didn't understand why. I was no one, and she was a star.

"She's an excellent singer, if a bit difficult at times."

An absurd sense of pleasure rippled through me. "Many adore her."

"Forgive me for my blunt nature"—Raoul paused to look down at me —"but she also puts off many people as well. I would like to see the directors give you a chance. Your talent might very well match hers. And she doesn't have half your beauty."

I blushed again, but this time it spread over my whole body, warming my core.

His good humor fled and his eyes appeared contrite. "I've put you in an awkward position. I should apologize, but I'm not sorry. Seeing you again after all of these years, Christine"—he paused, his tone growing serious—"I would like to call on you. To be your friend again."

My lonely heart lurched as if awakening from an era of dormancy. When we reached the fountain, we peered down at the water swirling with leaves and debris fallen from the onslaught of rain and autumn winds. I frowned, remembering Carlotta's warning. Did Raoul wish to court two women simultaneously? Though thrilled by the prospect of our growing friendship, I didn't see how he could be nearly engaged to another woman and yet still call on me.

Confused, I removed a glove and reached toward a red leaf, curled at its edges and floating atop the water like a tiny crimson boat. I pushed it gently and watched it glide over the surface until it snared on another leaf. What would Carlotta do when she discovered Raoul pursued me—even as just a friend? I would have to tread carefully. I couldn't risk dismissal from the opera.

Raoul peered down at me with guarded eyes. He seemed to be holding his breath.

"I would like nothing more." The words sprang out, surprising even me. Yet I felt a smile spreading across my face.

"I was hoping you would say that."

Timidly, I accepted the arm he extended. We wound through the park and down the avenue past a café, finally crossing the street in front of my apartment building.

"Will you still dine with us tonight?" I asked, my face aching from constant smiling.

"Indeed, as your maid so kindly invited me. I will see you soon." Raoul leaned in to plant a customary peck on my cheek and paused, inches from my face.

The world around me evaporated, except for the light on his honey-colored hair, the mirth in his eyes, the fullness of his lips.

He grazed my cheek and my breath caught.

"Good day, Christine. Until tonight." He tipped his hat.

It was so wonderful to be happy for a moment, to think of something else beyond the terrible machinist and my constant uncertainty at the opera house. Grinning like a schoolgirl, I watched Raoul stride away past the café across the street. And then I noticed him—a man at the café peered over the edge of his newspaper. When he caught me looking, he covered his face with it.

I frowned. His frame, his hat . . . I would swear it was Monsieur Delacroix.

~ 10 ~

Dinner with Raoul flew by in a haze of laughter and memories. Madame approved of his visit and made it clear she hoped he would come again soon.

When he had gone, she grabbed my hand. "He's perfect, Christine."

I sighed. "I know, but this was just a friendly call. He's soon to be engaged, from what I've been told."

"But he is not engaged yet." She winked and rolled toward her bedroom.

The next afternoon, as I drifted toward my dressing room at the opera house, the memory of Raoul was far from my mind. At every corner, I looked over my shoulder. If Joseph tried anything, I would be ready. My fingers closed around the ivory handle of Madame's two-barreled pistol, safely tucked inside my handbag. Heart beating wildly, I exhaled. I shouldn't carry a gun, despite Madame's insistence. I hadn't the slightest idea how to use it. The thing might not even be loaded, and I was too afraid of hurting myself to find out. Still, I hoped its appearance would prevent Joseph or Serge from bothering me.

A Schubert melody streamed from an open doorway through the corridor. I welcomed the distraction and poked my head inside the ballet practice room. A dozen ballerinas performed a *brisé* in unison before moving through a series of pliés, arabesques, and other moves I couldn't name. Their tutus bounced merrily with each leap, and their sinuous limbs glided from one step to another with simple elegance. I considered the strength they must possess. Though singing demanded muscular power from my legs to my throat, it didn't match the rigorous demands of ballet. Many days I watched the ballerinas backstage, massaging their bruised feet and stretching their aching muscles.

"Christine?" A soft voice called from inside the room. "You've returned!"

Meg slipped from her place at the barre in the back of the room and met me in the hallway, her steps seeming as light as clouds. "I'm glad you're well again." She kissed me on either cheek. "Come, I have something to tell you, but not here."

I followed her down a staircase and into a secluded room. An impish face made of bronze popped from the tiled wall, its grin mischievous and its watchful eyes trained upon us. Only one lamp burned in the room. The somber ambiance made me shiver.

Another place I should avoid being caught alone.

Meg leaned close and whispered, "It's Joseph Buquet, the machinist."

My stomach rocked violently. "What is it?"

Meg looked past me to ensure no one was listening. "He hasn't been seen in a week. I assumed you didn't know since you've been absent. Everyone is talking about his disappearance."

I swallowed hard and tried to slow my reeling thoughts. "He could have quit. Moved on. Has anyone looked into it?"

Her curls bounced around her cheeks as she shook her head. "Serge DuBois reported that the opera ghost attacked Buquet."

She looked down, her lashes sweeping the creamy rounds of her cheeks. "DuBois mentioned your name to the directors, too. He said you were a busybody, looking through the storage rooms, and that you should be questioned. Since you've been gone the length of Joseph's disappearance . . . Well, rumors have been raging."

Bile rose in my throat. I had been abused by the wretched man, had run for my life, and now Serge implicated me in Joseph's disappearance?

"I didn't harm him, Meg! I swear it! I wandered through a few of the storage rooms, it's true. Georges showed me around because I was curious about the sets and the mechanics of running a show. And then last week, I looked through some old costumes. I was feeling listless. I never get to perform, Meg. I—"

"You don't need to explain." She took my hand in hers. "Of course you aren't responsible for Joseph's disappearance. The very suggestion is absurd."

I squeezed her hand, grateful she believed the accusation baseless. "Will the directors dismiss me?" The blood drained from my face. "Or— You don't think I will be arrested?"

"No! Oh, Christine, I'm sorry. I didn't mean to scare you." She threw her arms around me. "The directors laughed in DuBois's face. They didn't believe for a single instant that a beautiful young woman, so innocent and sweet-natured, could harm a large man like him."

I remembered the coolness of the gun in my hand, the nightly lessons with the ghost. Innocent indeed. A shrill laugh escaped my lips.

Puzzled by my reaction, she looked at me quizzically. "I am glad you aren't upset."

Meg had proven herself a friend, in spite of her possible gossiping, and deserved a note of honesty. "I must admit, it alarms me. If the directors believe I'm a kidnapper, I don't know what I'd do. The gossip alone!"

"You need to dissociate yourself from the opera ghost."

I looked down. "I'm not sure how. People will see what they wish, regardless of what I do."

"I'll defend you. Try not to worry. Those who count think it's absurd your name has been brought into this." Meg linked arms with me. "Now, I need to get into costume."

Meg led me to the dressing room. Along the way, she babbled about who was kissing who, which singers were always late to practice, and the scandal of Monsieur Richard's new Russian ballerina mistress. My thoughts crowded out most of her words.

Joseph had disappeared? He must have fled the opera house, or perhaps he was still searching for the ghost underground. Somehow I knew, in the pit of my stomach, he hadn't left. I pulled my cloak tighter to ward off the chill seeping into my skin. I couldn't help but imagine the worst. He was here, somewhere in the building.

"I'll see you after the performance," Meg said, turning down another corridor toward the cast room.

"Good luck." I rushed to my dressing room and locked the door behind me. Without pause, I yanked the vanity drawer open and thrust the gun inside. I couldn't carry it around with me as I had planned, or I'd risk being caught with a weapon. The minute my lessons with the Angel concluded—or Joseph's whereabouts were uncovered—I would return the gun to Madame's desk drawer. It had been a foolish notion to accept it in the first place.

I paced the length of my dressing room. I should talk to the directors, but staying out of their sight might be better. Out of sight, and hopefully out of mind. I could call out to the Angel, but with everyone not yet on stage, it was risky. And what if he didn't show? The muscles in my shoulders tightened. I needed to talk to him and find out what had happened.

A flash of pale blue caught my eye in the mirror.

I whipped around. An envelope sat propped on the sofa's armrest. As I tore the envelope open, the scent of jasmine perfume wafted from the paper. I knew that smell—Carlotta reeked of it, as did her home. Sighing, I read the letter.

Christine,

Forgive my direct speech, but I will come right to the point. I am troubled by what I have heard regarding your comportment with the Vicomte de Chagny.

He called at your residence yesterday and from what I understand, you encouraged him. I thought we had agreed you would steer clear of him? Let me restate my point. He is as good as engaged. Should you continue to see him, I will have you terminated from your position.

Avec tout affection,

Carlotta A.

The "C" of her name was larger than the other letters and curled possessively around her name. Her punctuated surname looked as if the point had been made with force.

How did she know Raoul had visited me? I felt as if I could no longer move about the opera house—or the city—without being watched. I remembered the man in the café across the street. It must have been Delacroix. I hadn't been sure at the time, but how else would Carlotta have known about Raoul's visit? Though, surely Delacroix wouldn't spy on me; he could just as easily come to my home and ask me. Besides, what did he care if I befriended Raoul. None of it made sense.

A slight stirring came from behind the mirror on the far wall.

My heart leapt into my throat. "Angel?"

A sharp rap at the door split the silence. I cried out in surprise.

"Christine, are you all right?" the chorus director called from the other side of the door.

I exhaled in relief and scurried to open it. "The sudden noise startled me, is all."

In spite of his impeccable grooming and expensive clothing, Gabriel's pinched expression gave his weaselly features a frightening look.

"Carlotta won't be singing tonight." He tugged at the sleeve of his frock coat. "She claims she has a sore throat. She was perfectly well yesterday," he added warily. "In other words, there's no time to waste. You go on in an hour."

I sucked in a breath. I would be singing—tonight!

"I'll prepare immediately."

He eyed my day dress, his disapproval plain. Gabriel never appeared rumpled or in last season's coats, cravats, or boots. "Get into costume."

"I won't let you down." I drew myself up to my full height, until the outline of my form cast a shadow across the top of his blond head.

"See that you don't." He glanced down and gasped in outrage. Crouching, he rubbed at an invisible scuff on his shoe. When he glanced up at me, I concealed a grin. "They're Italian leather. Balmoral boots. They cost me a fortune, but they were worth every centime."

After a moment of scrubbing, he straightened and waltzed away with more grace than a queen.

I closed the door, and stood in front of the mirror. I would be

Marguerite tonight! This was my chance to prove I could fill Carlotta's shoes. I could do this. I *would* do this!

"At last you return."

I gasped in surprise. "You're here."

The Angel's chuckle echoed behind the mirror. "I am always here."

I stared intently at the glass as if it might fracture and fall away, revealing the Angel behind it.

"You rescued me last week." Emotion swelled and my words came out strangled.

"You cried out for me, dear one, so I came."

"I came to warn you. Those men wanted to find you and somehow bring you to their boss. I don't know that a ghost can be 'found,' but I was worried. I–"

"Everyone wants to meet the opera ghost," he growled. "Lure him from hiding and terrorize him. I will terrorize them instead."

I wrung my hands at the ominous shift in his tone. "Joseph Buquet is missing. Do you know where he is?"

"He is not missing. He'll turn up soon enough." Another gruff laugh echoed from behind my dressing room wall.

My stomach churned violently at the thought of the machinist finding me again. "Is it safe for me to stay at the opera? I can find work elsewhere–"

"You will not leave!" the Angel roared.

I flinched at his tone, but held my tongue. How quickly his emotions changed.

After a moment of silence, he went on, tone pianissimo. "Leaving would destroy your chances of becoming a star. It would also disappoint your father."

I felt a wave of shame, like a coward. He was right. If I didn't stay–sing Carlotta's part as long as they needed me–how would I ever know if I was good enough? And there was Madame as well. We would flounder without this income. Caught between fear and duty, I sighed.

"The machinist won't hurt you again. That's a promise."

"I thought I was safe last time," I said, tilting my chin in defiance.

"I am sorry you were accosted. I thought my first warning to him would be enough, but I should have known better. He isn't the brightest of men. I assure you, you are safe now."

I considered his promise; I had no choice but to trust the ghost. And he had come to my rescue—again.

"I'll stay. For now."

"Of course you will. Now, begin your warm-ups."

I went through my exercises, notes playing on my tongue, rhythm coursing through my veins. I could hardly believe my luck—taking Carlotta's place at last, even if temporarily. I tingled with anticipation.

"You're ready." The Angel's tenor vibrated in the floorboards. "Remember to use all that wells up inside of you while you sing. Strength, confidence. Feel the emotions in the song—*be* the song. Let it flow into your blood and project it outward. Wrap the room in your voice. I will be there with you, guiding you."

I closed my eyes as I envisioned myself on stage, commanding the room.

"I'll be watching from box five."

With that, the Angel went silent.

My eyes fluttered open. Hastily, I applied maquillage and changed into my costume. Within minutes, I rushed to the cast room in the east wing off the stage. Meg spotted me and made her way toward me, a smile on her face.

"I'm performing tonight," I said, breathless from my mad dash through the halls. "Carlotta has a cold. Can you believe it? I'm going to play the lead!"

Meg embraced me. "Now you'll show them!"

I smiled at my friend. I didn't know what I had done to deserve her kindness, but I was grateful for it just the same.

A ballerina burst into the cast room, terror etched on her features.

The excitement in the room shifted, and all gathered around the petite ballerina.

"Jammet, what is it?"

I joined the others, though all I could see was the topknot of her raven hair.

"It's Joseph Buquet, the machinist!" Jammet exclaimed. "He's dead! They found him hanging from a rope on the third mezzanine below the stage."

Everyone gasped.

I staggered backward in shock. He was dead? No. He couldn't be.

"Jammet, are you certain it was the machinist?" Meg asked.

"Of course I'm certain," she said. "I've just passed the directors and the magistrate in the hall. There's a load of reporters as well."

"Was it suicide?" another chorus girl asked.

"That's what the directors said." Jammet's eyes filled with tears. "They said it looked as if he had been dead for several days. I rather liked the man. He gave me sweets."

"He was a pleasant fellow," another said. "Always said hello to me."

"He didn't commit suicide," another man from the chorus said. "He wasn't the type. There's a murderer among us."

Lucille, the only contralto in the opera's chorus, replied in her husky voice, "I would bet my wages it was the opera ghost."

I stumbled, knocking into an empty chair. It tipped and crashed to the floor. Everyone began talking at once. Would the ghost murder anyone else? Could he be stopped?

"Christine, weren't you wandering on the third mezzanine before he disappeared?" Gaston, a baritone in the chorus, called out to me.

I leaned on the table for support. "I was looking through a storage room at the old costumes and sets. But I never saw Joseph."

"Two minutes," the stage manager called from the doorway. "Everyone at the ready."

Grateful for the interruption, I slipped away from the crowd toward the back of the room. The murmurings died down as the chorus members filed out, preparing to take their positions on the stage. Joseph did not commit suicide. The man was too determined, too strong, and very sure of himself—and I knew the truth.

The Angel had killed him.

His earlier words pushed to the front of my mind. *The machinist won't hurt you again. That's a promise.*

My hands began to tremble. It was my fault. The Angel wanted to protect me—he *killed* someone because of me. The strength of his attachment to me rocked me to the core, and the trembling spread until my legs felt weak. Sick. My tutor was a murderer—*ghosts* really could be malevolent.

At that moment, the show commenced and Faust's opening soliloquy floated through the doorway. Soon, I would go on. I wanted to flee to the safety of Madame's house, far from dead men, from dark angels, and pretending to be a real star.

"Christine!" the stage director hissed, grabbing me by the arm. "I hope you're ready. I never thought I would see this day."

"I am ready, Monsieur." My voice cracked. It felt as if I had swallowed a desert.

The director rolled his eyes. "It sounds like it. You do know the lyrics, right?"

"Yes, of course," I said, my voice still shaking. "I'll drink some water and do another warm-up exercise. I'll be ready in a flash."

"You had damn well better be, or this will be your first and last night on that stage. Gabriel and the directors will be watching your every move."

"*Je comprends.*"

My breath came in short bursts. I needed to calm myself. With exactly ten minutes until curtain call, I focused on the Angel's advice: strength, confidence, emotion. The advice of a killer. My friend and protector was a murderer. My head spun as my emotions tangled. I wondered where he was now, with the police and the newspaper reporters milling about the building.

"Can you believe it?" Meg's tutu bounced around her waist as she walked. "First, the ghost sends all of those letters and now Joseph Buquet. I asked Maman about it, but she wouldn't spill a word."

When I didn't respond, she pursed her bow-shaped lips. "Are you all right?"

Something about her expression melted my defenses, and I

grabbed her arm. "Oh, Meg, what if I'm terrible tonight? The stage director just warned me this might be my only performance. And if I'm blamed for Joseph Buquet's death—"

"It's not your fault. You didn't even know Buquet."

I didn't correct her assumptions. Friend or no, I couldn't tell her all that had happened. It would only create more panic.

"As for the stage director—the old bag—ignore him," she said. "You're a wonderful singer or you wouldn't be the understudy in the first place. Besides, Gabriel approves. No doubting yourself tonight, do you hear me?"

I exhaled a deep breath and embraced her. "Thank you. You can't know how much I needed to hear this."

"Of course. We're friends."

I managed a smile.

The stage manager poked his head into the room. "You're on, Daaé!"

With a deep breath, I followed him. I paced to my designated place on the stage and stood tall, ignoring the tremor in my hands. The curtains parted and light flooded the stage. A silent crowd stared—at me.

In the split second before the music began, I peered out at the theatre, gaining my bearings and gathering my nerve.

Impress yourself upon them, Papa had said. *Expand your presence and fill the space. Don't give the power to the strangers who gaze at you.*

A sea of faces looked on from the parterre. Above them, the wealthy perched in box seats, decked in finery and feathered hats. I envisioned them entering from the east wing, reserved for the gentry, hanging their overcoats in the private room adjoining their seats, and Madame Giry attending to their demands. Would they like a refreshment of champagne or some other delight? Could she assist them with reservations after the show?

Packed into the seats of the parterre, a crowd of working-class theatre-lovers anticipated the show. Without doubt, they had scrimped and saved for weeks to purchase even the cheapest seats.

All stared at me.

I willed my stomach to unknot and my mind to clear of the horrible news. *Focus, Christine.*

The conductor posed on his platform in a black smoking jacket, face lined with concentration and hands prepared to take flight. He tapped his wand on the podium, and raised his arms into the air. With a flick of his wrist, the music began.

Pulse racing, my lips parted in anticipation. At the right moment, I began. I pushed out the first notes, heart thundering in my chest until the lyrics streamed from memory and flowed over my tongue without effort. Like magic, the music wrapped me in a cocoon. I drew strength from within, power from the muscles in my diaphragm, and channeled the energy out through my throat. The exertion warmed my blood, and energy charged through my limbs as I belted out the lyrics to *"Je voudrais bien savoir . . . Il était un Roi de Thulé,"* a song about Marguerite's wish to identify the stranger she had met in the town square.

One song after another, I sang as if my life depended upon it. Perhaps it did. I couldn't keep my eyes from wandering in the direction of box five, in search of the Angel. Yet no one—and nothing—filled the box that I could see, neither human nor shadow.

When at last it was time for my final piece, "D'amour, l'ardente flamme," I faced the west balcony and flung out my arms. As I glanced up, there, in the balcony nearest the stage, sat a familiar handsome gentleman. He stared at me as if enraptured by my voice. My heart registered his face in an instant and thumped wildly.

The vicomte, Raoul de Chagny.

A flood of images crashed over me: Raoul on my doorstep, Carlotta's words of warning. Joseph smashing my head—his dead body swinging from the rafters. I squeezed my eyes closed, forcing myself to focus on the song, pushing the final notes higher.

The contorted bodies in the fire, the smell of charring flesh.

With every ounce of concentration I possessed, I sang over the memories, pushing through the encroaching darkness. Only a few more bars and I could escape, figure out what came next.

Papa's glazed eyes, his gasp of final breath.

Black dots speckled my vision as my fear strained against my will. It was too much. I couldn't—

The orchestra played their final notes, and my legs collapsed beneath me.

Applause began, slowly at first, but it caught like fire and ripped through the auditorium until it thundered from the rafters. The crowd jumped to their feet, cheering, chanting my name.

The cheering contorted into the roar of fire consuming wood. I panted, staring wide-eyed at the beautifully carved ceiling. All those dead bodies. Papa's dead body.

And then, it all went silent.

~ 11 ~

Aflurry of voices filled my head. Slowly, I opened my eyes. "She's awake!" Meg's voice rang through the fog like a bell. "Christine, you were brilliant! Truly brilliant."

"Who is your teacher?" asked Lucille, a ballerina. "You must have been training like mad. Your voice was so different in practice."

A groan rumbled in my throat as Meg helped me into a sitting position. I looked about and spied my vanity, now covered in carnations, roses, and several varieties of flowers I couldn't name.

"I fainted?" I asked, wrapping my arms around my middle. "How long was I out?"

"You were in such raptures over the music you swooned, right there on stage." Meg beamed. "It was incredible! The audience chanted your name as you were carried away."

I frowned. It wasn't raptures over the music, but an attack of panic, a tidal wave of overwhelming fright, confusion, and exhaustion. But I had done it. I had brought the crowd to their feet. Yet, no sense of satisfaction stirred in my belly. No joy hummed in my veins. I felt strangely cold and bereft.

"You were amazing!" Meg said, face beaming.

On her right, a doctor pulled a stethoscope from his case. He adjusted the pince-nez perched on the end of his nose. "Mademoiselle, you were overcome and fainted on stage. It would be prudent to ensure all is well."

Several others pushed around him, or called from the doorway. "Bravo, Mademoiselle Daaé!"

They clamored for *me*. They wanted *me*.

"Can we clear the room?" a male voice cut through the din. "Mademoiselle Daaé needs her space."

The music of that voice sent an arrow to my heart.

Raoul, in his elegant evening wear, ushered everyone out of the room except for Meg and the doctor. "Christine, are you all right? You sang with such conviction, you wrung yourself out. I saw you grow pale from my box."

Heat spread across my cheeks and neck. "I am quite well."

Meg grinned widely. "You'll keep Carlotta on her toes now."

Hearing the diva's name brought back her warning. I had to ask Raoul to leave, though every part of me struggled against the thought. He wanted to be friends; that was all. I didn't see any real reason to turn him away, and yet, I knew I must.

"Thank you all, but if you will excuse me, I need to rest." I crumpled inwardly as Raoul's face fell. He was bound to think me cold, but I had no choice. For now, I needed to stay on at the opera, and displeasing Carlotta endangered my position.

"I'll visit you later," Meg said.

I rose from the chaise. "That will be all, Doctor, thank you."

"If you insist," Raoul said. "But should you fall again, I won't agree to you turning me away."

"Of course. Thank you for your kindness." I nodded as he packed his things.

Everyone left but Raoul.

"I had to make certain you were all right," he said. "I'll be meeting my brother in the ballet room, and then on to the Grand Foyer for an aperitif after the next show. Will you join us?"

The clock on my vanity table chimed eleven thirty—the hour I was supposed to meet the Angel.

I walked to my dressing room door and held it open, anxious for him to leave. "It was lovely to see you again, Raoul, but I'm going to follow the doctor's orders and rest."

His brow puckered, and then he nodded. "Yes, of course. Good night." He hesitated at the door, a quizzical look on his face before continuing on his way.

I closed the door and pushed out a breath. Raoul had come to see me! In spite of my anxiety, my lips turned up in a smile—only an instant. What was I going to do about this? I sat at my vanity to rub away the rouge on my lips and cheeks, and discovered a single red rose tied with black ribbon, lying amid the lavish bouquets of flowers. I held it to my nose.

"You did well tonight," the Angel said.

I jumped. "You're here!" My pulse kicked up a notch.

The ghost was a murderer.

Regardless of his loyalty to me, I had to be careful. Should I anger him, he might turn against me, too. I smeared my handkerchief with cream and wiped my face clean of maquillage, rubbing hard until my skin glowed pink from the exertion.

"Monsieur le Vicomte cares for you," he said, his voice low.

"We knew each other as children. He is soon to be engaged." I unpinned the braided coils on my head, and they unfurled down my back. I released my hair, running a brush through the blond snarls until they grew silky again.

"You would do well to stay clear of him. The vicomte will only hurt you. Seduce you with his pretty visage and his money, and leave you when he has what he wants. He would never marry a musician's daughter, and certainly not a stage performer."

I pulled the brush through my waves again with force. I didn't like his implication: Stage girls were considered promiscuous, even if celebrated, and now I was counted among them. It seemed the Angel was no different from the men I'd had to endure at Madame's salon. The thought brought a sharp slice of pain. I had thought our friendship a special one.

"Perhaps I will be more than just a singer one day," I said, my voice tinged with resentment.

"What else could you ask for, selfish girl?" The air crackled with the Angel's sudden anger. "Did you not revel in the attention from adoring fans?"

"That isn't the point."

"That's precisely the point," he snapped. "I know what is best for

151

you." His voice grew savage, possessive. "You will do as you're told! You will take Carlotta's place permanently, and we will run the opera stage together."

The image of Joseph Buquet reemerged, his dangling body swinging from a rope on the mezzanine. My face grew pale in the mirror, brush suspended in midair over my scalp. I knew I mustn't provoke the ghost. At last I said, "I want nothing more."

"Very good. And you will steer clear of the Vicomte de Chagny as well." His voice turned menacing. "I don't want to hurt you, Christine."

My Angel threatened me, as if I were Joseph Buquet or the rest of them. A crushing wave of disappointment washed over me. I thought I was different to him, somehow, special. With a trembling hand, I lay the brush on the table. I would have to tell Raoul I couldn't see him again. Carlotta might threaten me, but she wouldn't hurt me. But the ghost—my Angel—might.

I cleared my throat of the sudden tears clogged there. "The Vicomte de Chagny and I are only friends, but I will do as you ask. As for tonight, I don't think I can practice. I'm too tired."

"So these are the thanks I've earned. You won't spend time with the Angel who has taught you everything. Who saved your life. Have it your way. Good night!"

The room went silent.

Brimming with emotion, I remained at my vanity. Of course I was thankful the Angel had rescued me from my attackers, but I couldn't justify murder in any form. He could have had the man arrested instead. And now he threatened me. I gazed at my reflection in the mirror, the way my bottom lip quivered. Would the Angel truly harm his protégé? He seemed to care for me a great deal, but I couldn't predict his next move.

After waiting several minutes to ensure he had truly gone, I tugged at the buttons on my costume, slipped out of the muslin bodice, and pulled at the stays on my overly tight corset. Just a little looser and I could breathe. As the ties released and I exhaled, a whisper of sound came from the wall.

I froze.

I would swear I'd heard the faintest intake of breath.

Disturbed by the thought of being watched—especially while undressing—I made the decision to wear my costumes home. My stomach turned over at the thought of my breasts bared and legs exposed to the Angel. Visions of a floating form with leering eyes—and Joseph's bloated face—haunted me until dawn shimmied beneath the edges of my drapes. Yet when I opened my eyes at last, only one image popped into my head—the gun.

I shot up to a sitting position. I'd forgotten to bring it home. Leaving it at the opera made me too nervous. After the show tonight, I would return it to Madame. With Joseph gone, I had no need to keep it anyway.

I ambled around the house all afternoon, exhausted from worry, before setting out for the opera house. Thick fog blanketed the city landscape with gloom. I wished I could duck inside the cover and disappear for a while. I dreaded the coming conversation with Gabriel; would I lead for another day or would Carlotta return to the stage, my performance forgotten.

But first, I must retrieve the gun.

I entered the west side of the building, shook out my umbrella, and headed toward the staircase that led to the cast rooms. At the bottom of the stairs, a man in a curious white suit and colorful turban met my eye, nodded, and swept past. I turned to look over my shoulder, wondering if he were this mysterious Persian that Meg had mentioned. Lost in thought, I continued on my way.

As I passed the director's office, I couldn't ignore the shouting and slowed my pace.

"This is ludicrous!" Madame Giry flew out of the room and rushed past me, tendrils of chestnut hair sweeping across her cheeks.

I stared after her, stomach churning. Madame delivered notes from the opera ghost to the directors. I wondered what had happened now.

"You will lose your job for this!" Carlotta shrieked as she emerged from the office behind Madame Giry. She waved a letter covered in red ink over her head.

Madame Giry ignored the reproach and picked up speed, turning at the end of the hall.

I shrank against the wall in silence, not wanting to become involved.

Carlotta stomped through the hallway, intent on catching the concierge—until she noticed me. She stopped suddenly, hands on hips.

"Well, aren't you just the rising star?" Her voice dripped with sarcasm. "The directors found your performance 'riveting,' I believe was the word they used. But I'm returning to the stage this evening, so you can save yourself the trouble of getting ready. My voice is in top form and I have many friends who will be here tonight." Her large brown eyes narrowed. "I hope you enjoyed your brief time in the light, because there won't be any more. Those ridiculous notes that are circulating do not frighten me, or the directors."

Her open hostility made my spine stiffen, and I hardened my resolve. I had proven my worth last night, despite being overcome at the end. This woman wouldn't bully me. Not anymore.

In the chilliest tone I could muster, I said, "I have no idea what you're referring to. I wrote no such notes."

"Someone is pretending to be a ghost, and leaving notes with instructions. Oddly, many of them reference you. We all suspect you're the culprit."

"Is that what the directors think?" I asked. "I would never do such a thing. At the very least, I have my pride."

Her eyes narrowed and she leaned closer. "You're playing a dangerous game, Christine. I know everyone in this town. One word from me and you're finished."

With that, she spun on her heel and stalked away in a cloud of perfume and conceit.

I groaned. This was the Angel's fault. I hadn't the slightest idea how to untangle the mess. All of those notes! The directors must see me as a pest—a jealous, foolish woman—in spite of their glowing account of my performance. Fury sparked inside me. If the Angel could have his way, I would also have mine. I would stand up for myself, my reputation. I was tired of being pushed around.

I barreled down the stairs to my dressing room. This ghost would show himself—now—and explain his motives! If he didn't, I would expose him to the directors. The charade was over, like it or not. As I neared the end of the hall, I stopped. A man leaned against the door of my dressing room with his back to me.

At the sound of my footsteps, he turned.

"Christine," Raoul said, a smile lighting his face. "I was hoping to see you."

I halted, too astonished to continue. My anger vanished, but the anxiety I had felt for the last twenty-four hours rushed up my throat. He couldn't be here, but God Almighty, the unexpected beauty of him set off a siren inside my head.

"H-hello, Raoul."

"Is now a bad time?" He tucked a book under his arm. "I can come again another day, but I was hoping we might talk." He ran his free hand through his tousled blond hair.

He isn't a gentleman, I reminded myself. Leading another woman to believe he would propose marriage, but seeking friendship with me at the same time, was wrong. It might destroy the woman's trust, her feelings. A voice whispered in my head, *And yours*. I shook my head. I had to resist his charms and see him for who he truly was. A man many longed to call their own, a man who had his pick of the town among women—a man who had already chosen his future bride.

"You were marvelous last night." His eyes gleamed. "Your father would have been so proud."

In spite of my resolve, warmth bloomed in my chest. "I'm honored you think so."

"The honor is mine."

His intense expression turned my bones to liquid. I looked down,

155

attempting to seal my emotion away. When I lifted my head again, he stood only an arm's length from me. I ran a hand along the slippery folds of my umbrella to avoid his gaze. My hesitation, and all of those warnings, rang like a tocsin in my head.

I straightened, cleared my throat. "I'm afraid I must practice, Raoul."

The hope in his eyes faded. "Oh, I apologize, of course. Another time." He held the book in his hands toward me. "I almost forgot. I brought something for you."

Against my will, my heart fluttered.

"I wanted you to have this." He pressed the volume into my hand. "I bought it some time ago, but it should belong to you."

Emotions whirled through me like a cyclone as I caressed the volume: *The Sharper Detected and Exposed* by Jean-Eugène Robert-Houdin, the master of magic. Raoul had given me a book of magic to go with the beautiful box he'd gifted me so many years ago. I gaped at him, touched by his thoughtful gesture—and the sight of the forbidden tome. But Raoul was unaware of my swearing off magic. And he remembered—from all that time ago—how illusions comforted me. With care, I cracked the book's cover, releasing the smell of dust and old paper, and skimmed the table of contents. Suddenly I couldn't remember why I had given up the pastime I loved most.

"It's an older volume." Raoul laughed nervously. "One of the few remaining original copies. You used to love illusions. I hope you do, still? You were quite good at them, as I recall. And your mother had loved them, as well, yes?" He probed my face with an intense gaze.

"It's beautiful," I whispered, suddenly breathless. I held the book to my chest. "I will cherish it."

He beamed at me. "I do so enjoy bestowing gifts on my friends."

I wanted to take his hand in mine, but I was far too fond of him already, and our time needed to come to an end. His generosity made what I had to say so much more difficult.

A sigh—or a soft groan—came from inside the wall near my head.

The smile on my face froze. I knew that sound.

"After the show tomorrow, I'll stay for an aperitif in the foyer. I hope you'll join me? I can introduce you to my brother again, and some of our friends. I asked yesterday, but you seemed distraught after your performance."

"Yes, I was overcome." Though I shouldn't meet with Raoul, I knew the directors would expect the most prominent members of the cast to attend the gathering, and now that I had played the lead, that group included me. I would attend this time, and tell Raoul I couldn't see him again after. Perhaps by then I could think of an excuse.

The groaning sound grew louder, this time near my feet.

My heart skipped wildly. I knew the Angel was nearby, or would be very soon.

"Thank you for the book," I said, opening my dressing room door.

He tipped his head forward in a polite nod. "I hope to see you tomorrow evening."

I nodded, a tight smile on my face. I'd barely made it inside my dressing room, when the voice sliced the air.

"You were good last night, but not *magnifique*," the Angel greeted me disdainfully. "Don't let the others' praise go to your head."

I removed my cape and hung it on a hook. "I sang with all I had, with my very soul. And that wasn't enough?"

"I want to feel your devotion, your love. It didn't shine the way it should."

I wondered if he meant my love for the music, or for him. I respected his talent, craved his guidance, but could not love a man-ghost who threatened me and killed without a second thought. How could he possibly think otherwise.

"You do not feel for me as I feel for you." His voice dipped to a middle C.

Cringing, I measured my reply. "You are a ghost, a voice inside my head. How could I love you?"

"A voice that has made you—saved your life—and guides you in your time of need," he snarled.

"I am grateful for your guidance," I said quickly to placate him, "and for saving my life. It's a debt I can never repay."

His hollow laugh shook the gilded mirror on the wall.

Frowning, I walked toward it. Was the wall hollow there, behind the glass? I touched the etchings on the outer edges of the mirror, pausing to see my tight lips and the tension gathered along my jaw.

"Grateful to me, yet you love the Vicomte de Chagny."

"I've hardly made his acquaintance. That is, not since I was a child." Though my words sounded assured, my heart throbbed at the thought of loving Raoul.

"Yet he is there when you swoon, and seeks you out to give you gifts."

My eyes drifted to the book of illusions on the sofa.

"He's renewing an old friendship. I assure you, he isn't interested in more. He's courting another woman. I'll avoid him when possible like we agreed."

A laugh that sounded more like a snarl, ripped through the room. "If you choose to pursue your relationship with the Vicomte de Chagny—or promise yourself to anyone else—I will never visit you again. Your music will leave you, and your protector will vanish. Your hopes of a career on the stage will collapse." When I did not reply, he continued, "No man can possess you, Christine, or he will pay."

I struggled against a flash of anger, and an unexpected wave of sadness. I would have to sacrifice my own happiness—and the ghost would prefer that—to keep me under his thumb. If he cared for me, or loved me as his words implied, he wouldn't ask such a thing.

Love did not take prisoners.

I gave the mirror my back. "I've had no proposals."

"You will soon. But remember who admires you most, who keeps you on the stage. Refuse them, or you and your nobleman will pay the price. Is that understood?"

I stared glumly at Raoul's gift without reply.

"My dear Christine, you don't understand." His voice took on a passionate tone. "I'm writing an opera that will make the crowd weep with its perfection, cry out at its magical sets! You will sing it with me on the most famous stage in the world." His voice softened. "Never fear, the music will seduce you, and in time, you will come to love me. Your pure heart is the only one that understands me, sweet Christine."

He took my silence for acquiescence and continued, "Until my opera is complete, you will take Carlotta's place. If the new directors refuse to remove her, I will deal with them. As for your fame, it will grow and the invitations will flood in from all over the city. But you will sing in one place only—at the opera house, with me. It will increase their demand for you."

A shiver ran over my body. He would "deal" with the directors? I didn't want to find out what that meant. I couldn't imagine disrupting the opera schedule for his piece, ignoring the directors' authority, and taking over the stage—all with the infamous ghost. I would be hated by all.

I forced a cheerful tone. "I look forward to hearing your opera."

He laughed, a more joyous tone. "I thought you might. Now then, prepare yourself for the show. I have matters to attend to, but I will return for our lesson."

Silence surrounded me.

He truly believed he could control everyone—and that I would love him for it! I plopped down on my sofa. What was I going to do? I leaned my chin on my hand, eyes wandering around the room, searching for an answer that wasn't there. At last they came to rest on the vanity drawer.

The gun! I'd forgotten it entirely.

I leapt toward the vanity and slid the drawer open. I reached toward the back, seeking the fabric of my handbag and the cold metal of the gun's barrel. Instead, my fingertips scraped upon wood.

My blood pumped faster. I swiped my hand through the back of the drawer again. Nothing. I bent to peer inside the drawer.

Empty.

Perhaps I had put it in another drawer? I yanked open each, one after the other, blood racing.

The gun was gone.

Think. I had to think. Had I left the building with it last night? I was so distracted; my mind was so foggy. I didn't remember doing so, but perhaps I had left it in the coach. Though not the most convenient of circumstances, that would be better than considering the weapon at large among the cast—or in the Angel's hands. But if he was a spirit, what would he need with a gun? Somewhere in my gut, I knew. There was more to the Angel than I had first assumed. And soon, I would learn the truth, one way or another.

In spite of the sinking sensation in my stomach, I forced myself to put on a happy face and made my way to the auditorium. How would I explain the gun's disappearance to Madame Valerius? I groaned as I reached for the door leading into the theatre. Inside, the cast murmured among themselves. The directors had called a meeting, presumably to discuss Joseph Buquet's death. I strolled down the aisle and slid into a seat, its usual scarlet a muddied crimson in the half-light.

Messieurs Richard and Montcharmin walked onto the stage.

I felt a pinch on my arm and turned to see Meg leaning forward in her seat. She winked when I met her eye.

"Attention, everyone. We called this meeting to discuss a tragic incident that occurred last night." Montcharmin rested his hands on his protruding belly. "As you know, someone died here, under our roof. A well-liked machinist by the name of Joseph Buquet was found hanged. Whether or not he committed suicide is unclear at this time, but we have spoken with Inspector Mifroid. He will be interviewing many of you soon. We ask that you comply with his requests."

"What of the opera ghost?" Pierre—the man with the scary mole—called out.

"We're looking into this nonsense." Monsieur Richard tucked his hand inside an open flap of his vest. "I'm sure there is a perfectly rational explanation, but let it be known, we will get to the bottom of this, and those responsible for the pranks will be brought to justice.

The police will be searching the premises for clues. Don't be alarmed. They are doing their job. Any other information should be brought to us immediately."

"The police will do you no good if it's a ghost," someone shouted.

The cast murmured.

I focused on making my face a mask. I didn't want to be implicated as the ghost's accomplice. Still, the police would come for me at some point, ask questions, and I would have to tell them the truth. At least, the partial truth. My name was all over those letters so I would have some explaining to do. For now, I needed to deal with the missing gun. I sank further into my chair. What if the inspector found the gun before I did?

"The ghost is real," Little Jammet whispered to another dancer.

Indeed he was, and this time I wouldn't make the mistake of trying to warn him. He had killed a man and threatened me. He could defend himself. Besides, the thought of confronting him . . . I shivered in fear.

"Just one more quick announcement," Montcharmin said. "Tomorrow after the performance, we hope you will join us for some merriment in the Grand Foyer. We would like to celebrate our transition here as new directors."

"And bring some cheer to the place, for God's sake," the other director said.

Everyone laughed.

"Refreshments will be served."

A light smattering of applause rippled through the room.

I stood, stomach full of lead, and started back to my room. I had to find the gun before the police did.

~ 12 ~

I plopped down on a chaise in Madame's salon, weary from the day's exertions. The last few hours, I'd torn apart my dressing room, searched the cast room, and gone through many of the storage rooms. I hadn't even found my handbag, let alone the missing weapon. Tears of frustration swam in my eyes. With a huff, I slammed my fist onto the seat beside me. Who had stolen the gun—and, more perplexing—what did they want with it?

"You've received another invitation," Claudette called merrily from the kitchen. Her work boots scuffed a melody on the floorboards as she walked from room to room. She handed me the beautiful stationery card. I would have to refuse the invitation, like the others. I hadn't forgotten the Angel's warning. So many warnings from so many directions.

I sighed heavily, and slipped my finger under the flap. The Duchess of Zurich requested I sing at her salon, and she would pay me more than I had ever made—double a month's salary at the opera house. I looked at Claudette, eyes wide. If I accepted her invitation, I would be able to replace Madame's gun before she noticed it missing. Though I didn't have the slightest idea how to buy one, I would figure that out later. Madame didn't expect me to return it soon, if ever, but I didn't want to admit I'd lost it. I needed to replace it and this was my chance.

"Well?" Claudette asked.

"I'm going to accept." I *had* to go. I would just have to lie. What was one more lie at this point?

"Good. The money will be helpful." Claudette nudged the edge of the frayed rug with her boot. "Say, can I ask you something?" Her usual bold demeanor shifted to one of timidity.

"Of course."

"It's about your book," she said. "I would like to read it."

"Which book?"

"The book the gentleman gave you. Monsieur le Vicomte." She studied her blunt fingernails.

"The book of illusions?" A lump formed in my throat instantly. Just the mention of the book stirred inklings of envy that Claudette could read the text and feel no guilt or self-loathing; envy that she could delight in the techniques and daydream about magicians without her throat closing from remembered smoke. She could enjoy the gift Raoul had given me, and I could not.

Noticing the conflict in my eyes, she rushed to reply, "I understand if it's too special to you."

"No," I replied firmly. "Someone should read it, or it will go to waste."

"Go to waste? You won't read it, then? Whyever not? Magic is part of who you are." Claudette put her hand on mine. "Always has been, even if you haven't practiced in a while."

I said nothing and glanced away.

"Christine?" She said my name with such soberness, I met her eyes. "I understand why you stopped playing cards. You feel responsible for your papa's death. But we both know that isn't the truth of it. Things happen, beyond our control. The good Lord takes you when he's ready. He wanted to hear your papa's music in heaven, I say. It's time you stopped blaming yourself. If you enjoy magic . . . Well, life goes fast. Embrace it."

Emotion swelled from the pit of my stomach, and rushed up my throat. Tears burned my eyes. All this time I had kept everything inside, forced away a part of me that was true and real. I knew that deep down all along–I knew it now. All I had allowed myself was to sing, to honor Papa. Everything I did, I did for him, to make him proud. Yet magic had been a part of Mother's gifts, too. Wasn't that just as important–to embrace all of who I was? Seeing Raoul again, holding the book of illusions in my hands, had unleashed something.

Claudette wiped away the tears slipping down my cheeks. "It's about time, isn't it?"

"You're right. I know you're right." I blew my nose and hugged her fiercely. "I've been so disgusted with myself. So afraid."

"You're a talented lady. With many gifts. Wasting them would be the biggest tragedy here, don't you know?" She smiled and offered me another clean handkerchief.

I exhaled, smiling through the tears. "You're right. You should—we should—read the book."

Claudette's expression turned sheepish again. "Now then, there's just one more problem."

"What is it?"

Her creamy skin deepened to crimson until her freckles were hardly distinguishable. "I don't read well. I was hoping you could read it to me, or at least help me?"

Stunned, I sat silently a moment before replying. I couldn't imagine not knowing how to read. It was one of the few pastimes Papa and I enjoyed together daily. In spite of our pitiful circumstances, we always had a few books on hand, and borrowed others whenever possible. I would help her. It would be a good exercise for me; to confront the panic, push past all of my pent up emotion. I was nineteen years old, an adult. I needed to act like one.

"I would be delighted to teach you," I said at last.

She kissed my cheeks and whirled me around. "We'll make a grand time of it."

I laughed and threw my arms around her neck. It would be grand all right, but I hoped not of the panic-inducing variety.

"I'll just fetch it from your night table." Before I could answer, Claudette strutted from the room, her gray skirts swirling behind her.

Nervously, I picked at a small flap of skin along my thumbnail until it tore and the skin underneath became raw and tender. I hope I didn't regret this.

"*Voilà.*" She placed the book on the table between us and scooted beside me on the sofa.

"Well"—I inhaled a deep breath—"I suppose we should start from the beginning." I opened the book of illusions, my fingers tingling as they ran the length of the page. So many things to learn. A rush of familiar emotion—wonder, excitement, comfort—flowed through me.

"It has been so long," I whispered. After a moment more of reverence, I grinned at Claudette. "Shall we begin?"

I returned to the magic book each day with ink-stained fingers, to take notes into the late hours until my lantern ran dry and my candles snuffed out. Memories of Mother rushed back: her beautiful voice, her spun-gold hair that cascaded down her back, the sleight of hand and other games she played with me. The illusions had tied me to her memory always. For the first time since Papa's death, I felt like myself again, but a newer, wiser version. A happier version. I had allowed the anxiety to drain away, and started down the slow path to forgiving myself.

Once I had devoured every page of the book, I retrieved my precious magic box. I smiled. Raoul had given me both the box and the book. He understood my heart then as he did now, and he didn't even know it. I had to thank him for his encouragement, for bringing me back to such joy. After the performance Friday evening, I would seek him out in the smoking room just as he had asked, but would keep it formal. I didn't have to tell him we couldn't be friends. I could keep him at a distance—after I expressed my gratitude.

I practiced my old illusions and new ones, though I was limited by the few trinkets I had used as a child. To what end I practiced, I didn't know, but I felt alive. I liked to sing, but magic! It challenged me and kept me awake at night, puzzling over new ideas. It made each day an adventure. I combed through my box of tools, throwing out broken pieces and sorting the rest.

I pulled the drawstring purse from my top dresser drawer and emptied all the money I had saved onto the bed. I had enough to pay the doctor this month and some for personal use, though perhaps I

should save it just in case. The salon money would cover the gun, but Madame might need something else. Abruptly, I grabbed my handbag and slipped my change purse inside it. I cared very much for Madame, but I needed new equipment. I had earned it.

I pulled on my cape and set out for the most popular magic shop in Paris: Mayette Magie Moderne. Nestled on a corner in the Latin Quarter, it abutted my favorite market. I descended from the hackney cab, walked uphill, and entered the small shop. As I closed the door, a bell jingled to announce my arrival. A single lantern burned inside, its flame glinting off the glass counter and the metallic instruments displayed in the front windows.

No one greeted me, but a door behind the counter sat ajar and a gentleman tipped in his chair, puffing on a Gambier clay pipe like the one I had seen the choral director use. I walked through the cramped space filled with displays of wands and top hats, handkerchiefs and gloves, magic coins, pamphlets, an array of books, and drawings of specialty items for order. I thumbed through a booklet with many types of mirrors. I wondered if the friendly machinist, Georges, would help me build a cabinet. I would need one for some of my newer illusions.

I ran my finger down the page and stopped on a picture of Platonized glass; a special mirror coated in liquid metal and heated until the platinum affixed to the glass. Curious, I peered at the drawing more closely.

The gentleman from the back room set down his pipe and joined me. "Can I help you find something?" He ran a hand over his full gray beard and peered at me with a curiosity that bordered on suspicion.

"I would like a set of handkerchiefs and a wand."

The vendor leaned over the counter and peered at me closely, an eyebrow raised.

His surprise could only mean one thing—a woman, unescorted and alone, wanted to purchase his wares. An illusionist's wares. He'd never seen that before, it was clear.

I shook off the discomfort of his shocked stare. At one time, the shopkeeper's gaze would have made me doubtful of my place. Not today, not now. I belonged here. There was no rule against female magicians and I would join their ranks if I pleased, even if I never performed in public.

"Also, I would like to know how much this glass costs, as well as one of these multipaned mirrors." I folded my gloved hands and rested them on the counter.

"Are you buying glass for an illusionist? If so, he should see the drawings himself and bring in specific dimensions."

Indignant at his insinuation—that I could neither choose which one I needed, nor be anything more than an assistant—I squared my shoulders. "With all due respect, I am quite able to choose a piece of glass with proper dimensions. I know exactly what I'm looking for."

"Very well," he said slowly. "It doesn't matter who wants it or who orders it, as long as you pay."

With an apologetic smile, he turned the book of drawings around to face him and flipped open a notebook. He shook his quill pen and rolled it between his hands to warm the ink inside. One by one, he recorded the items in his notebook in one column, then filled in the prices of each on a second column. "The handkerchiefs will cost you one franc each, the wand two. I have a smaller version of the glass pane available now if you want it. As for the mirrors, they will cost you fifty. In all, it will run you seventy-six francs."

"Seventy-six francs!" I shook my head. "The other shop I visited could give me the lot for thirty francs." Though a bald-faced lie, I knew the man was trying to swindle me, like any shopkeeper might a woman. One look at my gold embroidered red cape, lace collar, and lamb-hide gloves, and he assumed I had unlimited funds to spend. He didn't know they had all come secondhand from one of Madame Valerius's wealthy friends.

The expression on his face shifted from conceit to one of newfound respect. "I assure you"—he said—"this mirror is made with the finest materials. It even resembles one used by the great Robert-Houdin. But I can knock a few francs off and give you the lot for sixty francs without delivery fees, of course."

I met his gaze squarely. "Forty-five francs, including delivery, or I go elsewhere. You can deliver the order to my home as soon as it's ready."

"Done." A bemused smile lifted the corners of his iron-gray mustache.

A young blonde had come from nowhere, in pretty clothes, and bartered like a hardened businessman. I couldn't help but smile, proud of my determination to get what I wanted.

I fished a wad of bills out of my handbag, counted them, and laid them on the counter. "That should do it."

The gentleman scooped up the money and gave me another hard stare.

"Do you have something to say, Monsieur?"

He leaned further over the counter, as if he wanted to share a secret.

"*Oui?*" I said expectantly.

"Illusionists must guard their secrets, Mademoiselle. Be careful where you share them. Often, your friends aren't who you think they are."

I thought of the few friends I possessed—Claudette, Meg, and Monsieur Delacroix, maybe even Raoul. I could trust them . . . mostly. I remembered Meg's wagging tongue about all the goings-on in the opera. Still, I knew she meant no harm and had helped me many times.

I nodded. "Thank you."

"And, Mademoiselle?" His forehead scrunched, his voice turned somber. "Beware of ghosts. Conjurers tangle themselves in the spirit world and wind up being haunted themselves, and not just by those they summon, but by the living."

I knew all too well what it was to be haunted.

"I thank you again, Monsieur. Good night." With pride, I left the magic shop and joined the bustle of pedestrians in the street. Next, off to find tools.

"I think I need a bigger cloak to obscure the entire thing," I said, stepping back from the trunk.

As I suspected, Georges was delighted to help me build a cabinet with a false bottom. When I had shown the machinist my drawings, he looked stunned, but quickly got to work.

Claudette stood beside a large crate, hand on her hip. Not only had she been amenable to working on illusions, but she relished being part of my evolving skills. I couldn't imagine working through them without her.

"You're smiling," she said, untying her apron. It had been nothing but a nuisance each time she tried to escape the sack inside the trunk.

"You would make a wonderful assistant," I said. "A real one, on a stage. You're pretty and spirited. You've got just the right amount of showmanship, yet you seem to know when to be reserved. You're a natural."

And she was endlessly patient while we practiced. Since we had begun, I worked constantly. Why I needed to perfect these illusions was a mystery to me—it wasn't as if I would have the chance to perform them.

Except perhaps at a salon, a voice in my head said.

But it was an absurd idea. The *salonnières* would want me to sing, not perform illusions with my maid-assistant.

I ran a hand over my hair. "Let's wrap it up for tonight. I need a break."

Hungry from the evening's exertions, I devoured leftover potage and bread before heading to bed. After practicing all week during the day, and music lessons at night with the Angel, I felt the pull of deep fatigue. Within minutes, sleep seduced me and I found myself standing on a stage. In my dream, I pranced like a ballerina and twirled in a white costume adorned with sashes in blues and silvers that lapped like waves against my body.

Claudette walked toward me. She shimmered in her own costume layered with alternating patches of color that resembled fish scales. The dress ended well above her knees. As she moved, the light caught sparkles painted carefully along her brow and dotted across the rounds of her cheeks. Behind us, a set flat mimicked the sea with fish and corals, an octopus, and even a squid.

Claudette waved a long swatch of fabric in the same watery hues over my body.

I disappeared and a faceless crowd cheered.

A new set whirred as it moved into place. This time, a grand organ rolled to center stage, and bodiless skeleton arms appeared from hidden panels in the wall, cradling violins. On cue, the violins and organ played in unison—without the help of human hands.

The crowd applauded once more.

With a puff of smoke and a flash of light, I reappeared, this time in a billowing white gown and gloves. I raised my arms toward the ceiling of the theatre and sang an aria I didn't recognize. My voice carried over the instruments and filled the auditorium. As I sang, I glanced out of the corner of my eye at something moving in the wings of the stage. A shadowy figure stood in black redingote, bow tie, and top hat. A woman floated at the man's side, beautiful with her gleaming blond hair and blinding gown made entirely of crystals. Her face felt familiar somehow, but I couldn't quite place it.

The man raised his arms like a conductor and my voice responded, pushing the notes further. There was only one being my voice responded to in such a way—the Angel. Even as I sang, I puzzled over his presence at my magic show. Why would he be there?

He lifted his hand and my voice obeyed.

As he took a step closer, the lanterns on the stage threw light across his face.

Stricken, I stopped, midsong, and the crowd murmured.

The Angel wore a mask.

~ 13 ~

After I awoke from the dream, it took the whole day to shake the haunted feeling the mask inspired. When at last it was time to head to the Duchess of Zurich's home, I was relieved. Her home—if one could call it such—lumbered across an entire city block. Though imposing, the mansion was also elegant with its statuettes, gilded fence posts, and sweeping lawns. Candles lighted a ruddy brick walkway that lead to the front doors. Even in the early winter months, the grounds were a veritable wonderland with snow-dusted topiaries, lighted pathways through a maze of hedges, and marble fountains that gleamed in the twilight. A swathe of clouds floated lazily across a violet sky, finally eclipsing a fingernail moon still on the rise. I couldn't believe I was about to perform here.

A butler ushered me into the front hall, took my cloak, and showed me to my position and where the other performers would stand as well: a pianist, a trio of ballerinas, and—to my surprise—a conjurer. I didn't know why it should surprise me. Conjurers weren't uncommon at the larger salons, but I hadn't seen one in nearly four years.

I floated through the salon to a corner near the French doors. The wealthy mingled with one another; they laughed and conversed in a restrained way, faces prim. It suited me that they kept their distance. I had little interest in striking up friendships with those who would always treat me as inferior, even if their belittlement was disguised in a sheen of pretty manners and polite gestures. I gulped down the last of my punch, grateful for the alcohol it contained.

The hostess returned to the makeshift stage, interrupting my thoughts. "Ladies and gentlemen, please welcome Stéfan the Illusionist."

The conjurer stepped into position. Though I needed to warm up and prepare for my own show, I *had* to watch. I settled into a chair along with the audience.

Stéfan opened with a tepid introduction, followed by a series of amateur tricks. "And then it becomes a dove!" The conjurer threw his hands into the air.

Only the dove didn't spring from his hands. Instead, the bird poked its head out from the gentleman's sleeve and began to coo.

The audience guffawed and whistled.

I winced. Poor fellow.

The conjurer stuttered and began a new trick to cover his embarrassment.

I glanced across the room at our hostess, beribboned and feathered in enough lavish blues to make the most glorious of peacocks jealous. She was so absorbed in conversation with a gentleman that she didn't appear to notice the lackluster show. I wondered how in the world the duchess found this conjurer. Perhaps he had approached her. I scanned the faces in the audience. At least half of them leaned toward an acquaintance for a bit of gossip with their neighbor, or looked over their shoulder at the doorway, hoping they might escape without being noticed. The poor man didn't realize just how horrid he truly was.

I stood and inched along the outer edge of the room, scooting behind the curtain of the stage. I had hardly made it when the audience began to heckle the conjurer. Nervous I might receive the same treatment, I gulped down a glass of water and began my warm-up.

The duchess slipped behind the curtain in front of me, stuck her hand through the folds of the fabric covering the stage, and, without warning, and yanked the conjurer's jacket. He stumbled backward and fell on his rear. His hat tumbled from his head. A clump of wadded silk spilled from it to the floor.

More laughter arose from the crowd.

"I am sorry about the spill, Stéfan, but that will be all, thank you. You're sending people to the door," the duchess said, taking the stage.

The conjurer grasped the pole on his left to heft himself to his feet.

The pole couldn't support his weight and it teetered, causing the entire frame of the stage to sway. Those seated in the front row rushed from their chairs to avoid being slammed by the rods.

"Watch out!" someone shouted.

Two men jumped out of their seats and grabbed it just in time, pushing it back into place.

Several others laughed at the spectacle.

Had I been the hostess, I would have been mortified, but instead, the duchess dissolved into a fit of giggles. When she could breathe again, she raised her arms to regain everyone's attention.

"For our final performance this evening"—she said in a gay voice —"we welcome Mademoiselle Christine Daaé, soprano extraordinaire, straight from the Nouvel Opéra."

A smattering of applause arose and the murmuring settled some as people reclaimed their seats.

I stepped through the curtain and faced the crowd, clasping my hands together. Finding a point on the back wall, I envisioned hollowing out my insides to make room for the air I would need. Become a vessel for the music that carved a path through me, until it reached my throat and vibrated my vocal chords.

After a moment's pause, the pianist began.

As I sang, all evaporated but me—my father's daughter—singing with all my heart. Strength bubbled up from within and I drew upon it like a woman at a well, desperate to quench her thirst. That confidence—the same I'd felt when I bartered with the shopkeeper— again came rushing to the surface. The rapt attention of the audience pressed around me like a blanket, warming my blood, fueling my confidence further. I liked being on stage. No, I *adored* it; I felt more alive there than anywhere. For the first time since Papa had died, I could feel the first inklings of contentment, in spite of all else that ran amok at the opera house. In this moment, I understood—I knew— somehow that my time at the opera was limited. Someday soon, I would embark on my own path.

After a few songs, I bowed to the applause, warmed with elation and relief that the performance was over. Thirsty, I headed to the refreshment table. The duchess joined me, signaling the attendant at the table to pour her an aperitif of Bardinet.

She sipped the cherry brandy and winked at me. "You, young lady, were magnificent. You stepped in early without a fuss, and didn't show a monstrous attitude like many other singers I've known. I'll have Jacques pay you double. I hope you'll consider joining us again."

"Double?" I nearly dropped my water glass. "You're certain?"

"Never question someone who offers to pay you. Take it and be off, as quickly as you can, before whoever it is changes their mind."

I laughed at her candor. "Thank you, Madame."

"Have a nice evening." She winked.

I watched in amusement as she threaded through the crowd, laughing and nodding, her feathers bobbing. It had been worth it, risking the Angel's wrath. Now I could buy a new gun with one night's work, pay Georges for the cabinet, and still have money left.

After receiving payment, I made for the door. A footman led me to a waiting carriage. When I was deposited home, I rushed up the front steps and to my room. After counting the bills, I hid the money in an old handbag in the back of my armoire.

The clock chimed eleven. I needed to rest, but I didn't feel tired. Though it was late, exhilaration hummed in my veins. I felt less burdened, freed from fear and the weight of the unknown. My eyes fell upon the book of illusions on the bedside table. It had changed everything. I threw open the balcony door and a wintry gust whooshed into the room, whipping through my hair and under my skirts. In spite of the chill, I relished the air, felt emboldened by it.

I stepped outside and stared at the crows perched silently on the eaves of the neighboring house. They were still as death beneath the dome of ebony sky. I shivered, my mood dampening slightly. Were they sleeping, or were they watching me?

A scraping sound came from the far corner of the balcony.

Another bird, perhaps? I glanced in that direction, catching sight of several motionless lumps on the ground. Curious, I walked to the corner and bent down to inspect the mysterious items. With a gasp, I fell on my heels and scrambled backward.

A dozen crows lay dead, their eyes unseeing, with red ribbons tied around their broken necks. A single red rose lay next to them.

He had come—the Angel. The Angel of Death.

I had disobeyed him, by going off to sing elsewhere, and that angered him. The bubble of happiness around me popped and fear snaked through my body until I shook. Someone would pay each time the Angel's wishes went unheeded. This was his message. He could reach me beyond the opera house.

I would tell him about the gun—why I needed the money—and make him understand. He had to forgive my indiscretion. I dared another look at the dead birds. Something glinted near their bodies.

What in the world?

I reached toward the source of light, winking just above the bodies. My fingers met the cool surface of beveled glass. I frowned and leaned closer.

I snapped upright once more, the truth hitting me with unexpected surprise.

It was an illusion.

There was only one dead bird, its body reflected in fractured panes of glass like a prism. The Angel had tried to deceive me. I crouched in front of the glass to study its size and angles. The gears turned in my ever-curious brain. Had the Angel etched the glass himself, or purchased it somewhere? I could make use of something similar for my own illusions, perhaps. I raced inside for my notebook and quill pen to sketch its dimensions and take notes. As an afterthought I grabbed a lantern and threw my cloak around my shoulders. My exhilaration returning, I stepped into the cold night air once more.

The illusion was gone.

~14~

The following day, an angry hiss greeted me as I entered my dressing room. A rash of goose bumps ran over my arms and I quickly shut the door.

"Who's there?" I called, inviting the dark one to answer.

The sound of nails screeching against the wall sent a tremor along my spine.

"You left a dead crow on my balcony," I said. "Why? You know I am your willing student. There is no one who is able to teach me as you do, who inspires my music more. I already do your bidding. Why would you frighten me?"

"Already do my bidding?" The menace in his laugh seeped from the walls into the room, filling me with dread. "You aren't doing my bidding, dear one. Believe me, if you were, you would know it." His voice deepened. "I've told you not to sing for anyone but me, here, in my house."

I planned to tell him about the gun all morning, but now could not bring myself to do it. If he had taken it, he might be planning something awful. If it wasn't him, Lord knew what he would do to the person who had, perhaps implicating me further. I shuddered. No, I must keep it from him.

"I-I need the money," I said. "My benefactor is ill so we have many bills. She refuses to dismiss her footman and maid, and can't do any work herself so—"

"You are forgiven. This once. Promise me you won't ignore my wishes again."

"I've told you I would heed your wishes," I said with impatience. Though, as I said the words, I knew I would break my promise that very evening.

I glanced at the clock. As soon as the show ended—the show I was not a part of tonight—I would go to the smoking room and join Raoul, if only briefly. I had to thank him for the book. He didn't know how much it meant to me, how he had brought me back to life. He'd given me my magic, released dreams I didn't know I still had. A powerful warmth surged through me, drowning the dread the Angel's threats had inspired. I could hardly wait to see Raoul again.

"Good. We understand each other then."

"Perfectly," I said, sweetly.

"Now, do your exercises and we'll begin."

I hid my irritation at his dictatorial tone and did as he asked until my vocal chords were loose and I was ready to begin.

"I have new music for you to learn. You'll find the sheet on your chair."

I picked up the paper, entertaining the question that always nagged at me when an object appeared in my room: How had the Angel gotten it there? There had to be a removable panel in the room somewhere. Yet when Delacroix had searched my room, he'd found nothing. I made a mental note to look for it myself.

I picked up the sheet of music and read through the tortured but beautiful lyrics. Titled *Don Juan Triumphant,* this opera paralleled Mozart's *Don Giovanni,* about the scoundrel who seduced or raped women, and was eventually dragged into the fires of hell by demons for his penance. But the Angel's Don Juan would change his ways, all for the love of Amnita, an innocent and beautiful maiden, after he managed to capture and seduce her. Beside each role, the Angel had listed a cast member's name. Next to the virginal maiden, I found my own, and Don Juan would be played by the Angel.

I shivered at the implications. Capture and seduction by the Angel. Rape?

"Did you write this?" I asked, my voice hoarse.

"It's mine, yes. And I've passed it along to those fools who run my theatre. They'll give it a full run, like the other operas—with my choice of cast.

"I wrote it for you," the voice said quietly.

Torn between admiration, flattery, and fear, I said nothing. What was he plotting? Did he . . . have feelings for me, beyond what I had imagined?

I walked to the large mirror on the back wall; the place from which his voice seemed to emanate. At last I whispered, "It's incredible. The musical score is unique, powerful."

The mirror shifted and my form faded until it appeared to overlay another—a male in a dark suit.

I gasped and stepped backward, pulse racing. "Is that you?"

He wore a cape and a fedora hat pulled low over his face. A sort of fog surrounded him, the way I would expect an apparition to look. His arm reached for me and caressed the image of my face in the mirror.

"Yes."

I gasped. He couldn't really touch me, I reminded myself. Confusion swirled inside me like a gathering storm. Here was the image of the man-angel who had taught me like a tutor, led me like a father, and now showed feelings for me that inspired an icy rush of emotion in my chest; a mingling of fear and something I couldn't place. *He is a murderer*, my head screamed. *He has threatened me! But he cares for me.* And I care for him, I admitted slowly, in some way at least.

Confused, I focused on the glass. How had he done it? I snapped my fingers as I realized the truth behind the illusion—this was Platonized glass, like the panes I'd seen for sale at the magic shop. The open panel was behind the mirror—not the wall! I grinned in spite of myself. I knew his secret.

He dropped his arm and his image faded from the glass. "It is time to sing."

After several run-throughs, I had the song almost memorized.

"Good," the Angel said. "Now, one last time and we will conclude for the day. I want you to learn each of your songs, and be quick about it. The cast is already ahead of you."

I closed my eyes and sang, focusing on each note, each breath. On the second stanza, he joined me. Surprised, my eyes fluttered open and

I stumbled over the next phrase. His beautiful tenor never failed to astound me with its perfection. I regained my composure quickly, and our voices braided smoothly as if from the same weave, then parted, only to rejoin in a harmonious swell. His voice caressed my own, coiled around it, and clutched it with need.

When the final notes concluded, I breathed heavily. I had never felt such intensity singing. Regardless of his rough demeanor and his outrageous demands, the Angel inspired me to be better, to throw off the doubts in my abilities. I longed to please him, even if he manipulated and scolded me—even when he terrified me into submission.

"You have done well, dear one," the Angel said, his voice thick with emotion.

I smiled, basking in his praise. "It's a beautiful song."

"A beautiful voice filled with emotion and longing is precisely what the song needs to make it soar. You are truly coming into your own."

I drained the water glass on my table, mulling over his words. Singing filled me with longing, yes, but not the kind he hoped for. There was no joy there, no pleasure, or sense of certainty that this was right for me. Not anymore. Suddenly I longed to see Papa more than anything in the world. I needed his comforting presence—I needed some sort of sign.

"We'll practice again tomorrow," the Angel said.

Shoving down my confusion, I nodded. "I would like some privacy now, please. And then I will be on my way."

"Until tomorrow."

Though the Angel's absence left a strange void, I was glad for it. I didn't want to take the chance of missing Raoul tonight. The performance had ended almost forty-five minutes ago. Quickly, I checked my appearance. My cheeks were flushed and my green gown accentuated my slender waist. A lightness of mood swept through me and I smiled.

I walked the familiar path through the corridors, up several flights of stairs, and into the main hall, admiring its beauty as I went. Every eave or marble pillar showcased an intricate carving of mythical beings, instruments, or decorative leaves, vines, and flowers.

When I reached the grand staircase, my heart beat in time with my steps. How would I thank Raoul? I didn't know the words. I headed toward the anterior hall, willing my pulse to slow its frantic pace. Inside Le Salon de Lune, I searched each face, to no avail—he wasn't there. Before continuing on, I took a moment to admire the gilded mirrors on opposing walls, and stood in front of the glass, marveling at the way my image repeated into infinity as it curved away from me. Above my head, black owls flocked around the ceiling fixture supporting a silver chandelier. The pewter sky of the dome curved around their dark bodies and dripped into sharp icicle points down the wall. A smattering of stars glistened in the painted night. I'd only seen this floor once before, and I'd forgotten how beautiful the rooms were.

Cognizant of the evening slipping away, I didn't hesitate and headed quickly for Le Salon de Soleil, the other smoking room at the opposite end of the foyer. The west room featured the same infinity mirrors, but all glistened in gold leaf rather than silver. Salamanders— a symbol of the sun—crawled around the center chandelier on the ceiling, and a sun projected its shimmering rays down the walls. The opera house held as many facets of beauty as it did secrets, it seemed. I waded through elegant gentlemen sloshing their cognacs, lost in tall tales and political discourse, and ladies discussing *Nana,* the latest novel by Émile Zola, about a prostitute-turned-stage player. At Carlotta's party and again at the Duchess of Zurich's salon, I'd overheard plenty about the scandalous novel. I mentally added the novel to my list, to see what all of the fuss was about.

When I'd made it through the crowd to the opposite side of the room, my disappointment flared again. There was still no sign of Raoul. Stomach pitching like a ship at sea, I continued on to the ballet room. I slipped through the crowd, dodging dancers still in their costumes who leaned into gentleman in a flirtatious way or sipped coyly from a beverage purchased, without doubt, by the *abonnés* who sought their company. Once at the far end of the hall, I walked through the Salon de Glacier and circled back the way I'd come.

Where was he? Raoul was nowhere in sight.

Perhaps he had given up and left, or maybe he had forgotten his invitation altogether. So many women sought his company. Maybe he'd sought the attentions of someone else.

Heart growing heavy, I headed to the last room. The Grand Foyer's brilliance startled me, and I couldn't help but to stop and stare. Every surface glinted as if dipped in liquid gold. Of all the rooms, the foyer stood apart as the most stunning with its lavish murals, lusty ornamentations, and a series of golden chandeliers that spanned the hall in a neat row. Now I understood why the Nouvel Opéra had taken so long to complete—outside of war with the Prussians, revolts, and swelling ground water—it must have cost a fortune to decorate all in gold leaf, hardwoods, and rare marbles shipped in from all over the world. An unbelievable sight of beauty and opulence.

A shrill laugh jolted me from my thoughts and I continued my brisk pace through the room. Unwittingly, I held my breath, hoping against hope I was wrong; that Raoul hadn't left after all. But as I neared the western end of the Grand Foyer, my hope wilted. He had definitely left. I looked down to blink back the unexpected rush of tears, and tugged at the end of my glove. He would think I didn't care for him, and it was just as well, I tried to tell myself. I needed to end my associations with him anyway.

I scanned the room one last time and turned to go.

And there he stood, beneath the giant clock that sat atop the fireplace mantel at the farthest end of the hall. He was alone, his head bowed, his face contemplative. He swirled the spirits in his glass, sipped from it, and tucked the glass against him in an absentminded gesture.

The boisterous conversation faded, and the room around him seemed to brighten. I couldn't deny my feelings for him, and there was no use trying. I had always cared for him. Nothing had changed that, not even the years.

He turned, as if sensing my eyes on him.

I caught a glimpse of sadness on his features first—or was it resignation—before it gave way to a smile.

He walked toward me, sending my heart into a frenzied pace. The sight of him flushed all thoughts from my head. What would I say?

"Bonsoir." His lips brushed my cheek in greeting.

Tongue-tied, I searched for the right words.

"I thought you weren't coming," he said.

"I had to practice first," I said hoarsely, throat burdened with emotion. The urge to touch the curve of his mouth overwhelmed me.

"Yes, of course." He laughed and smacked his forehead with his palm. "I should have realized. Well, I am happy to see you now."

We stood for a long moment, smiling at each other but saying nothing.

A blush burned across my cheeks, my chest, and heat radiated from my skin. At last, I glanced away, over his shoulder at a golden lyre mounted above a doorway to the balcony. An old Norse tale Papa told me, about an enchanted lyre, streamed through my head for an instant, before the reason I wanted to speak to Raoul flooded back.

"I wanted to thank you properly," I said. "For your gifts. The book, and the lovely magic box you gave me when we were children."

His brow raised in surprise. "You still have the magic box? That gives me more pleasure than you know." He stepped closer. "I was afraid you would see my gift as childish, but I'm delighted you like it still."

"I had given up illusions since . . . well, since Papa died. I locked it away until recently. Your book prompted me to begin again." I looked down at my satin gloves, sliding one atop the other. "I'm not certain I would have taken up illusions again, had you not given me the book. I haven't been this happy in a long time."

His eyes crinkled at the edges and he leaned closer, until our faces were only inches apart. The faint smell of cognac mixed with his natural scent of seawater. I yearned to press closer still, into his arms.

"You can't know what it does to me to hear you say that." Soberness replaced his smile. "To make you happy, even in such a small way . . . You're a dear friend."

Tension vibrated between us. I moved closer.

"Raoul"—my tongue curled around his name, caressed its contours —"it's not in a small way at all. I've loved illusions always. I hadn't realized how much until now."

"I know," he said so softly, the din around us might have drowned out his words had I not been centimeters from him. He grasped my hand and squeezed it.

His touch sent a swarm of bees through my veins.

"Why, there you are, Monsieur le Vicomte!" Carlotta's soprano singsonged behind me. "We're ready to leave." She swept between us, ignoring me with blatant disregard and giving me her back. "The others are just behind. I'm afraid our restaurant awaits."

I had the sudden urge to shove her, watch her lustrous curls fly about her shoulders, hear the satisfying *thud* of her ample form connecting with the floor. I shifted my gaze to an oval portrait high overhead, trying to gain control of my emotions.

"Christine!" Monsieur Delacroix joined Carlotta, looking as pristine and handsome as ever. "What a delight to see you here." He kissed my cheeks and smiled warmly. "You usually hide in your dressing room."

Avoiding Carlotta's glare I said, "I thought I would enjoy the social part of the evening for once."

"A fine idea," Delacroix agreed.

Another woman joined them, at her side was the policeman, Inspector Mifroid, who I'd seen questioning the cast and crew the last couple of weeks. She flashed Raoul a pretty pout, and released her grip on the inspector's arm.

"There you are." The woman fluttered her lashes at Raoul. "We've been looking all over for you."

Was this the future fiancée Carlotta had referred to at her soirée? The woman sparkled in white silk crusted with beads, her hair was pinned in an elegant chignon, and black gloves tapered to her elbows. Her entire person glittered beneath the light of the chandeliers.

Pretty to be sure, and a catch for any man. My heart slowed at the thought of her hand in Raoul's, him beaming in her presence.

Against my will, my eyes darted to Raoul's face to assess his level of interest.

He smiled easily, though his shoulders appeared rigid. "I was having a brandy, and a moment away from the crowd. How are you, Claude?" He clapped Inspector Mifroid on the shoulder. "It's been too long, my friend."

"You owe me a drink." The inspector grinned. He was younger than most of the police officers I had seen, with round eyes and boyish pink cheeks.

"And a game of cards," Raoul said.

Carlotta gazed at Raoul. "There is plenty of brandy at the restaurant, gentlemen. Shall we go?"

"Before we go, Christine"–Delacroix cupped my elbow with his hand–"I wanted to tell you that I have an awards banquet on Monday, put on by the Académie des sciences. I've already spoken with Madame Valerius and she has consented to release you for the night."

He had asked for permission without talking to me first–and Madame had consented—without care for my own wishes? Everyone saw fit to choose for me without bothering to consult me. Anger reared up inside me again, streamed into my fingers and curled them into fists. When would my wishes be important? It wasn't that I didn't want to go, it was that I was never consulted in the first place, as if I were a child.

"It will be a formal affair. Wear something appropriate." He noted the expression on my face and hastily added, "As you always do."

I had yet to reply and he had the audacity to tell me what to wear? Still, I couldn't think of an excuse not to join him when I had nowhere else to be—except for practice with the Angel. And I wouldn't tell the professor that, for certain.

"Are you all right?" Raoul asked. "You're shaking."

So I was. Shaking from irritation at Delacroix and Carlotta's arrogance, and from the emotion Raoul inspired in me that I couldn't control.

"There you are," said a male voice, similar to Raoul's in timbre and pitch. His brother Philippe clapped a large hand over Raoul's shoulder.

Philippe wore a suit and cravat fit for a nobleman, but his broad smile suggested amicability, as if he cared more about being approachable than wealthy and superior. The gentleman possessed Raoul's fair looks, though his nose took up more of his face, and his eyes were sky blue with crinkles at the edges, instead of the seawater hue of Raoul's.

Mademoiselle Sorelli, the head ballerina, held fast to his arm. She had removed her tutu and now wore a silky skirt with folds cascading to her knees and a shawl with fringe about her shoulders. As usual, her lovely cheekbones looked as if they could cut glass. Her gaze caressed Philippe's face, her burgeoning love for him as apparent as the nose on her face. I pitied her. She could never be more than his mistress. Convention and his social status wouldn't allow it—just as I could never be with Raoul.

My humor darkened further and my legs ached with the need to flee.

"Philippe, you remember Mademoiselle Daaé?" Raoul said, gesturing to me. "From our summer in Normandy when we were children."

"Of course." Philippe kissed me on the cheek in greeting. "Once a lovely child and now a beautiful woman and singer. You were marvelous."

I smiled. "You are too kind."

"Our little Christine has come a long way from a poor musician's daughter, hasn't she?" Carlotta cooed, as if proud as a mother hen. Yet, jealousy burned in her eyes. "It is a shame her talents won't be on display. They asked me to return to the stage as soon as I was able, so I dragged myself from bed today, just so I could perform."

"And what a performance it was," Inspector Mifroid said.

I reddened in spite of myself. All seemed glad to welcome Carlotta back.

"We all begin somewhere," Raoul said, jumping to my defense. "Some of us are born into more humble beginnings, and others are blessed with wealth, both through no fault of our own. It's what we do with our lot that counts most."

Had we been alone, I might have reached for Raoul's hand and squeezed it. He was a gentleman and a truly good person. Pain rippled through me as I remembered once again that we could never be together.

"Quite right," Delacroix added. "In fact, a colleague of mine saw you sing and has asked me to introduce you to him. He would make an excellent match for you."

I glanced at Raoul, but he looked away. Once again, I had been served an "opportunity" without asking for it, never mind the fact that I was forced to suffer their condescension openly.

Annoyed, I steeled my voice. "It's a kind thought, Monsieur, but I really must be going. It's getting late. I won't keep you all from your reservations. Good night." I turned to go, moving swiftly away from the group that was too important, too high-standing in their social circles to welcome me.

"Christine, wait," Raoul called after me.

I pretended not to hear him. Without looking back, I forged on to the cast room, collected my cape and gloves, and hurried into the cool night air.

After a night of dreamless sleep, I headed to the opera house the next day, Raoul's words playing in my head, over and over.

You can't know what it does to me to hear you say that. To make you happy, even in such a small way . . .

My stomach flipped each time I thought of the light in his eyes, the warmth of his hand—until I remembered something else he had said.

You're a dear friend.

The buoyancy of my mood deflated each time those words rang in my ears. He seemed to have feelings for me one instant, but made sure to emphasize our friendship the next. Grunting in frustration, I entered the building and made my way to the cast room. I plopped down in a chair, sullen as the day's early winter sky.

I'd barely sat down when Meg swished into the room, the ruffles of her purple dress fluttering below the hem of her overcoat. "Have you heard?" Her eyes were bright with excitement. "The ghost demands we perform his opera. Everyone is learning their parts, and listen to this! He'll play the lead! Do you think he'll show himself?"

I nodded glumly. "I wonder how the opera ghost will perform on stage."

Meg grinned. "I guess we'll see, soon enough. Maman says the opera will be magnificent."

"Or a complete horror." Secretly, I wondered how the Angel convinced the directors to do his bidding this time.

"Oh, I just ran into Carlotta." She removed her coat, hung it on the wall. "She said something about the directors. You're supposed to meet in her dressing room in five minutes."

"Oh?" I unbuttoned my cape and slid it from my shoulders.

"She said it would be of great interest to you, whatever that means." Meg rolled her eyes.

I laughed at how much the gesture transformed her usually sweet expression. "You don't think she's sincere?"

"When is Carlotta ever sincere?"

The day Carlotta told me I would never take her place, she was hateful and insecure, but very sincere. The woman was a viper.

"Much as I dislike her, you should see what she wants," Meg said. "You never know. It might be important."

I sighed. "You're right."

"You'll have to tell me what she says." Meg's eyes gleamed with a wicked luster. "Though, if I am being too nosy, never mind me, of course."

I laughed once more at her expression. Reluctantly, I headed to Carlotta's dressing room. Her door stood ajar so I stepped just inside. "You wanted to tell me something, Carlotta. I—"

My voice shriveled in my throat. Raoul held a massive bouquet in his arms.

"Oh! I'm sorry. I—"

"Christine, how lovely to see you," Carlotta said. "Just look at these beautiful flowers. Some gentlemen have exquisite taste, don't they? All of that proper upbringing serves them well." She looked at Raoul with a knowing smile. "Thank you, Raoul. I'll pass them along to Mademoiselle DuClos."

Raoul bought a stunning bouquet for Carlotta's friend? I forced myself to swallow a groan. He did care about her.

Raoul gently set the flowers on a table. When I caught his eye, he opened his mouth to say something, but closed it promptly.

"I apologize," I said, choking on the roses' perfume. "I didn't mean to interrupt. Meg said you wanted to see me."

"Oh? About that, well, never mind." Carlotta fluttered her lashes at me like a dismissal.

Forgetting my manners, I stepped backward through the doorway and left; the image of Raoul's startled expression—and the triumph etched on Carlotta's face—burned in my mind. The Angel had warned me about Raoul, and he was right. I would only get hurt should I pursue my feelings for him. But as the pang rippled through me again, I knew I'd already allowed myself to go too far. It was time to stamp out my girlish notions and move on.

The evening of Monsieur Delacroix's Académie ceremony, I resigned myself to accompanying him. He was a friend, after all, and it was his big night. Usually I enjoyed my time with him, as long as we didn't discuss the opera ghost. We set off toward our destination, but the carriage didn't stop in front of the hotel where the banquet was to be held. Instead, we pulled into the drive of the Académie de sciences.

Delacroix stuck his head out of the window and shouted at the coachman. "Around to the back."

Puzzled, I frowned. "Why are we here?"

"I need to take care of something first. It will only be a few minutes, and then we'll be on our way."

"May I come in with you? I've never been inside a school before."

He hesitated a moment. "You haven't? That would make sense, of course. Fine, fine. You can see my office. Come. We must move quickly so we aren't late." He held out his hand to help me step down from the coach.

We covered the short distance to the door. Using his own key, Delacroix unlatched the lock and we ducked inside. The building smelled of musty volumes, ink, and unidentifiable odors, no doubt, from an array of experiments behind some locked door. I followed him with haste. Much of the hall lay in shadow at the late hour, though an occasional pool of light spilled onto our path.

"Éduard." Delacroix tipped his hat at a man who sat at his desk.

"Gustave?" the man replied. "Why aren't you at the ceremony?"

"I'm on my way," the professor called over his shoulder as we barreled down the corridor.

For some reason I felt the need to be silent, perhaps in reverence for the thousands of brilliant minds that had spent time under this roof, or maybe it was the deep quiet of the building. It could also be my foul humor. I couldn't erase the image of Raoul in Carlotta's dressing room, arms filled with flowers. Neither could I shake the feeling that Delacroix was on edge, that something wasn't right.

I followed the professor up two flights of stairs.

"Here we are." He slipped a heavy iron key into the hole and popped open the door. As he turned on a lamp, I came in behind him.

Bookshelves lined three of the four walls, and on the third, a large corkboard hung beneath a window, covered with dozens of photographs. Delacroix's desk filled the small office and lay beneath orderly piles of pamphlets and papers. In one corner of the room, a stack of booklets towered to the ceiling. With one gentle push, the whole thing would topple.

"Wait here," the professor said, tugging a lumpy envelope from one of the locked drawers in his desk.

"Where are you going?" I rubbed my arms to ward off the chill in the drafty room.

"I'll just be a few minutes." He flashed a bulky envelope at me, closed the door behind him, and his footsteps fell away.

Too curious to uphold my manners, I traversed the room at once to look at the photographs. I'd never seen so many in one place before. They were costly to make and develop, from what I understood. I bent over them—and jumped back. In one, a man faced the camera and a spirit drifted over his head, its hands resting on the man's shoulders. Another displayed a group sitting at a *table tournante* as a bright cylinder of light lingered above them. Still another, showed a woman at her sewing table as a spirit in a full-length white veil hovered before her, unseen. I shivered and rubbed my arms again. Many of the photographs were of the dead; though their spirits had left the bodies, often the souls remained on earth. At least, that is what Papa would have said. I was beginning to believe he was right.

I straightened, suddenly realizing I had never seen a photograph of Mother. Why hadn't Papa had her picture done? If only I could ask him. I moved to the section of the corkboard covered with newspaper clippings. Many of the articles announced conjurers coming to town, or causing disturbances in Paris and abroad, their spirit cabinets and apparitions in tow. I paused to read a piece of newspaper in the center of the board. Its headline read:

CONJURERS CONTACT THE DEAD, CAUSE SUICIDE

Dread swam in my stomach. Beneath the title, the author had drawn a caricature of a young man with a thin face and sunken eyes, almost skeletal in appearance, standing with an older gentleman. They were both decked in capes and top hats with evil, slanted eyes. A specter of a woman floated between them. In the front row of the audience, a man's eyes were round, too large for his head, and his mouth hung open. I leaned in closer to read.

Crespin le Grand premiered his latest act last night at the Theatre Margot in the ninth arrondissement. Audiences have come to expect his shocking performances, but Saturday evening's show reached new levels when he introduced his young apprentice, the Master Conjurer. The young illusionist called upon an audience member in the front row to volunteer the name of a passed loved one, after which, the illusionist called upon the spirit. It appeared in a faint wisp of smoke. Many altercations broke out in the crowd until local authorities arrived. Monsieur Jerôme Delacroix, the audience member who supplied the illusionist with the name of his deceased wife, refused to comment.

I stumbled backward a step. It was Delacroix's father and the Master Conjurer! My mind tumbled with the new information. Suddenly it made sense why the professor sought to disprove *spiritisme* so desperately. His father's obsession with his dead wife—Delacroix's mother—had only been stoked by the performance. I wondered about the timing. Perhaps his father had taken his life shortly after?

Heart racing, I scoured the rest of the board for clues but found none. Unperturbed, I bent over his desk and thumbed through a few of his papers. They were covered in figures and equations. I'd never find anything there, at least not quickly. I straightened the stack and peered at the dusty spines of his books, finding one scientific manual after another: books on geology, exotic birds or species in the Orient, methodologies and theories of experimentation, dissections. Scrunching my nose in disgust, I moved to another bookshelf and ran my finger over the tomes. The subject matter shifted. Not only were there books on spiritualism, but also on illusions. I paused on a copy of *The Sharper Detected and Exposed*, the same book Raoul had gifted me. Continuing on, I scanned the titles quickly until I reached Elliott's *Mysteries, or Glimpses of the Supernatural*. I pulled the book from the shelf. As I flipped it open, a sheaf of paper fluttered to the floor. Recognizing Delacroix's handwriting, I picked it up and read his notes.

> *Signs of the Supernatural include but are not limited to lights without a source, particularly those which pulse, objects moving of their own accord, cool breezes in an otherwise warm space, raspy whispers or the sound of garbled voices, the outline of a human form in freestanding space, and unexplained noises that appear to communicate with the living.*
>
> *Seen: two, rest yet to prove*

The night I sang in the courtyard a few months ago, there had been an unusual cool breeze. That wasn't atypical in the evening, even in the summer, but it had persisted. It was very odd, I must admit, and I had run indoors. I shook my head. It was purely coincidental. I hadn't seen anything else outside of the séance.

Delacroix's voice echoed from the marble floors in the corridor. Heart thumping, I stashed the paper back inside the book and shoved it back into place on the shelf. Disturbed by the photographs, the frigid office, and the talk of spirits, I lunged for the door handle—but paused at the sound of his voice.

"You said it would be enough." His voice was angry.

I strained to hear the other voice, but couldn't make out the murmuring.

"I deserve this," Delacroix went on. "You know that as well as I do. I shouldn't have to pay anyone off to begin with."

Paying someone off? I turned the handle and carefully opened the door, peeking around the edge. Delcroix's back was turned to me; he faced another man, who wore an immense top hat.

"We have company," the man said in a low grumble.

Delacroix whipped around and I stepped into the hall, pasting a smile on my face. "Are we ready, Monsieur? It's quite chilly in your office."

"Yes." He strode toward me, anger flashing in his eyes.

"Is everything all right?" I asked, taken aback by his expression.

The other man tucked the mysterious envelope inside his jacket and skulked off in the opposite direction.

"It is now." He brushed my cheek with his lips in friendly affection. "Let's be off, shall we?"

Within minutes, we made our way to our destination and were seated instantly at a table already filled with other people. After a brandy, Delacroix's brooding expression lifted. He seemed to cheer at the possibility of taking home his award, and I did my best to free my mind of everything but where I was at this moment: in the company of a friend, with fine food, and in a lovely dress. Without luck. My mind stirred with the images of the dead on the professor's wall, preened and photographed for eternity, and more disturbing, the news of his father and the Masked Conjurer. I should think the professor would feel some relief with the magician dead and gone. I glanced at Delacroix's dear face: his angular features, peppered hair, and piercing but lovely eyes. I knew why he didn't feel relief. There wasn't any when a parent died so unexpectedly. I understood this well. Still, it seemed unusually coincidental that both of us suffered because of the same magician.

I peered over the rim of my wineglass at the other professors seated around the table. They resembled each other with their uniform morning coats, pince-nez, and sober expressions. The professors' wives chattered while their husbands tended to their brandy glasses. I was virtually invisible, even in a gown the happy blue of a summer sky that was so different from the browns and rich burgundies scattered throughout the hall. I had hoped the color would brighten my mood.

"You must have a very good chance of winning," I said to Delacroix. "You're so diligent in your work." I thought of the large stacks of papers on his desk, the rows of scientific volumes.

"I hope so," he replied. "I've published five essays this year alone, helped rewrite the program of studies, and launched an investigative research campaign on spiritualism. Even Charles Paget can't boast a list so accomplished."

"Who else was nominated?" I asked.

Monsieur Delacroix smirked. With thinly veiled disdain, he said, "Paget is my competition, the professor with the bow tie and wrinkled coat, two tables over."

Professor Paget was opposite Delacroix in looks and stature, with disheveled hair, a full beard, and hunched shoulders. He embodied what I envisioned an intellectual to look like: as if it were a struggle to remember to groom himself, organize his papers, and keep a clean home.

"He's accomplished in the natural sciences?" I watched the man ignore those around him and, instead, scribble something in a notebook.

"Quite," he said through clenched teeth. "In fact, he seeks to disprove spiritualism as I do. He has just written an article about essence versus being. It's all over the papers."

I nodded slowly, grasping why he seemed so irritable. Delacroix saw the man as a threat to his own prestige, possibly even to his livelihood.

"I'm sure you'll write something better." I patted his forearm.

He relaxed some and smiled. "If the lovely Christine Daaé says it will be so, it will be!" He chuckled, his self-assurance returning.

"What is the award for, exactly?"

"It's a certificate that recognizes exceptional study in different branches of science. Four awards will be given tonight. I've been nominated for the Grande Médaille."

We finished a leisurely dinner of creamed vegetable soup, roasted hen, and pralines and meringues. Then a man stepped up to the podium at last, the speaker launched into a dry introduction to the history of the awards, past winners, and the honor of being associated with the Académie. The speaker's voice droned like a cello stuck on the same note.

I was going to need another glass of wine if the banquet continued like that. I glanced back at Professor Paget, who continued to scribble in his notebook. I wished I had brought my own. A new illusion niggled at the back of my brain: a trick of light, a large mirror, a projector . . .

My mind drifted and I lost myself in the new idea.

"And the award goes to"—the speaker paused for effect—"Professor Charles Paget."

Applause followed, snapping me out of my reverie. Delacroix's eyebrows shot up and he clenched his brandy glass. Shock registered plainly on his features and he didn't bother to hide it. He'd been passed over, humiliated.

Professor Paget wormed his way through the sea of tables to the stand, accepted his award, and returned to his seat. He picked up his pen immediately and continued to write as if nothing had happened. Neither happiness, nor pride radiated from him. I glanced at Delacroix again, afraid to see how Paget's unaffected acceptance bothered him.

"He shouldn't have won. I was assured—" Delacroix clamped his lips closed, aware he was about to say something he should not.

My eyebrows shot up. Had this been what the payoff was about at the school? Delacroix must have done something he shouldn't in the name of competition.

His face burned red and a vein on his neck pulsed just above his collar. "I think we are finished here." He stood, tossing his napkin on the table. "Come, Christine. This is an insult."

He pulled me through the room, and once outside, jumped into his waiting carriage.

Stunned, I climbed in behind him. Surely, he knew he looked ungracious to storm out in front of a slew of his colleagues. At the very least, I wished he would consider how he made me look: like his young mistress, tagging along after him.

"You can't be serious," I said, taking the seat across from him. "We're going to leave, just like that? What will the others think?"

"I don't give a damn about the others. If they can't see how ridiculous that decision was, they're idiots." He gripped my hand a bit too tight. "But this means I'll need to rely on you to make my project a success."

"Rely on me?"

"Contact the opera ghost. I know you've spoken with him, or perhaps have even seen him. Your name is all over the notes he keeps sending to the other players. I don't understand why you've lied to me to protect him, but enough is enough, Christine. You need to be honest with me. I need your help."

My hand flew to my throat in alarm. I wondered how much he knew. He knew enough to realize I had covered for the Angel, at the expense of our relationship. Now what could I say? I couldn't jeopardize our relationship any further. He had been nothing but kind to Madame Valerius and me, only to be betrayed by my lies. Regret crashed over me.

I cast my eyes to the floor, thoughts tumbling like mad.

His jaw set in a hard line. "Meet me in your dressing room tomorrow during the performance. We'll summon him. If he doesn't show, we're going underground."

~ 15 ~

I couldn't refuse Delacroix, and I couldn't warn the Angel—he might try to hurt the professor—so I decided to flee Paris to gather my courage, and make some decisions. The directors agreed to a fortnight away, since Carlotta's triumphant return to the stage rendered me almost useless anyway. I scratched out a quick note in my dressing room to the Angel explaining Madame's need for vacation and my own, knowing full well how furious he would be that I had left while we practiced his opera. For once, I didn't care. I had to get away. I considered writing Raoul as well, but abandoned the idea. It was better to just disappear. He would get the message that way best of all.

Madame's wealthy brother agreed to pay for the cost of the trip for both of us as well as Claudette; he knew as well as I that it might be Madame's last. Grateful for his kindness, I promised to secure him free tickets to the opera. We took the afternoon train northward the following day to Bretagne, debarked at the station, and hailed a coach to the Auberge Soleil-Couchant in the Bay of Perros. Madame's friends owned the inn where we stayed and lavished us with extra comforts. Once settled, we dined on a hearty seafood stew with champignons and cream sauce. After, we sat by the fire in the hotel's great room and enjoyed Calvados, the local apple brandy. Already I felt a bit lighter— safe from the haunted passageways of the opera house, and far from the unsettling effect of Carlotta's sneer. Tomorrow I would visit the beach to invigorate me, despite the raw winds. And Papa's grave.

The flames of the fire receded as the tinder burned away.

"I've something to tell you, Christine." Claudette cradled a teacup in her hands. "You won't like it."

I raised an eyebrow, but said nothing.

"I knew you wouldn't do it, so I did it for you."

"Do what, Claudette?" My tone grew impatient.

"I sent it. Your letter to the Vicomte de Chagny." Anxious, she stared at her cup. "I knew you wanted to send it."

A stone sank in my stomach. I thought of the wastebasket in the study stuffed with discarded letters. All except one. I had abandoned it on the desktop yesterday when dissonant squawking drifted from the salon. I'd rushed from Madame's desk to check on my canaries. Somehow, a tomcat had wandered in from outside, perhaps when Alfred had gone outdoors to beat a broom. The mangy animal batted the cage with its paw and slammed its body against it, rattling the perches and bells inside. My birds screeched and fluttered, hovering as far from the cat's swooping paws as possible. I shooed the offender outdoors and soothed my pets with a song, stroking their soft chests to calm them. Berlioz's little heart beat rapidly against my thumb for some time.

After that disturbance, I had forgotten the final letter, assuming I had tossed it. I explained my gratitude for Raoul's friendship, and insisted that we end it. Not only was it unfair to Mademoiselle DuClos, whom he intended to marry, but the Angel forbade it. In closing the letter, I had mentioned our intended holiday in Bretagne.

At least now Raoul knew, and I wouldn't have to explain when our paths crossed again. After I realized this, relief flowed through me. Raoul knew everything now, and I didn't have to confront him again. I thought of his face, the way he had beamed at me in the Grand Foyer. It was best I avoided him anyway.

"I saw the heap of crumpled paper in the wastebasket, but there was one note left on the desk. His name was printed at the top." She reached out to squeeze my knee. "I hope you aren't angry with me."

"I'm not angry, but don't do that again."

"I'll never meddle again. Promise." She held up her hands. "I had no right. I'm sorry. I just—I just knew you wanted to and couldn't."

Madame remained silent through the entire exchange, but glared at her empty brandy glass. To break the tension, Claudette retrieved the empty glass and within moments, she returned with a fresh pour.

I sighed. How could I be angry with Claudette? She was right. "I suppose he didn't write a response," I murmured.

"Perhaps he did," she said. "I posted it only yesterday."

If he replied, I would have to wait until I returned to Paris. And what if he didn't? My stomach flipped at the thought.

Claudette kneeled beside me. "It's clear he cares for you, no matter what else is going on. Why else would he visit your dressing room, or give you the book? Why would he come to the house?"

I dropped my face into my hands. "He does care for me. As a *friend*." The word tasted bitter on my tongue. "He said so himself."

"Being friends is never a bad place to start." She wrapped her arm around my shoulder.

"There's another woman, too. He left the gala the other night to have dinner with her and the others, and he bought her a huge bouquet of flowers."

"They are engaged then?"

My throat filled with cotton at the word. "Not that I am aware of."

When had I grown to care so deeply for Raoul? We hadn't spent much time together, yet here I was. Something about him held my heart captive, ever since we were children.

Claudette leaned closer, her cloud of red curls bouncing around her face. "Never mind the situation. As long, as you don't know his stance with this woman—from his mouth—you have a chance to win him."

I shook my head. "I'm not a desperate stage girl." Fatigue settled over me like a thick blanket; my bones ached with its weight. I wouldn't grovel, manipulate him, or ruin my reputation. If he wanted someone else, so be it. I'd have to find a way to move on.

"Well"—I set down my brandy glass—"I'm off to bed now, but I'll be going for a long walk in the morning. Would you like to join me?"

"Yes!" she said eagerly.

"For now, let's forget about Raoul, shall we?"

Claudette said nothing as I climbed the creaking stairs to my room.

⊙⟡⊙

Claudette and I rose early and ate a breakfast of baguette smeared with fresh butter and plum jam. I wrapped myself in gloves, an overcoat, and hooded wool cape. One layer wouldn't do in a town along the sea. But I welcomed the icy winds; their ferocity eroded my emotions until I could forget it all for a while.

"Are you ready?" I asked.

Claudette touched the woolen hat fastened tightly to her head. "You don't think it's too cold?"

I grinned. Claudette, though a maid, had always had a warm roof over her head. She hadn't braved winters in abandoned shacks as I had.

"We'll survive. We're dressed properly and there isn't even snow."

"True enough," she said, following me through the front doors of the inn.

We started for the stretch of yellow sand wrapping the bay. All was alive with sharp ocean air and cold sunshine. As we rounded the bend, the water came into view. Though tranquil near the shoreline, it heaved beyond the rocky point that extended into deeper waters. Clusters of boulders framed the edges of the inlet, serving as breakers for thrashing waves.

We strolled to the outer reaches of the cove where the sand tapered off. I had forgotten how rocky this part of the shore was and found myself climbing over hunks of pink granite turned this way and that; some covered in skeletal vines once resplendent with white blossoms, others crusted with barnacles or painted in layers of seagull waste.

"It's pretty here, in spite of the wind," Claudette said, looking out over the rock garden and beyond to the glistening waves.

"We'll have to return in the summer. You'll be thankful for the wind then."

The scenery blurred as a memory flooded from childhood, and I was swept back in time. I had been doing this exact thing one summer day—jumping from stone to stone, filling my lungs with sea air, and enjoying the holiday away from the city.

I had stopped for a moment to run a finger over my wind-chapped lips.

"One day I'll be at sea," Raoul had said from behind me.

"The navy?" I had asked.

"As soon as I'm able." He bent to scoop up a clump of seaweed. "Father doesn't want me to join, but it's my life. My decision."

My boots skidded on the slick stone.

Quickly, his hand darted out to steady me. "They're slippery in the summer when the algae grows."

"This way, you two!" Papa had called from ahead. He and Raoul's father led the way to a dock tied with many boats. They would sail and while away the afternoon, while I enjoyed the song of the sea from shore.

The past faded as I refocused my gaze on the waves. How my song had changed since then—from glee to sorrow, and now uncertainty. Somehow, I knew I must write my own song, but didn't yet know the words.

Beyond the rock bed, another inlet crowned with sand stretched wider and longer than the others; a perfect holiday oasis in warm weather. I shielded my eyes from the sun and peered at the series of abandoned docks, once populated by boats tied to every peg. Summer would come again, and with its warmth, life would fill this lovely little town.

Icy wind pelted my already-numb cheeks.

"I'm shivering," Claudette said. "Can we head back?"

Judging by the ascent of the sun, our walk had taken most of the morning. "I suppose I've tortured you long enough. Let's go this way, along the trail. It'll shield us a bit from the wind."

We trudged along an overgrown path that snaked through a series of cottages, the scent of dead grass clinging to the breeze. The inn was in sight.

Claudette wrapped her arms about her middle. "Did you bring the magic book? We could practice after we warm up."

"Yes, but I have to admit, I don't see the point of practicing sometimes."

She paused to place her hands on her hips. "Because it makes you happy, for one."

"That's true." I stopped beside her.

"And who's to say you won't be a real conjurer someday? Maybe . . ." She chewed her bottom lip.

"Go on."

"Maybe you should think about finding somewhere to perform. I could be your assistant."

I smiled. "You like it as well."

"It's better than scrubbing floors and washing sheets—not that I'm complaining. I'm fortunate to have such an accommodating mistress." She winked at me. "She treats me about as well as a relation."

I had daydreamed of that very thing—me on stage, Claudette as my assistant.

"There are so few female illusionists," I said. "Drawing a crowd would be almost impossible."

"Just because it hasn't been done much doesn't mean we can't try. You know how to present yourself to a crowd. You're beautiful and clever." She grinned. "And I'm ever-so-charming. We could woo them."

I laughed.

Glacial air whipped around us. We squealed at the cold and dashed toward the welcoming façade of the inn.

Once inside, I said, "The problem is, it's not just the lack of crowd. There's so much more involved in a magic show: the pageantry, the proper tone, the equipment."

"Luckily, you like to learn." Claudette grinned.

I couldn't help but smile back at her. "Indeed, I do."

I pushed the chicken around on my plate, watching it as it chased the baked apples swimming in brandied cream sauce. Though delicious, I didn't feel hungry. I couldn't stop thinking about my conversation with Claudette. Female illusionists weren't really allowed on stage; they would never be accepted by an audience. I recalled Papa's unease when he saw me practice cards. He'd only allowed it because he knew how much the illusions had helped me cope with losing Mother.

With a heavy sigh, I abandoned my meal and retired to a chair by the fire. I gazed into the flames curling around the edges of a blackened log. A vision of Raoul sprang to mind, of him standing by the fireplace in the Grand Foyer. That night he seemed genuinely happy to see me, yet when the others arrived, he acted as if I did not exist. Then there were those flowers in Carlotta's dressing room. I sighed heavily. I wondered when my feelings for him would fade, and when I would accept that his attentions were nothing more than a rekindling of our past friendship, an honor to our families, really. I pulled my cape tightly about me and snuggled against the chair's headrest. I'd been so anxious these last few months. Adding Raoul to the mix didn't help things. And now the illusions . . . If I were more honest with myself, perhaps I wouldn't be in such a strange position. I knew the answers, deep down: I was a second-rate singer, I would never wed a nobleman, and I didn't have the courage to tour as a conjurer, much less the financial means. I should be grateful for a paid position at all.

The clatter of horses' hooves arose from outside the *auberge*. The next moment, the front door opened widely. A gust of sea air blasted through the great room, and the flames of the fire writhed against the cold. Who could the new guest be—the inn was nearly empty this time of year.

My mouth fell open.

A handsome man in overcoat and hat stepped through the doorway.

Raoul de Chagny.

~ 16 ~

I turned around quickly, clutching and releasing my hands inside the muff in my lap. Raoul had come! He'd received my letter. My face grew hot at the thought of him reading those words. I didn't know whether to kiss Claudette or strangle her, yet here he was—to see me. There could be no other reason.

I turned once more, heart in my throat.

Raoul's gaze wandered over the dining area tucked away in the far corner, the small office where a patron could rent a room, the large fireplace ringed by a cluster of chairs, and finally, landed on me. His smile lit the room like a beam of light over stormy waves. He strode toward me without hesitation.

"Christine!" He sat across from me. "I received your letter and came at once. I had to see you." He held out a simple bouquet with an assortment of holly and evergreen branches in a cone of parchment paper, tied neatly with a ribbon. Its simplicity was beautiful. "For you."

"I— Thank you." I accepted the bouquet, heart thundering in my chest, and cradled it against me. I dared not hope he had feelings for me, yet here he was in the flesh, the moment he received my letter. The words I longed to say refused to come—that his presence inspired music in my head, that something about our connection felt magical.

"There's something you need to know." Raoul cleared his throat and placed his hands on his knees.

I braced myself for truth. He was engaged and he would prefer I not write him—or worse, he felt as I did, but couldn't marry below his station.

"I don't know how to say this." Raoul laughed softly to himself. "It's awkward, but here goes. When you came to Carlotta's dressing room that day, the bouquet you saw—"

209

"Really, Raoul, there's no need to explain. It's none of my concern. I had come to see what Carlotta wanted to tell me—"

A realization hit me like a gale of frosty air. *That* was what Carlotta had wanted—for me to see Raoul with the flowers for her friend, lest I get any more ideas about where his feelings lay. She'd never had anything to tell me in the first place.

"What is it?" Raoul touched my shoulder.

I smoothed my expression. "I just remembered something I need to do when I return to Paris."

I understood perfectly well. Raoul and Mademoiselle DuClos would marry, and I would remain Carlotta's understudy or leave the opera house altogether. She dictated what happened there, and I couldn't fight against her or the tide of her support. It was too strong. And that had to be enough, for now. Except . . . what would I do about the Angel and his promises? I grimaced. The constant back and forth made me weary. I felt trapped in the middle, tugged from every direction.

"Please, I feel like I must explain," he persisted.

"It really isn't necessary."

"I didn't purchase them for Mademoiselle DuClos or Carlotta. In fact, I don't know why Carlotta said what she did. I didn't buy the flowers at all. She asked me to carry them for her from the cast room. When she alluded to them being from me, I didn't correct her in front of you because I didn't want to embarrass her. It would be like calling her a liar and no gentleman would do such a thing. I assumed you understood, but judging by your expression—and your letter—you didn't."

A weight lifted from my shoulders. I was such a fool. Raoul, ever the gentleman, respected Carlotta's feelings. He hadn't known it would be at my expense. I glanced down at the holly bouquet in my hand. He *had* bought flowers—for me. Only me.

"I needed you to know"—Raoul leaned closer, his eyes locked on mine—"how much you have come to mean to me, Christine. I can't stop thinking about you. Your voice, your sweetness, your beauty." The words rushed from his lips as if a dam had burst. "By day's end, I feel as if I might go insane waiting for the next time we might meet."

Blood rushed to my face. Could this be true? I looked down at my hands to hide my eyes, afraid they would give away too much. "I thought you were soon to be engaged to Mademoiselle DuClos."

"Where did you hear that?"

"Carlotta," we said in unison.

He sighed. "That woman meddles in everyone's affairs. I haven't made a single advance, so I'm not sure why she has been lying to you. Unless . . ." He stared at me, surprise marking his features.

"What is it?" I pressed.

He shook his head. "It's nothing that concerns you, but believe me, I don't care for any woman but you."

Warmth surged through me until I thought I might burst into flame. "Raoul," I whispered his name.

His eyes, full of hope, searched my face. "You sought me out in the Grand Foyer, but then you wrote this letter. I don't understand why we can't be friends. Please, tell me what I've done to offend you."

I touched his hand with the lightest of caresses. "I care for you a great deal—but I just can't be with you, Raoul. I'm sorry I can't say more, at least for now. Perhaps one day I can tell you the truth."

He clasped my hand and held it against his face. "The day I came to congratulate you after your performance, just before I knocked at your door, I heard a man's voice. I have agonized over it every day since. Please, put me out of misery. Are you promised to another? Is he the reason you hide from me?"

I felt the blood drain from my face and pool in my toes. Raoul had heard the ghost's voice? The Angel's threats rushed back.

No man can possess you, Christine, or he will pay.

Raoul couldn't know the truth. It didn't matter how I felt about him; I couldn't put him in harm's way. I stood abruptly, sending my muff and the bouquet tumbling to the floor.

Raoul retrieved them and held them out to me. "Have I offended you?"

"You must have been hearing things," I said a little too forcefully. "I don't entertain men in my dressing room."

"With due respect, I know what I heard." His voice took on an edge. "There was a man in your room."

A spark of fury flashed behind my eyes. He assumed I would be alone with a man? I wasn't facile like some of the other stage performers, promising myself to men who paid me in baubles and pretty silks. I might care for Raoul a great deal, but I didn't owe him an explanation—neither could I give him one. If I revealed the Angel's secrets, Raoul would be in danger. Still, he need not insult me.

"There is no respect in your tone, Monsieur le Vicomte." I used his title, knowing full well it would get under his skin. "And it's late. Thank you for your sentiments, but I must retire to my room."

"Christine, wait. I have to know. Is there another man?" The muscle twitched along his jaw.

"Good night, Raoul." I headed for the staircase.

He followed me and scooped up my hand.

His touch set off a tingling in my belly. Though I wanted to throw myself into his arms, I had to remember my convictions—protect Raoul from the Angel, and protect myself from Carlotta. Being sentimental would only cause more trouble.

"Forgive me." Desperation overwhelmed his usually elegant demeanor. "I shouldn't have said what I did. I have no claim on you, or any right to question your ..." He paused.

I raised an eyebrow, appalled once more by his veiled accusation.

"Those you choose to befriend." He recovered quickly. "But please, Christine. Tell me. Who is it? I don't want to make a bigger fool of myself than I already have."

Something about the softness of his expression prompted the truth before I could stop myself. "The Angel of Music spoke to me in my dressing room. He is my tutor, and he has saved my life, more than once."

In a swift change of emotion, Raoul threw back his head and laughed. "An angel? You had me going there for a moment. Who is it really? Come, please tell me."

Stung by his ridicule, I tossed his gifted holly back at him and ascended the stairs. "Believe what you want, Raoul," I called over my shoulder. "It's the truth."

"Wait." He bounded after me. "I'm sorry, I—"

I closed my bedroom door in his face.

"I just want to understand," he called through the door.

I leaned against the wall and squeezed my eyes closed. Why must I give up what I wanted? I wanted Raoul. An unbearable ache spread through me. I wondered what it would be like to move to Bretagne permanently—or home to Sweden again—to escape it all for good. But running away wasn't the answer. The Angel would follow me. He'd known instantly when I had sought work outside the opera house—he seemed to know my every move.

"Christine?" Raoul's voice softened.

I moved to the window, trying to block him out. A full moon lorded over the sea, illuminating the black waves with a trail of silver. At the edge of my view, I could see the town square with its fifteenth-century church. The church's spire was crowned with an iron cross, and a stone fence encircled the adjoining cemetery—Papa's resting place. The church windows reflected the moonlight, obscuring any movement that might have come from within the building.

After some time, I pressed my ear to my door. Raoul's pounding had ceased, his voice had faded, and it appeared as though he had given up. I chewed my bottom lip and glanced over my shoulder at the flower vase the innkeeper had freshened with carnations.

I needed to visit Papa tonight.

Two hours later, when all had quieted in the *auberge*, I pulled on my cape and gloves. I reassured myself that I had nothing to fear in this deserted little town in the middle of the night, and I needed to see Papa tonight, alone and in peace. There was something sacred about a full moon on a cold, clear night, and I wanted to bask in it inside the churchyard.

With feet as light as air, I stole down the stairs and met the innkeeper's wife, who was poking the fire.

"I am going to the churchyard to my pay my respects to my father. Will you leave the door open, or perhaps lend me a key?"

She frowned and leaned over the fire with her tool to push a singed log into the center of the heat. "At this hour, on your own?"

"It's just across the square. I'll be fine."

"It's close, but Jeanne won't be happy to hear you've been out alone at night in the dead of winter."

I touched her arm. "Madame Valerius doesn't need to know."

As she sighed, her bosom rose and fell. "All right, but don't be long." She slipped a key off of her key ring and placed it in my palm. "Take a lantern with you." She motioned to one on the receiving counter.

"Thank you, but that won't be necessary. It's bright as day with that full moon."

I tied the key to a ribbon on my dress and closed the inn's door behind me, planning to make haste to the church, but something about the air made me pause. It sparked with energy and the clean smell of fresh snow. I looked at the sky. The full moon beamed, but patches of clouds blew in swiftly from the sea. I mustn't take too long or I might be caught in a storm. With assured steps, I walked across the cobbled square. The church sat like an old woman with its aged limestone and humped transept; its lifetime had spanned the rise and fall of kings, of republics, and thousands of tides. The building transported me to another time, of seafarers, Celts, and those who worshipped nature long before the god of the French Catholics. I had read about the Celts, and many other things, in the library at Madame Valerius's house during the three years I lost to grief.

I swung open the church door and stepped inside. It looked as I remembered it, though I hadn't visited since Papa's death. Its arched windows were fortified by iron ribs, and the granite flooring was the same pink as the stones from the bay. My steps echoed over the stone as I walked down the aisle in filtered candlelight. Visions of Papa's funeral flooded back: the mass drowned out by torrential rains that beat at the roof, and my exquisite pain. I sat in a pew near the front and stared at the crucifix behind the altar. The wood looked new and out-of-place amidst the ancient ambiance of the building. I bowed my head and said a prayer. Perhaps no one would hear me, but I had to try.

After several minutes of quiet reflection, I walked through the transept at the rear of the church. As I walked through a door into the churchyard, I clutched my hands to my chest. A sudden sensation of being watched settled over me. It was perfectly rational to feel unease in a graveyard, I assured myself, but no one was here—no one living anyway. I shivered, but continued on, following a series of stones to an outbuilding. Beyond the building, the cemetery sprawled across a patchwork of overgrown grass.

I frowned. Had the outbuilding been there before? I didn't remember it, but I had been so mired in grief my last time here, I must have missed it. Curiosity got the better of me and I headed to the building. It was small, a mere few meters wide with a roof and two large holes cut out of the stone to serve as windows, though no glass covered them.

I tried the latched handle. It wouldn't compress. I tried again with more force, and jiggled the latch. With a *click*, it popped open. Moonlight spilled through the windows, illuminating what appeared to be an altar. A set of shelves spanned the back wall, crowded with boxes the size and shape of small birdhouses. Each had a miniature roof and a cutout door in the front. I frowned. Why were there so many birdhouses in here? Perhaps the priests made them.

I looked over my shoulder to make certain no one was watching. No one stirred inside the church, or walked by on the street. The night was still as death. I grimaced at my thoughts. Pushing on, I ducked inside to take a quick look.

Each birdhouse was painted with a unique design of vines, crosses, or crests, even the occasional heart. On the front of each house, below the peephole, someone had written a name. I touched a painted heart and peered inside the dark hole.

The fleshless smile and hollow sockets of a skeleton stared back at me.

"Skull boxes!" I cried out, stumbling backward. It was a charnel house! A drawing from one of Madame's books resurfaced in my mind, and the information flooded back. Because of limited space, bones of the deceased were dug up after five years to make room for the more recent dead. Families honored their beloved by placing their skulls in a box. The tradition had died out in the last decade or two, but a few of the charnel houses remained.

I dashed to the graveyard, rubbing the goose bumps from my arms. What had I been thinking, to come here at night amid the cemetery's stillness, the shadowy church, the bones. Foolish woman. I would pay my respects to Papa and return at once to the warm safety of my room. As I weaved around the headstones, I noted with relief no fresh coffins had been interred recently.

Papa's headstone lay nestled beneath the bowed branches of a pine. Just as I reached the back row, it began to snow; a dry snow that gave the air a metallic tang and glittered as it fell, coating the markers of the dead in dazzling white. A breeze swept up from the sea, stirring the flakes into sparkling whorls. I reached out to touch them, but they melted instantly on my glove.

I knelt at Papa's grave. For several minutes, my thoughts swirled like the snowflakes.

"I miss you so much," I whispered as I pulled off the weeds and grass that had crept over the stone. "I love to sing, Papa. To perform is all we ever wanted, but ..." I stopped, searching for not only the words, but also for my true feelings. "I don't know how much longer I can remain at the opera. It doesn't feel right, somehow."

The breeze kicked up and the snow fell faster, turning the flakes from glitter to icy pellets. The moon ducked behind a fat cloud and all fell into shadow. I pulled my hood tighter to shield my exposed skin.

"I have been practicing my illusions. It's all I think of." Once I admitted my true desire, the words flooded my tongue. "I know it isn't what you wanted for me, nor is it likely I will ever be able to perform, but . . . Oh, Papa, give me a sign. Please, I need to feel your presence. I need to know that all will be well."

The beautiful whine of a Strainer violin broke the silence.

I stood abruptly, heart pounding in my ears. Could it be? But it was! I recognized the quality instrument Papa had played my entire youth at once—and his favorite piece, "Lazarus", a tale of death and rebirth. The melody, and the accompaniment of waves sweeping the shore, mesmerized me. I stood as frozen as the gargoyles perched on the gateposts.

Spirits were real. They must be. Papa was with me, still. Perhaps he always had been. Tears sprang to my eyes as the melody played. Was this his blessing?

The song ended and silence enveloped the cemetery once more.

A crash came from the charnel house.

"Who's there?"

My voice frightened a flock of crows nesting in the pine overhead. They cawed as they flew away, their black wings disappearing against the night sky.

Startled, I screeched and raced to the gate.

"There's nothing to fear. It is I." A familiar tenor floated through the churchyard.

It wasn't Papa, but *him*. Terror prickled up my neck. Would I ever be free of the Angel?

"You wouldn't throw away your talent. Waste it on magic tricks, would you? Illusions are dangerous. Take my word for it."

"You heard me?" I said, my voice hoarse. Despite the cold, the heat of embarrassment spread up my neck. Perhaps this was the sign Papa had sent—the Angel, the violin, the firm answer I sought—follow my path back to the opera where I belonged. Only I didn't feel as if I should.

"You spoke aloud, dear one. Of course I heard you, but I need not hear your words. I know your heart. And I'm here to reassure you, you are a singer. It's what your mother would have wanted as well. She would want to keep you safe, and to encourage your talents."

217

My mother? How could he know what Mother wanted? The cold of the gatepost seeped into my hand and into my blood. "Have you— Have you spoken to my mother?"

The Angel's tone grew sharp. "For now, we need to discuss the problem at hand."

"Which is?" I shivered as snow covered the tips of my boots, and the last of my body's warmth bled away.

"The Vicomte de Chagny, of course. He followed you here, professed his love, no doubt."

My patience wore thin and suddenly I felt very tired. "What does it matter? I am forbidden to see him."

"He's a sailor. One woman will not sate his appetite."

My hands curled at my sides. "I'm following your request. What more do you wish from me?" I grew tired of his demands, of this game. I grew tired of giving up everything and everyone for which I cared.

"I want you as far from that wretched man as possible." His voice echoed against the outside of the church buildings. "Return to Paris. The opera awaits, as do your lessons. If you don't, those fools at my theater will be extremely sorry. And so will you."

"As you command, oh great master."

Fuming, I slammed the gate to the churchyard behind me, and barreled across the town square to the inn.

The following morning I sat before the fire, coffee in hand. Madame Valerius was amenable to my returning to Paris, though I felt awful for asking her so soon after our arrival. I had been forced to lie, explaining the directors had sent me a telegram demanding my return. Madame and I decided she would stay on at the inn for the next two weeks while I returned to Paris with Claudette. Alfred would be sent there immediately to aid her.

The front door to the inn burst open.

A gendarme half carried a shivering Raoul with blue lips and disheveled hair. Monsieur Delacroix accompanied him.

"Raoul!" I cried, racing across the room.

"Put him in front of the fire," the gendarme said.

The innkeeper wrapped Raoul in a blanket while his wife handed Raoul a steaming cup of tea laced with brandy. "Drink this, Monsieur," she said. "It'll get the blood flowing."

I sat across from him, fear roaring in my ears. "Are you all right?" My voice cracked with emotion. This was my fault.

"What were you doing at the church last night?" the gendarme asked.

"I was following Christine," he said, his voice hoarse. He slurped a hearty dose of tea. "She left the inn so late, I feared for her safety." His face softened as he looked at me.

The gendarme rested his right hand on the pistol holstered at his hip. "So the better question is: What were you doing out, Mademoiselle? This man could have died. We found him nearly unconscious in the graveyard, covered in skulls from the charnel house."

My stomach folded in on itself as I imagined the skulls littered over Raoul's body.

The innkeeper's wife shot me a pleading look. If I mentioned she had given me a key, her husband would give her hell, and the police might as well.

"I couldn't sleep so I visited Papa's grave. The church was lit and unlocked, so I assumed it would be fine. It's so close—just across the square. Oh, Raoul." I kneeled beside him, tears threatening to spill down my cheeks. "I'm so sorry."

The innkeeper refilled Raoul's tea. "You're lucky you didn't get frostbite. I'll heat a bowl of beef stew. You need your strength."

"I was worried about you," Raoul said, his face still pale with cold. "And I wanted to talk to you. To apologize." His eyes moistened as he looked at me.

I felt my insides melt, my defenses vanish. How would I ever stay away from him?

"You haven't told us what happened yet," Monsieur Delacroix said, his tone curt.

I was startled at the professor's voice. I had forgotten he was there —and hadn't begun to process why he would be in Bretagne. Had he followed me out of concern, or did he plan to confront me about the ghost? I felt my face go as white as Raoul's. The Angel was here, too, and I had to keep Delacroix away from him. It seemed too coincidental, though perhaps my overactive imagination created links that weren't there. Suddenly I was glad I was leaving for Paris in a couple of hours. This little inn was too small for the lot of us.

"Monsieur Delacroix"—I stood to greet him properly—"what a surprise to see you here."

He kissed my cheek. "Yes, I am only stopping for a day on my way to Le Havre for business. I knew you and Jeanne would be here. She sent me a letter letting me know, so I thought I would look in on you. I do feel responsible for you both, after all."

Though relieved he had a legitimate reason for being there, his manner made me uneasy. He seemed . . . unsettled.

Raoul's lips regained their color, though his eyes still had the glazed-over look of fever. I wanted to smooth the lock of hair from his eyes, rub his hands between my own, and comfort him.

"We still haven't heard the story," the gendarme said, giving Delacroix a cold eye. The professor had overstepped. "How did you come to be surrounded by skulls?"

"I watched Christine walk through the church to get to the cemetery. Rather than risk her seeing me, I scaled the fence and hid in the pines surrounding the churchyard. There was a violin." He frowned. "And I heard voices. Christine sounded angry and fled through the church. I wanted to race after her, but"—he clenched his jaw—"I had to see who she was talking to first."

"And who was it?" Delacroix's eyebrow arched.

"I will ask the questions here, Professor," the gendarme said, pushing out his chest in an act of superiority. "Mademoiselle Daaé, if the person in question had something to do with Raoul's assault, we need to find him and make sure he doesn't attempt anything like this again. Then there's the matter of defiling the charnel house."

My lungs constricted. The Angel had intended for Raoul to die, or perhaps it was only a warning. But what could I tell them? To say it was a random thief wouldn't explain the violin. No thief would play the violin in the middle of the night near a graveyard. I hung my head, defeated. I had to tell them the truth. There was nothing else to say.

"At first I spoke to my father. When I asked him for a sign, a violin began to play. A Strainer violin, just like the one he owned while alive. Then I heard a voice. It was the Angel of Music," I added in a barely audible whisper.

The innkeeper and his wife stared at me in disbelief. The gendarme rolled his eyes.

Raoul groaned and leaned his head back onto his chair. "The Angel of Music again?" He's followed you here?"

A smile spread across Delacroix's face and his eyes shined with triumph, as if he'd finally won a game he had been playing unsuccessfully for some time.

"Yes," I said, shifting from one foot to the other.

"So you talk to ghosts?" the gendarme asked. "Are you one of those bizarre spiritualists then?"

I didn't answer, but looked down to study my hands.

Delacroix tipped my chin so he could see my eyes. "He followed you from the opera house?"

I didn't respond. I couldn't shake the feeling that the professor had known the Angel would be here, though the idea seemed absurd.

"What happened after you heard the voices?" The gendarme sighed, his impatience was growing thin. He didn't believe any of this, it was clear.

"Christine left while I waited in the shadows. After several minutes passed, this voice said, 'I know you are there, and if you know what's best for you, you'll keep your distance. From me, and especially from Christine. She belongs to me.'" He looked to me for verification.

I couldn't bear the sadness in his eyes and looked away.

Raoul grimaced. "Infuriated, I demanded the man show himself, told him to stop being a coward by hiding all the time. His laugh sliced right through me. I knew then this man had seen and done horrible things. I truly fear for you, Christine."

Monsieur Delacroix latched on to each word greedily. His overeager manner set me on edge; I found myself all but glaring at him.

"A cloaked figure stepped out from the far end of the tree line. I chased him and managed to grab hold of his cloak's edges. The man whipped around and—"

"Go on," Delacroix said, breathless.

My mouth gaped open. Raoul had seen him! Had had his hands on him! He was no ghost, no angel, just as I had suspected, but a man!

"He wore a mask covering half of his face. The other half . . ." He shuddered. "It was obvious he was badly scarred."

I froze. The dream I'd had rushed to my mind's eye. Somehow, deep in the recesses of my brain, I had known all along there was something to that dream, that mask. I grimaced at the thought of what lie beneath it. What had happened to the poor man to make him hate everyone—and himself—so much? I didn't understand why he thought I could make it better for him.

"After that, he hissed a warning and cracked me over the head," Raoul said. "I must have gone unconscious because I woke to the sound of the gendarme's voice." He glanced at the policeman with a grateful look.

"And we found you covered in skulls, half frozen to death." The gendarme rubbed his bearded chin. "Clearly this angel-man wanted you out of the picture."

I knew he did, but I couldn't tell them the truth. Raoul would be silenced indefinitely should I breathe a word. Tears of frustration stung my eyes. I felt like one of my precious canaries being batted by the tomcat; a songbird in a cage, beating my wings to escape a predator.

"He wants Christine for himself." Raoul glared at me as though I were the perpetrator. "And we don't know how she feels about him."

"Well, Mademoiselle Daaé, how do you feel about the Angel?" Delacroix sounded amused. "Please, enlighten us so we may know how to proceed."

"He's my teacher, nothing more."

"And a heckler, a liar, and likely a murderer," the professor said, his mouth twisted into a snarl.

I cringed at his vehemence. I'd never seen the professor so angry.

"Now, Professor, we don't know that he wanted to kill Monsieur le Vicomte." The gendarme folded his hands over his protruding belly. It was obvious he hadn't seen much in the way of criminal activity in the little town. "All we know is he assaulted him. We blindly assume Raoul is the innocent, but perhaps the Angel was provoked."

"That's preposterous!" Raoul jumped to his feet, knocking the empty glass to the floor. It shattered on impact. "I wouldn't threaten a man except in battle, or if he hurt someone I love. I can call upon twenty men to testify on behalf of my character."

The gendarme raised his hands and said, "Calm yourself. We need to examine all of the facts. No one is accusing you of a crime."

The innkeeper's wife scuttled between Raoul and the professor, sweeping up broken glass with a hand broom and pan.

I glanced at the wall clock. It was already ten o'clock and my train left at eleven thirty. I still needed to gather my things and fetch Claudette.

"Forgive me, gentlemen, but I must prepare my valise. My train departs soon."

"Train?" Raoul stood, his eyes full of longing. "You're leaving?"

"Not to worry, I'll see her to the train and back to Paris," Delacroix said firmly.

"Pardon me?" I said, taken aback by the professor's insistence. "My maid is coming with me. We'll be fine. You have business to attend to in Le Havre and I am quite capable of seeing myself home."

"I'll not hear of you traveling alone. Not after this mess." He fixed me with his vivid eyes. "It's too dangerous, Christine. Besides, the business I have can wait."

I couldn't make out the professor's intentions. He had arrived in a flurry only moments before, claiming important business; yet, after hearing about the scene with Raoul in the cemetery and my returning to the opera, he suddenly changed his mind. And then there was that smile of satisfaction. He was planning something. Still, to argue with him would only strengthen his resolve and cause him to question my loyalties. I didn't have it in me at that moment to argue.

"If you're certain it doesn't imposition you in any way. I wouldn't want you to abandon your studies."

"It's no trouble at all. I was headed to visit a friend who is a retired professor, so in truth, there was some business to be discussed, but little."

"Won't he miss your visit?" I said, more a plea than a question.

"Think nothing of it. It's far more important that I take care of someone I consider family." He smiled broadly.

"Very well, the train leaves in an hour. Please send your friend my regrets for detaining you."

Judging by his expression, he seemed almost relieved.

"I'll meet you here in the salon in a quarter of an hour. We should get to the station *tout de suite*. Vicomte, Officer," he said, tipping his head politely.

My eyes paused on Raoul's lips, now rosy with warmth. I looked down and cleared my throat. "I hope you recover quickly, Raoul. Please take care of yourself."

I turned before I could see the emotion in his eyes, and made a dash for the stairs.

~ 17 ~

During the journey back to Paris, the professor and I spoke little. I replayed the events in the cemetery over and over again—and how spooked and bedraggled Raoul had looked. My heart clenched each time, and I grew furious with the Angel. I didn't know what to do—how to resolve this. What's more, I couldn't reconcile the loss I felt. The Angel wasn't an angel at all, but as real and alive as me. Somewhere along the way I had grown to believe, or to hope at least, that spirits lived among us, that somehow he really was a spirit that looked out for me. Now I scolded myself for my stupidity.

The following evening I headed to the opera house, weary from lack of sleep and anxiety.

Meg Giry grabbed my hand the moment I arrived, pulling me into a shaded nook between the wall and a staircase. "Monsieur Montcharmin has been talking about you." Her caramel waves brushed her cheeks as she tipped her head near mine. "They've been quarreling about some notes they've received."

"Again?" I groaned. Why did the Angel insist on mentioning me? He was creating more enemies, which I did not need, especially among those who paid me.

"Are you in some sort of trouble?" Meg asked, eyes wide.

"No." I shrugged, trying to disguise my alarm. "I don't know."

"It's the opera ghost again, isn't it?" Her voice hushed when mentioning the Angel.

"He wants me to succeed, and doesn't care who he offends to make that happen."

"Be careful. You're making enemies, whether you intend to or not."

I sighed. "I know, but what am I to do?"

Meg shrugged. "Talk to the directors. Make sure they know you're not involved in this, and then we'll find a way to lure the ghost out into the open and figure out what he wants."

If Delacroix had been unable to flush the Angel out of hiding from his lair at the opera, we certainly couldn't. Besides, I knew what he wanted. He wanted me, in whatever form he could have me, and the stage—to be his and his alone.

"You're right." I nodded numbly. I had to tell the directors I'd returned early anyway. "Thanks, Meg. I'll talk with them now." ⸱

"Bonne chance." She kissed my cheek and scurried off to the practice room.

At the office door, I steeled myself for a reprimand and knocked. Regardless of what they had to say, something must change.

"Come in," Monsieur Richard's voice called.

"Messieurs, good day," I said. "I've put off the vacation to the sea after all. I wanted to let you know I will be here at your disposal."

"Very good," Monsieur Richard said. "And good timing, I'd say, eh Montcharmin?"

"Sit down, Mademoiselle Daaé." Montcharmin motioned me toward a seat. "We need to discuss a troubling matter with you."

"I'll stand, if you please." I stood at the edge of his desk, which was stacked with years' worth of ledgers beside a freshly inked letter. I sneaked a glance at the salutation. My pulse began to thump in my ears. The letter was addressed to OG, the opera ghost.

"Fine, fine." Monsieur Richard hovered over a crystal decanter filled with tawny liquid. He poured a splash into two glasses before raising his brow at me. "Care for a scotch?"

Surprised by his bold gesture, I frowned and said, "Thank you, no."

Women didn't drink spirits at this time of day, though in the theatre, one did many things outside the norm. Still, this was no social call. I wanted them to get on with their admonishments, if that's what this was about.

"You may have heard"—Monsieur Moncharmin paused to roll the scotch around in his glass before tipping it back to swallow the liquor in one gulp—"there have been notes circulating in the opera house, delivered by Madame Giry from the ghost. Oddly, most of them have your name in them. Would you care to explain your connection with the OG?"

Indignation rose inside me. After this little meeting, I would confront the phantom, demand he show himself, and cease all of this nonsense at once. If Carlotta was to rule the stage over me, so be it. I would happily accept my pay and remain as understudy until I could figure out my next move.

"The ghost has helped me with lessons, but I have never seen him. He is a ghost, just as you all have said." I thought of the violin in the graveyard and him clutching Raoul's cape. With effort, I shoved the image away and continued, "I come to work each day, practice in my dressing room, and hope to sing on stage. The notes, and any other ploys, are not my own. I am as appalled as you are, and detest how my name is ceaselessly drawn through the mud. Messieurs." I stuck out my chin.

"It is curious, his obsession with you, Mademoiselle." Monsieur Moncharmin stroked the curled ends of his mustache. "You're certain you've done nothing to invoke his attentions?"

I threw out my arms, my frustration bubbling over. "Just how would I have done that? I've never laid eyes on this . . . creature. How could I possibly force him to do anything?"

"He pushes your career." Montcharmin leaned forward in his chair. "At the expense of others."

"And he wishes to bankrupt us," Monsieur Richard muttered. "One hundred thousand francs indeed."

"How much?" I asked, taken aback. "Gentlemen, I assure you, I have nothing to do with his demands. If I hear from him directly, I will tell him to cease the notes at once. To leave you and the others be."

"A warning, Daaé." Montcharmin tipped forward at the waist, a shadow falling across the bridge of his nose. His eyes glittered beneath a graying brow. "We will have to dismiss you should further disruptions occur. Consider this your first and final warning."

"I can't account for the ghost's whereabouts. It's unfair to hold me responsible for his doings. Should you dismiss me, gentlemen, you will regret the loss of my talents. With me gone, you'll have no one to fill the lead when Carlotta feigns an illness." I tossed my hair in defiance, sending a golden cascade over my shoulder. "Now, if that is all, I have rehearsal."

They stared at me, silent and dumbstruck by my sudden change. I was no longer a naïve chorus girl, so easily managed and bossed about.

"Well, since you're here, why don't you join the chorus on stage this evening?" Monsieur Richard said at last.

"Perhaps that will appease him for now." Montcharmin nodded in agreement.

"I'll check with Gabriel." I stalked across the office. "Good evening, gentlemen."

I closed the door behind me, relishing the surprise imprinted upon their faces. I smiled as I headed to Gabriel's office. They may not like the notes, they might even dismiss me, but at least I had stood my ground.

After a quick meeting with Gabriel, I scooted to my dressing room. I'd had enough of the Angel's games. If he wished to continue as my tutor, I wanted to know who he was truly, and his intent after his opera went to stage. I would set my own rules—and boundaries for him as well. No more violence, no more threats, or I would turn him over to the police and leave him for good. From this point forward, I would be in charge.

I locked my dressing room door and flung my overcoat onto the sofa. I turned to face the center of the room. "Angel, show yourself at once. I demand to know who you are. I'm finished with your games."

Nothing but silence.

My temperature rose as my heart pounded a staccato beat in my chest.

"I have other ambitions, you know," I said. "I don't have to stay here. I'm tired of doing what everyone else expects of me. I'm tired of being threatened." Fury mounted inside me and courage flooded my limbs. "Show yourself at once!"

228

A *pop* and *click* split the silence, and the lights to my dressing room went out.

I opened my mouth to scream but a cool finger pressed gently against my lips.

"You summoned me, *ma chèrie*," said the smooth tenor I had grown to know so well.

My heart beat rapidly like a bird's, my pulse thrashing against my throat. I searched the blackness around me for a silhouette, a shadow, anything to shed light on the dark Angel. My courage melted like butter on hot bread. He was a man—flesh and blood—and a dangerous man at that.

"It makes no difference whether I am a man or a ghost. Yet you feel me upon you." A soft laugh vibrated in the air around me. "Yes, dear one, I am real. Alive. A man, as you are a woman, but I think you knew that. You have never believed in spirits."

That wasn't entirely true. My chest heaved as I tried to regain my composure.

A whooshing sound stirred a breeze around my face, and with it, the lights went on once more. I whirled around. He had disappeared again.

"Who are you?"

An eerie silence filled the room.

I stared into the mirror on the back wall, but saw only my own frightened reflection. He must have come from behind it. There seemed to be no other way into the room, unless the armoire had a false back. I glanced at it and turned back to my reflection. No, this made the most sense, though the glass might be too heavy to move. I would search the room later.

"Why does it matter what my name is?" His voice echoed from the walls.

"Because it does," I insisted. "Tell me. I wish to know you. That isn't possible unless I call you by name."

"You wish to know me, do you?"

The lights flickered. My form faded in the mirror and the silhouette of a man in a hat and cape replaced my own.

I gasped and stepped backward several steps.

"It's me, *ma chèrie*. Come closer." The hand in the mirror motioned to me.

My pulse hammered in my ears. I didn't—I couldn't—be near him.

"After tonight," he said, "Carlotta will be unable to perform."

"You aren't going to hurt her?" I willed my voice to remain even.

"What do you take me for, Christine? I am an *angel*, remember?" The beautiful voice fractured into a terrifying laugh. After he regained his composure, he said, "My name is Erik. That's all you need to know for now. In time, I will reveal my true identity to you."

"Prépare-toi," he said. "This will be the last time you play a role of such insignificance." His breath tickled my ear.

I jumped at his nearness, throwing out my hands. My fingers met a patch of skin, grooved and ridged in an unnatural way. I yanked my hand away, repulsed by the sensation.

"Do not touch me!" he snarled.

"I'm sorry. Forgive me, I—"

"Enough! I have things to tend to. I must go."

The lights flickered a final time.

"Erik?" I spun around on my heel. He had gone.

I glanced at the clock on my vanity. There was no time to waste. The show would begin soon. I tied my hair back in a low, flat queue to resemble a boy's from the past century, dressed in culottes and shoes with buckles, and rushed through my warm-up exercises. My part as a boy was small, but nonetheless I needed to be ready.

After I dressed, I headed to the cast room on the wing of the stage, mind racing. I couldn't imagine how Erik knew Carlotta would be unable to perform after tonight, unless he was planning something sinister. My stomach clenched at the thought. I should warn the directors—or Carlotta—but what could I say? I had no proof he would truly enact a plan, and what's more, they would blame me for his schemes.

When I reached the holding room near the stage, I joined the other cast members. Neck taut and tension high, I felt a headache coming on. I walked back and forth, rolling my shoulders forward. If my vocal cords weren't relaxed, I would sound like a squeaky wheel.

The next instant, Carlotta pushed herself to the edge of the stage to await her cue. When she received the signal, she glanced in my direction and threw me a false smile.

Too anxious to be obsequious, I looked past her.

The curtain went up. Light flooded the stage and Carlotta's voice projected perfectly over the orchestra. I watched the diva intently, stomach swirling with equal parts anticipation and fear.

When my cue came at last, I leapt out from behind the folds of fabric. As I opened my mouth to sing the part of Siebel, Faust's student, my eyes were drawn to the box seats where I had once seen Raoul. There he sat, eyes glued to the stage, pain contorting his features. I refocused on the audience, pushing my own pain—and him—away.

Carlotta joined me in the faux garden carrying her bouquet of lilacs. She launched into the ballad of the "King of Thule" with such alacrity and beauty, I held my breath. She hit the perfect octave, showed perfect pitch. I glanced down at the dull buckle on my shoe. I could never compete with her vocals. The woman was a true star.

And then it happened.

The next syllable, Carlotta's voice cracked. Her lyrics came out as a croak.

The orchestra stopped abruptly.

My hand flew to my mouth in surprise. She sounded like a toad!

Much of the audience gasped in shock. They had never seen such a thing; Carlotta's performances were always flawless.

Horror marring her features, Carlotta wrapped a hand around her throat.

Guilt and pity—and horror—washed over me. How could Erik have known her voice would falter midsong? Perhaps through a potion, but that didn't seem likely. I glanced at the box seats where Raoul and his brother sat and at the box on the far right side of the stage—box five.

Erik's box. The directors had taken the seats instead, and now leaned over the railing, mouths agape.

Carlotta threw out her arms, signaling the orchestra to begin again. The crowd stilled, their faces set into masks of concern. The maestro's troubled expression smoothed and he tapped his wand on the edge of the podium. With a burst, the song began again.

Carlotta filled the pool of light at center stage. She held her head high, the glitter from her fake jewels sparkling. The horns bellowed and the jaunty cadence of strings joined in the melody. She inhaled deeply and began. The first few notes floated out over the audience, wrapping them in the perfection of her voice.

I held my breath. In spite of my feelings toward the woman, I hoped she would make it through the song. I didn't wish such embarrassment on anyone.

As she began the next stanza, I squeezed my hands into fists.

The audience leaned forward, holding its breath.

The diva's voice croaked. This time it was a series of spasms, like those of a tree toad.

Carlotta cried out, bosom heaving.

The audience exclaimed. Many jumped to their feet. Something was amiss, and everyone in the room could feel it, as if a malevolent cloud had rolled over the seats and floated toward the copper ceiling.

My arms crawled with goose bumps. What had Erik done?

Carlotta stomped across the stage and ducked behind the curtain.

I jumped out of the way as a bevy of her friends raced to console her. The moment she left the stage, the audience dissolved into a melee of confusion. Someone shouted for people to remain seated. Charles, the stage director, signaled for the curtain to close. As it swept closed, someone screamed.

I looked out at the audience with a tightness in my chest. This was it. The horrible something for which I'd been waiting.

The massive chandelier suspended above the audience began to sway. With each swing, the brass fixture gained momentum. Screams filled the auditorium as the screech of rending metal echoed through

232

the theatre.

I looked at Raoul's seat, scarcely able to breathe. He watched in shock as the light fixture swung in broad strokes overhead.

"Ladies and gentlemen"—Charles projected over the confusion—"please exit quickly through the far doors. Quickly!"

Just then, the cable lengthened as it unraveled from a support in the ceiling.

"Run!" I screamed.

My voice blended with the chorus of shrieks and chaos.

With a resounding *snap*, the chandelier's cord gave way and smashed down onto the rows of seats beneath it. Glass exploded and metal twisted on impact. The unlucky few who had not escaped to the safety of the hall were crushed to death beneath the weight of brass, steel, and shattered glass.

My legs felt weak. The room began to spin. People were hurt—dead! —and it was at Erik's hand. I knew it. I knew he would do something terrible again, because of me. I gasped for breath, cursing the stays I had pulled so tightly to hide my breasts beneath the male costume.

"Get the gendarme!" The stage director shoved me aside. "*Dieu*, someone has been killed!"

In the next instant, the floor gave way beneath my feet.

An inky darkness swallowed me. The sounds of mayhem and fear disappeared—but for my screams. My stomach dropped as I flailed in empty space.

I was falling.

~ 18 ~

After what felt like minutes of hurtling through space, I landed on something soft, grunting at the impact. I must have triggered a trapdoor on the stage, though I couldn't think how. I remembered the stage director pushing past me. The screams, the body trapped beneath the chandelier . . . and Charles's words:

Someone has been killed.

I bit my knuckle to hold back the sobs clawing at my throat. This was my fault. If I had had courage enough to tell Erik I didn't want to sing, didn't need his help, those lives would have been spared.

I had caused the death of my father, of Joseph Buquet, and now I was responsible for this.

Anguish poured down my cheeks in a river of tears. I didn't belong here. I would never be better than Carlotta, and I didn't care. Every moment I spent at the opera house endangered others. And oh, Raoul. I hated being here. I wanted to go. I didn't want to sing anymore.

My sobs ceased abruptly, and bewilderment stole over me. I didn't want to sing?

I don't want to sing.

To sing for enjoyment, yes, but not for money, fame, and fortune—or to be the center of the Paris music world. That wasn't me. It had never been my dream. I blinked rapidly to clear the tears and wiped my nose on my sleeve. I had done it all for Papa; I thought it had helped him somehow, and eased his grief over Mother. The music Papa and I created had soothed us both. But the cost of it now—

Something stirred behind me. I peered into the darkness but was unable to make out a single shape.

"Who's there?" My voice came out shaky, heavy with emotion.

A scratching sound followed a squeak.

A rat. I cringed, remembering the fat city rats I'd seen too often in our temporary homes. Their fur slick with filth, rustling through piles of rotted hay, or their pointed nails scraping inside the walls. I ran a finger over the scar on my left hand. A rat's bite had left its mark; the wound had bled and stained my dress. Papa had made me soak my hand in steaming-hot water for three days to ward off infection.

I dusted dirt from my culottes and looked up at the ceiling, trying to make out the grooves of the trapdoor. The panel had closed and sealed perfectly. Too perfectly. I couldn't make out a single crack where light seeped through to guide my way. Panic squeezed my chest.

"Help!" I shouted. "Help! I'm trapped!"

Suddenly a hand covered my mouth, an arm snaked around my middle. Someone dragged me backward. I struggled, but couldn't break free of my captor's steely grip. He whipped me around and pulled my arms together, binding them roughly in front of my body with something that felt like rope.

I screamed again as a blindfold slipped over my eyes.

"Do not fear," a silky tenor whispered in my ear. "It is only me. I have something to show you."

Relief crashed over me, followed by dread. If I had nothing to fear, why did he bind my hands and blindfold me?

As if reading my mind he continued, "You know I would never hurt you, dear one. You are my apprentice. My responsibility."

A hand sheathed with a leather glove ran down the side of my face and traced my lips.

I recoiled from his touch. "Madame Valerius will worry, especially when she hears about the chandelier. Please, Erik, let me go."

The chandelier that killed at least one and wounded others, for which he was responsible—for which *I* was responsible.

"Not to worry. I've sent her a note and informed her you will be visiting friends for a while."

A while? My knees buckled.

His grip tightened around my waist. "It's all right. Come, I will look after you. Now duck your head. The tunnel ceiling is low." He steered me forward with a gentle hand.

We walked for some time in silence.

Finally, I couldn't bear to hold the burning question inside me another moment. "Did you sever the cable supporting the chandelier?"

"You think me capable of murder?"

"I don't know." Perhaps the chandelier had been an accident, the cable weak. Yet I knew the truth already.

His low laugh echoed off the walls of the tunnel.

Afraid to say the wrong thing, I remained silent. If I incurred his wrath, Lord knew what he would do. As we walked on, I was thankful for the boy's costume I was wearing.

We turned again and the atmosphere shifted from musty to damp. When the stench of sewage and sulfur permeated the air, I knew we were no longer beneath the opera house. The sound of trickling water reverberated in the underground cavern.

"We're in the sewer?" I choked on the pungent odor of human waste. Much longer in the bowels of the city, and I would vomit. I strained against the ties binding my hands; panted as the thick air expanded in my throat and chest. I had to remain calm. It wouldn't help if I panicked.

"Have patience. All will be revealed to you very soon. For now, I have a story for you." He paused to maneuver me around a bend. "There once was a young girl. She was beautiful—so beautiful everyone's eyes followed her wherever she went. She sang like a songbird at her father's insistence. In fact, he claimed the Angel of Music guided her."

I splashed through a puddle and cringed as my stockings were soaked through. In that moment, I was grateful for the dark.

After several minutes of silence, he continued. "Across town there was a man who possessed a gift of his own, one that would not only put him in the public eye, but make him infamous. It would cause him more pain than he could ever imagine."

When Erik didn't continue, I asked, "What was his gift?"

"Illusions."

My footsteps faltered. "Illusions," I echoed, my voice hoarse.

"Tricks and trifles. Making others believe what they wished to see; reflecting their dreams back to them with tantalizing imagery and pretty tales. Constructing trapdoors, false cabinets, movable mirrors. Yes, illusions. This man could read his audience—he knew what triggered their imagination. How to transport them to a place of magic."

Magic. My heart pounded harder at the word.

"What happened to him?"

"Many loved his show, but others feared him and wanted to expose him as a fraud. He was harassed and accosted."

Suddenly, the blindfold fell away. A ladder led upward to the ceiling. I pivoted to take in my surroundings, but my eyes detected only the faintest light. Walls ran on either side of us and a recessed shaft below brimmed with sewer water. Beside me, my dark angel loomed. His black suit, hat, and flowing cape blended with the walls, yet the silhouette of his face gleamed white.

I gasped.

A porcelain mask covered half of his face, just as Raoul had said—just like my dream. A memory resurfaced, an afternoon with Claudette.

Did you see that man? she had asked.

Which? I didn't see anyone.

Claudette had frowned. *He's disappeared now. Wears a mask o'er half his face...*

I covered my mouth with my hand. Had Erik followed me all this time, tracked me like an animal? But why? I grew light-headed as one thought followed another. Perhaps he had planned to bring me to the opera house. But ... it was Monsieur Delacroix who helped me gain an audition.

"Angel—Erik—" I clutched the bottom rung of the metal ladder to steady myself. "Do you wear a mask to cover a scar?"

"That is one reason, yes. And also not to be recognized." He motioned toward the ladder. "Enough talk. Go."

I mounted the ladder, mumbling another prayer of thanks I wore boy's clothing. Soon, I felt him climbing below me. My stomach churned at his proximity and I forced myself to focus on the metal rungs. After another two meters, we would reach the top.

Another step, and another—and the sole of my right shoe slipped on the slick metal. I cried out in surprise.

A hand steadied me.

"Careful," Erik said. "Here, you'll need me to open the sewer cap anyway."

He climbed until his body was directly over me, around me.

I breathed heavily at the nearness of him, head swimming. Confusion roiled inside me. With a hand at my waist, he guided me the reminder of the way. Once he removed the sewer cap, he carefully maneuvered around me and pulled himself through the hole. I reached for his outstretched hand, eager to escape the stink of the sewer. His hand's cold boniness surprised me and I nearly let go. I screeched as my other foot slipped.

"Steady," he said, hauling me up through the hole.

As I reached the surface, cool night air bathed my face. I scanned the street around me, trying to get my bearings. We stood on a side street about a kilometer from the opera house. My heart stalled. It was a street I recognized from my nightmares.

Erik spun me around gently. In my ear he whispered, "My former place of employment. And the place where"—his voice cracked—"my love perished."

A theatre in the throes of reconstruction loomed before me.

I gasped, mind reeling as the pieces came together. The throwing of voices behind the walls, the Platonized glass, the trapdoors. Erik's long black cape.

"It was you."

He nodded, mask pearlescent in the moonlight. "I am the Masked Conjurer."

~ 19 ~

Did you know my father?"

"In a sense," he said.

"I almost died," I whispered, my eyes fastened on the theatre's new roof. The last time I had seen it, it had been a charred, gaping hole. The image of a hand with broken fingers flashed into my mind, of being lifted from the ground and carried from the theatre. It was the last thing I had seen before going completely unconscious that night. "Someone rescued me."

He leaned closer, amber eyes glittering. "*I* rescued you. You lay against your father's body. I wasn't sure you were alive, but I had to try."

My throat flooded with emotion. The Masked Conjurer—my dark angel—had rescued me, even then. I swallowed hard, and stared ahead to regain control of my emotions. A stray cat meandered in the alley next to the theatre, its burnt-orange fur visible each time it stepped into a pool of light.

When I could speak without my voice wavering I said, "There were men who rushed the stage, set everything on fire."

"Yes." His voice took on an edge.

"I'm sorry you lost someone you loved in the fire. Your assistant." How could I not feel sympathy for someone who had lost so much. Erik had given up his magic and the woman he loved, lived as a ghost of his former self. He had lost everything, just as I had that night.

"I have found a way to console myself." A smile resembling a grimace stretched his thin lips over an overly large set of teeth.

His skeletal smile startled me from my temporary lapse into sympathizing for such a man. He wasn't the same person he once was. Kidnapping and murder had become his consolation.

Pulse skipping, I glanced at the alley several meters ahead. It was a dead end. A series of dark storefronts spanned the rest of the block, and a large field flanked the other side of the theatre. There was no clear escape. Should I run, I had no place to hide at this hour. Perhaps he would release me when we returned. Perhaps he needed to explain himself, and then he would let me go as he did every evening. For now, the most sensible thing to do was remain calm, act as if all was normal.

"Have you lived in the opera house since then?" I asked, attempting to keep my voice even.

"These last four years. I've built a home there, one that is complex, but a home nonetheless."

I nodded. So complex, in fact, that neither Delacroix nor any of the others trying to hunt him down had managed to find him.

A damp breeze stirred the hair on the back of my neck. I shivered. "Please, Erik. I'm ready to go home."

"As you wish."

In a swift movement, he covered my mouth with a handkerchief.

Chemicals burned my nose and throat. Before I had time to react, my head grew foggy and the world dissolved.

I awoke in a four-poster bed beneath a deep blue velvet coverlet. I shot up, staring at the strange surroundings. Given the dank air, I knew I must be somewhere below the opera house. I groaned. I had asked Erik to bring me home, not to *his* home. As I imagined what he had in store for me, fear followed revulsion. Some part of Erik was evil —at the very least, broken and unstable—and I was at his mercy.

I slipped from the bedcovers and my skirts swished around my legs. *Skirts?*

I rushed toward a mirror, turmoil roiling inside me. I was wearing a boy's costume when he took me hostage. Now I wore a scarlet ball gown with full skirts, trimmed with ribbons along the hem. The neckline dipped low and curved over the contours of my breasts in a daring fashion, and demi-sleeves draped my bared shoulders. With my palm, I covered the vast expanse of milky-white skin laid bare. The gown was lush, sensual. I had never worn anything so overt. What's more, I had no recollection of how I came to be wearing it.

Erik's hands must have been upon me, unfastening my chemisier, slipping down the culottes, tucking me into the expensive silk. A tingling stirred somewhere inside me, but was quickly squashed with disgust. I turned to view the back of the gown; it swept about my ankles, but I couldn't feel it against my legs. I lifted my skirts to my knees and realized with relief that he had not removed my trousers. I peeked down the front of the dress and saw my corset, felt along my back and it was still tied overly tight so I might look more like a boy on stage. I leaned against the glass and breathed a sigh of relief. He hadn't done anything too indecent.

Reassured, I strode to the bedside table. Ignoring the tea tray of ham, bread, and a pot of jam, I reached for the square of stationery tucked just under the plate's edge. Erik had left a note?

I will return soon, my love. Eat, and rest well.
—E

My love. I shivered at the implication of his words. The way his burning amber eyes had drunk me in. He might protect me, respect my wishes, and release me as he had in the past, but I couldn't be certain. Erik had no qualms about threatening me—and kidnapping me against my will. I crumpled the paper.

I had to find a way out—now.

Scanning the room, I took in an armoire, a few luxurious tables, and many chests fanning across the cavernous room, along with a writing desk and a set of nude statues serving as candelabra. Dozens of candles blazed everywhere, even from sconces on the walls. At last, I spied a lantern and started toward it. To my dismay, the gas well was dry. With an irritated huff, I stared into the black corridor leading away from the cavernous room. That had to be the way out, but if I got

243

lost, who would find me? *He* would, and he would be outraged I had tried to escape.

It was a risk I would have to take.

More afraid of the man than the unknown of the dark, I trudged forward. As the light behind me faded, humidity coated my skin and the smell of water permeated the air. All of a sudden, I slammed my head against an overhang. I cried out in pain and surprise. My head spun with stars, and I blinked away instant tears. With a light hand, I touched my forehead and winced at the already-rising knot. Reaching out in front of me, I felt along the outcropping of wall. A hole large enough to move through opened along the passageway. I ducked through it and carefully stood, arms stretched overhead. I breathed a sigh of relief as I stood tall again.

After several strides more, a pinpoint of light shone in the distance. I hurried toward it until I could finally make out its source. A lantern hung from a peg affixed to the wall, emitting a red glow. I picked up my pace, excitement winding through my limbs. A way out!

Suddenly, the ground beneath my feet grew softer, and my heels sank into the earth. After another few steps, I understood why. The lantern illuminated the placid surface of a small lake. A boat tethered to a dock floated on the water—on the opposite side of the lake.

My heart sank. I cursed my weakness. Why did I have to be afraid of water? My knees trembled at the thought of sinking to the bottom, of cold water rushing down my throat and into my lungs. Of creatures lurking in the water's depths.

But it might be the only way out.

With a steadying breath, I walked to the shoreline. The inky well seemed unearthly in its calm. Yet, in spite of the undisturbed surface, I couldn't make out the bottom—it was just too dark. I stared glumly at the boat, and back at the shoreline again.

Don't be such a coward, Christine. You should at least try.

With a surge of courage, I waded into the lake. I gasped at the cold, but continued forward, pushing away the terror of all that black, fathomless water. Water seeped into my shoes and stockings, crept higher along my ankles and calves, swept over the crest of my knee. I squeezed my eyes closed and began to hum Beethoven's Concerto Number Five to block the terror mounting in my chest. I pushed forward another step.

That instant, the bottom gave way. I screeched, and then careened downward, plunging into the depths. Water filled my mouth and darkness enveloped me as I sank. I thrashed in the icy water, reaching for something—anything—to latch on to, to pull myself out. But there was nothing—only me and an endless dark pool.

This was it. This would be the end. But what choice did I have? I could suffer torture and death at the hands of a madman, or drown quietly, swiftly, never to be heard from again. My lungs burned as I struggled against the pull of the water, and the heavy gown.

Just then, my feet hit rock. I scrabbled along it, frantic to reach the surface. When the tapered edge inclined sharply, I pushed off with my feet, shooting to the surface like an arrow. As my head broke the surface, I gasped, sucking in blessed air. I crawled along the bank through shallow water to the shore, water streaming down my shivering body. Sobs racked my lungs until I'd left the water completely.

I slumped on the shore, gasping, sobbing. I couldn't do this. I'd have to find another way out. Dejected, I pulled myself to my feet and followed the path back to the bedchamber. I collapsed on the bed. Somehow, I would have to use my wits to escape.

After changing into a dry chemise, I crawled into bed for a spell to recover. Sometime later, I awoke to the sound of music. Confused, I sat up and looked around, recognition coming as I glanced around the room. My dejection returned. I was still in Erik's lair.

The music grew louder, the notes cresting like a tidal wave. A lusty, booming sound pulsed through pipes that could only come from one instrument—the organ. A voice drifted over the sounds of the instrument, almost painful in its beauty. Erik may have been a great conjurer, but he was a brilliant musician. I frowned, thinking how odd it was that we should have such similarities.

I wrapped a shawl around my shoulders, covering the top half of my chemise, and followed the music to a large mirror near the armoire. Puzzled, I knocked on the glass. A shallow thud sounded beneath my knuckle. There must be a double-paned, movable panel behind it. I hit my forehead with the palm of my hand. Of course—his mirrors. A conjurer was always wedded to their mirrors. I felt along the wall, searching for an outline or crack. Giving up, I pushed on the surface of the mirror. None of the corners, or even the center, would give way. Frustrated, I checked the floor beneath the armoire. After several minutes, I was ready to give up. Huffing out a breath of frustration, I kicked the baseboard beneath the mirror.

With a swift motion, the panel clicked and swung open.

I grinned. Things were never as they seemed, especially in the home of an illusionist. I stepped into the passageway, careful to leave the door open behind me. Cool air rushed beneath my chemise as I walked farther from the warmth of the bedchamber. After several more strides, the passageway widened to a great room.

In that moment, Erik began a new song. Notes blasted around me and eased into a melody, filling the room with music. On the back wall, a series of pipes gleamed in the light. Beneath them, the organ stood as elegantly as the music that poured from it. Erik's form swayed with passion as the notes swelled into a crescendo.

I stared, mesmerized by the music, and his spidery fingers moving swiftly over the keys. On his left hand, he wore a golden wedding band. His great love, lost in the fire—had they been married? I moved closer, my heart throbbing in tune with the music, until the final notes echoed against the walls. Such beauty he had created, on an instrument I did not even like! I had always found the organ too heavy and macabre, but Erik somehow made it ... seductive.

I paused to take in the scene. He began again, this time with a softer tune. His voice danced along with the music, then soared above it.

Tears sprang to my eyes at its raw power and regality.

The music stopped abruptly.

"What are you doing here!" Erik whipped around, snarling through clenched teeth.

"It's beautiful. I've never heard that piece before. Are you the composer?"

"How did you get in here?" he demanded.

"You must play your music publicly. It's too beautiful to keep to yourself."

He forgot his anger for a moment and said, "Soon, my opera will play, and that is good enough for now. I will reveal more of my pieces in time."

Then it hit me—the path to my freedom, the way I must deceive him.

Suppressing my relief, I said, "Do you plan to take the stage when your opera premieres, or will you sing your parts from the wings of the stage? Your mask covers your face. A face, I know, I would hold most dear no matter what happened to it." I paused to look into his eyes. Hope danced within them and I went on. "With your mask, no one would know you were the Master—"

"My enemies would hunt me like a stag, gut me, and leave me to die."

The gloom in his voice made me want to weep. How desolate, how tortured he was. No one deserved the heartache he suffered day after day. And yet ... *And yet he was a murderer.*

"Surely the police—"

"Can do nothing!" he thundered. "No, I am safer here, safer with a mask and in the shadows." His sadness sucked all the air from the room.

I flinched at his sudden anger and fear flared in my belly. Yet I pressed on and inched closer. "Is there no one who can help you?"

"I have no one. And it's just as well. They would only become a victim to the violence that follows me."

Violence *had* followed him, both by his own doing and because of those who wanted to destroy him. But Joseph Buquet was dead without proof of his murderer, or alternatively, his suicide, and it had been years since the fire. No one knew he was here—except Delacroix. I imagined how determined Delacroix would be to bring Erik to justice after my kidnapping. Some part of me felt guilt for adding to Erik's suffering, but mostly the thought gave me relief.

"Who is after you?" I asked, softening my tone. "Buquet is dead."

"If I tell you too much, it will endanger you. Illusions, while fascinating, are dangerous—another reason a beautiful young woman should never become a conjurer," he said, rising from his bench. "They make people believe something is real, when the truth is a different thing entirely."

"I understand that conjuring the dead is an act. Spirits aren't real." I waited for his confirmation. Surely, he didn't believe in an afterlife. A conjurer couldn't. Meeting Erik as a man, not an angel or a ghost, had only strengthened my opinion.

He whipped around. "Spirits are quite real. I may present an act"— his voice went soft—"but I assure you, they are quite real."

Shocked by his assertion, I said nothing. I directed my gaze to the tuft of dark brown hair falling over his forehead just above the line of the mask. I wanted to believe Papa's spirit lived on, and Mother's as well, but there was no proof, no real sign it was true. An image of Delacroix's list of supernatural activity came to mind, scrawled on the slip I'd found inside one of his books. And then there was that night in the courtyard when I thought I'd felt something. I shook my head. The night in the courtyard was my imagination going wild at the late hour, under a full moon.

A deep laugh rumbled in his chest. "If you could see your expression. Your innocence is sweet, dear Christine."

I frowned. "I simply want to understand the truth."

He paced from one end of the room to another, hands held behind his back, face bent forward. "Truth is what you perceive. Facts are malleable. They reflect the beliefs of the purveyor. You must know what you believe, and play on the beliefs of your audience, to be a great performer. The audience wants a world that promises more than they can see. That is the principle of conjuring. It's the principle of everything."

I clasped my hands as I watched him stalk back and forth. I had agitated him—the opposite of what I needed to draw him in, to make him believe a false truth as he had just explained to me. He must believe I was falling for him and that we could perform his music together so he might become a star again. All in the name of our love.

Our love. I shivered.

Erik's voice raised in volume. "Those who wanted to prove I was a fraud caught me, and beat me to a bloody mess. I was on my way home from a show one evening when the fools followed me. Threatened to reveal my secrets unless I paid for their silence. I chose silence."

Knowing I should comfort him, I moved closer. The wretched man had been through so much. He longed for what we all did—to be admired, to be loved, to indulge in our passions. He didn't deserve all he had suffered.

"They came after you again, the night of the fire?" His posture stiffened as I lay a light hand on his shoulder.

"I was followed for months," he said, his voice weary. "They appeared to be just a few thugs from the rue St. Denis, nothing more. One night, I turned the tables and followed them instead. They reported to someone who didn't want to be seen."

Rapt by Erik's tale, I moved closer still. "Who was it?"

"You don't need to know."

"But I won't tell anyone. Besides, I'm sure I don't know him."

"They almost killed you once. If they discover we are linked, they may try again."

"The fire," I whispered. "Whoever it was is responsible for Papa's death."

He nodded.

I remembered Joseph Buquet's conversation that day, months ago in the costume storage room.

We'll get the ghost, Joseph had said. *Bring him to the boss for questioning.*

"Was Joseph Buquet working for this unseen man?" I asked.

"He was one of them, yes. I have him to thank for a cracked rib. And he had his hands on you," he growled.

"I wasn't badly hurt." I forced a sweet look, pursed my lips for effect.

"Now there's no chance of him bothering you again." He revealed his cadaverous grin.

Eager to change the subject, to put him at ease, I said, "Will you play your piece for me again? It's one of the most beautiful songs I've ever heard."

His eyes locked with mine a moment, then he turned and began to play—demonstrating the full power of the music.

I moved toward him, mesmerized by his gleaming mask, his hunched form bent as he lost himself in his memories, his pain, and in the passion that flowed through him to the keys. I couldn't help but wonder what he looked like beneath his mask. What was so horrible he had to hide it, even from himself? I had to know—to make him believe I could love him no matter what he looked like. Heart in my throat, I inched closer. A buried memory arose to the forefront of my mind, one I hadn't remembered until now. The night of the fire, the crowd had gasped when the Masked Conjurer first stepped into the light. I'd missed it because of the man blocking my view of the stage in front of me. Was Erik hideous even then, even before the mask?

The music blasted against the walls, drowning out the sound of the racing pulse in my ears.

Only a short distance remained between us.

I lunged for the mask. In a second, I slipped it off his head. It clattered to the floor.

He screeched in horror and leapt to his feet. "No! How could— I trusted you!"

I covered my mouth in shock and shuddered with revulsion. Much of his scalp was burned, leaving a river of lumps and ragged flesh that ran across his left cheek; the skin below one eye sagged, baring much of the socket. On the side of his face where he hadn't been burned, his cheekbone poked out at a sharp angle. Even before the scarring, he was fearsome to behold.

"Are you satisfied?" he screamed. "You see a man already born with the face of a devil, made more hideous by those who despise him!" He swept his sheet music to the floor, and launched the music stand at the wall. Its wooden leg split as it cracked against stone.

Breathing heavily, he stormed toward me.

I arranged my features into a serene expression, hoping the fear didn't shine in my eyes. *He must believe.* Yet I backed away—until I met the wall.

When he reached me, he pinned me in place, one hand on each shoulder. His fingers dug into my flesh as his eyes blazed with fury. He leaned closer, his scarred face only inches from mine. I didn't turn away, determined not to show my disgust at his buckled skin—melted by fire and mended by hate.

"You had no right." His tone turned oddly calm, yet I knew the danger lurking there. "Now you see the monster who watches you each night, who longs to make you his." His grip on my shoulders loosened.

"I wanted to see you," I breathed, willing my thrashing heart to slow. "To show you . . ." I focused on his eyes, trying to ignore the rest of his hideous face. Through stiff lips, I said, "You aren't a monster. You're . . . you're beautiful. A tremendous musician—and illusionist, once. We will show the world your genius. Together."

The rage in his eyes gave way to joy. Softly, he slid the shawl from my shoulders and let it slip down my body to the floor. With the tip of his index finger, he traced circles on my cheek and my neck.

I swallowed hard against the lump of fear in my throat.

Slowly, he pushed open the lace collar of my chemise. A groan emitted from his throat, and something inside of me sprang to attention. My heart thundered in my chest as his cold fingers found my collarbone, and slowly inched down the slope of my breast.

Tears rimmed my eyes as confusion raged inside me. I felt such sympathy and regret for the man, and kinship in a way. I cared for him, longed to comfort him, and yet his touch brought deep sadness. I would never love Erik the way he wished—and I hated the lie I must tell him. But it was the only way.

"Please, Erik. I don't— I'm not—"

He wrenched away from me as if awakened abruptly from a dream.

I took in the scarred face, the wild look in his eyes, the trembling hand. God help me, but the man looked like a demon.

"You look at me with pity!" He seized my arm and dragged me toward the passageway, shoving me back into the bedroom. "Stay there until I decide what to do with you!"

The wall collapsed in on itself and slid back into position.

I staggered to the bed, tears streaming. I wept for his tortured soul, for all he had been through. I wept in fear of what was to come. But I could never be the salve for his diseased spirit, or make him well again. I was just another pawn in his game.

~ 20 ~

Erik stayed away for hours and I began to believe he'd abandoned me in his dungeon beneath the opera house. I turned over idea after idea, in search of both a way out and a way to escape him for good, but I couldn't imagine how I could ever dupe him. He had followed me for years. I covered my face with my hands. For years!

I tried to return to the organ room, but found the spring trigger no longer worked. Frustrated, I walked the circumference of the vast bedroom, running my hands over the wall, knocking as I went. There had to be another door somewhere, a hidden passageway to my escape. But after an exhaustive search, I found no doors or openings, even after moving heavy furniture. Dismayed, I crossed my arms over my chest. Now what? I glanced around the room, eyes traveling over candelabras and tables, bouquets of roses. And trunks. It was curious there were so many of them. I bent over one of the larger trunks to eye the lock. It wasn't complicated. If I had a pin, or some sort of metal wire, I might be able to open it. Stalking to the small vanity Erik had set up for me, I dug through the drawers and found several pins. If I could open a German trick lock, I could solve this simple one.

After several minutes, I smiled at the satisfying *click* of a lock giving way. My studies had served me well. I threw open the lid and sifted through a pile of scarves, a flattened birdcage, an array of small mirrors and ropes, and even a top hat. My heart leapt in excited surprise. Magician's supplies!

I closed the lid and moved to the next trunk. One by one, I opened them and rummaged through their contents, discovering everything from clothing to tools. I found smaller boxes packed with gears and metal pieces of a type I had never seen before. Kneeling beside the trunk, I pulled out the box and sifted through the pieces, sliding their parts and fiddling with their hinges.

A clock chimed from somewhere in the room. I startled at the intrusive sound. How long had I been at it? I stood, dusted off my skirts and headed for one of the two remaining trunks. Once opened, I picked through stacks of books and papers, choosing a solitary notebook bound with leather casing. I sat back on my heels to read. As I flipped open the cover, a dozen or more photographs and drawings fluttered to the floor around me. I bent to retrieve them—and froze. My own face stared back at me.

Erik had taken photographs of me? One showed me at the vanity table in my dressing room, putting pins in my hair, another of me removing my makeup, still another as I read a libretto. All taken from behind the mirror. My stomach shifted like high tide and nausea swelled within me. What else had he seen?

I dug through the remainder of the pile, finding a photo of me on the balcony at Madame's house, a drawing of me in her garden, and one of me in my chemise. He had been watching all along—everywhere—even while I was at home. I swallowed hard and looked up. Was he watching me now from somewhere in the walls? The man was more deranged, more obsessive than I had imagined.

I straightened the pile of photos and dug through the remaining contents of the trunk. The title printed on the face of another well-worn notebook caught my eye: *The Masked Conjurer's Illusions, Volume One.*

He wrote down his illusions! I plucked it from the pile and held it to my chest.

The echo of footsteps came from the dark corridor.

I jumped to my feet and turned.

Suddenly Erik was upon me.

"What do you think you're doing?" he demanded.

The heavy volume slipped from my hands and struck the top of my foot. Suppressing a yelp, I bent to retrieve it.

"I didn't know where you were."

He wrenched the book from my hands. "You are going through my things."

"You left me here alone with them." I stuck out my chin defiantly.

He tossed the book down and lunged at me, scooped me up, and threw me over his shoulder like a rag doll.

I screamed in surprise.

"Quiet!" he growled.

"Where are you taking me?"

"To the bed."

My biggest fear resurfaced—that he would possess me in the most intimate way or, worse, torture me while he played out his fantasies.

"Please, Erik"—I panted in fright—"I beg you to respect me."

Heaving a sigh of exasperation, he dropped me onto the edge of the bed like a sack of sand. I bounced as I landed on my derrière, and pushed away from him against the pillows.

"I won't disrespect you in that way. Not now." He leaned over me until his breath was upon my cheek. "But one day you will ask me to."

Like hell. Still, I forced myself not to lean away from him, ever-aware of my mission.

"Don't go through my things again," he snarled. "Or there will be consequences."

"I just . . . I just want to know you. Your music." I swallowed, plunging deeply to find my courage. The words came out in a whisper. "Your illusions."

Candlelight danced across the surface of his mask. He reached for me.

I froze as he brushed a curl from my forehead, ran a gloved finger down my cheek and neck—and across the exposed mounds of my breasts again. My insides squirmed as he leaned forward and planted a kiss on my forehead. After, he jerked upright and stalked to his trunks. Within seconds, he unlocked one and fished out a stack of notebooks.

"You wish to know me," he said. "This is the best way. My secrets."

Taken aback by his sudden change of heart, I remained silent.

"Well?" he growled. "Would you like them or not?"

255

I shifted on the bed. "I don't understand."

"I've taken you against your will. The least I can do is prove to you I am a man of heart, a man of great knowledge."

I stifled my response. The redeeming facets of his character disappeared under the weight of his crimes. Still, I wouldn't turn down his offer. This was the best way to gain his trust—and the best way to learn his illusions!

I accepted the two volumes gratefully. "Perhaps you might teach me?"

Conflicting emotions raged in his eyes, then a knowing smile followed by confusion. "I thought singing was your passion. Your father—"

"Taught me to sing, yes, and encouraged me every day. I do love to sing, but—" I wasn't sure how to finish the thought. "Something has changed."

He shook his head. "Women are assistants, not illusionists. You can read the volumes, but I won't teach you." He reached for the ribbon at my elbow and caressed it between his thumb and forefinger. "It's too dangerous."

"Not always." I looked away, embarrassed by how small my voice sounded, how uncertain.

He chuckled. "Nearly always, dear one."

Annoyed by his dismissive laughter, I stuck out my chin. "There was Nella Davenport the illusionist and the Belgian, Datura."

"You have studied."

"A conjurer told me about them once, when I was young. He showed me how to do a few simple illusions. I have practiced on my own since then." I sniffed, put off by his incredulity. I was perfectly capable of learning, regardless of my sex. After a moment's pause, I lowered my eyes. Voice soft, I added, "Illusions comforted me when I lost Mother. She used to reward me with sleights of hand—a ball or a wand or a deck of cards—when I finished my singing lessons. She loved them. Illusions remind me of her still."

Now I wanted to be an illusionist as she had—regardless of the difficulty, despite the hours of practice needed, the money to get started. I could perform at salons, gain an audience slowly. I didn't have to live out someone else's dreams, even if they were dear Papa's. I had my own.

Erik studied me without a word.

Maybe if I showed him how we were alike in our love of magic—that I identified with him—he would be lulled into teaching me.

"Perhaps, I could learn from you, as your apprentice. We are so alike, you and I. Both singers, both passionate about wonder and magic and make-believe. This is why we felt an immediate affinity for one another, *n'est-ce pas*? I just . . . I just want to work with a master." I forced out the final sentence. "With someone I care for deeply."

"I shared my music with you, and even gave you my books." The edge returned to his voice. "Now you want me to teach you conjuring? Rather demanding, aren't we?"

I smoothed the silk skirts of my gown, measuring my next words. His need for acceptance and self-admiration seemed more important than anything else—greater, even, than winning me. I looked up from beneath my fringe of lashes. "Just think of all you can teach me. That which no one else has done before, or will be able to do ever after. Your expertise is unparalleled."

"I was an apprentice at one time, long ago." He shook his head. "But you're a talented singer, and music suits you. You wouldn't have to struggle the way you would as a magician. As a singer, I can ensure you're in the lead, as you deserve. It's safer, more assured."

"I want to learn illusions," I said firmly. "And you're the person I want to teach me."

He glared at me. "Headstrong woman."

I had never thought so, but I liked the idea and smiled.

"If I taught you"—he went on—"it would mean you have to stay here, a little longer, at least."

A thought I hadn't considered. Realizing my mistake, I swallowed hard, but squeezed his hand in a show of good faith. "Yes, it would."

He was startled by the unexpected display of affection, but then his smile unfurled, displaying his long white teeth. His thin lips all but disappeared.

I cringed inwardly. He looked more skeletal than human. I reminded myself this was the same man who had taught me exquisite music and rescued me in my darkest need, and forced a smile in return.

"Very well, dear one. Why don't we begin?" He motioned for me to join him at a table. "The first thing you must learn is how an illusionist thinks. How he views the world around him.

"The basic principle," he went on, "is to play on the way a normal individual perceives an object and the space it encompasses." He performed a series of illusions with a small ball. The object disappeared into his sleeve, and then into his pockets.

When he finished, I plucked the ball from his fingers, careful not to make contact with his skin, and repeated each of his illusions.

Surprise crossed his face. "You are proficient at sleight of hand."

"Quite." I smiled.

He sat taller, as if to prepare himself for the challenge of impressing a worthy student. I felt I was, and I smiled again.

"Good. On to the next principle," he said. "You can make the audience believe they have a choice when you are leading them by the power of suggestion. If done well, they will always choose what you wish them to."

I nodded. "For example, the number illusion. Choose a number between one and seven, but not four. By suggesting certain numbers, you have planted them in the person's mind. Highlighting them, in a sense."

He bared his skeletal smile once more. "A simple example, but it seems you understand this principle as well."

"I suppose the next theory you will explain is the use of ambiguous language, or perhaps the simple tactic of distraction. As you show the crowd a colorful array of scarves, your assistant inserts a rabbit into your top hat upon the mirrored table. The true illusion happens elsewhere, outside of the scarves."

His smile twisted into a grimace. "If you know all of this, why did you ask me for help?"

I clamped my mouth closed. I had to remember his fragility.

"I understand the principles well," I said, "and I am proficient at sleight of hand. I've learned a bit about box illusions with mirrored panels. The bullet catch as well, though I've never actually attempted it. I am interested in more challenging illusions. Freeing oneself from chains." My voice dropped. "How to conjure spirits, and most importantly of all: how to disappear."

He crossed his arms over his chest, his black jacket bunching at the elbows. "If I share all of these with you, what sort of act would I have left to call my own?"

"But you won't perform again."

"One never knows."

I felt my face fall, my hope deflate. Those were the illusions I wanted to learn. I thought of the séance Monsieur Delacroix had facilitated that hot summer evening, months ago. He had appeared smug until I had gasped at the mention of the Angel and ran from the room. Had it made him doubt? I knew contacting spirits was a contrived act, but I had begun to question if spirits were real anyway—until Erik's true identity had been revealed. Now I knew for certain: A soul returning from the grave was also merely an illusion, conjured by those who wished to believe.

"You said yourself, I am merely a woman. What are the chances I would ever use your illusions? Anyway, I would need my own ideas to make a name for myself."

He steepled his fingers. "Why don't you perform an illusion for me? I'd like to see you in action. Keep in mind, your delivery is as important as your act. You are a player on a stage, and the crowd wants to be amazed. They want to fall for your persona, to believe in your skill. You must make them love you—or hate you—but eliciting a strong emotion is essential. Indifference is death."

Suddenly I felt timid. I didn't have a routine in mind, and I had no props. I didn't know what my act would be or the themes I'd use. I had only seen two conjurers' shows; the rest I had learned from books. What I knew about being on stage came from the opera. I thought of my time as a page boy or a pupil, a butterfly, a courtesan, and the myriad of other roles for which I had posed in musical productions. I had had plenty of time and experience being someone else in front of an audience. But who I truly was—who I wanted to present to the world—I had yet to discover.

"I don't have my props. I only possess a few, anyway, and nothing elaborate. I'm a beginner. This is why I need your help."

He considered my plea while studying my face. I longed to look away from his troubled eyes, the grim mouth, and the shining mask; but that would shame him, and the delicate new thread connecting us would snap.

He sighed heavily. "I can't say no to you." He swept across the room, cape billowing behind him, and fished a set of drawings out of one of his trunks. "We'll raise a spirit from the dead. I can't lay out the full illusion here, but I can show you how it's done."

He spread the drawings out on a table. "See how the cellar below the stage is deep? This is where you hide the body." He pointed to another drawing with a plane of wood set at an angle. "The person lies here against this tilted plane. You project a bright light straight at the individual, and above him, there is a large pane of glass on the stage. That throws the person's muted reflection into the air. When the person below stage moves, the ghost moves, too, and there you have your spirit."

My eyes bulged. "It's brilliant! How did you figure out the lighting?"

"Most illusions are about lighting, ingenuity, and—"

"Science," I said, smiling. "Inventions, gears, and machines. My favorite things."

"Indeed." Something shifted in his eyes, as if he were seeing me for the first time—as if he realized he didn't know me at all. "You surprise me, Nanette."

"'Nanette'?" I snapped to attention, heart jumping into my throat. "That's my mother's name."

"Isn't it your second name as well?" he asked, looking away.

"How did you know?" I asked, unease turning my stomach.

His tone turned impatient. "Would you like to see more or not?"

After a moment of hesitation, I nodded. "I'd like to see as much as you'll share."

He smiled his skeletal smile.

~ 21 ~

Erik and I practiced new illusions: flowers that multiplied inside a cone and cascaded to the ground, pulling endless ribbon from a top hat, a disappearing act with the help of a special cabinet or trunk, and—one of his favorites—escaping from handcuffs. In spite of myself, I read his notes hungrily, soaking up his instructions and anecdotes. He'd sketched illusions performed by other celebrated conjurers in his notes as well: Hermann's card-throwing, the Davenport brothers' spirit cabinet, Pepper's ghost, and Dekolta's vanishing birdcage. But we spent the majority of our time on the theatrical skits he insisted were the most important element of the show.

"Costume and dialogue emphasize the magic of the illusions," he said often.

"Where did you learn how to do all of this?" I asked one day.

"Much of it is self-taught. Some I learned from watching others, but the most difficult and interesting of my illusions I learned while living in Persia."

Persia? There was much more to Erik than I expected. And then I remembered the shadowy man I'd seen once in the music chamber, and Meg's mention of his friendship with Erik.

After hours of demonstrations, he would lead singing practice, and I would do his bidding without complaint. Still, his patience wore thin when I fatigued or when I needed to eat, and he grew truly frightening when I wanted to spend time alone.

Though I absorbed the instruction and delighted in my newfound knowledge, I yearned to go home. Madame needed me, I worried about Delacroix's reaction to my disappearance, and I couldn't wait to show Claudette all I'd learned. Nor could I stop thinking about Raoul. Did he assume I had run away with Erik? The thought vexed me to the point of nausea. No matter how much Erik shared with me, no matter how much time I spent in his presence, I feared what he might do. When I didn't learn a new song as quickly as he liked, he would snap, raise his voice, and belittle me, or clutch my arm too hard. At times, he would gaze into my face with adoration, then startle out of his reverie as if realizing, for the first time, who I was. By lesson's end, his eyes would shift from vivid to angered, or worse, to sorrowful. He walked a narrow line between madness and lucidity, and I wondered how long it would be before he tipped into a world of eternal night. I didn't want to be there when that day came.

After a lengthy lesson and a particularly irritable exchange with Erik, I collapsed and fell into a deep sleep, for how long I couldn't tell. When I closed my eyes, Raoul's face appeared. I thought constantly of Madame and Claudette, my family. Were they looking for me? If only I could send them a message somehow.

I didn't see Erik for hours? Days? Food and pretty cakes appeared on trays at regular intervals in the bedchamber as if I were a noble waited on by an invisible servant. Without daylight or clocks, time became fluid, a stream of unending moments. I revisited the organ room many times in an attempt to escape, trying in vain to find the passage Erik used. It was too well-hidden. I wound my way along the passage to the lake again and stood at the water's edge, yearning for a boat to magically appear on the dock nearest me. My time there needed to come to an end. I had learned enough, and longed to go home with every inch of my being.

Despairing, I rifled through Erik's trunks again in search of something—anything—that might give me a clue as to how to escape. While sorting through his notebooks, I noticed a stack of papers I hadn't seen the first time I'd gone through his things. Carefully, I unfolded the series of labeled drawings.

My mouth fell open in surprise.

The drawings were maps of the opera house, its various floors and system of underground passageways. Heart beating wildly, I traced the space marked "bedroom" with my fingertip. The room narrowed into a passageway—the one I had discovered—with its end flanked by an oval marked "lake." On the shore opposite the tunnel, a set of steps led to the next floor up, but from there, a series of trapdoors, another tunnel, and three more flights of stairs led to different points in the building, none of which led outside. One of the tunnels lead to the main hall.

Rushing back to the bed, I began copying the maps onto blank paper in minute detail. My hand cramped as it flew over the page, sketching each path, room, or hidden door. I paused when I came to the bedroom sheet again. In the corner adjacent to the room, Erik had drawn a large box. I frowned, pulling the map closer to make out the fine print. It read: rotating door.

There was another way out!

I leapt from the bed and turned the map in my hands until it aligned with my position in the room. The wall behind the armoire should pivot, according to the drawing. I strode to the correct spot, and glanced at the paper once more. The door worked with a lever and counterweight. I studied the floor and the wall in search of the telltale lever. There it was, hidden behind the back leg of the armoire. I slid my foot into the space beneath the furniture and mashed down on the lever. The pivot triggered and the wall turned rapidly. Heart pounding, I faced what appeared to be a storage room of foodstuffs, oil, and pieces of furniture. A deep recess spanned the back wall. Hope filled me until I felt buoyant.

I raced toward it and stepped inside the darkened hole. To my chagrin, there were no escape doors or staircase, only a slide. I climbed onto the bottom of the slide and peered up to see where it led. Its curvature twisted and disappeared into a dark chasm. The slide provided a way into the lair, but no way out. Disappointment speared me through. Back to finding another plan.

"Christine!" The Angel's voice echoed from a distance.

My heart leapt in my chest. I glanced down at the carefully copied maps. I would keep them, just in case. I folded the notes hastily, one by one, and stuffed them inside my pantaloons.

"Christine, answer me!" Erik's voice grew closer.

I raced to the door, yanked the counterweight, and the panel rotated.

"Hello, Erik," I called as I rushed into the bedroom. "I'm dressing. Give me a moment more of privacy, please." I tossed the books into his trunk, and dashed back to the bed, pulling out the remaining copied pages. When all had been secured, I straightened my skirts and smoothed my hair. "Thank you. I'm ready now."

He stalked into the room and stood over me, breath fanning hot across my neck.

I strained not to grimace at his nearness, or to stare at the scar that ran along one side of his jaw and bulged in places along his neckline. Instead I focused on his eyes, which smoldered like the embers of a fire. They beheld me with such intensity, I grew fearful of what thoughts lay behind them. Against my will, I shuddered.

"I'm so hideous to behold, you shiver at my appearance." He gripped my arm harder than he ever had before.

"No, that's not it!" I cried out, in part from the agony of his grip. "I am cold, is all. It's very damp down here and I've only just changed clothes."

He stared at me, seeming to try to ascertain if I was telling the truth.

"You know I care for you. In fact, I should think you know how much by now." I placed a trembling hand on the uncovered half of his face. "You can trust me. But I must . . . I need to go home to see my family and assure them I am well."

He put his hand over mine. "You care for me."

"Yes," I said, swallowing. I needed to push him just a bit more. "We have practiced quite a lot. I know most of my lines for *Don Juan Triumphant*, and the cast—"

266

The mention of the cast snapped him out of his brief reprieve from anger. "I'll deliver you from this torture at once."

The urge to protest rose up inside me. In spite of my disgust, I wanted to soothe him, to assure him things could change in his life if he only tried, and that I could help him, but I didn't voice any of that. It wasn't true, and I was desperate to be delivered from this oblivion. He could lord over his dungeons, his dark corners and fathomless night, without me. I yearned for the light.

"I know you want to get away from me, so we'll go. Now!" He pushed me through the bedchamber and along the pathway without lantern or torch.

"You're hurting me," I said, tugging against his grip.

He shoved me again with force, and I slammed into the cold wall.

I rubbed the shoulder that had borne the brunt of the impact. Any sympathy, any kinship I felt with my dark angel evaporated instantly with his cruel behavior. In its place, fear and disgust returned. I had to escape him for good.

We walked in silence to the shore of the lake. This time the skiff was tethered to the dock nearest us.

"Get in," he said.

I obeyed and stepped into the boat, keeping my focus on the seat rather than the fearsome water below us. With one shove, Erik could push me overboard and hold me underwater. Today he seemed in just the mood to do it. I knew I had to tread carefully. As I sat, the edges of the paper hidden in my pantaloons scraped against my skin. I froze. If I moved too much, they would rustle and alert his attention. Should he discover them, all was lost.

Erik switched on a lantern swinging from a curved pole that extended from the bow of the boat. Its beams radiated a shallow halo, reflecting off the black face of the water. I remained silent, containing the relief coursing through me with each paddle stroke, until the dock on the opposing grew near. I was almost free!

After debarking, we stepped out of the boat and continued on a winding path from one floor to another and, at last, we stopped.

He gripped my arms once more and pulled me to him.

I held my breath, waiting for his next move.

"Your little intrigue with my illusions is done." The cool porcelain of his mask nearly touched my face. "Singing is your life. Go, be a diva. You won't have trouble with Carlotta anymore. She'll play a minor role from now on. I've seen to it. We'll sing together, you and I, along with the cast for *Don Juan Triumphant*. Once the show is a success, I will tell you what to do from there."

"You didn't . . . hurt Carlotta, did you?" As much as I detested the woman I didn't wish her any harm.

"Not yet." His voice was cold. "If you stay away from Raoul, no one else will suffer harm. Including your Madame." His eyes narrowed inside the slits of his mask. "And you." He wrapped his hand around my throat and squeezed softly but firmly, the cool leather glove against my skin. "Do what you are told, or you will face my wrath. Is that understood?"

"Yes," I said, my voice shaky.

He released me, hit a lever with his foot, and a panel behind the mirror of my dressing room wall opened. When it slid shut, I fell into the chair at my vanity for a moment to gather my wits.

I stared into the mirror, wondering if he watched from the other side. Tears of relief gushed down my face, but I didn't feel weak and lost any longer. Erik may have his wishes for me—as Papa had, as Madame Valerius and Delacroix had—but I had plans of my own. I would play Erik's game to protect those I loved a little longer—until I created a way to escape him once and for all.

~ 22 ~

I fell into Claudette's arms the minute I returned home, and told her everything.

She embraced me for a long time. "I was so worried," she said, her brown eyes watery. "Madame is oblivious. She believed you visited Meg's family home. But two weeks away from Paris without a word to anyone? It didn't sound like you, especially since you were supposed to be singin'. As soon as the Vicomte de Chagny came by the house looking for you, I knew something wasn't right. He said he spoke to Meg Giry, and found out she wasn't on vacation as the letter claimed. When another letter arrived that said you were well and not to worry, we didn't alert Madame, but I was giving it two more days before I called on the police."

Trying to sound nonchalant I said, "Raoul came by the house?"

"Yes." She tugged on one of the folds of my black silk gown. "What on earth are you wearing?"

I didn't bother to glance at the extravagant gown. "What did he say? Did he leave a note?"

"I don't think I've ever seen you show so much of your skin. Goodness. One can almost see your—"

"Claudette! Please answer me," I said, exasperated by her blathering.

"Aye, Monsieur le Vicomte! He stopped by three days ago, was it?" She nodded. "Three days. Apparently, the directors plan to turn the lead over to you, but when you didn't show, they had to cancel the performance. When Monsieur le Vicomte heard, he questioned the cast. No one had answers, so he came here, looking for you. We agreed that if you didn't show in two days, we would get the gendarme involved. Oh! And he left his address. You should visit him, or write him a note. He's sweet on you." Claudette smiled. "Very sweet."

A hundred thoughts flitted through my head. Should Erik kidnap me again, no one would think to look for me inside the labyrinthine hell below stage. I needed to share the maps with someone I could trust while I decided on my plans. I knew just the fellow.

"Let's get a carriage."

Within minutes, we rumbled over cobbled streets across town. When the carriage pulled into the drive of Raoul's estate, my breath caught. The house was as beautiful as I had imagined. A dozen windows looked out over an expanse of lawn dotted by fruit trees and flowering bushes that lay dormant for the winter. The front walk wound between rows of elegant topiaries, and chestnut trees lined the edges of the lawn. I could only imagine the property's beauty in the spring.

Before Claudette and I reached the front door, two butlers held the oaken doors wide.

"*Bienvenue*, Mademoiselle," one man said, though he didn't look at me directly.

"I've come to see Monsieur le Vicomte. Is he at home?"

"Christine!" Raoul's voice echoed from some unseen room. "You've come!"

Despite my reserve, despite my constant struggle to suppress my feelings for him, my heart leapt at the sound of his voice.

He raced down the grand staircase into the front hall, his expression contorted with worry. "Are you all right?"

I nodded numbly, unable to move as a tidal wave of emotion engulfed me. "I– Oh, Raoul," I whispered.

He crossed the foyer at once and gathered me in his arms.

I stiffened at the unexpected contact, and emotion clogged my throat. How could I ever explain? How could I tell him what he meant to me? I melted into his embrace, reveling in the sensation of his arms around me, his breath on my hair, his warmth. "I'm all right," I breathed.

Claudette inched away from us, pretending to study the artwork in the front hall.

"I was about to call in the gendarme." He pulled back a fraction to gaze into my eyes. "Where have you been? Don't say you were with Mademoiselle Giry, because I've already spoken with her. I was worried sick."

"I . . . well. I—"

"Meg Giry said she thought the opera ghost had kidnapped you," he added, his tone grave. "Is this your 'Angel of Music'? The same man who accosted me in the cemetery?"

I looked into his concerned face. This man was prepared to go to the police. He had interviewed the cast and been worried out of his mind. An overwhelming need flooded my senses. I reached out to touch his cheek and stopped at the change in his eyes.

"Was it him, the Angel of Music?" His tone took on an angry edge.

"It was," I admitted, my voice soft.

"Did he hurt you?" He cupped my cheek with his hand.

"No." I sniffed, trying not to cry.

"But he held you against your will." He slammed his fist against the stairwell banister. "Evil bastard."

A strange need to defend Erik arose inside me. How could I describe his loneliness, his haunted face, and the ruins of his career, his life? He'd lost everything. Regardless of his wrongdoings—even with his threats—I could not hate him.

"He's not all evil," I said, my voice wavering.

Raoul pulled back in shock. With tight lips he asked, "Do you love him?"

"Why do you ask such a thing? As I fall into your arms."

"He left me for dead and kidnapped you, yet you defend him!" A realization crossed his face, then evolved into a scowl. "You went with him willingly, didn't you?"

"Of course not!" My anger sparked like a match. "He kidnapped me, yes. And no, I do not love him. Not in that way. I pity him. He has been beaten and nearly killed, driven underground by his enemies. He lost the only woman he has ever loved in a fire—and now he loses—"

"Christine, he has *murdered* a man, perhaps more than one. He

271

would turn on you, should the mood strike him."

"I have thought of that, which is why I'm going to tell you a secret. But I am not going to tell you unless I have your word that you won't share this until I am ready."

He grimaced. "I don't like the sound of this, but I suppose I have no other choice. Of course you can trust me. I would never do anything to harm you."

"I have a map of his chambers and the underground of the opera house, should he . . . should he take me again," I added, swallowing hard. "I'll keep it locked in the trunk where I store my tools and things. All you will need to do is fetch Claudette and she will know where to find the key. But until then, we leave him be."

"Why don't we turn over the map to the gendarmes?"

I shook my head. "There is more at stake than I can tell you."

He looked away, frustration stamped on his features. "I just don't understand you, Christine."

"Nor I, you." My anger began to swell again. I thought of Carlotta's warning, Erik's demands. I couldn't breathe. "You tell me how I should behave, yet we aren't family, or . . . anything. You have no claim on me."

Raoul paled. "Please forgive me. I have been presumptuous. When it comes to you, I lose my head. I . . . You're right. I have no claim on you. Since our trip north, you have made it clear you don't want that sort of attention from me."

"That was not my intention at all, Raoul."

He stepped closer. "I don't understand. One moment I feel we have an understanding—a shared emotion—and the next, like I am as unwanted as cold rain."

My hand found its way to the curve of his cheek. "I have tried to steer you away, yes, but that doesn't represent my true feelings."

Without hesitating, he wrapped me in his arms again.

My will collapsed and I burrowed against him, taking in his scent of seawater and sunshine, reveling in the feel of his body pressed to mine. When he pulled back, I frowned. I didn't want him to leave me, not ever.

"Is everything all right?" I asked.

"More than all right." His eyes darkened. Slowly, he raised his hand and traced my lips with his fingertip.

My lips parted at his touch, and my blood warmed. Somewhere a throbbing began inside me. He shouldn't touch me in this way, but I ached for him.

Claudette cleared her throat.

I tried to pull away, but Raoul held me tighter. He leaned his forehead against mine. "You are so beautiful."

I sighed, dizzy with pleasure at his nearness.

He lifted my chin with a gentle hand.

For a split second, I thought of the many reasons I should put distance between us.

Then his mouth met mine.

All thoughts drained from my head, all protestations vanished. The softness of his lips, the moan that rumbled in his throat, held me captive. As his kiss deepened, my arms moved of their own accord and wrapped around his neck. I leaned into him, threading my fingers in his hair. A passion swept over me and I wanted to be closer still—I wanted him to devour me. I pressed my body against him.

The sound of footsteps echoed in the hall.

We wrenched apart.

"Pardon me." Philippe descended the staircase, a satisfied smile on his face.

I wanted to crawl into a hole and die.

"Hello, Philippe," I said, utterly mortified. My face flamed hot. "I was just leaving. Thank you again, Raoul." I nodded at him, gathered what little dignity I had left, and headed for the door.

Claudette didn't hesitate, following close behind and grinning like a jackal.

"Wait, Christine!" Raoul reached for my hand and held it to his heart. "Are you going to the masquerade ball tomorrow evening? At the opera house, of course. I plan to be there. If you would save me a dance? I would like to speak to you afterward, in private. There is much to say."

"Yes, there is," I whispered.

Raoul smiled. "Until tomorrow night."

"Until tomorrow night."

Philippe winked at me as he passed behind his younger brother.

In spite of my embarrassment, I smiled again, then turned to go.

As I stepped into the night air, I didn't have a care in the world. My blood hummed with the memory of a perfect kiss. Tomorrow night, I'd meet Raoul at the masquerade ball. Erik would be furious if he were to find out, but I didn't care. I couldn't turn Raoul away. I wanted this, wanted Raoul in my life, too much. There had to be a way for us to be together, and I would find it.

The next day, as I prepared for the masquerade ball, I dreamed of Raoul, his lips, his arms around me. I had to be with him somehow, regardless of the consequences. With him at my side, I could face Carlotta's scheming. As for Erik—he need not know my true feelings. The beginnings of a plan glimmered in my mind, some way to end this charade. Though I had yet to work out the details, I knew one thing for certain: All would happen on the opening night of *Don Juan Triumphant*. Until then, I would continue on with Erik as we had before, and I would keep Raoul in the dark. Until then, I couldn't guarantee anyone's safety, but appeasing Erik was the best way to try.

Claudette helped me with the last pieces of my costume. I stared into the mirror, taking in the gold butterfly mask whose wings fanned across my cheeks in a graceful arc. My hair bounced with long ringlets, and shimmered with jeweled studs. The gown had been more difficult; I didn't have the funds to purchase a new one. Madame Valerius had asked a favor of a wealthy friend, who had insisted I borrow her daughter's gown. I accepted with glee and relief. The dress had been worn only once, and sat forgotten in an armoire—until tonight. I stroked its rich silk, the color of summer peaches; the full skirts tucked and folded in a dozen layers, mimicking a waterfall of amber waves. I wondered how I would ever bring myself to return such a dress. I wanted to wear it day and night, to sleep in it.

When the carriage pulled in front of the theatre, my heart fluttered with anticipation. Raoul's fervent kiss, his speech, played over and over again in my head.

There is much to say.

My hopes soared as I entered the opera house. With a lightness of step, I continued to the front hall and luxuriated in the magnificent scene before me. The directors had outdone themselves. Hundreds of patrons flowed up and down the main staircase toward the Grand Foyer clutching their masks, some feathered and beribboned, others stitched with shimmering thread, still others sparkling with sequins and jewels. The more adventurous wore masks that mimicked animal faces. I gazed at a woman with a mask made of porcelain, its design painted to resemble the petals of a flower. I touched my own mask, covering all but my lips and a small section of my forehead. Would Raoul recognize me? I saw no one I could identify in the crowd.

As a group of gentlemen dressed in ghoulish plague masks passed me, I recalled one of Papa's stories. Ever fond of history, he had recounted many tales of the king's court to a willing subject, enthralled as I was by their grandeur and intrigue.

"The masquerade ball began in the late medieval court of King Charles the sixth," Papa had read from a borrowed text.

"What did they wear?" My nine-year-old mind had wanted him to paint a picture with his words.

"Velvet robes and jewels. Masks and animal fur. They dressed as stags and horses, boars. Some dressed to look like members of the court."

I'd listened, engrossed by the tales of games and drunken merriment, lust and abundance—something I couldn't really understand in our impoverished state. Some of the costumes had even caught fire during the court's reckless celebrations.

"Once, enemies to the crown used masks to get close to the king. It was then that masquerades were deemed too dangerous, and were outlawed for a time," he had said.

Papa had made a mask for me, too, of a beautiful songbird.

Now I followed the flow of traffic up the marble steps. I couldn't help but compare the gentlemen's costumes to those of the ladies. Many men wore their usual formal attire of black tails, white vests, and cravats. But I was happy to see those who deposed their suits in favor of culottes and coats sewn with golden thread, as well as wigs and extravagant hats made to look like jesters from the monarchy. Even a warlock or two roamed about.

A Mozart melody floated through the hall and mingled with the hum of voices. As I entered the Grand Foyer, my nerves flared. What if Erik caught me dancing with Raoul? Would he come after me? I shook my head. He wouldn't expose himself so publicly. The whole of Paris would know the opera ghost was a fraud, merely a man with desperate intentions. I forced the thought from my mind. Tonight I would enjoy myself without worry. I stopped beside the balcony doors, fastened tightly against the winter cold, and scanned the crowd for Raoul.

Messieurs Montcharmin and Richard approached before I noticed them.

"Mademoiselle Daaé, good evening." Monsieur Montcharmin tugged on the end of his pointed mustache. "Aren't you lovely."

"Thank you, Monsieur. So I am recognizable?"

"There aren't many fair-haired young ladies with such radiant beauty gracing these halls."

"Very kind of you to say." I smiled. "It's a lovely soirée. All of Paris must be here."

"We have already tripled our donations for the year," Richard said, resting one hand on his belly. "It seems our ploy has been a success."

"How marvelous."

"I've heard there's a new talent in music making the headlines," Monsieur Richard prattled on, making polite conversation. "A Richard Strauss of Germany. Some are predicting he'll join the list of the greats, or so says Herr Auttenberg. He's visiting to watch the performances on our stage next week. Good of him to come. Perhaps we'll invite Monsieur Strauss to meet with the music director sometime."

"The world can never have enough beautiful music," I said, smiling.

We watched the crowd for a moment, as a nervous silence stretched between us. I steeled myself for the reproach I knew would come. Not only had I disappeared for two weeks, but Erik's opera meant I would be in the middle of all the trouble again.

Monsieur Richard clutched a suspender cradling his belly. "You disappeared for a fortnight without a word, Mademoiselle."

"Yes," I said. "I had to leave unexpectedly. I apologize, messieurs, but I had no choice in the matter. It was urgent."

Montcharmin stroked his mustache. "Urgent. I am sure."

I twirled my handbag nervously. Erik's threats kept me employed, I knew. What director would keep on an understudy who left on a whim.

"As you know"—Monsieur Richard broke in—"Carlotta has not been herself. We would like to offer you the starring role in her stead for a while. Soon, we will be beginning a new program, as I am sure you've heard." He threw me a pointed look.

"Yes, sir. I . . . the cast practices for—"

"*Don Juan Triumphant*," we all said in unison.

I clutched my handbag to my body, imaging the ways Erik had convinced the directors to do his bidding. I knew his bribery took on one form only: mortal threats.

"But we need to be certain you won't disappear again," Montcharmin said. "We'll increase your salary, of course, as the lead."

I forced a smile. "How could I say no, gentlemen? Thank you for the opportunity."

"It won't be permanent, mind. But we would like to try it for a while. Until—"

Richard silenced Montcharmin with a glare.

I knew what that look meant. They wanted me to lead until they dealt with the opera ghost. But no one could "deal" with him until I had.

Monsieur Richard released his suspender and clinked his glass against Montcharmin's. "*Fantastique.* You start tomorrow."

The two men scurried off, no doubt to secure more donations. Too edgy to remain in one place, I headed to a refreshment table.

"May I get you something?"

My heart leapt into my throat. The voice I had yearned to hear all day filled my ears with music. I turned to find Raoul, resplendent in formal evening attire and a simple black mask.

I smiled, heart bursting with gladness. "You aren't wearing a costume."

"There's something too close for comfort about masquerading as the nobility of yore while still carrying a title, *n'est-ce pas*?" He closed the distance between us.

I laughed. "You were always eager to shed your title."

"Titles mean so little in today's modern world. I am a man of the *République*."

I thought of the way women swooned around him, longing to become his duchess; the way men respected him instantly for his property and his family name. He couldn't be more wrong. Titles still meant a great deal, and were dismissed easily only if one possessed a title.

"Your humility is admirable," I said. "It always has been."

"And you"—he gathered my hand in his and held it to his lips—"are admirable. More than admirable. You're stunning."

Euphoria coursed through me. All was well with the world, if only for the moment, and I wanted it to never end.

The musical ensemble concluded their song and the sound of applause filled the hall. When the first notes of a waltz followed, the dancing began anew.

"You promised me a dance." Raoul leaned closer and held out his arm, sparking a blush that spread beneath my mask. "Shall we?"

My stomach somersaulted as he led me to the dance floor and placed a hand at my waist. As we whisked over polished floors, I couldn't wipe the smile from my face. A graceful and experienced dancer, Raoul's gaze remained steadfast on mine and he never seemed to consider his steps. So much emotion shimmered between us, it robbed me of breath.

I loved him. By God, how I loved him.

"I have dreamed of this moment," he said. "Of taking you in my arms and sweeping you across the dance floor like we were the only two in the room."

My blood hummed in my veins. "Aren't we?"

He brushed his lips over the tip of my nose, then pulled me closer until our bodies nearly touched—a scandalous position—in front of everyone.

I yearned to be closer still.

"Tell me what you are thinking," he said.

A laugh bubbled in my throat and broke free. "I find it curious how we go from one emotion to the next, from the depths of fear and despair to the heights of joy, so easily and without warning."

"I want to be your source of joy always," he said, his voice husky.

"To be here with you is a dream." My heart nearly burst with happiness.

We danced another song, and another. When the third ended, we paused to catch our breath.

"We'll wear holes in our shoes tonight." I laughed as he clinked his punch glass against mine.

"I'll be happier for it."

I gazed at him, memorizing his features, the beauty and the signs of pain etched there, the soul in his eyes.

"Come away with me somewhere, away from the crowd." He scanned the room as if looking for an escape. "I'd like to talk alone."

"To the roof, perhaps?" I knew there was a hidden staircase just off the former emperor's apartments. I'd found it the first time I'd gone exploring. We would be alone there for certain.

"It's this way," I said, boldly taking him by the hand.

His fingers closed around mine, and I led him through the foyer, dodging the merrymaking guests, until we reached a quieter wing of the building. After pausing to look around, I ducked through a door that appeared to open into a storage room.

Raoul frowned. "What's in here?"

"Shh, he'll hear us." I pulled him inside. Once the door closed, I whispered, "You'll have to come closer or it won't open. Here, right in front of me."

"Who? What in the world—"

I covered his lips with my finger. "He's always listening."

Raoul pressed against me and placed his hands on my waist possessively. His scent rushed my senses like an opium cloud and I felt like a woman drugged. I wanted to lose myself in him.

"What next?" he asked, his tone guttural yet soft.

I groped along the ceiling for the crack I knew was there. At last, I found the lever and pulled it. The revolving door pivoted. We found ourselves in another cramped room, but this time, a staircase spiraled upward toward the ceiling.

"Amazing," Raoul whispered.

I smiled in the dark. "Follow me."

We climbed the staircase as quietly as possible. At the top, Raoul flipped open the latch and we climbed onto the roof. A sliver of moon carved the night sky. Scattered pockets of shadow chased the moonlight in a delicate, silvery dance across the rooftop. City lights winked in the distance.

"It's colder than I thought." I shivered at the bright cold, wishing I had the added protection of my cape. "We won't be able to stay for long."

"It's frightfully cold tonight." He rubbed his hands together. "So I will come right to the point, save the rest for another time." He pulled his mask over his head. "First, let me see you."

I pulled up my mask.

He cradled my face in his hands, ran his thumb across my cheek. His touch left a trail of heat on my skin.

After a moment, I forced out a whisper. "We must be careful. If Erik discovers us . . . He has threatened to harm you, and me as well. He may be planning something this very minute."

The joyous expression on his face melted. "Someone must put a stop to this nonsense."

"I will, soon," I said quickly. "I just need a little more time, until *Don Juan Triumphant* premieres. If we're hasty, we will all lose this game he is playing."

"I'll go along with this a little longer, Christine, but only because I trust you." His jaw set in a hard line, his eyes looked fierce in the pale moonlight. "I'm worried for your safety."

"Please, let me do this my way."

He leaned his forehead against mine. "I trust you, my love."

Another burst of joy returned the smile to my face. I sighed and wrapped my arms around his neck.

"I have something I need to ask you." His breath puffed around us like a steam cloud in the cold. "Seeing you again, after all of these years, has lit a fire inside me I didn't know was there. I can't eat. I walk the grounds of my estate at night like a ghost, unable to sleep. I think of nothing else but the sweetness of your voice, the softness of your lips." He gathered my hands and held them against his heart. "Put me out of my misery. Tell me you love me, too."

Emotion welled in my throat. He loved *me*, a musician's daughter, a second-rate opera singer—a woman stalked by an insane man posing as a ghost. He loved me. I touched his cheek with my fingertips. "I have feared my love for you, tried to deny it, but it's useless. It consumes me."

His eyes watered, and he kissed my hand. "Then let us be apart no longer. Marry me. Be my wife and I will cherish you and protect you always."

I felt as if I could catch a breeze and fly, drift among the stars like a night bird. Somehow, I'd found something meaningful and real— something that was not an illusion. Raoul wanted *me*, loved *me*.

A single tear slipped down my face. "I want nothing more."

He crushed me against him and twirled me around. We laughed, jubilation distracting us from the cold for a moment. Then his lips covered mine in a slow, tender kiss.

I kissed him back, my need for him turning greedy, and my body tingled in places it never had before.

His hands slid over my back and cradled my head as he held me against him.

"Oh, Raoul." I gasped between breaths.

"My darling," he said, kissing me again. His hands moved slowly over my shoulders, down my arms. Gently, he probed my ribs and slowly moved upward. He peered into my eyes, as his hand moved higher still, and cupped my breast.

I arched against him, desire flaming inside me.

He groaned, and began to plant kisses below my ear and along my neck. When his lips reached my breasts, my head grew dizzy. I watched him, stroked his hair, as he freed me from the neckline of my low-cut gown. Softly, he took my nipple into his mouth. I gasped as his warm tongue circled my flesh, his hand massaged the fullness of my breast. My knees went weak. Too consumed, I couldn't think—didn't want to think—about the impropriety. We would be married, belong to each other at last. That was all that mattered. On that glorious day, his eyes, his hands, his tongue, would roam everywhere. I shivered with pleasure.

He raised his head and smiled at my expression. "It pleases you, my love?"

Breathless, I nodded. "Yes, my darling, but we must stop."

"I know." He kissed me softly, then helped me adjust my clothing. "I'll dream of you in the meantime."

We held each other for some time, shivering with cold, yet burning with our new secret.

When I could no longer feel my fingers, I pulled from his embrace. "As much as I don't want to, we should return."

"Yes, my brother will be looking for me."

We retraced our steps in silence, though a full orchestra trumpeted inside my head. I was in love. I would marry—marry Raoul!

But soon after we returned to the Grand Foyer, my smile waned.

Carlotta strutted toward us in a gown straight from Renaissance Italy with its puffed sleeves, intricate gold thread, and crushed velvet. Matching scarlet and green feathers waved triumphantly on either sides of her mask, and her lips were slathered in bold rouge. I groaned and drank deeply from a glass of punch.

"What is it?" Raoul asked.

Before I could reply, Queen Carlotta descended upon us.

"Buenosera." She greeted us in Italian. "We must speak immediately, Raoul. I've been looking for you all night."

Ever surprised by Carlotta's audacious nature, I gawked at her opulence, her bosom barely contained by her gown, and the way she inserted herself into any conversation.

I glanced at Raoul. He shifted from one foot to the other. He seemed uneasy in her presence always, though she appeared nothing but kind to him, if heavily flirtatious. But she flirted with everyone, even women at times, if it suited her mood. I held my breath, waiting for her to chastise him about her friend, Mademoiselle DuClos.

"That is quite a costume, Carlotta," Raoul said. "You always stand apart from the rest of us."

Given his tone, I wasn't sure if he meant it as a compliment or an insult. I knew what I thought of the matter. Classic Carlotta, showy as ever. I sipped from my glass, and wished she would be on her way. The evening had been magnificent so far and she did nothing but cast a shadow on the festivities.

For an instant, I lost myself in a dreamy haze. The look on Raoul's face while we danced, his beautiful words, his touch—I could scarcely believe it. I would be his wife! I smiled broadly in spite of myself.

"We need to talk, Raoul," Carlotta insisted. "Now."

Her tone jolted me back to reality and I glanced at Raoul.

"Can it wait?" His irritation snuffed out the light in his eyes. "I'm enjoying the company of Mademoiselle Daaé at present."

She laughed a brittle sound laced with sarcasm. "It will wait another six months to be exact, for a total of nine."

All humor left his face and panic filled his eyes. "Nine months?" He choked on the words.

I looked from one to the other, trying to follow their meaning. Nine months? The only significance nine months held that I could think of was . . . I stared at Raoul, my confusion mounting. What was this about? The ebullience I'd felt for the last two days began to dissipate like day-old champagne.

"It's exactly what it looks like! Our rendezvous has cost me, Monsieur le Vicomte, and now it will cost you." Carlotta placed her hand on her abdomen and looked pointedly at me, though she addressed Raoul.

My chest tightened as my gaze locked on to her hand on her stomach, hidden beneath the billows of her gown. When I met her eye, her smile turned vicious. A series of images flashed behind my eyes: the flowers that day in her dressing room, her constant warnings to stay away from him, the way she stared at him.

The room began to spin.

The warnings Carlotta had made weren't to preserve her friend's relationship with Raoul—they were to preserve hers.

"You are with child?" Every ounce of color drained from Raoul's face.

"Indeed, my dear vicomte."

My happiness imploded as tremors of shock shook me to the core. Raoul had bedded Carlotta? Could this be true? Carlotta was vindictive, I knew, but she wouldn't lie about this. Would she? At the very least, she couldn't lie about their shared intimacy.

I glanced at Raoul. His face blanched—all I needed to know.

I closed my eyes against the despair, the sight of Carlotta's hateful glee. What a foolish girl I was. We couldn't marry; it was impossible. He would ask for Carlotta's hand instead. It was the honorable thing to do. He wouldn't damage the family name—and she knew it.

I stumbled through the crowd, rushing past guest after guest, the stiff smiles of their masks mocking me, the swirl of colors and macabre costumes. I'd built a wall around my heart after Papa died, but Raoul had found a way inside. He knew me as I truly was. Yet I had known nothing about him after all. Anguish blinded me as I pushed toward the door.

"Christine!" Raoul shouted my name from somewhere behind me.

I squeezed my eyes closed, wishing I could block out his beloved voice. Erik's wretched face popped into view, his words of warning about Raoul. My dark angel loved me as well in his twisted way, but he saw me as a dream, a fictional woman who could rescue him from his despair and self-loathing. I wanted none of it—neither him, nor Raoul. I wanted none of this opera house. I had to get out, leave. Go far from Paris.

"Wait, please! Christine." Raoul persisted in his chase.

I pushed hard past a man blocking my path, desperate to escape. He spun around to see who the rude person had been.

Monsieur Delacroix looked bothered by the offense and then amused. "What on earth? Christine, are you all right? Where are you going in such a hurry?" He clutched a cigar in his hand and stood in a circle of men, none of whom wore masks or costumes.

I cursed the tears pricking my eyes. "I need to go home. Something has come up."

"Let me escort you," he said. "You look distraught."

Though grateful for the kind offer, I couldn't bring myself to be with anyone right now. "I will be all right. Stay, enjoy the ball."

An errant thought pushed through my despair—Delacroix was Carlotta's lover. Did he know about the pregnancy and her relations with Raoul? Fresh pain burned through me and I clutched my handbag until the sequins dug into my skin.

"You should speak to your mistress *tout de suite*," I said, not bothering to keep the bitterness from my voice. "She has some news to share."

"I don't have a mistress," Delacroix said, frowning. "Do you mean Carlotta? She's just a friend of mine. Really, Christine, what's going on?"

She wasn't his mistress? I groaned. Then the child had to be Raoul's for certain.

The lights flickered in the Grand Foyer. The music stopped abruptly.

All turned to stare at a figure making his way through the room.

I followed their eyes and stopped.

A man dressed head to toe in crushed red velvet weaved through the crowd. His cape, fringed in black tassels, waved behind him. His hat sat at an angle on his head, exaggerated and overstuffed with large feathers like those the king's fool might wear. Yet it was neither his suit, nor hat that drew the most attention, but his mask. The porcelain surface resembled a skull. Only one man could embody Red Death so completely.

Le fantôme de l'opéra.

Bumps ran over my skin when his eyes locked on mine.

As Erik progressed through the room, guests parted like waves, making way for this god of the underworld.

And he came for me. The opera ghost, my dark angel, my tormenter.

How happy it would make him to learn of Raoul's news. He would have nothing to fear from the vicomte's attentions again. Raoul would forget me, as I must forget him. Tears dammed behind my eyes. Why did Erik have to make a spectacle of himself now, of all times? I couldn't handle his antics, not now.

"Good evening, patrons," his voice resounded in the room. "I see you are enjoying my masquerade."

Despite the large crowd, complete silence met his greeting. "No matter what those cretins say, this is my theatre. They are under my command." He opened his arms to encompass the room. "All of you are under my command."

Palms open, Erik flicked his wrists. All of the doors slammed shut.

Screams sliced the air. Fear gushed through the room like clouds of smoke.

In fascinated horror I watched him draw closer. How had he managed such a feat? My mind raced through the pages of notes I had read, the tools in his trunks, and my own knowledge of machines.

Perhaps some sort of spring system or hydraulics?

I looked to Delacroix, suddenly remembering his feverish need to expose the opera ghost. The professor set his glass of spirits on a nearby tray, his eyes never leaving the opera ghost. Slowly, he approached Erik like a fox stalking a rabbit.

"It's you!" Delacroix called out. "I knew it was you! When the rumors began and the strange events continued. No other conjurer could execute such stunts successfully—they haven't your skill level. You are the Masked Conjurer!" His eyes narrowed and he bared a grim smile. "Behold, patrons!" Delacroix boomed. "Your ghost is a fraud! He is but a mortal man. And a demented one at that."

"Your lackeys were too stupid to notice me stalking them," Erik replied. "This is my building. They had no hope of defeating me here. I wouldn't let them beat me and leave me for dead *again*, to set fire to my theatre and ruin me a second time. Joseph Buquet was beneath even you, Delacroix." He let loose a maniacal laugh. "Ladies and gentlemen, it isn't I you should fear, but this desperate, murderous tyrant before you!"

Patrons gasped in surprise. Several women fainted. Another screamed.

I stared at them in utter shock. The professor's lackeys? *He* had sent Joseph Buquet—but, no. I shook my head. The professor was too kind, too good. Surely, he couldn't hide such a vile side of his nature. Unsteady on my feet, I leaned against a pillar. *He* was the man who hadn't wanted to get his hands dirty—the one responsible for the theatre burning that night. My thoughts became a morass of panic and disbelief as I processed the news. I forced myself to breathe, gulping in air.

Think, Christine.

A series of memories flitted through my mind. Delacroix helped me get an audition at the opera. I closed my eyes, remembering how he hadn't bothered to look at the list while I searched for my name. He'd bribed the directors or, at the very least, promised an exchange of favors. The night the machinist attacked me, the professor had been waiting outside in his carriage. Had he sent the machinist in to deal with me as well, or just with Erik? Nausea roiled in my stomach.

But something still didn't make sense. The professor wanted me to help track Erik's movements, but he could have used any of his criminal friends. Why would he go to such lengths to use me—an innocent young woman—for his quest? He used me as bait, but why? I was missing something. What could I be missing?

I did know one thing: He was the man responsible for Papa's death, and all those others who had burned to death that night, nearly five years ago. He had almost killed me—and then he had fed me to the wolves.

The professor's piercing eyes flashed and his hands balled into fists. He looked as if he might explode.

It was too much. This was all too much. Tears flooded my eyes and streamed beneath my beautiful golden mask.

Erik pointed at Delacroix. "In his desperation to further his career, the professor has cost many their lives."

In spite of the wretched accusations, all stood captivated by the spectacle before them. Disbelieving as I was.

I looked at Delacroix—a man I thought I knew, whom I had called friend. He had helped me so often, and cared for Madame. I didn't know how I would ever tell Madame the truth, or if I could.

"You accuse me of falsehoods!" Delacroix shouted. "I am a scientist, an academe, and a gentleman. You, Monsieur, are a madman. Someone fetch the police!"

No one dared move.

"Arrest that man!"

No one moved.

Two of the gentlemen in Delacroix's circle looked at one another as if deciding whom they believed.

Furious at the inaction, Delacroix rushed Erik like a bull. When the professor reached him, he threw his arms forward to grasp Erik—but his hands met air. He stumbled forward several paces before regaining his composure.

Erik reappeared at the other side of the room.

The onlookers gasped. Those standing near the ghost scurried quickly away.

The professor's face purpled in rage. He rushed the conjurer again, determined to reach him before he disappeared. Just as Delacroix raised his hand, *le fantôme* swished his cape, the lights flickered once more, and he was gone.

Erik's haunting laughter echoed above our heads.

The doors burst open.

A collective cry sounded in the room—one of astonishment and relief. And a hint of surprised pleasure. After a moment's hesitation, the crowd broke into applause.

"Whether a conjurer or ghost, that was an incredible show," a woman said behind me.

Other murmurings of delight rippled through the room. The best spectacle in the city was right there at the opera house, as always. Assuming it was part of the festivities, the guests roared with applause and laughter for several minutes before continuing their conversations as if nothing had happened.

Delacroix had proven nothing, except that he was a fool.

I watched him, too stunned yet to move. This man, who had kissed my cheek and escorted me to dinners, had murdered Papa, even if indirectly, and had stolen Erik's life from him. Anger and disgust boiled inside me. I felt ill at the sight of him, at his corrupted ambition. Most of all, that I had trusted him.

The professor knelt and ran his fingertips over the floorboards, searching for a trapdoor. He wouldn't find it; Erik was too good. Given the illusion, I suspected Erik had used a projector to display his image. I felt a perverse sense of pride at Erik's brilliance. He had escaped his pursuer again—this time in front of the entire city of Paris.

Delacroix looked up, his expression was shrewd and fury coiled in his eyes—a killer's face. He had always unnerved me. Now I knew why. He met my gaze and titled his chin defiantly, as if daring me to speak.

For the first time in my life, pure hate spread beneath my skin like poison.

When he registered my expression, he got to his feet and started toward me. "Christine, we need to talk."

I turned on my heel and fled.

No one was who they seemed. Not even me. I wasn't a naïve young woman—someone who could be manipulated, who believed in façades and lies. I knew all along Carlotta was plotting against me, that Delacroix made me uneasy. And that my time with Raoul was a dream, too good to be believed. Why hadn't I listened to myself?

That would end now.

As I dashed to the door, I tore the golden butterfly mask from my face and tossed it to the floor.

Act Three

"*Past the Point of No Return.*"

—Andrew Lloyd Webber's
The Phantom of the Opera

~ 23 ~

During the following days, I ruminated on all of the terrible things Delacroix had done. I couldn't reconcile the man who had cared for Madame Valerius and taken me under his wing with this murderer. His kindness had been a ruse, a bandage for his guilt, and his dedication to me a penance to make amends for the wrong he'd done. But that wasn't all. Joseph Buquet's attack and Erik's undoing were Delacroix's fault, too. I shuddered at the memory of Buquet's hands upon me, and of all the terror I endured. The professor had been so reassuring, so attentive. His need to avenge his father's death went beyond reason.

I tapped the quill pen in my hand against the desktop. There was still a missing link. Why had Delacroix believed I could lure Erik out of hiding? With so many connections to the opera house, he shouldn't have needed me. The professor was too calculating, too careful to choose just anyone. I dropped the pen and watched it roll to the edge of the desk. At least he had respected my wishes so far. I thought of the letter I'd sent, demanding he steer clear of Madame's house in exchange for my silence. How furious and disgusted I'd been when I'd written it. I wanted to involve the police, but what proof did I have of any of this mess? Everyone from the ball thought the play between the Red Death and the professor was merely an entertainment act.

As for Raoul, I couldn't even think his name without tears, so I didn't think of him. I locked away the memory of his kiss, his scent, the way he had devoured me with his gaze, his lips. It was too painful. We couldn't be together and that was that. *The End* of our story.

I sorted my pile of notes. Claudette and I had practiced our illusions diligently each day since that horrible night. I returned to sing at the opera to be paid, and for that reason alone. Oddly, Erik didn't visit my

293

dressing room, haunt the corridors, or speak to me at all. He seemed to understand my distress, or perhaps he was up to his own schemes. Either way, I was more than grateful for the reprieve. I knew it wouldn't last. *Don Juan Triumphant* began its run in a matter of days. But there was one thing I *did* know—I would get my revenge on Monsieur Delacroix, and escape from Erik. And the only way was to leave Paris, and soon.

I closed the Robert-Houdin book, and fished the list of illusions out of my notes. In my despair, I had thrown myself into our practice more than ever. Claudette and I had even created a preliminary act to give our performance cohesion, and the illusions as much impact as possible. Each illusion centered around a skit: a young lady collected money from a banker as the coins dissolved, a princess in a tower met a witch and disappeared to her escape, a singing mermaid lost her love at sea and conjured his spirit. In truth, we needed a theatre with equipment and trapdoors, but for now, we had to make do with the bare minimum. The more complex illusions would come in time. Instead, we focused on those we could manage on a smaller scale. Christmas was nearly upon us, and provided ample opportunities for fetes and salons—the perfect time to strike out and try our hands at a real performance.

I pushed up from the desk and pulled a carton of props to the center of the room. As I opened the lid, Claudette set a vase filled with white roses on the table.

"Another bouquet for you." She hummed as she looked about the salon. "If any more arrive, where will I put them? We're out of space."

I tucked a strand of hair behind my ear. Vases of roses, carnations, and other hothouse varieties covered every surface. Raoul had sent flowers each day for the last three weeks, but I refused to see him. Yet, I tortured myself with visions of him being intimate with Carlotta, and their eventual marriage. I'd have to suffer her smugness when she flashed a large diamond ring and insisted everyone call her Vicomtesse de Chagny. Though she loved to sing, *La Italiana* had proven she wanted nothing more than comfort and wealth. I winced as pain pulsed in the cavity beneath my ribs. I had to move past this somehow. Somehow...

"I don't know." I gave Claudette my back, and bent over the box to pluck out a screwdriver and magnifying glass. "Throw them out for all I care." I pulled out a series of colored scarves connected to one another on one long thread. "Let's practice." I tossed the scarves on the heap and stood at one end of the settee.

Claudette joined me, and we pushed the furniture aside.

"And now, ladies and gentlemen"—I called out to the empty salon —"you see before you my assistant, Claudette."

She folded forward in a bow, one foot before the other in a pretty ballerina pose and smiled her best smile.

Piece by piece, our act unfolded.

After a time I paused, staring at her maid's dress, trying to place my finger on what was missing. Our act was coming together, and we were becoming more comfortable with our roles, but it all seemed too similar to those of other illusionists. We didn't have a special spark to set us apart.

"What is it?" Claudette asked.

"Nothing. Let's go through it again."

When we began the show for the third time, Claudette stumbled on the ties around her legs while trying to free herself.

"That wasn't fast enough," I said, looking at Papa's pocket watch. Now I understood why conjurers' assistants wore scant clothing.

"The fabric keeps getting in the way." Claudette blew out a breath and the copper curls on her forehead took flight.

"I'll have something made for you. Something that sparkles, but is tasteful. Perhaps in green to match the shade of your eyes."

Claudette grinned. "We're really doing this?"

"We're really doing this." I smiled. "In fact, we have our first show next week."

I pressed my face against the window of my balcony door. Torrents of rain gushed down the rooftops. Wind rattled the shutters and whipped water against the windowpane. The rawness soaked into my bones, driving me to the fire. I whiled away most of the day, tinkering with an idea for a special hinged box and trying to ignore the sweet scent of rose blossoms. Raoul continued to deliver them. Each time he arrived with flowers, I forced myself to stay in my room, though the urge to chase him into the street and watch his retreating form plagued me. Worse still, he waited for me outside my dressing room at the opera house after each performance. I passed him at a brisk pace, head down. When he called after me, reached for me, I dodged him and raced out of sight.

I lay my hand atop the stack of his unopened letters, secured neatly with a ribbon. What could he still have to say?

A soft knock sounded at my bedroom door.

"Come in."

Claudette entered, crossed her arms. "He's come again."

"Raoul?" I said, unable to hide the hope in my voice.

She nodded. "The least you could do is to thank him for the flowers. Besides, you're miserable, and you can't avoid him forever."

I jumped up from the bed. "I'll see him, but only for a minute."

I followed Claudette to the salon, head high in spite of my turbulent stomach.

Raoul stood awkwardly in an elegant green coat that was too big for his frame—the first time I'd ever seen him unkempt. He had lost weight.

"Christine—"

"Mademoiselle Daaé, if you please," I corrected him. Distance between us must be established. Or I might launch myself into his arms.

He looked down, trying to hide his surprise at my abruptness. "Right. Mademoiselle Daaé." He paced a second and then stopped, and covered the distance in two quick strides. He reached for my hand and held it to his heart.

Surprised, I stepped back—and met the wall behind me.

"Have you read my letters?"

"I'm afraid I haven't had time." I looked over his shoulder, trying desperately to ignore the way his hand felt over mine, the soft thud of his heart beneath it.

"My darling, I know what you must think of me, but the situation is not as it seems. Carlotta—"

"Is your lover. Or was your lover. It doesn't matter now. I don't see what's so difficult to grasp. You have a child together." Anger welled inside me. I had never been as destroyed or as humiliated as I had that night. I had let him kiss me, touch me. Propose marriage! Only to be tossed aside like an old shoe and trampled upon by his lover. By Carlotta!

"Christine, please. She isn't my lover. Let me explain. When I'm finished, if you still wish for me to go, I will do as you ask."

I crossed my arms over my chest.

Claudette cleared her throat. "Pardon me, Monsieur, but I can put on the kettle or bring an aperitif?"

"Thank you," he said. "Brandy would suit me fine."

I glared at Claudette, and turned back to him. "If you must go on, do it quickly."

Relief crossed his face. "I'll start at the beginning. Four months ago, I was at sea. We docked in Naples for a fortnight before I returned to Paris. A friend of mine"—he looked down—"my closest friend, Marc, went to a tavern with me one night. We stayed out very late. After a few hard drinks, I was ready to go back to the barracks and sleep it off. Marc wasn't. He told me to go, that he'd head back after another round. It was a hot night, swampy, without moon or stars. The streets were mostly deserted, but I thought it best to take a hackney, especially in the state I was in, since I didn't know the town well."

He balled his fists at his sides. "Marc never made it back to the barracks. He was knifed outside the tavern in the alley. As you can imagine"—his voice cracked—"I was devastated. Had I been with him, we could have taken the ruffians, or maybe dodged them altogether."

He paused for a moment to contain his emotions. "I've known Marc since I was a boy. His health was always fragile, but he insisted on joining the navy. I had promised his mother I would look after him. Telling her what happened . . . I will never forgive myself."

I clasped my hands to keep from smoothing the wavy locks on his forehead, from soothing his pain. I reminded myself I was angry with him—where he went from there did not concern me. He had someone else to care for him now.

"Over the next several days, I drank myself into oblivion." He looked over my head, his mind in the past. "A fellow mate tried to shake me out of my stupor. He knew I loved the opera, so he insisted we see a local star. She'd gone on to be a lead diva in Paris, but had returned for a brief visit."

"Here we are," Claudette said brightly.

We moved to the sofa in the salon. I busied my hands with handing Raoul a glass of brandy, willing them not to shake.

"After the show, Carlotta and the cast joined us at a tavern. We started talking. She was away from Paris on vacation for a few weeks. She had agreed to sing that night as a favor for a friend. We had many drinks. The night wore on. Christine, I was in a bad way."

"She comforted you," I said, my voice soft.

"In a way, I suppose." His face was drawn. "I followed one horrible mistake with another. We all went back to her friend's house—he was the theater's owner—and I found myself alone with her, but it isn't what you think. We talked more about what had happened with Marc, and then I passed out on the sofa in her room. That's all that happened. I swear it, Christine. She tried, by God, but it didn't happen. Now I know why she wanted to seduce me. She wants a rich husband and a title." He scowled. "I've spoken to her about giving the child to a loving home, or allowing me to pay for its expenses, even though it's impossible that it's mine. She won't agree, but I know she cares nothing for the baby."

He studied my face, searching for a sign of acceptance.

"You wouldn't leave her and the child to fend for themselves." I set

298

down my glass. "That's not the kind of man you are. Even if it's not yours."

He nodded, hope filling his eyes. "So you understand?"

"I do, yes. The only way to not look like a cad, and to protect your family honor, is to marry her." Pain tore at me. He was a good man, and now he would never be mine. I closed my eyes to hold myself together. His regret was real, yet there was nothing to be done. She would ruin him, one way or the other.

"I'm so sorry I hurt you, *mon amour*. The night of the ball, I was going to explain. I didn't want there to be secrets between us. I couldn't ask"—his voice became soft—"I couldn't ask you to be my wife without you knowing the truth, yet it was so cold and we lost ourselves in passion . . . Christine, I do not love her. I never have and certainly never will. And I am not the father of her child. It isn't even possible. I have—I have never touched her."

Tears pricked my eyes. We would have been happy. But now, I could never accept him—not unless Carlotta released him. Even then, I couldn't banish a child to a life without a father.

I sniffed and forced myself to stand. "I'm afraid this doesn't change anything, Raoul. The fact is, you're going to marry Carlotta."

He took my hand without hesitation, and cradled it in his palm. "I love you. I've loved you since the day I met you all those years ago in Normandy. Your sweet nature, your cleverness. Your kind heart. All of the games we played . . . You were magical then, and you still are. I love you fiercely, Christine Daaé, even as you shun me now."

Unable to hold back the flood any longer, tears slipped down my cheeks. I would never experience that love. It was all so unfair, so cruel.

"You're crying." His face crumpled. He pulled a handkerchief from his jacket pocket and dabbed my cheeks gently. "You love me, too."

"So much." I choked on my tears. "But we can't be together and you must go. Go, and leave me alone."

"My darling," he whispered, determination brimming in his eyes, "I will find a way for us to be together. I won't be trapped by Carlotta."

"I'm the one who feels trapped, Monsieur le Vicomte." I pulled away to avoid his touch. "I have my own life, my own dreams. Please, you must go."

"I'll find a way to make this right. I can't accept giving you up, Christine. I won't."

I held open the front door for him. "Goodbye, Raoul."

He gave me a last mournful gaze and turned to go.

When he'd gone, I sank to the floor and wept.

The following evening I scampered up the drive to the Duchess of Zurich's home. She had been kind to me in the past, and generous, so when I approached her about hosting me at her salon, she seemed delighted—until I mentioned my illusions. She agreed to them only if I sang a concert first, an easy term to accept.

"Good evening, Duchess."

"How lovely it is to see you again, Mademoiselle." She kissed each of my cheeks.

I smiled, but nerves fluttered in my stomach. "May I present Claudette? She is my assistant."

Claudette's eyes grew round as she took in the woman's home. She hadn't worked for anyone but Madame Valerius, and likely had never set foot inside a house so grand.

"How do you do?"

"Very well, ma'am, thank you." Claudette curtsied.

The duchess smiled. "You two may begin when you wish. We love entertainment."

"Thank you," I said, returning her smile. "We'll prepare now."

I led Claudette to the curtain behind the stage area. The salon was as I remembered, filled with expensive furnishings, generous refreshments, and a pianoforte in the front of the room. The instrument might be in the way for our show, but Claudette and I would work around it. We rushed about, setting up a small table and positioning the few props we needed.

My heart beat wildly as more people filed into the room and began to seat themselves. We were really going to do this!

Claudette fumbled with the scarves, and nearly knocked over the small table.

I looped my arm through hers and pulled her behind the piano. "You can't twitch during the show. I'm nervous, too, but we have to appear calm or they will sense our discomfort. They have to believe what we're selling them, or our illusions will fall flat. They'll laugh at us."

She glanced at the growing audience. "I'm sorry. I've never been in front of people before. They're all staring at us. Gives me the jumps."

I squeezed her hands in mine. "Don't make eye contact. If we blunder, we try again, all right? It won't be so bad, I promise."

"Well, there are worse things," she said, her face expressionless. "Like kissing Albert."

We both giggled at the thought of puckering up to the footman.

"Ready, then?"

She nodded. "Mind if I have a drink first?"

"As long as it doesn't make you sloppy."

"It'll help."

"Very well, but not too much."

She scurried off to the refreshment table and came back with a whiskey. In seconds, she gulped down the entire thing.

"I thought you were going to take it easy!" I glanced at the almost-filled set of chairs.

"You forget I was raised by an Irishman. An evening isn't set to rights without whiskey."

"Right." We both knew she hadn't had whiskey in ages. "Well, why don't you stand behind the piano until we begin."

I turned to the crowd and pasted a smile on my face, knees quaking. We had practiced the routine so many times I had dreamed about it. But what if I made a fool of myself? I glanced over my shoulder to seek reassurance in Claudette's casual smile, but her back faced me.

Swiftly, she tipped her head back and downed another whiskey.

"Claudette," I hissed.

She spun around, but rather than guilt, her eyes shined and a smile lit her face. She had managed to kill the nerves, all right. I drew a finger across my neck and mouthed the words "no more." She scuttled back to her spot behind the piano.

If she messed this up, I would strangle her.

The Duchess of Zurich joined me at the front of the room. "Please welcome Christine Daaé, diva from the Opéra de Paris. From what I've been told, she has more for us this evening after her concert. She is an illusionist as well."

Several in the audience emitted cries of delight, some nodded, a few smiled. No one could resist an illusionist—unless they were terrible. I gulped. I could not be terrible.

I sang the first song, and when finished, I looked out at the sea of faces. Not a dry eye remained; they were enraptured by the music, by my voice. It was then, that it struck me. I must use both of my talents together. There was no reason why I should give up one for the other. My voice could be a part of my illusionist persona and my show. It would be my mark, what set me apart from the others! Joy rushed through my veins. I could honor both Papa's wishes and my own, together.

When I finished my final song, I bowed at the hearty applause, a gleeful smile on my face.

The duchess stood again and said, "Messieurs, Mesdames, thank you for coming this evening. Now, may I present to you—well, once again I give you the Great Christine Daaé."

Though I cringed at the introduction—I needed a stage name—the crowd clapped again, many with doubtful expressions on their faces.

Claudette joined me, and I performed my easiest illusions first: sleight of hand with a ball, then with cards, and then another illusion in which I made flowers appear in an empty vase with the help of a hat.

When the vase wobbled and began to tip, Claudette's hand shot out to steady it.

The crowd tittered with laughter.

I blushed and my voice wavered as I began the next illusion.

We performed four small acts, and all were successful—mostly. The last illusion we bungled completely. I tripped over the edge of the table, knocking over a stand holding a "false" wooden egg.

"Slippery little guy," Claudette said, snatching it up before it reached the audience.

They howled with laughter.

I burned with embarrassment until a smattering of applause broke out, followed by cheers.

Claudette winked at me.

They loved us! What could have been a disaster turned out both entertaining and humorous, because of Claudette. I broke into a smile as another realization dawned on me. Claudette couldn't be stiff or mysterious. That wasn't who she was. Why force her into that role? Her contribution to our show was humor and cheer, and the crowds would love her. Together, we would make an excellent team.

At the end of the act, we curtsied. Our presentation needed work, but we'd survived our first show.

Claudette squeezed me with all her might. "We did it!"

I laughed at her enthusiasm, but I beamed with joy as well. "Indeed we did."

As the audience dissipated, we packed up our things. Everyone moved to another part of the house for refreshments—all but one man, who remained in the final row.

When I caught his eye, he clapped again, slowly.

My heart stopped.

Monsieur Delacroix winked and a sardonic grin stamped his face. "Bravo, Mademoiselle Daaé. So you're an illusionist now. *Bravo.*"

~24~

Are you friends with the duchess or did you follow me here?" I began packing the props into our bags at once. I couldn't get out of there fast enough.

"I know all of the places you go." His smile sent a shiver over my skin. "You've been busy with your illusions. Having costumes made, buying your props. Practicing at all hours."

The lacy collar at my neck tightened as the air grew thick and hard to breathe. Delacroix had been spying on me, stalking me, just as Erik had. Were they so different, these men who sought to control me?

"What do you want, Delacroix?"

He grinned again. "Now, now. There's no reason to be rude to the man who has made your life possible."

"Don't you mean the man who ruined my life?" I snapped, surprised by the strength I felt.

"Do you think you would have been chosen for a role at the opera house had I not intervened? You have a lovely voice, it's true, but the choral director had no use for an inexperienced girl on his stage. Look at you now. You're the main event."

"You paid for my position," I said, incredulous at his assertion. "Why did you do it?"

"Two reasons. I owed it to you after the loss you suffered in that fire. And also, I wanted to lure the Master Conjurer out of hiding. I had had no luck tracking him myself, but you were the key."

"Why me? You could have asked Carlotta to lure him out."

He snickered. "You never knew, did you?"

"Knew what?" I demanded, growing impatient with his game.

"His stage assistant was blond and blue-eyed, just like you. Beautiful and devoted, like you. A lovely singer, but truly a magician, just like you. One could say you were as alike as ... mother and daughter."

My body went cold. It couldn't be—Mother had died of some illness. "No." I shook my head vehemently. "Mother died."

"Mother and daughter," he emphasized the words. "The sad tale of the Daaés. Nanette met the conjurer at a show in Sweden. Oh, the Master Conjurer was always a frightening man to behold, but that didn't scare her. She fell in love with his magic and his passionate demeanor, so unlike your father's reserved nature. She left for Paris within a fortnight of meeting the illusionist. Your father loved her so much, he let her go—provided she agreed to leave you behind. He couldn't bear to part with you. She resumed the use of her maiden name—Mademoiselle Cartelle—and joined Erik's act. They traveled together and became inseparable, until the night of the fire. She perished there, just as your father did. Rather ironic, don't you think?"

My head reeled. I leaned against a column for support. Was this true? I closed my eyes, searching my memory for clues. That night of the fire, the assistant wore a beaded costume. A glittering mask covered much of her face, but her blond hair shone like a halo in the dim stage lighting.

The room began to spin, my breath shortened. Mother had betrayed Papa, and left me behind. Papa had let me believe—made me believe—she was dead, to protect me. I couldn't ... I couldn't fathom ...

Erik had rescued me. He had called me Nanette! All along, he knew.

I stared at Delacroix, unable to speak, barely able to breathe.

Alarm in her eyes, Claudette tucked her hand under my elbow to steady me.

Erik's obsession made sense at last—his need to be near me, his longing for me to love him. The many times he had snapped out of some almost-trance, looking at me as if he didn't really know me. And he didn't. He knew *her,* my mother—he wanted only *her.* Relief and pain and disgust folded together and I doubled over with the force of it.

The few memories of Mother that remained suddenly twisted and changed. The small illusions and sleights of hand, the way she encouraged my sense of wonder, and yet, she thought so little of me and of Papa, she abandoned us both. *This* mother, I did not long for. *This* mother made me ashamed I had ever belonged to her, that I was like her.

Delacroix folded his hands. "When the opera ghost saw you, another angel with a heavenly voice to match, I knew he would be instantly besotted. I daresay, he's even more taken with you, my dear Christine, than he ever was with your mother."

"Shut up!" I said through clenched teeth. "Stop talking! You didn't know her." My voice faltered. Neither had I.

He chuckled at my vehemence.

Claudette squeezed my hand. "Let's get home. Madame will worry." I heard the veiled panic in her voice.

He gripped my shoulders. "No need to worry about Madame Valerius. She's safe at my house. For now."

My fury gave way to a fear so potent, I thought I might retch. "What do you mean?"

"She'll be staying with me until I get what I want."

"What do you want?" I whispered, blood draining to my toes. "I've protected your secrets, though I have every reason to expose you."

"And you'll continue to protect me, or you'll regret you ever crossed me. Do we understand each other?" I tried to pull free of his grip, but his fingers tightened. "You'll go to your Angel of Music." He smirked. "Steal his precious notes on raising the dead and bring them to me."

I glowered at him. "Why do you need them? It's not as if you believe in spirits anyway."

"What I do with the information is none of your concern."

"It won't give you prestige. Your colleagues will laugh at your obsession."

His grip on my shoulders tightened. "I suggest you hold your tongue."

"You're hurting me!"

"And I will hurt your dear Madame, should you not do what I ask."

"You wouldn't," I said, my voice hoarse. "She's your friend."

"Her husband was my friend. She's just an unfortunate little old woman, who will not know what hit her. Perhaps that would be better, don't you think? She can't walk. Her health declines by the day."

Delacroix wanted to frighten me. He wanted me to bend to his will. I wouldn't. Not this time.

I met his gaze. "If you harm her in any way, I will see to it that you never work again."

He laughed until tears gathered in his eyes. When he stopped, his expression grew fierce, his lips thin against his bared teeth. "I am surprised at your bravado, Christine. Don't you remember the night your precious papa lay dying in your arms? How you almost perished yourself? I'm not afraid to do what I must."

I blocked the painful image from my mind and returned his ire. "You've worked all your life to prove your father wrong. He couldn't conjure your mother through his séances, could he? She will never come back, and your father didn't love you. You should be glad your mother can't see who you've become. She would be disgusted by your wickedness."

His hand connected with my cheek in a powerful blow.

I tumbled backward, pain radiating across my face.

"Christine!" Claudette caught me just before I fell.

I blinked away the instant tears. He hit me! In a public salon. I looked around, blinking hard to clear the instant tears away. Had someone else noticed? My heart sank as I realized the party had moved to the dining room. There was no one to witness his abuse.

"You think that hurt?" He massaged his hand. "There is more in store for Madame Valerius, and for you, if you don't bring me those notes."

I glared at him with all the fury I felt, throbbing cheek be damned.

He leaned toward me until I could feel his breath on my face. "You have one week."

~ 25 ~

The following day, with a load of powder applied to my bruised and sore cheek, I took a quick ride in a hackney cab and dashed through the opera's corridors without a word to anyone. The building was eerily silent at that early morning hour, except for a faint hum, as though the walls were breathing. My heart pounded in my ears. If I failed, Madame Valerius would be murdered in cold blood by a man she had trusted for years. I couldn't let that happen. She and Claudette were all I had left.

I unlocked my dressing room door. When I swept into the room and lit a lantern, my eyes bulged in surprise. The mirror was already ajar, as if in invitation. I shook my head. How did Erik always know? It appeared I wouldn't be able to snag his notebook or the photos secretly. I would have to ask him for them and hope for the best. Perhaps if I told him about the professor's threats, he would take pity on me.

A mirthless laugh rumbled in my throat. Erik wasn't the type to take pity on anyone. I would have to take my chances.

I grabbed a lantern and stepped into the dark. After several minutes of following the winding path downward through the labyrinth, the air clumped together in a damp mass, and the odor of mold drifted through the tunnel. I was almost there.

As I descended the final staircase, two angry voices broke the silence. I ducked beneath the overhang of the tunnel, extinguished my lantern, and perched in the shadows.

A woman in a brown day dress had her back to me. Erik stood across from her, his mask gleaming in the dull light. Something else gleamed in his hand.

I edged closer. Was it—? I gasped.

The delicate hilt of a familiar two-barrel pistol glinted as he waved it about.

Bile rose in my throat.

"Stop this, Erik," she said. "You're terrorizing the cast and the patrons. If you know what's good for you, you'll leave. If you don't, I'll go to the inspector. I'm tired of protecting you."

My breath grew ragged. I pressed my back into the wall and my lantern clinked lightly against the stone.

"Who's there?" Erik raised Madame's gun. "Show yourself!"

I remained still, hardly breathing.

"You're imagining things," the woman said. "Put down the gun."

Erik turned to point the gun at her. "You know about all of the terrible things I've done. Tell me why I should release you."

"I would happily bury your secrets and you know that."

"And so you shall." He fired.

The woman crumpled in a heap to the ground.

I screamed, too stunned to contain it.

"Show yourself!" Erik roared.

"What is the matter with you?" I stepped out from my hiding place, heart battering my rib cage, and bent over the body. I covered my mouth in shock. Madame Giry, Meg's mother—the woman who delivered Erik's notes—lay dead at my feet.

I fell to my knees. A bullet hole oozed blood between her eyes. "Erik, what have you done? Have you no sense of decency? She has been nothing but kind to you, and you shot her!" How could I ever love you? You're as much a monster as Delacroix."

Erik lowered his hand. Voice soft, he said, "What are you doing down here, Christine? Have you missed me?"

Too angry to hide the truth, I glared at him. "I came for your notebooks. And to learn the truth about my mother."

He flinched. "Do not speak of her!"

"She left my father for you, didn't she? You took her away from her little girl." Hot sorrow welled to the surface like tar.

"Nanette wanted to join my act," he growled. "Your father wouldn't let her follow her dreams. And then we fell in love. We planned to come back for you. We tried to, but your father kept moving. He took you on the road to hide you from us."

"Mother wanted me?" I whispered. The tears began, blurring my vision. All of that moving, the years of homelessness and no friends, suddenly made sense.

"Of course she did." His tone grew gentle. "But your father would not let her have you. He was too furious she had left him."

Papa hadn't wanted to lose me, no matter what, but because of it, he had borne the weight of heartbreak, disease, and a violent death. Despair swept over me. How we had suffered from all of the lies, and the senseless pain life rendered. I wiped my tears on my sleeve. "She died alongside him, where she belonged."

"I don't want to talk about this anymore!" he shouted.

"Fine. Give me the notebooks and I'll go."

He stalked toward me. "Haven't I given you enough?"

"Delacroix threatened my benefactor's life, and mine. Would you see me killed by your enemy? You have already lost so much because of him."

He glared at me, a savage look in his eyes. Finally, he said, "You may have the books on one condition." A ghoulish smile showed beneath the porcelain edge of his mask. "Afterward, you come away with me, and we will wed."

"Marry you?" I asked, incredulous.

"Let me guess," he retorted. "You want to marry that pathetic nobleman. The scoundrel who impregnated that Italian cow. He deceived you, yet still you care for him. What does he possess that I do not?" He paused, anguish brimming in his eyes.

"When you love someone, you don't imprison them," I seethed. "You can't force me to marry you."

He went still, and in a tone as sharp as a blade he said, "Should you choose to run away with your precious Raoul, I will find you, and he will join your parents."

My brave words died in my throat. He meant it. He would find me and destroy my happiness at all costs. Fresh tears poured down my cheeks. "If I do as you wish. If I marry you, will you grant me a last request?"

"That depends." He stepped closer, the scent of death wafting around me.

"I wish to perform one final show before I . . . disappear. One week from tonight."

"The night my opera begins," he said, his voice laced with excitement. "We will perform together—one grand show, and leave at the pinnacle of our fame. Wait here, one moment." He stalked to the bedroom and returned.

"Here." He thrust his notebooks at me. "They're yours. Now be on your way. Pack your things and say your goodbyes. After our opening night's performance, you will become my bride. I will take you some place safe, far from this madness, forever."

The man was truly beyond reason.

With a last tearful glance at Madame Giry's body, I clutched Erik's notebooks against my chest and fled up the staircase to freedom, all the while my thoughts raged like a storm. I had one week—one week to make an escape plan, one week to free Madame, and one week to make the professor pay for what he had done. Then, I—and I alone—would disappear. But for now, I had an even bigger problem.

Madame Giry's lifeless body beside the lake. The gun that killed her could be linked to Madame Valerius—and me.

If found, I would be wanted for murder.

I hated to admit it, but I couldn't pull off my plan on my own. Despite my reservations and the words we had exchanged, I raced straight to Raoul's house. If he cared for me as he claimed, he would help me.

When the front doors swung open, Raoul greeted me, his face pale.

The moment I set eyes on him, my tangle of emotion burst forth and without reservation, I threw myself into his embrace.

He wrapped his arms around me fiercely. "What is it, *mon amour*?"

Sobs racked my body. "Erik shot Madame Giry, a woman who works at the opera house. With my gun." What would I do, should I be arrested and tried for murder?

He held my head against his chest. "I can speak to the inspector, but I can't promise anything, I'm afraid. If you're implicated, you may never sing again. So much could go wrong . . . run away with me, Christine. Please." He searched my face. "We'll leave everything behind. Start a new life. I have plenty of money—more than I could ever spend."

For an instant, hope and longing masked my pain. "What about Carlotta?"

The muscles along his jaw twitched. "She could live here while I—"

I pulled out of his embrace. "She would leech every last centime from your coffers. Destroy your reputation, and mine."

The glum look returned to his face. "You're right. I don't care about my reputation, but I care about yours. And my brother's. The woman can destroy me, but not those I love. I can't allow it. But there must be a way."

How much did I care for propriety? I intended to become a conjurer, come what may, and the thought of life without Raoul—the idea was too bleak to imagine. I chewed my bottom lip. Perhaps I could make Carlotta see reason. She wouldn't want me to go to the society pages with her association to Delacroix, a murderer.

I smiled.

Neither would she wish to be seen as a whore who lied about bedding a nobleman to win a title and his fortune.

"I'm going to talk to Carlotta. I think I can make her see reason. If you never bedded her, her lies are going to stop. *Now.*"

Raoul clutched my shoulders. "You are the best thing in my life." He touched my hair softly, and pulled me to him again.

I sighed at the tingle of his body against mine. I wanted him so desperately: his love, his support, his friendship. I would do anything for him. He was my home—suddenly I knew that truth to the marrow of my bones.

He brushed his lips over my earlobe and under the curve of my jaw. I melted into him as the heady scent of his skin washed over me. For a few moments, I forgot about my mother's past, my promise to the phantom, the professor's threats.

"Raoul," I sighed his name.

"Mon amour." He ran a hand over my shoulders and down my back until it cupped my hip.

I looked up to meet his eyes.

His lips covered mine, coaxing my mouth open. His sadness from the last few weeks turned to urgency and leaked into his kiss, until the intensity took my breath away. As I tasted him, all else fell away. I pulled him closer, running my hands over his shoulders, his back, lacing my fingers in his hair. Consoling him, being what he needed—taking what I needed.

He rested his forehead on mine. "I'll take you away from here. You can do your illusions as much as you like, or sing. Whatever you wish. As long as we are together."

I lay my cheek against his chest, mind spinning. I remained that way for some time, thinking, scheming, and at last, I pulled from his embrace. The final pieces of my plan fell into place. First Carlotta, then Erik, then Delacroix. But to succeed, I would have to put my illusions to the test.

"First, there is business to tend to. Much to put to rest." I explained my plan, watching his face change from incredulous to furious, to hardened acceptance. I outlined his role and the others, explained the delicate nature of Erik's mind, all the while never admitting my complex emotions toward the conjurer. Raoul wouldn't understand how I despised the phantom, yet cared for him deeply; the way I looked up to him, yet felt him the lowest of men. What mattered now was to move forward, to put all into action—to save myself and everyone else I cared for.

Raoul took my hand in his. "I will speak to the inspector and also arrange for backup. As you wish, I will also alert the directors, and a few fellows from the navy who can help us—the moment you give me the sign. I don't like this, Christine. Should something go wrong—"

"Nothing will go wrong. We will take precautions, have a secondary plan ready, just in case."

A weak smile crossed his face.

"Promise me you will do exactly as I say, or all will be lost. *All*, Raoul. I know Erik and Delacroix better than anyone. You must trust me."

After a moment of hesitation he nodded. "I trust you."

I smiled faintly in relief and brushed my lips across his cheek. "First, I'm going to pay Carlotta a visit."

There was only one way I could confront the diva. I had to go to her home, unannounced.

When I reached Carlotta's apartment on the Place des Vosges, I knocked with insistence.

No one stirred.

I worried my bottom lip with my teeth. I had talked myself into coming all morning and now she wasn't home? She *had* to be home. I needed her to be home.

I knocked again, this time more loudly.

No answer.

I turned to look at the neighboring park behind me; its fountain lay dormant instead of burbling, the flower beds lay vacant, and the cobbled street was slick with a coating of half-melted snow.

The door opened, swicking over a mat in the entryway.

"Can I help you, Mademoiselle?" a footman asked.

"I am here to see Carlotta."

"She isn't expecting visitors." His mustache twitched as he spoke. "May I ask who is calling?"

"Mademoiselle Daaé. It's about the opera," I said. "We are friends and colleagues. She'll want to see me right away, I assure you." I pushed past him, rushing through the salon.

"Mademoiselle!" the footman's voice echoed in the stairwell. "Please allow me to announce you. Mademoiselle Arbole is in her bedroom, dressing. I'll just get the maid to let her know you're here. You may wait in the salon."

"Oh, that isn't necessary. Really," I said, not slowing. If I waited, she might refuse to see me. Now was my only chance.

I padded quickly through the hall to the series of bedrooms on the second floor. Two doors stood open and a third, closed. I lunged for the closed door and turned the latch. It was locked.

"Mademoiselle, please," the butler called.

Breathing hard from racing up two flights of stairs, I rummaged in my handbag for a hairpin.

"Mademoiselle Daaé, I insist you wait until I have spoken with my mistress." His voice grew louder as he approached.

With a steady hand, I picked the lock in a second. The door swung open.

Carlotta sat in a window seat, back to me. She appeared to be daydreaming. Without pause, I stepped into the room. It was now or never.

"I need to speak with you," I said, my tone bold, unwavering.

Carlotta stood, a startled look on her face. The lingerie she wore fluttered about her knees and covered very little of her breasts, its dark silk stretched taught across her abdomen—it looked as flat as ever.

I smiled, relieved. Though I knew in my heart Raoul had told the truth, here was the final proof. Not only had she lied about Raoul, she had lied about being pregnant in the first place.

"You aren't pregnant," I said.

She pulled on an overcoat and tied its sashes. "What are you doing in my house?" she snapped. "You have no right to be here! Julie! Gerard!" She screeched for her maid and butler.

"You lied to him, to me, and to everyone," I continued, my voice calm. "Why?"

"Stupid girl. For security, of course. Now I will lose everything because of you, you thieving, talentless wretch!" She barreled toward me, hands outstretched.

In an instant, her hands were in my hair.

"Get your hands off of me!" I screeched in pain as she yanked at my curls. At that moment, every ounce of anger, frustration, and the pain of every loss I'd ever felt, ignited in one fiery mass and exploded. I shoved her with all my strength.

She catapulted backward and landed hard on her derrière. Stunned, she didn't move.

"I came to call a truce, to strike a deal," I said. "Not to fight with you."

"Why would you do that?"

Gerard burst into the room. "Are you all right?" He glared at me and helped Carlotta to her feet. "Shall I throw this woman out?"

Carlotta's eyes narrowed. "You have one minute to say what you came to say and then you are never to set foot in my house again, or I'll have you arrested."

I crossed my arms over my chest. "Apologize to Raoul and set him free. I, in turn, will perform one last show. I swear, after that, I will never return to the opera. You will become the star again, and all will be set right. However, should you continue this charade, I will go to the papers and the police, tell them about your lies. Maybe I'll add a few of my own, beginning with how a certain diva worked in a brothel in her youth. It might interest them as well, that you've bedded a murderer, who also bribes his colleagues to win awards."

"You don't understand my predicament," she snarled. "You are young and beautiful. Every man would fall at your feet. You haven't wanted for anything your entire life."

"You know nothing about me!" I hissed. "Of the years I lived in barns and condemned buildings, enduring the kind of cold you fear will stop your heart one night while you sleep. Of watching my father die in my arms and losing all I had, all I was. Of the guilt I felt for following my heart, and yearning for forgiveness that will never come, because it lies beyond the grave."

I threw my hands in the air. "You are beautiful, a magnificent singer, and still of child-bearing age. All of Paris adores you. Everyone will meet your demands, Carlotta, and you also have your choice of gentlemen. All but one. You cannot and will not have the Vicomte de Chagny.

I crossed my arms over my chest. "I feel no sympathy for you. You have nearly cost me the man I love and my happiness. You've manipulated and belittled me, one time too many."

She stared at me, thunderstruck while I paused to breathe.

"You can have your stage, your throngs of admirers, and the self-pity in which you wallow. After my final show at the opening night of *Don Juan Triumphant*, I am through. You'll never see me again. But only if you set Raoul free. Otherwise, I will make your life hell. If you don't believe me, try me."

Carlotta posed by the window, pale lips pulled tightly closed. She flicked her frizzy hair over her shoulders and down her back.

"Do we have a deal?" I asked, hand on the door latch. "Or are you prepared to lose it all?"

For the first time since we met, her eyes filled with admiration and respect.

She nodded. "We have a deal."

That night I stared at the shadows playing across the ceiling. One more week and Madame Valerius would be free, one week and the Master Conjurer's legacy would be wiped clean. I would escape my association with Madame Giry's death, and disappear forever. If all went well, Raoul and Claudette would be at my side.

A scraping noise sounded near the armoire. I sat up in bed, heart pounding, and peered into the darkness. Between the professor's threats and Erik's constant spying, I knew I wasn't safe. Someone was always watching.

The scraping came again.

"Who's there?" My voice seemed too loud for the dead of night.

I stared at the crates sitting atop each other against the wall—the few belongings I would bring with me when I fled. I'd spent the remainder of the day putting elements of the plan in order, and packing. I lay back down, pulling the covers all the way up to my earlobes. It was probably a mouse. No one could fit behind those crates. I turned on my side to face them, just in case.

I closed my eyes in the hope that sleep would soon come.

The scraping came again, then a coolness settled over me. My eyes flew open. What in the world was that? With a shaking hand, I reached out, my fingers meeting the cool draft. I yanked my hand back. The sound of my racing pulse filled my ears. Could it be?

"Is it you, Papa?" I whispered.

Another cool brush touched my cheek.

I shot up. Peering into the dark again, I tried to discern a shape. It was him. It had to be.

"Papa?" I said, my voice soft. "So much has happened. I'm frightened."

The coolness brushed my face for the second time.

I froze, not daring to move, all the while every nerve stood on end. He was here. He was really here. Conjuring spirits might be an illusion, but souls were not—just as he had said, just as Erik had said, just as I had hoped, but not dared to believe all this time. Warmth and the lightest sense of elation rushed through me. I lay back down, straining my eyes to catch a glimpse of light or some sign of Papa. He was *here*. Tears streamed from the corners of my eyes and soaked into the pillow. Papa had been right all along. The Angel of Music *did* look after me. Papa was my angel.

I lay in the dark for some time without moving. Eventually the sensation dissipated and I burrowed under my covers. When I awoke after hours of deep sleep, my anxiety about the path ahead had vanished and only clarity remained.

I knew what I must do.

I wrapped a shawl around me and went to the study to write some letters. The first I addressed to the Académie des sciences—they must know what Delacroix had done, about his bribery of the other members, about his henchmen. They could see to an investigation and confer with the police inspector. The second letter went to Madame Valerius, and the third to Meg. In it, I explained what her friendship had meant to me, but nothing of my plan. I couldn't risk her spreading gossip, especially if she saw my name associated with Madame Giry's death. She would despise me. A knot formed in my throat, and after a moment of hesitation, I added:

Things aren't as they seem, dear friend. That is all I can say. I am so sorry for your loss.

The next letter went to the police, and the final I addressed to Delacroix himself, to be delivered on the opening day of the opera. I folded a copy of the map I had penned carefully, omitting select chambers and traps he need not know about, and tucked it into the envelope alongside the letter. I would give him the secrets behind the illusions he so desperately wanted, but he would have to get them for himself.

I smiled.

And when these things were done, I would leave Paris—in operatic style.

~ 26 ~

T hank you for meeting me." I slid into a seat across from Georges the machinist at a café the next morning. Our table nestled against the back wall, away from the window. I didn't want to chance being seen. "What I'm about to tell you is confidential. Life-threatening, in fact. You must promise to keep it to yourself."

He raised an eyebrow. "What's all this, Ma'moiselle? I have to admit, I was surprised to hear from you."

"First, I need you to promise me you won't tell a soul." I batted my eyelashes at him the way Carlotta did around men, and tried to appear coquettish.

"Have you got something in your eye?"

I coughed. "No, I—"

He grinned. "You have my word."

We ordered coffee, and I unfolded a couple of sketches I'd spent most of last night designing.

"Did you design these?" He scratched his unshaven cheek with a thick finger, muscled from years of working with his hands.

"I did, yes. And I need you to build it. Here's the cabinet. I've bought a mirror for it already. It should be fastened along this panel here." I indicated the proper placement with the handle of my spoon. "Once it's complete, I need it placed on the third mezzanine, next to the scene flat depicting a church. It has to be in that exact spot. I've designed a special trigger here, which must connect with the lever in the wall."

"When do you need it finished?" he asked.

"Friday morning."

"Friday?" He leaned back in his chair. "The timing will be tight."

Wordlessly, I nodded.

Amused, his lips quirked into a half-smile. "May I ask what you are planning?"

I studied him a moment. This man had every reason to fear Erik, just as the other machinists did after Buquet's death. Some had even found jobs elsewhere as the rumors spread about the ghost, and after the chandelier fell. I had prepared a long answer for this question—I knew it would come—but that wouldn't do. Not now.

"I need to catch a ghost," I said.

His eyebrows shot up, but after a moment, he nodded. "I'll do it."

"I can't thank you enough, Georges." I paid him for the materials and his time.

He pushed up from his place at the table. "I haven't much time and a lot to do. I'll be on my way. Be careful, Ma'moiselle."

As I watched him set off down the street, I smiled. I would be more careful than I'd ever been in my life.

Opening day of the opera, I went over the details of the plan with Claudette all morning.

"Remember, the timing must be perfect." I wrenched my hands as I paced. "Once the show begins, take the lantern in my dressing room and make haste. Erik may not let me finish the show. He likes to cause havoc and since it's my last show, his antics could be worse than usual.

"I haven't seen him a few weeks. He is either remaining in hiding for his own safety or planning our getaway plan." I shuddered at the thought. If he captured me again, all would be lost.

"Above all," I continued, "he must believe he's in control. If that doesn't work, we revert to the backup plan."

"I'll be ready, not to worry," Claudette said.

"What if he doesn't show?" I said, chewing on a nail. "Erik, I mean. What will I do then?"

"That's what the backup plan is for, remember?"

I nodded, but couldn't suppress my nervous energy.

She locked the last of the trunks. "When can Albert ship these off?"

I glanced at the clock on the wall. One o'clock in the afternoon and we had readied everything. "He should take them now. Albert?" I called.

"*Oui*, Mademoiselle?" He rushed from the back of the house.

"Do you have the letters and the tickets?"

"Yes. Have you finished with the trunks?"

"Both mine and Madame's. Remember to drop the letters first and then ship the trunks. Keep watch at Delacroix's house. When he leaves, meet the police inspector. If all goes well, I'll see you shortly after."

"Yes, Mademoiselle."

"And, Albert?" I lay a hand on his arm. "You'll take good care of them?" I glanced at the gilded cage across the room. Bizet chirped happily while Berlioz and Mozart hovered around the bowl filled with seed. I looked away, afraid I would become emotional.

"Of course. Your canaries will like the country."

I leaned in to embrace him.

He stiffened at first then relaxed and returned my affection. "You will be missed a great deal, Mademoiselle." Sadness filled his brown eyes.

"I'll miss Paris, too," I said, my voice soft.

He squeezed my shoulder. "I had better be going. The timing will be tight."

"Thank you. For everything."

He dragged the trunks toward the door to load them in the carriage.

I swallowed hard and focused on a carton on my lap, filled with odds and ends. I would miss Albert and Madame terribly, and my sweet canaries, but I couldn't put them at risk.

After Albert had gone, I looked at Claudette and let out a breath. "It's time for the show."

☙❧

The curtains swept open. The crowd seemed to throb with a palpable energy—not a seat remained vacant—and I drew upon it, pulling it into my lungs and through my limbs. The audience had come in part for the show, but mostly to see the composer of *Don Juan Triumphant*, the infamous *fantôme* who had held the cast hostage for his production; the man who terrorized all who crossed him. How would they react when they saw him at last? Anxiety streaked through me. Everything must go as planned. I couldn't predict Erik's moves, but I knew one thing. To profess my affections was my best chance to entrap him.

I swished across the stage in a snow-white gown that clung to the curve of my hips, and revealed the roundness of my breasts and shoulders: pure as a maiden, yet inviting sin. But the sin I would commit tonight would not be the sort for which my Don Juan hoped.

The orchestra began, and the first notes of the song surged from my throat into a beautiful melody over the strings. As I sang, I stared out at the crimson seats and saw the magnificent chandelier, now fully restored. Policemen stood along the outskirts of the room, just in case. I said a silent prayer of thanks as each song flowed into the next without incident.

A conjurer depended upon timing above all else.

Just then, Erik—dressed in his black suit, cape, and fedora—took the stage.

I breathed the slightest sigh of relief. He had come. The time had come.

The audience murmured as Don Juan stalked across the stage like a panther, singing his song of seduction. I remained calm while he circled me like his prey, ran his cold fingertips across my shoulders. Tonight, he would become my prey.

The audience was locked on to the stage, mesmerized by his voice and the sight of him, the opera ghost.

Despite my elaborate plan and my nerves, despite all that had transpired between us, I felt myself fold into his rhythm, and my spirit float along with his soaring, beautiful voice. A twinge of pain twisted in my chest. I pitied him, for all he had lost and had yet to lose, for the heartache he would continue to suffer. Most of all, I pitied him for never feeling the love we all deserved. But it wasn't meant to be.

When the song ended, I shuttered all thoughts of our connection, our hours of practice in music and magic. Our would-be friendship.

One song more, and it was time.

Erik caught my eye as he sang the final notes of the song. He winked, and spun away from me to take his proper place for the next scene.

Heart pumping in my ears, I glided to my own position.

Overhead and backstage, the fly boys pulled the ropes and managed the levers to change the backdrop. I imagined Georges looking on, waiting for me to strike. He should have the cabinet in place by now. I exhaled deeply to calm my nerves.

The stage floor opened to make way for a new set that mimicked a bedroom. The song I had waited for all week, at last, began.

My eyes darted to the exit doors.

Erik's voice rang out like a beautiful songbird with perfect pitch.

I leaned and whispered into his ear, "I've decided. I choose you."

He stared at me for one beat, incredulity and hope in his eyes.

I held his gaze, forcing a look of adoration.

He smiled broadly and kissed my hand. He believed me.

Just then, the exit doors flew open and Inspector Mifroid raced toward the stage. The directors and a pack of policemen followed at their heels.

Just as I planned.

The audience writhed in their seats, anxious to see what would happen next.

Still stunned by my declaration, Erik hesitated.

"We must go. Now—this way!" Taking advantage of his shock, I tugged his arm, leading him toward the wings and away from the trapdoor I knew he would choose.

We twisted through two more corridors and descended farther into the bowels of the building. At last, we reached the third mezzanine.

"Wait! I have a rock in my boot." I stooped over my foot at the perfect spot. Georges did not disappoint. Not five feet from us stood the cabinet, exactly as I had designed it, positioned over the trapdoor no one knew was there. No one but Erik and me, and now Georges.

"You can do that later," he snapped.

"Please, it's cutting into my foot! My toes are bleeding."

"Make it quick!"

As I began to unlace my shoe, footsteps echoed behind us. I breathed a sigh of relief. Claudette and Raoul had arrived.

"Wait here," Erik said.

If he left, he might disappear himself into another part of the building. The plan would fall to pieces.

"Please, Erik!" I called. "Don't leave me. I'm frightened without you."

"Do not worry, my love." He rushed back to me and cupped my face in his hand.

I willed myself not to flinch at his cold, bony fingers. "I-I need you at my side."

"I'll return for you, always. You are my heart, my soul, Nanette."

I chilled to my core. He had called me by my mother's name again, even now. I was not my mother–I was more than she had ever been–and I did not love him. I could not–would not–be the person he wanted me to be.

The clamor of feet in the stairwell grew louder.

"Just wait here." He turned to go again. "I'll be right back."

Panicked, I flung myself at him, placing a kiss upon his cheek.

Stunned, he staggered. After an instant of pause, he gathered me to him, pressing his mouth against my lips.

Revulsion swept through me as his teeth bumped mine, and his fingers found their way into my hair.

"Christine!" Raoul charged into the room, knocking us askance. "I won't let you do this! I know you don't love him."

"You can't take her from me!" Erik shouted.

Raoul threw all of his weight, and pinned Erik to the ground.

Erik shouted and struggled, regaining his footing and knocking Raoul in the jaw. Raoul's head snapped to the left—but years as a sailor had served him well, and before Erik could move much more than a foot away, Raoul lunged at him again.

I shrieked as Erik went down hard and Raoul crushed him under his weight. After several swift punches, the mask skittered across the floor and Erik's raw, bloodied face was laid bare for all to see.

"Look at your prince!" Erik shouted. "He tortures me, but I love you still, Nanette! Nanette! Don't leave me!"

I tried to block out Erik's tortured cries, his agony. The man was a murderer—forlorn and alone, but also a thief and a killer, a man obsessed, who would hold me against my will forever, or kill me trying to make me love him. This was the only way.

A policeman's whistle split the air. The angry voices of a mob drew near.

In seconds, the crowd stormed onto the mezzanine.

"On your feet!" Inspector Mifroid shouted.

Raoul yanked Erik to his feet. "This is the man you're looking for. The so-called opera ghost."

Inspector Mifroid gripped Erik's shoulders as two other policemen came to his aid.

"Nanette," Erik wailed in a feral tone. "Nanette!"

A lump of emotion clogged my throat. In a shaky voice, I said, "I can't let you hurt anyone else, or destroy yourself. This is the only way."

Inspector Mifroid twisted Erik's arms behind his back and locked a pair of handcuffs in place.

"You'd better make it several pairs. And a rope," I said.

The inspector raised an eyebrow. "Are you sure that's necessary?"

"He's the Master Conjurer, remember?"

He nodded, motioning to his men to follow my instructions.

Erik's nose dripped with blood. His hair stood on end. His scarred flesh appeared more frightening than ever. He gazed at me, his eyes filled with betrayal and agony.

"I'm so sorry," I said, unexpected pain tearing through my chest. "But this had to be."

"We would have been happy." He howled in grief. "We will tour again together some day, Nanette."

Pity flooded my heart. I closed the gap between us, and plucked the handkerchief, folded into a neat triangle, from his breast pocket. Gingerly, I wiped the blood oozing from his nose. In a soft voice I said, "Mother would have been happy to tour with you, Erik. She loved you and relished your talent. That's clear to me now, and I can see why. You cherished her, understood her. But I am not Nanette. I am Christine, my own person, and I will never love you the way you wish me to. I hope, in time, you can find peace."

I crumpled the handkerchief and let it drop to the floor.

The onlookers watched in paralyzed silence.

"There's nothing to see here, everyone," Inspector Mifroid addressed the crowd. To his men he said, "Take him to the station."

Erik locked eyes with me a last time. "I'll never forget this."

"Goodbye, Erik," I whispered.

Three policemen hauled him toward the door, his form twisting in their grip. He shouted at the crowd, but they jeered in response, or stared in stunned horror at his face, until he disappeared from sight. Much of the audience followed, rapt by the spectacle.

Silently, I inched toward the cabinet. Another foot more and I could slip from sight.

"Mademoiselle Daaé," Inspector Mifroid said.

I stopped cold.

"I need to speak with you. There's a matter of a pistol to discuss. And a deceased woman."

I nodded, a knot in my throat. Madame Giry's death would haunt me if the final pieces of my plan failed. I glanced at the cabinet, desperate to get away. The time was now.

"Inspector," one of the policemen called from the doorway. "He's already gotten out of the cuffs! We need something to tie him with."

"Here," Raoul led him to a corner packed with crates and tools and assorted items.

I ducked inside the cabinet and stomped the lever. Its spring triggered another lever in the wall—like magic. I felt the now-familiar sensation of the floor opening beneath me as the opera house swallowed me.

"Thank you, Georges," I whispered.

The sounds of angry voices faded as I slid down a shaft the length of two stories. When I reached the bottom, I was surprised to find my cheeks wet. I wiped the tears away and stood. I was doing the right thing, I reminded myself. Now, I needed to focus on the plan. Delacroix should already be waiting for me.

Heart quickening, I raced along the paths in the dark that I had memorized. When I made it to the passageway with the slide, I dove down it, racing toward the storage room that connected to the bedroom. In seconds, I waded through barrel after barrel of oil until I reached the far corner. I dropped on all fours to feel along the floor—and found it. A slight crack in the shape of a half-moon jutted out a few feet from the wall. I positioned myself in the middle of the hidden panel. The wall swiveled instantly, and I found myself in the room I'd come to know so well.

And there, in the middle of the room, stood Delacroix. He had come, as I knew he would.

"You're here," he said, a cold smile crossing his face. "I thought for sure you would send him after me. I've been waiting." He opened his jacket to show me a gun tucked inside his pocket.

I inhaled a sharp breath, trying not to panic at the sight of a gun. "You found your way just fine, I see."

He held out his hand. "Enough talk. Show me his notebooks. I want them now."

The professor assumed he could command me as he had before, but he knew nothing—yet—of my newfound courage, or of what I had already done. Tomorrow, he would discover I'd written a letter to the Académie, informing them about his attempt to buy the medal he so desperately sought, detailing the threats he'd made to their former award-winner's wife, Madame Valerius, and the dangerous ways he'd collected information with his henchmen.

I fiddled with the lock on the trunk for a moment and threw open the lid. Three notebooks sat on top of the pile of sundry items. I exhaled a small breath. Claudette had made it! She'd swapped the real notebooks for the copies we'd made, filled with fake tricks and food recipes, newspapers clippings and pamphlets. We had spent an entire evening making them. Yet, should Delacroix open a journal quickly, he would think they were Erik's notes.

I thrust the notebooks at him. "Here."

He clutched them to his chest. "Tell me about the spirits. How did he raise the dead?"

I shrugged. "It's in the journals."

He gripped my arm tightly and squeezed. "Show me how it's done."

"We don't have the equipment here, and we need a third person." I looked him in straight in the eye. I must let him know I wasn't afraid. I wasn't the naïve girl he'd known for the last four years. I yanked free of his grip.

"Show me." He waved the gun around.

"It's there, in the notebooks. Study them yourself." I called his bluff, praying he wouldn't sort through them now.

He glanced around the room. "Where is he?"

"You promised you'd let Madame go." I ignored his question.

He stepped closer and pushed the barrel of his gun against my forehead. Through clenched teeth he said, "Where is he?"

I knew, in that moment, my instinct had been correct. It wouldn't be enough to ruin his career and leave town, or even to send his enemy to prison. Just like Erik, I had to escape him in the only way that appeared permanent.

Death was my path to freedom.

"The police have detained Erik," I said. "Arrested him."

He dropped his hand to his side.

In a split second, I threw myself into the armoire. The force made the panel pivot swiftly—just as Delacroix fired a shot. Too late. Inside the storage room, I dismantled the counterweight rapidly to prevent him from following me. I would have to wait it out, and risk going back through the room later. And the only way I could leave, would be the passageway across the lake to escape.

"You're hiding him! Where is he?" Delacroix roared and pounded against the armoire.

My heart thrashed beneath my ribs.

The gun fired again. The ricochet of a bullet sent me to my knees. I panted in fear. It couldn't get through the stone, I reminded myself, or the wood paneling. I was safe—for now.

After some time, Delacroix's footsteps receded. He didn't know the storage room was a dead end. I'd left it off of his altered map completely, hoping he would assume I had escaped.

The final pieces of the plan remained. I had to destroy all evidence of Erik's lair to protect his secrets. From one illusionist to another, it was my gift to him; to the man my mother had loved.

Most important of all—I had to fake my own death.

I clasped Mother's rose pin to my bosom; it was the only thing I knew that could withstand excessive heat. It had survived one fire—it could survive another. When the wreckage was picked over, they would assume I had burned to death, as well. Ashes to ashes.

I selected the largest barrel of oil I could manage from the stockpile, and reattached the counterweight. I said a prayer that Delacroix had really left, and pumped the lever with my foot. The panel swung around.

Delacroix had gone.

Without pause, I turned the oil barrel on its side and rolled it from the bedroom and down the passageway to the lake. Using all of my strength, I hefted it onto the dock. Unscrewing the tightened cap with two hands, I rubbed the skin on my palms raw. I winced in pain, but worked at it until oil gushed from the opening, spilled over the dock, and slipped down its edges into the water.

Pockets of oil plunked into the lake and rose back to the surface. As more oil spread, the pockets joined to form a stream that snaked across the lake. Once the barrel was empty, I released it into the water as well.

I ran back to the bedroom, grabbed several candles, and one by one, set the drapes, the bedding, and the rugs on fire. As I started back to the dock, candle in hand, Delacroix's voice echoed from some hidden alcove in the underground chamber.

"Who's there?" he shouted.

I slipped behind a rock pillar and held my breath.

A shadow moved in the dimness. My heart thumped.

Lord, let it not be Erik, escaped somehow.

I strained my eyes and made out a slight form, petite, but definitively male.

"Show yourself at once, or you'll be sorry." Delacroix stepped out from his own shaded nook and raised his gun.

The figure didn't move.

Smoke billowed from the chamber, and spread across the lake.

My pulse thundered in my ears. The terror that came each time I smelled fire ignited and my hands began to tremble. Soon, it would be too late. The emergency cistern would collapse, the chamber would be flooded, and we would all drown.

Delacroix advanced another step. "I know you're there, conjurer! Don't be such a coward, lurking there in the shadows. Face me like a man!"

I wanted to scream at him, but the surprise might cause him to shoot.

The hidden person advanced a few steps.

The gun fired. A body fell to the ground with a *thump.*

I covered my mouth with my hand, squeezed my eyes closed, praying it wasn't somehow Claudette, lost underground. Fear seized my throat, my stomach, and a rush of panic took hold. But I had given her a detailed, map, I tried to reason with myself. She knew my plans to set the place on fire. She wouldn't be stupid enough to hang back, but if she were lost somehow . . .

Delacroix lowered the weapon and bent over the figure. He

stumbled backward, face blanched white with fear and disbelief. Whoever it was, he had made a mistake.

Smoke wound around my ankles. Any minute I would be coughing and giving away my position.

Noticing the smoke, Delacroix snapped out of his horrified trance. He glanced down at his map, and raced toward the only exit I'd indicated.

I exhaled a breath as he escaped through the tunnel opposite the lake—a different exit from my own. The stairwell to my safety lay on the other side of the lake.

As his form retreated from view, I darted to the body. I choked on a flood of relief as I realized it wasn't Claudette—or Erik. It was a man in white costume and multi-colored turban with toffee-colored skin, his expression now in a permanent state of relaxation. I knew him at once, though I'd seen him only once before. The Persian; a shadowy figure I would never know.

Something crashed from the bedroom, collapsing under the fire's destructive force. I glanced down at the poor man once more. An idea came, unbidden. I had planned to leave my pin somewhere in the bedroom, but now there would be the remains of a body, too. Disgust twisted my gut. This is what my life had come to—never again would I travel this path.

Quickly, I removed Mother's pendant, kissed it, and whispered, "Your final gift to me is freedom. You owe me that much."

I bent over the body and pinned the jewelry to his shirt with care. Smoke filled my throat and I coughed. The memory of another horrible night vibrated in my mind, my gut, on my tongue. Time to run.

I raced to the boat tethered at the dock, paying mind to the flame that had slowly made its way along the first few boards. I sucked in a breath and boarded the boat, loosening the rope tying it in place. I shoved off and began to row as fast as I could. Realizing I could row faster backward, I turned the boat in a circle, all the while heaving, praying.

Let me make it. Please, let me make it without falling in.

When I had paddled halfway across the lake, the flammable oil pooled in the middle of the dock, burst into flames. In seconds, the blaze spread across the slick river of oil on the water's surface. Horrified, I watched as the flames moved toward me at lightning speed. My muscles screamed as I pushed faster, harder. Soon the fire would engulf me, too.

Smoke burned in my lungs. *Go,* I chanted in my mind. *Go!*

Only a few more feet and the flames would take the boat. I wasn't going to make it. I would be trapped by fire again and, this time, there would be no one to rescue me. I was on my own.

Then it happened.

The fire split in two, and darted toward the shore in opposite directions. Away from me. As if my boat was surrounded by a protective shield.

Tears flooded my cheeks. I wasn't alone after all. *Thank you, Papa.*

I pushed hard, ignoring my raw hands.

The next instant, I crashed into the edge of the dock and flung forward on my knees. Too busy watching the fire, I hadn't gauged how close I was to freedom. I stood and the boat rocked violently. With a screech, I launched myself at the dock and scampered over the edge.

A siren wailed over the roar of the fire.

I knew what came next. The cistern would release its contents. Water would rush like rapids through the caverns, and drench the fire to save the grand palace above it. I took a last look at the dark world, ablaze with light. And turned to go.

I darted up three flights of stairs, raced across two floors, and back to the third mezzanine.

As I tripped into the room, I cried out. "I made it!"

"Christine!" Claudette dashed toward me and threw her arms around me. Raoul followed. "You're all right! What happened? Did you see Delacroix?"

I worked to calm my breathing. "The cistern will collapse any minute and the fire department will arrive. Did they manage to take Erik into custody?"

334

Raoul smiled. "I saw them lead him outside myself."

The darkness that engulfed me began to lift. Relief flooded my heart, and I stepped into the protective circle of Raoul's arms. "I love you."

"And I you, *mon amour.*" He brushed my lips with his.

Claudette cleared her throat. "I hate to break up the romance, but shouldn't we get going?"

I took Raoul's hand and the three of us groped along the wall to find the hidden staircase I knew was there. Within minutes, we found it, climbed two flights of stairs, and spilled out into the emperor's former apartments.

I paused for an instant to look at the two people I loved most in the world. "Thank you. For believing this could work. For believing in me."

"We always will."

Raoul squeezed my hand, and Claudette threw her arms around me.

"Let's get the hell out of here," I said, without a backward glance.

~ 27 ~

A train whistle split the night air, announcing its impending departure. I knelt beside Madame Valerius's wheelchair and embraced her gently. Albert and the police had freed her from Delacroix's home, and her loyal footman had escorted her to the train station immediately, trunks in tow.

"There, there, child." She stroked my hair. "I will be in good hands at my brother's, especially with Albert at my side."

A genuine smile crossed Albert's face. He was loyal as always, and grateful to be going with his mistress to Giverny, a beautiful town outside of Paris. She would spend her final days surrounded by peace, beauty, and family. I would never divulge what I'd learned about the professor and, with any luck, she would miss the story in the papers. I had instructed Albert to hide it from her, if possible.

Tears pricked behind my eyes. "I can never thank you enough for what you've done for me."

"I would give you all I have and more, all over again," she said, her blue eyes wet with emotion.

"Christine, we must go." Raoul touched my shoulder.

He was right. It was getting late and if we were to make the last train out of Paris, we'd have to hurry. I kissed Madame's cheek one last time.

Claudette followed suit. "It was a pleasure to know you, Madame."

She grasped Claudette's hand in hers and squeezed.

With a final parting wave, Raoul, Claudette, and I headed to our escape.

We arrived in Le Havre early the next morning. At my insistence, we rode until we reached the town of Mantes the previous night, and rested just long enough to board the first morning train to the seaport town. Once we arrived at the port, I exhaled a sigh of relief.

A seaman tipped his hat. "Your luggage has already been stowed aboard. We debark in two hours."

I laced my arm through Claudette's. Raoul took my free hand in his.

"This is it," I said, looking out at the docks bustling with sailors, passengers, and seagulls. "We're off on an adventure."

I had done it—pulled off a grand illusion—escaped my tormentor and traitorous friend, made right my parents' deaths. I was free. Seagulls swooped overhead and the tangy odor of seaweed filled the air. I smiled in spite of my fatigue.

"We'll have to work on your English, Ma'moiselle," Claudette said with a wink.

"And our act," I said.

"Find a place to live, and adapt to a foreign land," Raoul added.

"With my dearest friend and my fiancé, I can do anything."

Raoul unleashed his exquisite smile and pulled me into his arms. His face bent to mine. After a lingering kiss, he swung me around. I threw back my head and laughed, releasing the last of the tension from the past few days, months—years. Maybe even a lifetime.

I would be the illusionist I longed to be, with a new start in America.

Ovation

New York City, 1891

I looked out at the packed theater. Claudette and I had filled every show, along with the two male illusionists who shared our stage. A bevy of stagehands clamored at our heels. I'd found my most talented helpers performing in the streets, and at a local fair. When I'd asked Harry Houdini to join our show, he had leapt at the chance. He was a gem. In time, I might make him a more regular act.

Even ten years later, I didn't have the nerve to send for news from the Opéra de Paris. In the beginning, I feared being discovered by the authorities every moment, should my name be implicated in Madame Giry's death. Over time, my worry dissolved. My life in Paris was over. There, I was dead. In America, I had become someone new, an intoxicating woman who performed magic and made others believe the impossible. Christine was buried at sea. Her torment of that horrible year and the deaths of her loved ones drowned with her. But a newer, stronger self had emerged: a wife, best friend, and conjurer: Allegra the Great.

My talents created a show unlike any other. No conjurer sang as I did. No one fused illusions with drama, accompanied by scores from the greatest opera house in the world. Not as I did.

In my fine velvet gown and feathered hat, I walked to the opposite side of the cabinet centered on the stage and pulled the curtain closed to obscure Claudette. Immediately, she ducked behind a mirrored panel out of sight. When I opened the curtain, she had disappeared.

A collective gasp resounded through the theatre, followed by applause—and laughter as she quickly reappeared in a clown's costume.

I was the only female conjurer consistently on stage, but I'd heard of a few others making their way across America. Perhaps one day I, too, would travel with my own show. For now, I was happy expanding my audience in the great city of New York, the city of dreams.

"Ladies and gentlemen, I bid you good night." I bowed, and Claudette followed suit. When I straightened, I looked at the west balcony where Raoul always sat, ever supportive of his conjurer-wife.

He smiled and waved.

My eyes narrowed as something appeared behind him, a pool of darkness shifting among the balcony drapes. Raoul turned to look over his shoulder.

The next instant, I blinked and the shadow had disappeared. I shook my head to rid it of ghosts. It couldn't be— Could it?

Author's Note

The path to finishing this book was a twisty one. Layering well-known canon with my own ideas, and giving new dimensions to a large cast of characters that are beloved, presented no easy task. *The Phantom's Apprentice* went through many, many drafts and gave me more angst than I care to admit. How can one possibly make such a melodramatic story feel real—and relevant—today? Thankfully, the Muse held me at gunpoint, and I found my way to "The End." More than anything, I'm grateful for the incredible learning experience and growth this book provided. We writers like to do this to ourselves—push, push more, push harder still, in spite of the painful doubt and endless hours of hard work—all in an attempt to inspire readers, entertain them, and, most of all, to say something meaningful. I hope I've done at least one of these things, if not all.

A Note on Ghosts, Spirits, and Spiritualism: From the 1840s until about 1920, a movement called *spiritualism* gained in popularity. Its philosophy centered on a belief that spirits wanted to commune with the living, that they continued to evolve in the afterlife, and their guiding presence was very real on Earth. During this era, society saw the rise of Gothic novels and the occult, as well as the use of mediums and turning tables for séances. When mixed with a rapid series of new technological inventions and advancements, including electricity, mass transit, photography, and much more, people grappled for the essence of what mattered: their loved ones and the evolution of their souls.

Spiritualism evolved into a religious sect in some circles, and like with any religion, beliefs were tied to its principles and emotions ran high. There was much debate over the validity of spiritualism; scientists and philosophers sought to disprove (or prove), the likelihood that spirits were real. Many illusionists tapped into that emotional pool and manipulated it for their own gain, especially as advances in projecting images and different types of glass emerged. Suddenly, they could "create" apparitions. Riots did indeed break out after conjurers' shows from time to time. Viewing the dead caused a fright, and created endless controversy.

Gaston Leroux, the original author of *The Phantom of the Opera*, lived during this time and created a Gothic story woven with ghosts and, ultimately, a monster of a man who knew a few tricks a magician might use—playing with light and throwing voices, mirrors. It was from those pages that I gleaned my inspiration for an Erik who was driven underground by the shadows of his former life as a magician, and a Christine Daaé, who wanted to be more—and became more—than the fragile flower we have come to love in Andrew Lloyd Webber's stage version.

Acknowledgments

The list of those I must thank for encouraging me to finish this book is endless. To begin, I must thank my insightful agent, Michelle Brower, who worked through revisions with me, and bolstered my spirits when I needed it. I am beyond lucky to have you in my corner.

Author friends and critique partners who read early drafts—you're my guiding light and my tribe. I adore you and couldn't imagine writing in isolation. Special thanks go to Susan Spann, Kris Waldherr, Julianne Douglas, Hazel Gaynor, Janet B. Taylor, Sonja Yoerg, Kerry Schafer, Therese Walsh, Diane Haeger, Greer Macallister and Aimie K. Runyan. I'd also like to thank Christopher Gortner, who talked me through troubling developments and offered many words of wisdom. Thanks to Stephanie Cowell as well, opera expert, who patiently answered all of my questions. Another big thanks to those very talented individuals who helped with design work, formatting, editing, and much more: LJ Cohen, James T. Egan, Kris Waldherr, and Lara Robbins.

To my children, who now know Andrew Lloyd Webber's music by heart, and to my husband for listening to more opera than he ever wanted. This book has made converts of us all! Finally, thanks to my family, friends, and dear book club for being steadfast in your support and love.

About the Author

Heather Webb is the international bestselling author of historical novels *Becoming Josephine, Rodin's Lover, Fall of Poppies*, and *Last Christmas in Paris*. In 2015, *Rodin's Lover* was a Goodreads Top Pick. To date, Heather's novels have sold in multiple countries worldwide. When not writing, she can be found flexing her foodie skills or looking for excuses to head to the other side of the world. She lives in New England with her family and one feisty rabbit.

Connect Online
Website: www.HeatherWebb.net
Facebook: Heatherwebb, Author
Twitter: @msheatherwebb
Instagram: @msheatherwebb

Made in the USA
San Bernardino, CA
23 June 2020